GRAHAM MASTERTON is best known as a writer
of horror and thrillers, but his career as an author
spans many genres, including historical epics and sex
advice books. His first horror novel, *The Manitou*,
became a bestseller and was made into a film starring
Tony Curtis. In 2019, Graham was given a Lifetime
Achievement Award by the Horror Writers Association.
He is also the author of the Katie Maguire series
of crime thrillers, which have sold more than
1.5 million copies worldwide.

GRAHAM MASTERTON

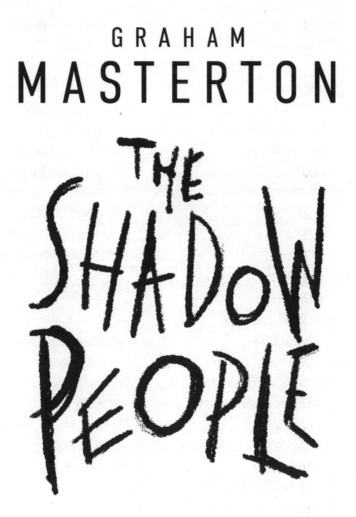

THE SHADOW PEOPLE

HEAD of ZEUS

First published in the UK in 2021 by Head of Zeus Ltd

9 7 5 3 1 2 4 6 8

A catalogue record for this book is available from
the British Library.

ISBN (HB): 9781800243361
ISBN (XTPB): 9781800243378
ISBN (E): 9781800243347

Typeset by Divaddict Publishing Solutions Ltd

Printed and bound in Great Britain by
CPI Group (UK) Ltd, Croydon CR0 4YY

Head of Zeus Ltd
First Floor East
5–8 Hardwick Street
London EC1R 4RG

WWW.HEADOFZEUS.COM

To my nightingale, Karolina Mogielska

'Where were you hiding, before you were born?'

'In the shadows.'

'Where will you be hiding, after you die?'

'In the shadows.'

'Where does your lord and master dwell?'

'In the shadows.'

I

As soon as he had smashed down the office door with his sledgehammer, Ron could smell meat burning.

'Blimey,' he said, stepping over the door. The air inside the office was filled with a fine haze of smoke, which shuddered in the draught that he had let in. 'Somebody's having a barbie.'

The office was derelict now, with half of the plasterboard hanging down from the ceiling where a pipe must have frozen and then burst. The desks and the chairs were still here, exactly as they had been on the day the Royale carpet factory had closed down. There was even a Diamond Jubilee mug from 2012 on one of the desks, with a forgotten pair of spectacles next to it, and a khaki parka drooping sadly on the coat stand.

The smell of scorching meat, though, was pungent and fresh, as if it were still sizzling on the grill.

'Squatters, most likely, innit, bruv,' said DuWayne, coming up behind Ron swinging his long wrecking crowbar, which he would be using to lever up floorboards. He sniffed, and sniffed again. 'Mmm, that's making me feel well hungry. I didn't have no breakfast yet.'

'Well, if you're lucky, they'll have left some for you.'

Ron crossed over to the open doorway on the opposite side of the office. It gave out onto a long corridor, with a staircase at the end of it. The stairs led down to the main factory floor, where Ron and his five-strong gang would begin their demolition.

He and DuWayne walked along the corridor to the top of the staircase. On either side, framed photographs were still hanging of the Royale factory in its heyday. The stairs were dimly lit by sunshine filtering down from a grimy skylight. Ron leaned over the banisters and called out, 'Anybody down there? If there is, you'd better hop it, and quick! We've come here to knock this whole building down!'

'Yeah!' shouted DuWayne. 'If you don't want to be flattened like a carpet pattern, get on your feet and beat a retreat!'

Ron said nothing. He was used to DuWayne rapping. DuWayne would even rap when he ordered a cheeseburger at McDonald's. They listened for any response from down below, but all they could hear was a faint crackling noise.

'What does that sound like to you, Dewey? Let's hope the place ain't on fire.'

'It would save us all the grief of knocking it down, wouldn't it?'

'It don't *smell* like no fire. Still, we'd best go down and have a butcher's. I just don't want no trouble with no squatters, that's all. You was off on your holidays when we pulled down that insurance building over on Ludgate, wasn't you, but there was half a dozen homeless in it and they didn't half give us a ruck getting them out of there. Poor old Biffo got his jaw dislocated.'

They clattered down the stairs in their steel-capped boots. The double doors to the factory floor were open only three or four inches, but that had been enough to let the smoke drift upstairs to the office. The door's hinges were rusted and the floor beneath them was covered with fine grit, but DuWayne pressed his shoulder against them and managed to scrape them open.

The factory floor itself was bare, since all the massive carpet-weaving machines had been sold off when Royale went bankrupt. On the right-hand side of the floor, though, there were still rows of metal shelving where the finished carpets used to be stacked, and on some of these shelves there were heaps of dirty-looking blankets and pillows.

'Told you,' said Ron. 'Bloody squatters. I bloody hate bloody squatters. Think they've got a God-given right to break in anywhere they bloody want to.'

'That's where all the smoke's coming from, bruv, down there,' said DuWayne. He pointed to the far end of the factory floor, where there was a brick recess that looked as if it had once had a fireplace or a furnace installed in it. This factory had originally been built in the 1870s for making hansom cabs for the London carriage trade, and the coachbuilders would have needed a furnace to beat the metal parts into shape. The furnaces were long gone, and now the recess was jammed with three large supermarket trolleys, each of them half-filled with smoking charcoal. Most of the smoke was twisting up the chimney.

'You're right, they was having a barbie,' said DuWayne. 'They must have scarpered when they heard you shouting down the stairs. Let's see if they've left anything worth noshing.'

The two of them walked the length of the factory floor, with Ron whistling tunelessly between his teeth. Apart from the blankets stacked on the shelves, there were heaps of rubbish to show that squatters had been living here. Underneath the windows on the left-hand side, the wall was piled up with crumpled shopping bags and bottles and broken cardboard boxes and dozens of empty soup and sardine tins, as well as ripped-up lengths of curtain material that looked as if they were stained with blood or something else dark brown.

'Bleeding animals, these squatters, I tell you. Worse than animals. At least my Tiger makes half an effort to bury his crap.'

As Ron and DuWayne came closer to the recess, they could see that the bottoms of the supermarket trolleys had been covered over with slates. The squatters had probably taken them off the factory roof so that they could fill up the trolleys with charcoal briquettes. Ron guessed that they must have lit the briquettes at least two hours ago, because they were ashy grey now with a faint orange glow and giving off so much heat that the recess appeared to have transparent ghosts dancing all around it.

Ron went up to the nearest trolley and looked inside it, shielding his face with his upraised hand. He could see two curved racks of ribs, already beginning to char, and what looked like three legs of pork lying side by side, their skin bubbling up into crackling. He could see other cuts of meat jumbled up in there too – neck and shoulders and shanks – although they looked as if they had been roughly hacked apart, rather than expertly sliced by a butcher.

DuWayne peered over his shoulder. 'No burgers. That's a pity. I mean, like, what's a barbie without no burgers?'

'No buns neither, mate, and no Kraft cheese slices. Sorry about that.'

He moved along to see what was roasting in the next trolley. It was then that he stopped dead still, and gradually lowered his hand, because he couldn't understand at first what he was looking at. DuWayne almost bumped into him.

After a moment of stunned silence, he said, 'Jesus Christ, Dewey. I mean, holy bloody Jesus bloody Christ.'

'What is it, bruv?'

The second trolley was piled up with human heads, their faces blackened by the heat, like some hideous parody of a 1950s' minstrel show. Some of their eyeballs had burst, so that their sockets were hollow. Others were staring up at Ron and DuWayne with irises that were milky and cooked. All of their mouths were wide open as if they were silently screaming, their lips stretched back over their teeth. By the length of their frizzled-up hair, Ron could see that at least three of them were women.

'This is all people,' he said, and he could hear himself saying it as if somebody else were speaking it into his ear. 'This whole bloody barbecue. It's *people*.'

DuWayne said, '*What?*' and then he saw the heads too, and turned away, retching, his hand pressed over his mouth. Ron took out his phone to see if he could get a signal, and then, with a trembling index finger, he jabbed out 999.

'Emergency. Which service?'

'Police, love. It's too bloody late for an ambulance.'

2

'You free, Pardoe?' asked DS Bristow.

'No, skipper,' said Jerry, looking up from his keyboard. 'I'm still writing up the statements from that Extinction Rebellion ruck. It's coming up in court tomorrow.'

'You can leave that for now. It's an LOB anyway. There's been an attempted armed robbery at WH Smith in the Tandem Centre, with ABH.'

'WH Smith? You're having a laugh, aren't you? What were they after? The *Daily Mail* and two rolls of Sellotape?'

'I don't know what exactly. But it seems like a couple of weirdos started to take stuff off the shelves and when the shop assistants tried to stop them these weirdos went for them with shanks. Two of the assistants sustained minor injuries but a third one got quite badly cut.'

'Gordon Bennett. What about the weirdos? Did they get away?'

'One of them did, but there were two officers already at the centre on another matter and they've detained the other one. Apparently he's an FBU so they're waiting for backup before they try to fetch him in. CSIs are on their way.'

Jerry saved the statements that he had been typing out and switched off his computer. As far as he was concerned the case he was preparing was a waste of time anyway, or LOB as DS Bristow had put it – a Met Police acronym for 'load of bollocks'. FBU stood for 'fucking big unit', which meant that the suspect who had been detained was physically large and violent and not easy to restrain.

'Take Mallett with you. He's in the canteen. He's come to the end of his shift but he's done sweet FA all day so he might as well earn his keep.'

'WH Smith,' Jerry repeated, as he shrugged on his new brown leather jacket and zipped it up. He was pleased with this jacket. He thought it made him look like Robert Redford before Robert Redford got all crinkly. 'What kind of twonk tries to pull an armed robbery on WH Smith?'

'Perhaps they were after the latest *Harry Potter.*'

Jerry went downstairs to the canteen, where he found DC Bobby Mallett trying to chat up PC Fiona Pitt. Almost every officer in Tooting police station had tried to chat up PC Fiona Pitt, because she was blonde and skinny with cornflower-blue eyes and lips that were were permanently pouting. She could have been an influencer on Twitter. The only problem was that she was engaged to a successful middleweight boxer called Billy 'Warhammer' Wilson.

Jerry sat down at the table next to PC Pitt and winked at her. She gave him a sarcastic smirk back.

DC Mallett said, 'I've just been explaining to Fiona here that boxing – well, it's hardly your lifetime career, is it? Most boxers are all washed up by the time they're thirty, and that's the lucky ones. And does she really want to wake up every morning and see a bloke with a nose like an aubergine lying next to her?'

'Do you mind?' PC Pitt retorted. 'Billy's nose is *beautiful.* What's an oboe jean, anyhow?'

'You wait until some kid ten years younger gets into the

ring with him. That's what happened to my Uncle Harry. He was only an amateur but he took on one fight too many. Now he looks like somebody smacked him in the face with a tea tray.'

'We've got a rumble in the jungle, Edge,' Jerry told him. 'There's been a stabbing at the Tandem Centre.'

Everybody in the station called DC Mallett 'Edge' because it was short for ''Edge'og'. He was short and tubby, with prickly black hair and bulging brown eyes and a blob of a nose, and he had a way of bustling along like a woodland creature in a hurry.

DC Mallett checked his watch. 'No way, Jerry. I'm on Code Eleven. I finished at three.'

'No, you didn't. One of the suspects is still on the premises and Bristow wants us over there prontissimo.'

'How long is it going to take us? I'm supposed to be taking my mum out to the Toby Carvery this evening for her supper.'

'Great romantic dates of our time. Sorry, Edge.'

DC Mallett puffed out his cheeks in disappointment. 'Oh, well. So much for our little tête-à-tête, Fiona. Maybe we can carry it on tomorrow.'

He stood up, and blew PC Pitt a kiss with his fingertips, but from the way she rolled up her eyes Jerry could tell that she would rather be watching her nail varnish dry tomorrow than continue the conversation that Edge had started today. She probably had no idea what a 'tête-à-tête' was, in any case.

'So what's the SP?' asked DC Mallett, struggling to zip up his nylon windcheater as they walked across the station car park.

'Two numpties were trying to rob WH Smith and stabbed three shop assistants who tried to stop them. Serious injuries, by the sound of it. One of the numpties was collared and he's still there now.'

'This fucking zip's broke. Lost half of its teeth, like my granny.'

They climbed into their unmarked Ford Focus and took a left along Longley Road, with their siren whooping and the blue lights in their radiator flashing.

'WH *Smith*?' said DC Mallett, after a long, frowning pause.

'Don't ask me, mate. We'll just have to see what this numpty's got to say for himself.'

It took them less than ten minutes to reach the Tandem Centre and park outside WH Smith. An ambulance was still there, although a police van with reinforcements had not yet arrived. Jerry knew that Extinction Rebellion were holding another demonstration in central London today, and scores of officers would be occupied in cutting free eco-warriors who had chained themselves to railings or superglued themselves to the road.

He and DC Mallett went up to the ambulance. The rear doors were open and they could see two paramedics bandaging the arms of a redheaded young woman, who was staring up at them as if she didn't know who they were or what she was doing here.

One of the paramedics saw the two detectives and she shuffled her way to the back of the ambulance to talk to them.

'The poor girl has nearly a dozen lacerations on her hands and her forearms,' she told them. She spoke with a Belfast accent, and very quietly, so that the redheaded young woman couldn't hear her. 'They're not too deep, but there's so many of them, criss-cross, this way and that, like. Whoever did this to her, they must have been in some kind of a terrible frenzy, I'd say.'

'How about the other assistants?' asked Jerry. 'Do you know how they are?'

'One of them was cut up the same as this girl, but cut across the throat too. Fortunately the manager had first-aid training and he stopped the bleeding, so I'd say that she's probably going to be okay. The other one though, she was stabbed several times in the chest and stomach and by the time we got here she was barely alive. I haven't heard yet but my guess is that we've lost her.'

The redheaded young woman suddenly started to sob. The other paramedic crouched down beside her and took hold of her hands and said, 'There, there, love. Don't get upset. It's all over now.'

'But why did she want to *hurt* me?' the young woman wailed. 'Why was she so *angry*? I only asked her to stop pulling down the display.'

Jerry frowned at the paramedic and said, '*She*, did she say? "Why did *she* want to hurt me?" She was stabbed by a woman?'

'The poor girl's in a right state of shock. I think you'll understand when you go inside and see for yourself.'

Jerry and Edge went into the shop. The manager was standing by the magazine shelf near the entrance, talking to one of the uniformed police officers. He was bald and bespectacled, with a little moustache that Jerry's dad would have called a 'thirsty eyebrow'. He was still highly agitated, and even though he had rolled up his right shirtsleeve, Jerry could see that it was soaked with blood.

Four other shop assistants were still milling around, three girls and a spotty teenage boy. They all had the same distracted expression on their faces that Jerry saw on almost every witness to a stabbing or a shooting or a fatal traffic accident.

It could take weeks or even months before every grisly detail stopped playing and replaying in their mind's eye.

'Collins,' said the manager, when Jerry and DC Mallett showed him their ID cards. 'Peter Collins. Actually, I was christened Colin Peter Collins. Just my parents' little joke.'

Yes, squire, bleeding hilarious, thought Jerry, but he didn't say so out loud.

The uniformed officer knew them already. PC Brookes, his name was, and he was a size taller and a size larger than most human beings, with a face the colour of uncooked pastry, so that he looked as if he had spent his entire working life in a windowless basement.

'I expect you'll be wanting statements from myself and my staff,' said the manager. 'We can go to my office if you like. More private.'

'We need to interview the suspect first,' Jerry told him. 'Do you have any idea what he was after?'

'Well, yes. But I'm baffled, to be honest with you. He and his companion were attempting to steal crayons and felt-tip pens and oil-painting sets from our art section. They were pulling them willy-nilly off their display hooks and cramming them into this black dustbin bag. But the odd thing is that this is the second time in three weeks that we've had art materials stolen. The first time we didn't catch them at it.'

'Crayons and felt-tip pens and oil-painting sets? That was all? They didn't go for the till, or anything else more valuable?'

'These Spektrum oil paints are £19.95 but they're on special offer and we don't really have anything else more valuable. We do stock an expensive book on technical word-processing, £95, but I can't see why anybody would want to steal that. Myself, I can't understand a word of it.'

'Okay. Let's go and have a word with this oil-paint pincher. Where is he?'

'In the storeroom,' said PC Brookes. 'We've arrested him for GBH and we've read him his rights. Matt Williams is looking after him.'

The manager led Jerry and Edge to the back of the shop, and PC Brookes followed them. The shelves in the storeroom were stacked with books and padded envelopes and hole punches and bottles of glue and it smelled of stationery, but there was another smell too – a rank sour smell of body odour. A bulky round-shouldered man with wild brown hair was sitting handcuffed on a folding metal chair.

Jerry realised at once why the assistant had called the man 'she'. He was wearing a filthy cream dress with short puffy sleeves, although he was so fat that the dress had split under both armpits. The hem reached down only as far as his knees, so that his hairy shins were bare, and he wore no shoes. His feet were filthy, with bruised toenails.

'Well, well, and what have we here?' asked Jerry. A few years ago he would have been able to add a sarcastic comment like 'Little Miss Muffet?' or something similar. These days, though, there were strict rules in the Met about how to address transvestites and transgenders and anybody who identified as something other than what they actually looked like. Besides, a transgender woman called Diana had recently moved into the flat next to Jerry's and Jerry really liked her.

The man stared at Jerry but said nothing. He had piercing eyes that were almost colourless and his eyelashes and the corners of his eyes were crusted with sleep. His forehead and his cheeks were burnished with grime. Close to, he stank so badly that Jerry could understand why PC Williams was standing in the far corner of the storeroom, with his hand cupped over his nose and mouth.

Enough to make a maggot gag, that was what Jerry's dad would have said.

'Do us a favour and leave the door open, would you?' said Jerry, taking out his phone. Then he turned to the man in the dress and said, 'What's your name, sunshine?'

The man growled deep in his throat but didn't reply.

'I'll ask you again. What-is-your-name? You speak English, don't you? Or don't you? What is *vôtre nom, monsieur*? What is *su nombre, hombre? Jak mash na imię*?'

The man growled once more, but still said nothing. He didn't even shake his head to indicate that he was refusing to answer.

Edge said, 'You may not know it, mate, but you've committed a crime and if you don't give us your details after committing a crime that's an offence in itself.'

'Yeah,' Jerry added. 'As if you're not giving us enough bleeding offence already, the way you pen-and-ink.'

'He never spoke to us, neither,' said PC Brookes. 'Not a word. Maybe he's Tom Thumb.'

'This is your last chance,' Jerry told the man in the dress. 'Who are you and why were you trying to nick all them crayons and felt-tip pens?'

The man continued to stare fixedly at Jerry and growled yet again.

'Forget it,' said Jerry. 'It's like trying to get sense out of a fucking bulldog.'

At that moment they heard the bustle of stab-proof vests and the squeak of boots making their way through the shop. Four officers had arrived to take the man in the dress into custody.

'Who's this, then?' said one of them, as they entered the storeroom. 'Lady Gaga's grandpa?'

The man made no attempt to fight back when the officers tried to lift him out of his chair. Instead, he went completely limp, and sagged sideways. Two of the officers had to grasp his arms while the other two took hold of his legs and between them they carried him out through the shop like big game hunters carrying a dead lion. As they heaved him into their waiting van, his dress rode up and Jerry and Edge could see that he was wearing nothing underneath.

'Bloody hell,' said Edge. 'That's a dong-and-a-half.'

'What about the other suspect?' Jerry asked. 'The one that got away? What was he dressed as?'

'It's all on the shop's CCTV, so you can see for yourself,' said PC Brookes, as the van doors were slammed shut and they watched it being driven away. 'I couldn't tell you for sure if it was a he or a she. He was all wrapped up in blankets, dark grey blankets. He had them pulled up over his head like a hood, and only his legs were showing. As soon as we turned up he was out the other door like shit off a shovel, wasn't he, Matt?'

PC Williams nodded vigorously. 'Off like a fucking rocket.'

'You've sent out an APB?'

''Course, yes. But he'd only have to dump those blankets and you'd never recognise him.'

'It depends, doesn't it? If he was dressed the same as his mate, he might have been starkers, and there's a fair chance you'd notice him then.'

'I'll tell you who we ought to contact first,' said Edge. 'St George's Mental Health Department. See if they're missing a couple of nutters.'

'*Edge*,' Jerry admonished him.

'Oh, yes. Sorry. Two patients who have mental conditions.'

Jerry looked across at the black plastic rubbish bag that was still lying on the shop floor, surrounded by scattered crayons and coloured pencils and boxes of oil paints.

'I'd still like to know why they wanted to nick all that gubbins, whether they were nutters or not.'

3

'Keep the media well away,' said DCI Saunders. 'I don't want even a whisper of this getting out. Not a squeak. Not until we know what the hell we're dealing with here.'

'Cannibals, if you ask me, guv,' said DS Barry Welch.

'I was planning on having a barbecue myself this weekend,' said DC Joan Harris. 'I've even bought the rack of ribs ready. But, *ugh*! There's no way I'm having it now.'

'Didn't buy any human heads, did you?' DS Welch asked her, but DCI Saunders gave him a caustic look and he said, 'Sorry, didn't mean it. Poor taste. Sorry.'

DCI Saunders was nicknamed 'Smiley' in the Met because he had absolutely no sense of humour at all. He was tall, with grey slicked-back hair and an aquiline nose, and a permanently resentful look on his face, as if every crime was committed with the express intention of irritating him personally.

He was standing with DCs Jeffries and Loizou beside the brick recess on the Royale factory floor, along with two other Major Investigation Team detectives and three uniformed officers from Walworth police station, as well as four firefighters.

The air was still smoky and still smelled strongly of burning meat, but the firefighters had completely wrapped up the three shopping trolleys with yellow Kevlar fire blankets. Normally they would have used dry powder extinguishers, but DCI Saunders had told them not to because their thick phosphate residue was likely to compromise the evidence. All he and his team could do now was wait for the charcoal briquettes to cool down and for a team of forensic experts to arrive from Lambeth Road.

He looked at his watch. 'Where's Malik? He's taking his sweet time, isn't he? Gorman, go down and see what he's up to, will you? I only asked him to check the basement, not to go off on his holidays.'

'Okay, guv.'

DC Gorman went across to the open door that led to the factory's basement. DC Malik had been sent down with PC Bone to make sure that nobody was hiding there, and to see if there was any evidence that might identify who had dismembered and started to cook the human bodies in the shopping trolleys.

'Babar!' he called out, at the top of the stairs. 'You found anything down there yet?'

There was no answer, so he called out again. 'Babar!'

There was still no reply, and it was totally dark down there, so he came back and asked one of the firefighters if he could borrow his flashlight.

'Maybe they've found some other rooms down there,' he said to DCI Saunders. 'I'll just go down and make sure they're okay.'

'Only Malik could get himself lost in a cellar,' said DCI Saunders. 'He got lost in Wimbledon nick once. Showed up twenty minutes late for a briefing.'

DC Gorman switched on his flashlight and descended the creaking wooden stairs into the basement, holding on to the handrail in case he lost his footing. The basement had a low ceiling and appeared to run under the whole of the factory floor. When Royale carpets were still in business, they had used it to store offcuts and rejects and spare machine parts. A few sagging rolls of carpet were still lying in the far corner, dark with damp, as well as two spiky rotors for separating wool fibres and a rusty metal frame. Elaborate spiderwebs hung down from the light fittings, but in recent years they had trapped nothing but dust.

'Babar! Where are you, mate?' DC Gorman shouted out, pointing his flashlight left and right. 'Babar!'

He paused, and listened, but all he could hear was water dripping. He had thought there might be other rooms down here that DC Malik and PC Bone were exploring, but his flashlight showed him that this one basement was all there was. So where the hell were Babar and Bone?

He ventured further. He was beginning to feel distinctly uneasy, as if somebody were hiding in the darkness watching him. He thought he heard a clattering sound, like a brick being knocked over, and so he stopped again, and flicked his flashlight all around him. Off to his left he suddenly caught sight of two feet protruding from behind a long roll of maroon carpet, and he recognised DC Malik's tan-coloured Chelsea boots.

'Babar?' he said, and hurried across to the other side of the basement. When he came around the end of the roll of carpet though, and saw DC Malik lying on the floor, all he could say was 'Shit.'

DC Malik's head had been smashed – so violently that his skull had been broken into five or six large curved pieces, like a broken vase, and his brains had been splattered across the concrete, glistening beige lumps that had fanned out nearly fifteen centimetres in every direction. His face had been flattened into a bloody two-dimensional mask, and a jumble of shattered teeth had burst out from between his lips.

His olive-green Barbour jacket had been unzipped, and the plaid shirt that he was wearing underneath had been forcibly torn apart. His stomach had been sliced open, from his breastbone downwards, and all of his insides dragged out into a messy disarranged heap – heart and lungs and prune-coloured liver and slippery coils of intestines.

DC Gorman took two stumbling steps back. He was so shocked that he almost lost his balance and fell over. He had seen plenty of dead bodies before, but even after fatal road collisions he had never seen a body as pulverised as this. DC Malik had not only been brained and disembowelled, but beaten again and again, as if his assailant had been furious with him.

'Bone?' he called out, although his voice was hardly more than a croak. 'Bone, are you there? Bone! For Christ's sake answer me!'

He listened. His mouth was swimming with acidic bile, and he was praying that he wasn't going to bring up his breakfast. Yet again there was no answer, only that steady dripping sound.

'*Bone*,' he whispered. Then he started walking stiff-legged back to the staircase, sweeping his flashlight left and right, terrified that somebody or something might come running at him out of the darkness. He ran up the stairs so fast that he slipped halfway up and bruised his knee.

When he emerged from the basement door, he saw that DCI Saunders was still waiting impatiently for the shopping trolleys to cool down. The forensic examiners had arrived, four men and two women, and they were opening up their aluminium cases of equipment.

'Well?' asked DCI Saunders, as DC Gorman came across the factory floor. 'Found anything useful, has he?'

DC Gorman was about to tell him that DC Malik had been killed when he blacked out. His knees gave way and he pitched sideways, hitting the side of his head against the concrete. His flashlight rolled across the floor and ended up against the toe of DCI Saunders' shoe.

'What in the name of—?' said DCI Saunders. 'Jeffries, Loizou – get down there and see what's going on. Take a couple of uniforms with you. This is getting more and more ridiculous by the minute. Gorman? Are you all right? Gorman?'

Less than three minutes passed before DC Jeffries reappeared. His face was colourless with shock, like a black-and-white photograph of himself.

'Malik's brown bread, sir. He's been – I mean, Christ, it's like some wild animal's attacked him. He's been literally torn to bits. Head bashed in. Guts hanging out. Never seen anything like it.'

'God almighty. What about the officer who was with him?'

DC Jeffries shook his head. 'Bone? No sign of him anywhere – not so far, anyhow, but there's stacks of old rubbish down there, carpets and stuff, so we're still looking. We've tried his r/t but he's not responding.'

DC Gorman was sitting up now. A female firefighter was crouching beside him, dabbing the graze on his forehead with an antiseptic wipe.

'You all right, Gorman?' asked DCI Saunders.

'Yes, guv. Sorry. Hell of a jolt seeing Malik like that. He and me, we've been working together for years. Ever since we passed out from Hendon.'

'Right. I think I need to take a look for myself. We'll be wanting floodlights down there for a start. And you CSIs can come down too. It seems like you've got your work cut out for you today, and no mistake.'

'I'll come down with you, guv.'

'No, Gorman, you stay here. Don't want you conking out again. We'd have to carry you back up the stairs if you did and you're not exactly a lightweight.'

Two of the forensic team went off to fetch LED floodlights from their vans outside, while DC Jeffries went back down the basement stairs and DCI Saunders followed him. As they crossed the basement floor they saw one of the uniformed officers standing guard over DC Malik's remains. DC Loizou and the other uniformed officer were right down at the far end of the basement, their flashlight beams criss-crossing each other as if they were fencing with light sabres.

DCI Saunders went up to DC Malik's body and stood looking down at it for almost half a minute without saying anything. DC Loizou came to join him.

'Guv? There's been a hole broken into the wall back there, big enough to climb through, and it looks like it leads into a tunnel. Whoever did this must have escaped that way, and they must have taken PC Bone along with them. There's no trace of him anywhere in here.'

'I ask you,' said DCI Saunders, unable to take his eyes off DC Malik's body. 'What kind of a raving psychopath can kill somebody like this? We can only hope that they bashed his head in first, so that he didn't suffer.'

He paused, and then he said, 'All right. Let's take a look at this hole. You say it leads into a tunnel?'

'It looks like it. And a fair-sized tunnel too.'

They went to join DC Jeffries at the far end of the basement.

The hole in the wall was about a metre and a half high and a metre wide. It had been made by chiselling out sixty or seventy bricks, which were still lying scattered around it on the floor. Then it had been partially hidden from view with rolls of sodden carpet stacked upright on either side. DCI Saunders bent down to peer inside it, but it was completely dark, and even when DC Jeffries lent him his flashlight, all he could see was bricks. However, he could feel a faint draught on his face, as if somewhere the tunnel led out into the open air.

He was still looking when the whole basement was lit up with circling lights. Two forensic examiners were coming down the stairs with portable LED lamps. One of them went over to join the officer standing over DC Malik's body while the other came up to DCI Saunders.

'Jesus,' he said, nodding back with a sad expression in the direction of DC Malik. 'Messy.' He was already suffering from pattern baldness even though he looked as if he had only recently left school.

'That's the understatement of the year,' said DCI Saunders. 'But now we've got ourselves some decent light, let's take a look inside this hole and see where it leads to.'

DC Jeffries and DC Loizou climbed through the hole first, followed by the forensic examiner with his LED lamp and then DCI Saunders.

DC Jeffries had been right: it was a circular tunnel, about three metres in diameter. Its curved walls were all brick, although the floor was covered in loose clay soil and rubble. The forensic examiner shone his lamp along it, but they couldn't see any end to it, only more darkness.

'This is Victorian engineering,' he said. 'They were still using bricks to line Underground tunnels in those days, instead of concrete.'

'So you think it's a Tube train tunnel?' asked DCI Saunders.

'By the look of it, yes, almost certainly. We're at least ten metres below the surface here, so I'd say it was built around 1890, when they first started using electric trains instead of steam. There's been no tracks laid down though, so obviously it was never used, and I can't say I've ever heard of it. It runs east to west too, but the Northern Line is the nearest Underground line, and that runs north to south. Maybe this was dug as some kind of extension, but then for some reason they abandoned it.'

'Well, somebody's found it. More than likely the same squatters responsible for those barbecues upstairs. What we need to do now is find out how far it goes, and where to, and see if we can discover any trace of PC – what was his name?'

'Bone, sir,' said DC Jeffries.

'*Bone*,' DCI Saunders repeated, in a dull tone, as if it were an omen.

DC Loizou had been walking further along the tunnel, and suddenly he stopped and called out, 'Guv! Come and take a look at this!'

They all went along to join him. When the forensic examiner shone his lamp onto the floor of the tunnel where DC Loizou was standing, he lit up a circle made out of scores of burned-out night lights. Inside this circle lay a litter of human bones, arm bones and shinbones and triangular scapulas, as well as five half-decayed pigeons with their sternums and their ribs showing through their dusty grey feathers.

'Bloody hell. I'd say they've been holding some kind of ritual,' said DC Jeffries.

The forensic examiner lifted his lamp so that it shone onto the wall that overlooked the bones and the dead pigeons. 'There – you may very well be right.'

Painted onto the bricks was an elongated figure with a goat's head, with horns, but a naked human body. Its eyes were yellow and its skin was orange, although its hands were scarlet, as if it was wearing red gloves, or had dipped its hands in a basinful of blood. DCI Saunders thought it resembled the way that Satan had been depicted over the centuries in various paintings and etchings of the Black Sabbath and gatherings of witches. The figure was very crude though, as if it had been painted by a child.

'You know what we've got here, don't you?' he said, and his fellow officers could hear that his voice was shaking. 'It's a *cult*, that's what this is. I've only run into this kind of malarkey once before – a bunch of devil-worshippers in Clapham, and they weren't a patch on this lot. Just old blokes in dressing gowns and the worst thing they ever sacrificed was stray cats. But there's no question about this, not to my mind. It's a cult.'

4

'So – are we going to have another crack at getting him to talk?' asked Edge, taking a last drag at his cigarette and then flipping it across the pavement.

'If he won't, I reckon we might have to call in Dr Basmati,' said Jerry. 'I mean, the geezer can't be a hundred per cent, can he, going around in a dress and trying to rob crayons? Maybe Dr B can help me to give *these* up too.'

He held up his cigarette and stared at it as if it had magically appeared in his hand from nowhere. 'It's that Linda. She got me smoking again. Her dad's got pneumonia and she's worried sick about him.'

'She's a bit of all right though, isn't she? Worth getting lung cancer for.'

'Well, she's better than a poke in the eye with a burnt stick, let's put it this way. Come on, let's go inside and see if we can get more out of our friend than growling and grunts.'

Jerry dropped his half-smoked cigarette into the gutter and together he and Edge went back into the station, past the reception desk, and along the corridor to the custody suite. Inside one of the cells, they could hear a drunken man singing 'who's taking you home tonight, who's the lucky boy?' and inside another, a woman was warbling what sounded like a religious chant, and spasmodically clapping.

'Quite lively for a Monday,' Edge remarked. 'Only need to collar a couple more and we'll have a barbershop quartet.'

They found the custody sergeant standing outside the cell where the man in the dress had been locked up, talking to DS Bristow.

'We're going to have another crack at getting him to talk,' said Jerry. 'If he can't, or he *won't*, then we might have to think about getting him assessed by a shrink. Then again, we might still have to, even if he *does* talk. Depends what he says.'

'Before you do that, he's going to need a shower and something respectable to wear,' said DS Bristow. 'You can smell him from here. And if he wants legal representation, there's no brief that's going to allow us to interview him in this state. Come to that, there's no brief that's even going to want to sit in the same room with him.'

Jerry opened the hatch in the cell door and peered inside. DS Bristow was right. The smell of stale sweat and dried urine was so strong that he was glad he still had the taste of tobacco in his mouth. The man was lying on the bunk with his back toward the door and his dress had ridden up almost to his waist, baring his huge hairy white buttocks.

'How's he been?' Jerry asked the custody sergeant.

The custody sergeant gave a dismissive shrug. 'Haven't had a squeak out of him. Four officers carried him in and dropped him down on the bunk just like that and since then he hasn't moved. I've asked him if he wants anything to drink or eat or if he wants to make his phone call, but he hasn't even told me to eff off, like they usually do.'

'Right, then, let's get in there and see if we can persuade him to clean himself up.'

The custody sergeant unlocked the cell door and Jerry and

Edge went inside. Jerry went up to the man in the dress, leaned over him, and said, 'Hey! Are you awake?'

The man didn't stir, so Jerry took hold of his shoulder and shook him. 'If you're asleep, mate, how about waking up and paying some attention? You're under arrest for grievous bodily harm and it could well turn out to be murder, so lying there like a log isn't going to do you any good.'

The man lifted his head, and then shifted himself over onto his back, staring up at Jerry with undisguised hostility. He didn't seem to care that he was completely exposed from the belly downwards. His penis looked like a knobbly sweet potato.

'Let me repeat the caution that you've been given, sunshine,' said Jerry, using his most officious tone. 'You do not have to say anything. But it may harm your defence if you do not mention when questioned something which you later rely on in court. Anything you *do* say may be given in evidence. And that includes growling.'

The man said nothing but continued to stare at him. His sweet rancid smell was overwhelming and Jerry almost wished that he would tell him to eff off, like so many other prisoners. He was trying to breathe in little restricted snatches, but the smell seemed to be seeping into his sinuses and he could even imagine that it was permeating the fibres of his clothes.

'Okay, your choice, *don't* say anything,' Jerry told him. 'But there's a couple of things you *are* going to do, whether you like it or not. You're going to take off that filthy frock and have a long hot shower. There's no way you're appearing in front of the Crown Court stinking like a dung heap and dressed like Dorothy on her way down the yellow brick road.'

He turned around and called out to the custody sergeant. 'Sergeant Miller – you've got a pair of sweatpants and a T-shirt big enough for matey here, haven't you?'

But the second he looked away, the man rolled off the bunk, stood up, and slammed Jerry against the wall. Jerry tumbled to the floor, and the man kicked him twice with his horny bare feet, once in the shoulder and again in the ribs. Edge tried to grab the man's arm, but the man swung around and hit him so hard that Edge fell backwards against the stainless steel toilet in the corner of the cell, toppled sideways, and was wedged between the toilet and the wall.

Jerry shouted out, '*Keith!*', but the custody sergeant had been keeping a watchful eye on them through the hatch and had already unlocked the door. He barged into the cell wielding a baton and without hesitation he struck the man three or four times on his upraised arms, as hard as he could. The man backed away, and promptly sat down on his bunk, his arms still raised to protect his head.

Jerry gave Edge a hand to wrestle himself out from the side of the toilet, and then both detectives stumbled out of the cell, followed by the custody sergeant, with his baton still lifted, in case the man tried to attack them again.

'Bloody hell,' said Edge, leaning against the wall outside and brushing down the sleeves of his windcheater. 'Bloody King Kong isn't in it.'

Jerry was rubbing his shoulder where the man had kicked him. 'The bastard needs de-stinkifying. And dressing in something decent too, even if it's another frock. We can't have him looking like that, even if he only appears in court by video link. It'll be front page in the *Sun*. Tooting Cops Nab Cross-Dressing Gorilla.'

'I'll rustle up some reinforcements,' said DS Bristow. 'Don't you worry, we'll clean him up even if we have to taser him. You remember those illegal immigrants we had a couple of years back?'

'Oh, that dirty protest. Don't remind me. They covered themselves in so much of their own shit they ended up looking like the Three Bears, minus Goldilocks.'

'We cleaned them up all right, didn't we?'

'Yes, but they were half-starved and weak as piss. This geezer – he's something else altogether. He's like something out of the Stone Age.'

Jerry and Edge went to the canteen for a mug of tea and a cheese sandwich while they waited for the next shift to come on. Jerry picked up his sandwich but he could still smell the man in the dress, or at least he imagined that he could, and he set it back down on his plate.

'Don't you want that?' Edge asked him.

'No. I forgot. Cheese is against my religion.'

'I'll have it if you don't want it. I've been confirmed in the Church of the Holy Cheddar.'

Jerry sat and watched Edge wolfing down both of their sandwiches.

'Do you get the feeling that there's more to this geezer than meets the eye?'

'What do you mean?' said Edge, with his mouth full.

'I mean, where's he been sleeping? He's obviously homeless.'

'In a cesspit, by the smell of him.'

'Yes, but he's well fed, isn't he? Yet I've seen no reports of anybody looking like him shoplifting or turning up at food banks or charity soup kitchens. You could hardly miss him, could you?'

'I don't think he's going to tell us. Personally, I'd say he's got a screw loose.'

'*Edge.*'

'Sorry. Mentally disordered. Or maybe he's foreign, and doesn't understand what the fuck we're talking about. But maybe Brookes was right, and he simply *can't* speak. I wish her indoors suffered from that. She'd talk the rear wheel off a Land Rover. You never know though. With any luck we'll collar his accomplice – you know, blanket boy, and maybe *he'll* fill us in.'

A uniformed PC came across the canteen and up to their table. 'DS Bristow said you needed some muscle to deal with a BU who's banged up downstairs. We're ready and waiting.'

'He's not just a BU, he's an FBU. How many of you are there?'

'Five, including myself.'

'That should do it. We need to strip him, give him a shower, and then dress him ready for a formal interview or examination by a doctor. There's some question whether he's mentally vulnerable, in which case he'll have to be sectioned.'

Jerry and Edge quickly finished their mugs of tea and followed the PC downstairs to the cells. Four other uniformed officers were waiting there in their shirtsleeves, as well as the custody sergeant.

'Hold your noses,' said the custody sergeant, unlocking the man's cell.

The man in the dress was lying with his back turned, as he had been before. Four of the officers went up to him and one of them patted his shoulder.

'Come along, mate. Time for a wash and brush-up.'

At first the man remained motionless, but then the officer patted him again. Instantly, he reared up off his bunk, took hold of the officer's left arm and sank his teeth into the side of his hand. Jerry was sure that he could hear a crunch.

The officer let out a shout of agony, and flapped his hand so that blood sprayed up the cell wall. His fellow officers rushed at the man, seizing his arms and gripping his wild tangled hair. They forced him face down onto the floor of the cell, and one of them kept him pinned down with a knee on his neck. Two more wrenched his arms behind him and managed after more than half a minute of struggling to lock a pair of handcuffs onto his wrists.

The man still kept on kicking and growling and rolling himself from side to side.

'Do you reckon he's on something?' asked DS Bristow. 'PCP or bath salts or something like that?'

'He's acting bonkers, and he's hyper-aggressive,' said Jerry. 'But if it's PCP he would have come down hours ago, and he doesn't seem to have a high temperature, does he?'

'Mentally disordered,' said Edge.

'What?'

'Not "bonkers", Jer. Mentally disordered.'

'Oh, fuck off.'

The four officers managed to heave the man up off the floor. This time, he didn't go limp, but threw himself violently left and right before buckling his knees so it took all of their strength to keep him upright. When he stood up straight again, he stamped his feet and tried to headbutt the officers as they gradually levered him out of the cell door and into the corridor.

They dragged him along to the shower room, where there was a stainless-steel shower cubicle. One of the officers took out a Stanley knife and cut the man's dress open, from the collar down to the hem, and then sliced off the sleeves. When the tatters of his dress were pulled off him, the man went berserk, growling and snarling and hurling himself against the wall, first on one side of the shower room and then the other, with the officers desperately trying to keep hold of him.

They tried to push him into the shower cubicle, but he dropped down onto his knees and doubled over. They tried again and again, but even when they lifted him clear off the floor they found it impossible to force him in through the opening and onto the shower tray. He was too heavy and too bulky. In the end they gave up and lowered him onto the floor again, where he stayed, not moving.

'What the hell do we do now?' asked the custody sergeant.

Jerry said, 'There's a hose out there in the car park, isn't there?'

'Well, yes. For washing the motors.'

'It's not in public view, is it? Let's take him out there and give him a good hose down.'

DS Bristow couldn't help shaking his head. 'If Inspector Lambert gets to hear about this, it wasn't my idea. In fact, I wasn't even here, was I?'

The four officers lifted the man onto his feet again. He slowly screwed his head around, like Regan in *The Exorcist*, scowling at Jerry and baring his brown, broken teeth, as if he were promising that one day he would have his revenge for being arrested and humiliated. As the officers led him toward the back door of the station, however, he shuffled and hopped along with them, since he obviously had no idea what they intended to do to him. Jerry wondered if he even believed that they were going to set him free.

A woman constable opened the door to the back corridor just as they were escorting the man outside. She took one look and then, startled, she immediately closed it.

Jerry took a bottle of Radox shower gel from the shelf in the cubicle and went out into the station car park. The sky was grey and there was a prickle of rain in the air. The officers had stood the man up against the wall next to the hose, and now they were backing away. The man was looking confused, obviously unsure what was going to happen to him next. Although he was so big-bellied, he was muscular too, with bulging biceps and thighs. Jerry saw that his hairy body was marked in several places with diagonal white scars, as if at some time he had been attacked with a machete.

One of the officers unwound a length of hose from the hose reel, and Jerry called out, 'Okay, fire away!'

The officer turned on the tap, and started to spray the man with it. Jerry was surprised that the man stood unmoving, his eyes closed, his chin slightly lifted. He cautiously approached him, and waved to the officer holding the hose to point it away for a few moments so that he could squirt shower gel over the man's shoulders and between his legs.

The man opened his eyes and although his expression was still hostile, it was strangely questioning too, like a two-year-old, as if he couldn't understand what Jerry was doing. Jerry couldn't remember any suspect ever looking at him like that.

He stepped back and the officer went on spraying, finishing up by directing a narrow jet of water at each of the man's feet. It was starting to rain properly now, although it was a very fine drizzle.

'Right, that'll do it!' said DS Bristow, looking up at the sky. 'Let's get him back inside and get him dressed.'

The officers had just taken hold of the man's arms when a woman in a smart navy-blue suit and a matching headscarf came around the corner of the building and into the car park. She crossed directly over to Jerry and said, 'Heavens above, Jerry, what's going on here?'

'Skip! Where did you spring from? I thought you were still working up in Redbridge.'

'I was. I am. I was right in the middle of investigating a protection racket against Pakistani shopkeepers. But I've been taken off it and sent down to see you.'

DS Jamila Patel raised her right hand like a racehorse blinker so that she wouldn't have to see the man's dripping white buttocks as he was jostled in through the station's back door.

'Sorry about the strip show,' said Jerry. 'Our detainee here was suffering from a severe BO problem, and we couldn't persuade him to take a shower. Let's go inside before we get as wet as him. What are you supposed to see me about?'

'There's been a major incident in Lambeth and for some reason DCI Birkenhead wants you and me to get involved.'

'Major incident? What kind of major incident? Can't say that I've heard anything.'

'That's because it's been totally embargoed, not only to the media but to all the other borough command units too. When I tell you all about it, you'll understand why.'

Jerry opened the back door for Jamila and they went inside. He hadn't seen her for nearly a year now, not since the last case on which they had been partnered, but he often thought about her. Her superior rank and their official working relationship meant that he couldn't tell her how attractive he found her. Not only did he find her clever and sharp, but he was mesmerised by her huge chocolate-coloured eyes, to the point where he sometimes forgot to listen to what she was saying, and her lips always looked as if she were waiting for him to kiss her. Which she wasn't, of course – or if she was, she hadn't told him.

Along with his pleasure at seeing her again, though, he felt an underlying sensation of dread. The only time they were assigned to a case together was when it involved a deeply disturbing threat that no other officer could understand.

5

As Jimmy and Cathy left their pew and started to walk down the aisle toward the front door, the Reverend Canon Helmsley hurried to catch up with them.

'I'm *so* sorry, folks… I saw you come in earlier but I had to answer a phone call from Bishop Abango. I don't like to sound unchristian, but he does go on a bit. How are you both? I hope you'll be coming to the fête next Sunday?'

'We're bearing up,' said Jimmy. 'We're just finding it hard to believe that it's a whole year now since Sam died. We only came in to say a little prayer for him.'

The Reverend Helmsley laid a hand on each of their shoulders. He was a big man in his fifties, with a ruddy face, while Jimmy and Cathy were only twenty-four and twenty-three, and both of them were very slight, so that they looked more like his children than his parishioners.

'I can assure you that little Sam is safe in the arms of Jesus. Of course he cannot play in this world any longer, but I can assure you that he is playing happily in Heaven. It will be many years before you can see him again, and I understand how painful that is, but you *will* see him again, believe me, and he will know you, and your family will be joyfully reunited.'

Cathy's eyes filled up with tears, and Jimmy dug a crumpled tissue out of his pocket and handed it to her.

'Thanks for that, reverend. We're trying for another at the moment but we didn't want Sam to think that we'd forgotten him.'

'Oh, he can see you,' the Reverend Helmsley assured them. 'He can see your grief. He will know how much you love him and miss him and he will know that he is never out of your minds.'

Jimmy and Cathy left the church and stepped out onto Kennington Cross. It was raining hard now, and the pavements were glistening with reflected street lights. Jimmy put up his collapsible umbrella and they hurried around the corner to Stables Way, at the back of the church, which had once been a mews but was now St Anselm's car park.

'What do you want to do now? Fancy going to Amici for a pizza?' asked Jimmy, as they reached their silver Seat. Apart from the Reverend Helmsley's ten-year-old Mondeo, it was the only car there.

'I don't know. I'm not all that hungry. Let's get in the car first.'

Jimmy opened the passenger door for her. As she was about to climb in, however, he was seized by his shoulders from behind, twisted around, and thrown down onto the wet tarmac. He tried to struggle back onto his feet, but somebody took hold of his anorak collar and started to drag him backwards.

'*Let go of me!*' he shouted. '*What the hell are you doing? Cathy!*'

Straining to lift his head, he saw that Cathy had been knocked to the ground too, and that two or three figures were hunched over her. He couldn't make out who or what they were, but they were all wearing what looked like duffel coats, with floppy pointed hoods.

'*Cathy!*' he screamed. '*Let her go, you bastards! Leave her alone!*'

It was then that he was clubbed so hard on the back of the head that he blacked out.

When Jimmy first opened his eyes he had double vision, but he blinked, and blinked again, and gradually everything came into focus. He saw that he was lying in a large gloomy room, lit only by the street lights outside. It was carpeted, but there was no furniture, and no bulb in the light fixture that was hanging from the ceiling. He could see that it was still raining from the sparkling drops that were trickling down the window.

He managed to sit up and rest his back against the wall. His head was throbbing, and when he reached up and gingerly touched his scalp, he could feel a lump underneath his hair. It was so tender that he sucked in his breath.

It all came back to him in a jumble: being dragged back along the ground, and seeing Cathy pushed over too. He could only guess that he had been hit on the head, because he couldn't remember it.

'Cathy?' he called out. 'Cathy, are you there?'

He reached into his anorak pocket for his phone, but it had gone. His wallet too. He stood up, pressing one hand against the wall to balance himself. He had no idea where he could be. He could see that the carpet was brown, with a swirly pattern like snails' shells, and that there had once been pictures on the walls, because each of them had left a dusty rectangle. There were two doors, one immediately on his right, and another on the left, next to the window.

'Cathy?'

He opened the door on his right, and saw that it was a

shower room, with a lavatory and a washbasin. The mirror over the washbasin was broken into three triangles, and so his reflection was broken too. Wan-faced, curly haired, more like a fractured ghost of himself.

As he came out of the shower room, the door next to the window opened inwards, very slowly, but for a long moment nobody appeared.

'Who's that?' Jimmy demanded, crossing the room. 'Who the hell are you and what have you done with my wife?'

The door was pushed open wider, and a fiftyish man came in, dressed in baggy jeans and a torn green sweater. He looked like an ex-boxer, with grizzled grey hair and a broken S-shaped nose. He was followed by two younger men, one with near-together eyes and ratty shoulder-length hair and the other with snakes tattooed on his neck and a lopsided Mohican. Both were wearing dirty tracksuits, one beige and one scarlet with grey stripes down the legs.

They came up to Jimmy and encircled him. The fiftyish man grunted in the back of his throat but none of them spoke.

'Where's my wife?' Jimmy repeated. 'What have you done with her? If you've hurt her... if you've touched her—'

The fiftyish man grunted again, and the two younger men seized Jimmy's arms.

'Let go of me, will you!' Jimmy shouted at them. 'Get your filthy hands off me!'

He tried to wrench his arms free, but the two younger men were too strong for him. The fiftyish man beckoned them and they started to drag him toward the door.

'What do you want? Who are you? You've already stolen my phone and my bloody wallet! And what have you done with my wife? Where is she?'

Still the men said nothing. They humped him through the

door and along the corridor outside. Jimmy saw that every door they passed had a number on it – 323, 324, 325 – and that outside one of them there was a hotel housekeeping trolley, still stocked with cleaning sprays and piled up with dust-covered towels.

'You're in *so* much trouble,' he warned the three men, even though his voice was shaking. 'The second we get out of here I'm calling the police. I don't know what you want from us, but I swear to God you're going to pay for it!'

The men pulled him right along to the end of the corridor, and the fiftyish man opened up the very last door. He tried yet again to tug himself free, but the fiftyish man turned around and raised his hand to him as if he were going to slap him, staring at him with such ferocity that Jimmy tilted his head back, and stopped struggling.

He was bundled through the door and into a room that was more than twice the size of the room in which he had woken up. It was crowded with at least twenty people, both men and women, who were all sitting on the brown-carpeted floor in a semi-circle. The smell of body odour made the air in the room almost unbreathable, and Jimmy could immediately see why. All the men and women looked filthy, with dirty faces and straggly hair, and they were wearing worn-out coats and sweaters and ripped jeans and some of them had blankets draped over their shoulders. Most of them wore grubby trainers or boots with no laces, but a few of them had blackened bare feet.

Behind them, the walls were thickly scrawled over with crude, multicoloured pictures. Jimmy could see strange wolf-like animals with bristling fur, as well as massive spiders and predatory birds with rats hanging from their beaks, dripping blood. In the centre of all this chaos, and by far the most dominant figure, was a painting of a naked man with the head of a goat. He reached from the floor to the ceiling, with his arms stretched wide, and his erect penis was encircled not with pubic hair, but with a coronet of thorns.

As soon as Jimmy was pushed into the room, the men and women all began to thump with their fists on the floor, and to set up a weird, high howling, like distressed dogs.

'Where's my wife?' he shouted, almost screaming. 'What have you done with my wife?'

None of them answered him, and he wasn't sure if they even understood him. They seemed to be incapable of speech. But then one of the younger men gave him another push, and he staggered into the centre of the room, and saw for the first time what was on the left-hand wall.

It was Cathy, naked, and she had been nailed to the wall with her arms out wide, as if she were imitating the man with the goat's head. Her head was drooping down and her eyes were closed, and Jimmy couldn't tell if she was breathing. The nails had been hammered through her hands, her elbows and her knees, but Jimmy's heart almost stopped when he saw that her feet were missing. They had been roughly cut off at the ankles, exposing the gleaming white ends of her tibia and fibula, encircled with ragged strings of skin.

Her legs appeared to have stopped bleeding, but in order to collect the blood that must have dripped from them before, a glass had been placed underneath one of them, and an ashtray underneath the other.

'That's my wife! That's my Cathy! What have you done to her, you bastards? I'll kill you for this! I'll kill you!'

Jimmy lunged toward her, but the men gripped his arms even tighter and held him back. He struggled with a strength that he never knew he possessed, fuelled by grief and rage and overwhelming fear. Gradually though, the men forced him down onto his knees, levering his arms up behind his back at such an acute angle that he heard the tendons in his armpits crackle. He was breathless now, and sobbing, but in spite of his pain he couldn't stop himself from lifting his head up again and again to look at Cathy, pinned to the wall like some medieval martyr.

The crowd of men and women in the room were all climbing to their feet. They had stopped howling, but several women were making whelp-like whining sounds in the back of their throats and two or three of the men were growling. They surrounded Jimmy and those closest to him leaned forward and sniffed, and grunted, as if they liked the smell of him.

'Please,' Jimmy whispered. 'Please let us go. Please let me get Cathy to a hospital. I'm begging you. I'm not rich but I'll pay you whatever you want. I can borrow money. Please. Just let me get my wife to A & E.'

Even if they understood him, the crowd ignored him. The fiftyish man gave a complicated growl and waved his hand and the two younger men hoisted Jimmy back onto his feet again. One of them then held him steady while the other pulled off his anorak, one sleeve after the other. He was too exhausted and hurting too much to resist.

The younger man tossed Jimmy's anorak into the crowd and it was caught by a man who was wearing nothing but a thin yellow cardigan and filthy shorts. The man put it on immediately, and zipped it up, shaking his twisted brown dreadlocks and crowing with pleasure. Next, the younger man pulled off Jimmy's sweater, and then his shirt, and threw those too, to men in the crowd.

Both younger men then forced Jimmy down onto the floor, on his back. Once they had prised off his shoes, they unbuckled his belt and dragged off his chinos, followed by his boxer shorts. When he was naked, they lifted him up and half-carried him over to the wall, next to Cathy. As they pressed him against the plaster, he turned toward her and saw her lift her head a little and open her eyes, although she didn't look in his direction.

'Cathy,' he croaked, but she must have been semi-comatose, because she dropped her head back down again without answering.

The two younger men kept him flat against the wall, while the fiftyish man approached him carrying a mallet, with a row of six-inch steel nails between his lips, like monstrous teeth. He raised Jimmy's right arm and took one of the nails out of his mouth. Jimmy felt the point of the nail pricking into the palm of his hand, and then the fiftyish man gave it five hard blows with his mallet. The pain that Jimmy felt as the nail pierced his hand was enough to make his spine jerk as if he had been given an electric shock.

The fiftyish man then nailed Jimmy's right elbow to the wall, and followed that by banging nails through his left hand and his left elbow, and then each of his knees. As the nails drove through his kneecaps, the agony he felt was so intense that he screamed, and brought up lumps of half-digested salad. Yet still he remained conscious.

The younger men let go of him, and stood back, smiling in satisfaction. He was left there, unable to move, tears running down his cheeks and vomit sliding slowly down his chest, unable to believe that this was really happening to him and Cathy, unable to believe that such unbearable pain could even exist for a second, let alone go on and on without any relief.

Was this really him, or was it some kind of nightmare? They had just left church, where they had been praying for God to comfort them in their grief at losing Sam. Where was God now? Why wasn't God tearing open the ceiling of this room and reaching down to free them from these nails and take them up into His arms?

The fiftyish man came up to him and stared at him, baring his teeth. Jimmy tried to say something to him, but his throat was clogged with sick and he couldn't begin to form any words. Eventually the man shrugged and turned around, pushing his way through the crowd of men and women before he disappeared.

Once he had gone, the men and women shuffled in closer, stamping their feet on the floor and making strange snuffling sounds, although none of them touched him. He didn't look at them, but only at the painting on the wall opposite, of the man with the head of a goat. His pain had grown so overwhelming that it had exceeded his ability to feel it, and his thoughts began to coagulate. This goat-headed man – was he the key to what was happening to Cathy and to him? Was this some kind of satanic ritual? Why had they cut off Cathy's feet?

He wondered if Jesus had endured the same kind of pain when He was hanging on the cross. But then God hadn't come down to rescue Jesus either. God had ignored them when they had lost little Sam and now they were suffering this hellish torture, and still He hadn't appeared.

Whatever he and Cathy had been brought up to believe, no matter how devoted they had been to the Bible and St Anselm's, perhaps there was no God, after all.

6

It had stopped raining by the time they arrived at Montford Place. DCI Saunders was waiting for them outside the Royale carpet factory, grim-faced, arms folded. He was talking to DC Jeffries and one of the forensic examiners, a short, wide-shouldered man with a thick neck and a comb-over to hide his balding scalp.

Jerry didn't recognise the examiner until he and Jamila had climbed out of their car and walked across to the factory entrance. It was then that he realised it was Tosh Brinkley, with whom he had worked on a gruesome double homicide case about five years before in Colliers Wood. It had involved dead grandparents found dismembered in a compost heap, wrapped in their respective cardigans. He couldn't believe how much Tosh had aged.

'Evening, guv,' Jerry said to DCI Saunders. Then, 'Wotcher, Tosh. Long time no see.'

'Well, well, well, if it isn't Jerry Pardoe! Haven't seen you in donkey's! Somebody told me you'd packed it in!'

'No, mate. But they've had me on quite a few funny old cases recently. Me and DS Patel here. Skip, this is Tosh Brinkley, Lambeth Road's leading specialist on multiple murders. The more the merrier, as far as Tosh is concerned.'

'We're looking at multiple murders here?' asked Jamila.

DCI Saunders nodded. 'Thirteen altogether, in what looks like some kind of ritual.'

'*Thirteen?* Are you joking?'

'I wish I was. But during the course of searching this building, we've lost one of our detectives too. When he went down to check out the cellar he was very brutally attacked by persons unknown, and killed. Not only that, the PC who was with him has gone missing. It was DC Malik who got done, I don't know whether you know him.'

'Babar Malik, yes,' said Jerry. 'He was seconded to Tooting last summer for a couple of months. Bloody hell. He was one of the nicest blokes ever. Have you collared whoever topped him?'

'No, we haven't. And we don't have any idea where our missing PC has been abducted to either. But you'd better come inside and see the crime scene for yourselves. I'll be totally frank with you, I simply don't have the words to describe what's happened here. It's more than a multiple homicide. It's a frigging nightmare.'

He led them up the concrete steps to the office door, through the office, and then down the main staircase to the factory floor. DC Jeffries and Tosh Brinkley followed close behind them.

'This place has been marked for demolition for the past three years,' he told them, as they made their way down the stairs. 'It was held up by some kind of a wrangle over planning permission and it's only this morning that the demolition team went in to start knocking it all down.'

'What's that smell?' asked Jamila. 'Has somebody been cooking?'

'I'm afraid they have. I hope you haven't had your supper yet.'

They walked the length of the factory floor to the alcove.

The firefighters had unwrapped the Kevlar blankets from the shopping trolleys now that they had cooled down enough to stop smoking.

Jerry looked across at the blankets heaped on the shelving. 'Somebody been living here, then. Squatters?'

'Only in the past five or six months. That's when the office staff next door at the Beefeater Distillery first noticed them, anyway. They notified the council but the squatters weren't being a nuisance so the council let them be. Better to have them living in this abandoned factory than sleeping on the streets, that's their policy. And it saves them having to fork out for shelters.'

As they neared the shopping trolleys, Jamila flapped her hand in front of her face. 'That smell…'

Four forensic examiners in noisy white Tyvek suits and blue nitrile gloves were taking photographs and samples from the shopping trolleys, but they stepped back so that Jamila and Jerry could take a closer look. In the first trolley, the ribs and shoulders had now charred black, although there were still some fissures of scarlet where the skin had bubbled up and split apart.

'What are we looking at?' asked Jamila. 'These pieces of meat – they're not what I think they are, are they?'

'Take a shufti at the next trolley, then you'll see,' said DCI Saunders.

They moved along and looked into the second trolley, crowded with human heads. Almost all the heads had smouldered right down to the bone, with a few tufts of shrivelled hair on the top of their skulls. Their teeth were exposed so that they all appeared to be grinning, as if they thought that being decapitated and having their heads roasted over hot charcoal was some kind of huge joke.

'Thirteen,' DCI Saunders repeated.

'Do we have any idea who they are?' asked Jamila.

'Not so far. But the forensic team are taking DNA and we'll be seeing if we can match them to any mispers.'

'We'll be able to reconstruct most of their faces too, if we have to,' put in Tosh Brinkley.

Jerry pointed to the third trolley. 'What's in there?'

'Take a look for yourself. Offal, I suppose you'd call it. Livers, kidneys, tripe.'

Jerry went up to the trolley and stared at the incinerated heap of intestines and internal organs. He saw a pair of withered lungs that had partly turned to ash, and a folded stomach. He felt the same way whenever he saw a body that had been smashed in a traffic accident or deliberately disembowelled: people could look so beautiful on the outside, but under the skin all of us are a hideous mess of pipes and tubes and slippery bags full of foul-smelling liquids. There were no exceptions, whether you were Quasimodo or Kim Kardashian.

'What do you reckon, guv? Is this a cremation or is it Gordon Ramsay's Kitchen Nightmares? I mean, do you think they were being cooked to be eaten?'

'Hard to tell conclusively, but when you see what's down in the basement I think you'll agree that we're dealing with a cult here.'

'There's a considerable pile of faeces over in the far corner,' said Tosh Brinkley, with no attempt to hide his relish. 'We'll be testing that back in the lab. If there's any trace of cannibalism, trust me, we'll find it. Not only that, it'll give us a wealth of information about the lifestyle and the health of your cultists – what drugs they might have been on, for example. I always say that you can interrogate a suspect for as long as you like, you'll never get him to tell you as much as his stool sample.'

'Let's take a look down in the basement, shall we?' said Jamila. The burned-meat smell of the shopping trolleys was beginning to make her feel nauseous, even though she usually prided herself on her strong constitution. She had waded along backed-up sewers, after all, with excrement bobbing against her boots, and she couldn't count the number of suspects who had vomited curries in the back of her car.

'You take them down there, would you, Jeffries?' said DCI Saunders, looking over DC Jeffries' shoulder. 'Ken Wallace has just turned up from the press office. We need to have a serious word about how we're going to present this massacre to the media.'

DC Jeffries led Jamila and Jerry through the basement door and down the steps, and Tosh Brinkley came too. Brilliant LED lamps had now been set up at every corner of the basement, giving it an unnatural, overlit appearance like a film set. Three more forensic examiners in white suits were gathered behind the long roll of maroon carpet, where DC Malik was lying. One of them was kneeling down and taking footprints from the floor around his body with an electronic dust lifter and a sheet of black plastic film.

'I'm warning you,' said DC Jeffries. 'It's not pretty.'

Jamila and Jerry made their way around the carpet. When they saw the devastating results of the attack on DC Malik, neither of them spoke.

'I'd say you're looking for a raving bloody psychopath,' said one of the forensic examiners, his voice muffled behind his mask.

'What do you think he was hit with?' asked Jerry.

'I'll be able to give you a conclusive answer once we've taken the poor bugger back to the morgue, but at a guess I'd say that the indentations on his skull were inflicted with a bushing hammer. That's one of those hammers with a face like a meat tenderiser. They're usually used for roughing up stone pathways to make them less slippery.'

'But he has been attacked with such *violence*,' said Jamila. 'I've never seen anything like this. Well, only once, back in Pakistan, when a girl tried to run off with a boy that her father didn't approve of. He used a flail and he reduced her to a pulp.'

Jerry shook his head. 'I don't know what Malik could have done to piss off *anybody* as much as this.'

'And the PC who was with him—?'

'PC Bone. Vanished. But we think he was taken into this old tunnel. My colleague Simon reckons it was dug as a Tube tunnel back in Victorian times but never used. Simon's a bit of a train spotter.'

Jerry looked down again at DC Malik's disembowelled body. He wasn't religious and he certainly wasn't Catholic but he felt like crossing himself as a blessing to a fellow officer who had met such an appalling death. He would have asked Jamila where Muslims go when they die but this wasn't the right moment.

'So where's this tunnel?'

'Right in the back of the basement here,' said DC Jeffries. 'Come on and I'll show you. It's been used for some sort of a ritual, although I couldn't tell you what for the life of me. Devil worshippers, something like that.'

'Now I'm beginning to understand why they called on us.'

'Well, you two have got the chops for dealing with this weird stuff, so I hear. Quite a reputation, in fact. I was surprised they didn't play the theme from *Ghostbusters* when you turned up.'

Tosh was trying to sound light-hearted but Jerry could tell that he was just as upset by the state of DC Malik's body as they were. They followed him to the back of the basement, to the hole where the bricks had been chiselled out. The forensic team had set up LED lamps inside the tunnel too, and they were taking dozens of flash photographs, so that the scene where the ritual had been held appeared to be flickering and jumping.

Jamila and Jerry climbed inside the tunnel and looked around.

'Who's that, then?' asked Jerry, nodding toward the painting of the man with the head of a goat. 'Looks a bit like Satan on his day off, doesn't he?'

'*Kha janthonah*,' said Jamila, under her breath.

'What?'

'It's nothing. I'll tell you later. It certainly looks as if some sort of ritual has been carried out here, doesn't it? All these bones! How many people do you think have been killed to produce so many? Look – there, and there, and there – *seven* scapulas, so that's four victims at the very least.'

Jerry peered into the darkness further down the tunnel. He could feel the faint draught that was blowing along it, and he thought that he could hear a distant rumbling sound that could have been a train. 'Do we know where this leads to?'

'DC Griffiths and four PCs have gone down to see if they can find any trace of PC Bone. I haven't heard anything from them yet but the r/t reception down here is dodgy to say the least. That was a good fifteen minutes ago so the tunnel must stretch quite a way.'

One of the forensic examiners lowered his camera and said, 'It's only a guess but I'd say it was originally dug to connect Vauxhall main-line station with Kennington Underground. In the end they probably decided there wouldn't be sufficient west-to-east traffic to justify it.'

'You must be Simon,' said Jerry.

'That's right.'

'So, Simon, you reckon this tunnel could link up with the Tube line at Kennington? If that's the case, you could use it to catch a train and go off anywhere, couldn't you?'

'Of course. Or if you went at night, when they switch off the traction power for engineering works and cleaning, you could simply walk along the track. Not at the weekends, when they run the Night Tube, but otherwise the world is your oyster.'

'I see. Thanks.' Jerry turned around to Jamila. He saw that she was still staring up at the satanic painting on the wall, her hand lifted to her mouth as if she were trying hard to remember something.

'He's really got you thinking, old goat-bonce, hasn't he, skip? What about, if it's not a rude question?'

'Like I said, Jerry, I will tell you later. It may not be relevant at all. I will have to look up one or two things first.'

She took out her phone and held it up so that she could take a picture of the goat-headed man. Then she said, 'Look – they're coming back.'

A wavering light was shining around a curve in the tunnel, growing progressively brighter, and they could see distorted shadows on the wall like a procession of ghosts. DC Griffiths and the four constables who had accompanied him came into view, and it was immediately obvious from the expressions on their faces that they had come across something grim.

DC Griffiths was tall and lanky with a prominent nose and heavy eyebrows. He came up to Jamila and Jerry and DC Jeffries with all the demeanour of a funeral director greeting a group of mourners.

'We've not found him,' he announced, in a sorrowful Welsh accent. 'We've found evidence of what's happened to him though. His uniform. It looks like it was torn off him. Bloodstained, I'm afraid. We've left it in situ for you forensics to examine it.'

'Oh, Jesus,' said DC Jeffries. 'No sign of PC Bone at all, apart from that?'

'Nothing at all.'

'You went right to the end of the tunnel?' Jamila asked him.

'Right to the very end. It bends around to the north for a bit and then it joins up with the Northern Line, although it's almost totally blocked up with slag. There's just about enough room for somebody to climb through, but we didn't proceed any further ourselves because of health and safety. Well, it's the live rail, isn't it, and the trains.'

'Six hundred and thirty volts direct current, the live rail,' put in Simon. 'And twenty trains an hour in the Kennington to Morden section, even off-peak. One every two minutes during rush hour.'

'Jerry—' said Jamila. 'We need to go and take a look at this uniform.'

'If you do that, I'll go back up and get Smiley up to speed,' said DC Jeffries. 'Most likely he'll send a couple of units to Kennington and Oval Tube stations to see if our suspects have shown up at either of those. If they're dragging poor Bone along with them, and they've taken off his uniform, they're hardly going to go unnoticed, are they?'

When DC Jeffries had gone, DC Griffiths said to Jamila and Jerry, 'This is like some bloody dream, this is. You know what I was working on this morning? Some gang stealing catalytic converters out from underneath cars in the Wimbledon station car park. And now I'm here in this tunnel and there's all these ribs and dead pigeons and this picture of the Devil on the wall, and I'll bet you anything Bone's been done away with.'

'Name of the game, isn't it, mate,' said Jerry. 'You coming, Tosh?'

'Right with you, mate.' He turned to one of the women forensic examiners and said, 'Margaret? Can you come along too, love?'

Jamila and Jerry accompanied DC Griffiths and three of the four constables along the tunnel. Tosh Brinkley and the woman forensic examiner packed up their aluminium cases and followed them.

'What's your opinion about what we're dealing with here?' asked DC Griffiths, as they walked along the tunnel. He lifted his flashlight to shine on his face.

'Can't say for sure yet,' said Jerry. 'Some sort of devil worshippers though, by the look of it.'

'Devil worshippers? It's a whole bunch of fucking psychopaths, in my opinion. We had some down in Wales once, when I was stationed in Blackwood. They thought they were Druids. Shocking, what they got up to. Dancing around in the nip and drinking each other's blood and all that business. Daft as brushes, the lot of them.'

They had covered nearly a kilometre before their lights illuminated the bloody clothing that was lying on the rough clay rubble. Every few minutes, they heard an Underground train rattling across the end of the tunnel, and felt the breeze of its passing.

They gathered around the ripped-apart remains of PC Bone's uniform. His high-vis yellow jacket was patterned all over with bloody handprints, his white shirt was in tatters, and his trousers had been torn apart. His boots lay beside the tunnel wall, with their socks still hanging out of them.

'Jesus,' said Jerry. 'It's like he had a fight with the Incredible Hulk. And lost.'

'Well, whoever or whatever assaulted him, there's plenty of evidence,' said Tosh. 'There's fingerprints, there's blood, there's footprints all over the shop. Margaret, do you want to get the lighting set up so that we can begin to take pictures? I'll get Simon and Munish along here so that they can make a start on the footprints. They're always the first to be compromised, the footprints.'

Jerry walked a little further along the tunnel. He could see two long parallel ruts in the soil, with deep indentations at intervals on either side. It looked as if PC Bone had been dragged along backwards by somebody digging in their heels to give them leverage.

He reached the heap of broken bricks and slag that almost completely filled the tunnel up to the ceiling. As DC Griffiths had said, there was a gap at the top that was just big enough for somebody to climb through, even though Jerry reckoned they would have found it a struggle to pull a lifeless body behind them. It was through this gap that he could see the lights of the Tube trains racketing past, and feel their slipstream.

He flicked his flashlight left and right to see if there were any footprints or traces of blood on the broken bricks. Down in the corner, next to the wall, he caught sight of what looked like a hand, as if a body was buried underneath the slag but hadn't been completely covered up.

When he went over to look at it more closely, he saw that the hand wasn't attached to a body. It was a man's hand with a gold wedding ring on it, and it had been amputated at the wrist – hacked at three or four times by the look of it, to expose the bones, and then twisted off. But it had also been bitten. A semi-circular lump of muscle had been taken from one side, just below the little finger, and there were tooth marks left in it.

Jerry looked around, but he couldn't see any sign of the bitten lump of muscle on the ground. Maybe the biter hadn't spat it out, but had chewed it and swallowed it. He couldn't help thinking of the man in the dress, and how he had crunched his teeth so deeply into the officer's hand when they were trying to take him out of his cell. And what about all the human body parts that had been roasted in those shopping trolleys, up on the Royale factory floor? Were those all intended to be eaten?

Jamila came up to him. In the darkness of the tunnel, her eyes reflected the light like a cat's. 'What have you found there?'

Jerry shone his flashlight on the hand. 'This could be PC Bone's. Whoever took him, they obviously didn't think that we'd be coming after them so soon. Looks like they might have stopped here for a bite to eat.'

Jamila looked down at the hand and slowly shook her head. 'At any other time, Jerry, in any other situation, I would have thought that you were making one of your terrible jokes. But even if I am badly mistaken in my ideas about this case, I am quite sure that you are not.'

7

Jimmy had lapsed into a strange nightmarish sleep. Even in the darkness of his dreams though, in which blurry figures appeared to be sliding in and out of doorways and climbing stairs, he had continued to feel the nagging pain in his hands and his elbows and his knees. It was like hearing a dentist's drill, endlessly screeching in another room.

After about an hour, he was woken up by a bustling sound, followed by feverish whispers. He opened his eyes to see that the men and women had gathered around him in a semi-circle, and that they were all holding up lighted candles and night lights. They were clearly excited, and their excitement seemed to have intensified their smell. Sweat, and urine, and dried blood, and something else too, a distinctive herbal aroma, like thyme.

The man who was now wearing Jimmy's anorak started howling and rhythmically stamping his feet on the floor, and the others joined him. A few seconds later, the women started to accompany them with a high, tremulous ululation. They howled and ululated louder and louder, and stamped their feet until the floor shook.

Half-deafened and numb with pain, Jimmy turned his head to look at Cathy, nailed up beside him. Her head was still hanging down, and her eyes were closed, and Jimmy wondered if she was dead. In a way, it would be a blessing if she was. Even if God didn't exist – even if there was no sunlit Heaven where she could hug their little Sam again – even if death was simply like being asleep for ever – anything had to be better than the never-ending agony of being pinned to this wall, and mutilated, and surrounded by these howling, ululating creatures.

Jimmy turned back to the men and women, looking from one face to the other, trying to see if he could make any kind of connection or elicit even the slightest flicker of sympathy, but he had no response from any of them. Both men and women stared at him glassy-eyed, baring their teeth as they howled and stamped, and sticking out their tongues lasciviously as if they were performing a *haka*, that threatening Maori dance that the New Zealand rugby team acted out before every match.

This wasn't a challenge though, like a *haka*, because Jimmy and Cathy were helpless, and in no position to fight back. Jimmy also saw that as well as sticking out their tongues, they were pretending to bite at their fingertips. He was overwhelmed with a sudden dreadful suspicion that made him shiver, even though he was nailed to the wall, and he almost tore his right hand away from the plaster. Could it be that they were *hungry*?

They kept on howling and stamping for another three or four minutes, and Jimmy saw that some of them were actually salivating, their chins dripping with spit, even though they came no closer. Then, abruptly, one of the men let out a weird *ooh-aah-yee!* sound and they immediately stopped stamping and fell silent. The fiftyish man with the broken nose had entered the room, and was standing by the door with a ragged shawl draped around his shoulders like the tallit shawl worn by rabbis. In one hand he was holding a sagging plastic shopping bag. He made no sound, but lifted the other hand, and all the men and women shuffled back toward the wall that was decorated with the image of the goat-headed man, to give him plenty of clearance. All of their candle flames dipped in unison, as if something were approaching from the corridor outside, causing a silent draught to blow in front of it.

The fiftyish man stepped back, and opened the door wider. A woman appeared, at least as tall as he was, and enormously obese. Her head was covered by a grey knitted balaclava and two hats perched one on top of the other – a wide-brimmed fawn fedora with a black bowler cloche hat wedged onto its crown. She was dressed in layers, with a purple fringed rug wound twice around her neck. Underneath the rug she was wearing a brown ankle-length overcoat, which was unbuttoned to show a herringbone jacket and a dirty white turtle-neck sweater. Her huge belly hung pendulously over the top of her waistband, as if she were carrying a dead lamb inside her sweater. Her mustard-coloured corduroy skirt was spotted and stained, with a fraying hem, and the heels of her rumpled boots were worn down.

Her face was moonlike, with clotted eyelashes and a snub nose and strawberry-red lips. She was heavily made-up, with eyeliner and blusher on her cheeks, and a beauty spot. All in all, she looked like a giant matryoshka doll.

She made her way slowly into the centre of the room, and as she did so the men and women held up their candles and started to hum. She ignored them, and approached the painting of the goat-headed man, and they parted to let her through. She reached up and pressed her hand flat against the man's erect penis, closing her eyes for a few moments as if she were drawing strength from it. Then she turned around and beckoned to the fiftyish man, and let out an extraordinary squeal from the back of her throat, more like a puppy than a woman.

The fiftyish man reached into the plastic bag that he was holding and brought out a wedge-shaped object, like a small brown shoe. He waved it from side to side and so it took Jimmy several seconds before he was able to focus on it and realise that it was a severed human foot. Its skin was crisp and bubbled and its toes were tightly curled over, as if it had been fried.

The fiftyish man handed it to the woman and she crossed over to the wall where Jimmy and Cathy were nailed up. She looked at Jimmy with an expression that was soft and almost affectionate, and she even smiled.

'Why are you doing this?' Jimmy whispered.

The woman continued to smile, but said nothing.

'Why can't you just let us go? You have no idea how much this hurts.'

The woman made a noise like a cough, but with her mouth tightly closed, so that it sounded as if she were trying to tell him that she didn't care.

'Please... I need to take my wife to a hospital. Please. I'm begging you.'

If the woman understood him, she showed no sign of it. Still smiling, she lifted the severed foot and held it within an inch of his face, and it was then that he could see that its toenails were painted pale blue, even though some of the varnish had flaked off when it had been fried, or however it had been cooked. It was one of Cathy's feet.

With great theatricality, the woman slowly spun the foot around and around and then raised it to her mouth and bit into the side of it. As soon as she wrenched the flesh away and started to chew it, the men and women in the room began howling and keening and stamping their feet again, and chanting a word that sounded like 'Hed-*dah*! Hed-*dah*!'

Jimmy couldn't bear to see the woman eating the flesh from Cathy's foot, and for a few moments he squeezed his eyes tight shut. But then he felt a scratching, jabbing sensation against his bare stomach, and when he opened his eyes he saw that the woman was prodding him with Cathy's toes, demanding his attention.

After that, he watched dully as she used her teeth to worry the skin and muscle away from the foot bones. She kept her eyes on him as she chewed, unblinking. Eventually she spat out a pale-blue toenail, and then held up what was left of the skeletal foot like a trophy.

'Hed-*dah*! Hed-*dah*!' the men and women chanted.

The woman gave Jimmy one last enigmatic smile and then she turned around and walked back across the room to the figure of the goat-headed man. With some difficulty she lowered herself down on one knee and reverently laid the bones of Cathy's foot on the floor in front of him. The men and women hummed again, and kept on humming when the fiftyish man took hold of her elbow and helped her to stand up.

The woman clapped her hands, and the men and women carefully set down their lighted candles and night lights all along the skirting board, so that the room was still illuminated, but from below, so their faces all looked like Hallowe'en masks. They gathered around Jimmy and Cathy again, and this time they were all grinning, as if the woman had now given them permission to satisfy their hunger.

Three of the men slid carving knives out of their jackets. One of them came up to Jimmy and pricked him in the chest with the point of his knife. He was unshaven, with a bandana around his sweaty forehead, and two of his front teeth were missing. Jimmy looked into his eyes, trying to understand what he was thinking, but it was like looking into an animal's eyes. The man was obviously feeling some emotion, but whatever it was, it was incomprehensible.

'What are you going to do?' Jimmy asked him. 'Kill me?'

The man leaned so close to him that Jimmy could smell his foetid breath.

'You're not going to kill me, are you?'

The man gave a complicated snort, but didn't answer. He raised his knife and Jimmy felt an ice-sharp pain just below his breastbone, followed by a cold sliding sensation all the way down to his genitals. He closed his eyes, hoping that he had fallen asleep again, and that this was nothing but a dream. But then his insides suddenly felt as if they were dropping out of him, that same feeling he had on a roller coaster when it went plunging downward from its highest point.

He opened his eyes and looked down. The man had cut him wide open and all his intestines had tumbled out and were hanging in bloody festoons between his thighs. He was in such shock that he found the sight fascinating more than frightening, but he understood in a detached way that he was going to die. He turned toward Cathy to tell her one last time that he loved her.

It was far too late. Even if she had not died earlier, she was being rapaciously attacked by a man and a woman with knives, who had not only disembowelled her but were prising her ribs wide apart so that they could crack them free from her spine, and were cutting thick slices of flesh from her thighs.

As his sight gradually faded, and darkness began to fill up

his brain, he saw the woman grip Cathy's hair and start to saw off her head.

He died before he could see the woman tossing Cathy's head into the hotel laundry trolley that the young man with the Mohican had wheeled into the room, on top of her intestines and her liver and the flesh from her hips. His own bowels would follow, and his ribs, and finally his head. All that would be left of Jimmy and Cathy, nailed to the wall, would be their spines and their pelvic girdles and their leg bones, with a few red rags of skin and flesh attached to them. Only their arms would remain, spread wide, as if they were worshipping the goat-headed man on the opposite wall.

8

Jerry was cramming sausage and sourdough bread into his mouth when Jamila said, 'I still can't be sure.'

'Sorry,' said Jerry, covering his mouth with his hand in case he spat some out while he was talking. 'You can't be sure about what?'

'That painting on the wall – that man with the head of a goat. Goats appear in almost every religion in one form or another, did you know that? In some of them they represent goodness and purity but in others they represent evil. Jesus in the Bible separated the sheep from the goats on Judgement Day, didn't he? The sheep were blessed and sent to heaven and the goats were cursed and sent to hell, and even now we refer to goats as being bad, don't we?'

'Not me, skip. But then I can't say I know any goats, not personally, so it's difficult to form an opinion.'

They were sitting next to a bare brick wall in Mud, the Australian coffee house on Mitcham Road, only two minutes' walk away from Tooting police station. Jerry had been ravenously hungry. When he had returned to his flat from Kennington late last night, he had eaten nothing more than a Bombay Bad Boy Pot Noodle, and even that had been hard to swallow after seeing Babar Malik's smashed-up body and PC Bone's severed hand with a bite taken out of it.

He had ordered Mud's wild mushroom special, which was two slices of sourdough with two poached eggs, a grilled sausage, red onion jam and a heap of mushrooms in pesto sauce. Jamila had ordered nothing more than a cup of lemon tea.

'I was so struck by that man with the head of a goat because my aunt in Peshawar used to have a picture in the hallway of her house on Warsak Road and it was almost exactly the same.'

'You're joking.'

'No. It was only a small picture, and it was very dark and dirty so that you could hardly make out what it was. But when I was young and I went to visit her, it always used to fascinate me, especially since it had a *ghiin*. That means willy.'

'So why did she have a picture like that? Don't tell me she was a secret devil-worshipper.'

'I was always too afraid to ask her, but when I was about twelve or thirteen I was spending the weekend with her and she caught me staring at it. That evening she explained what it was, and why she had it hanging there.'

Jerry prodded some more mushrooms onto his fork and said, 'Go on.'

'She said it was a picture of Balaa, who was one of the gods of Pragata. In the Kalash religion, there are two realms – Onjeshta, the realm of purity, and Pragata, the realm of impurity and evil. Balaa means "monster" and he was one of the most powerful gods of Pragata. Sometimes he was called "The Shadow God" because he lived in the darkness before you were born and the darkness after you die. He was best known for his power to protect evil people from justice. If you were a murderer, or a thief, he would make sure that anybody who had seen you committing a crime would either lose their memory or suffer a fatal accident, so that they couldn't give evidence against you.'

'Just as well the Merton Abbey mob never got to hear about him. If we hadn't had all those witnesses who saw them shooting that geezer – well, we'd never have got them all banged up.'

'My aunt told me that about ten years before, her eldest son, Ghazan, had a fight with another boy at his school who was a bully. He had stabbed him and the boy had died. At least twenty other children were in the playground at the time, and some of them did not like Ghazan at all, so they were prepared to stand up in court and say that they had seen him do it.'

'You're not going to tell me she got in touch with this Balaa?'

Jamila nodded. 'She said a prayer to Balaa, begging him to make all of the children who had witnessed Ghazan killing this bully completely forget everything that they had seen. But she knew there was a high price that she would have to pay.'

'From what I've read, you can get off a murder charge in Pakistan if the victim's family stands up in court and forgives you, can't you? Which in real life usually means you've offered them a sizeable bung. What's a monkey in rupees? That's the money they have in Pakistan, isn't it?'

'That's right. A monkey? Five hundred pounds? That works out at more than a hundred and five thousand rupees. But the family of the boy that Ghazan had killed were not prepared to forgive him, not for any amount of rupees. She had to pay Balaa, but not with money. And this is what disturbed me so greatly about what we saw in that old carpet factory, and in that tunnel.'

'It didn't exactly fill me with joie-de-whatsit either.'

'Before he will consider helping you, Balaa demands that you eat human flesh, as a sacrifice to show your devotion to him. He also demands that you remain loyal to him for the rest of your life and say a prayer to his image every day. That is why my aunt had his picture hanging in her hallway.'

'Don't tell me she ate some human flesh.'

'All she told me was that the daughter of the woman who lived next door to her had a stillborn child.'

Jerry was about to help himself to some more mushrooms, but his fork froze in mid-prod.

'You're having a laugh, aren't you? She ate next door's baby?'

'She was crying by then, and she couldn't tell me any more. But that was the implication, yes. The thing is though that it looks as if the members of this cult, whoever they are, they're doing the same. Eating human flesh and saying prayers to this goat-headed creature who looks like Balaa.'

'So who do you think we're looking for? A bunch of Pakis? Sorry – people of Pakistani origin?'

'I have no idea, Jerry. The resemblance between the painting on the wall in the tunnel and my aunt's picture, it may mean nothing. You can find so many pictures of demons with goats' heads, in so many different cultures.'

'What's the plan, then?'

'We can ask around in the local Pakistani and Bangladeshi communities, in case anybody has heard about this cult. Maybe they thought nothing of it, and dismissed it as a rumour, but it still might give us a lead. I can go and see my friend Chakshan Varma at the Muththumari Amman Temple in Upper Tooting Road and perhaps also visit the Shree Ghanapathy Temple in Wimbledon.'

'Okay. While you're doing that, I can drop into some of the

Indian restaurants along the Broadway and see if they've got wind of anybody eating anything apart from bhuna gosht.'

'Very well,' said Jamila, with an unexpected smile. 'But I shall be checking your breath afterwards. I know that you are addicted to curry.'

Once Jerry had finished his mushroom special, they walked back to the station. They found Tosh Brinkley and Simon the train spotter waiting for them in the reception area.

'Have you been waiting long?' Jamila asked them. 'I thought you said nine-thirty.'

'No, only five minutes. Hardly any traffic for some reason. It's like the end of the world out there.'

They went upstairs to the office that Jerry shared with Edge, although Edge was in court today. Tosh had brought his laptop and he set it down on Jerry's desk and opened it.

'It's going to take at least another week to complete a full examination of all the human remains we collected from the Royale factory. But I thought you'd find it useful if I gave you a preliminary report, so you'd have a clearer idea of what kind of offender you're looking for. And Simon here has been doing some research on the location and where PC Bone might have been abducted to.'

'Well, that could be very helpful,' said Jamila. 'DCI Saunders sent two units out, one to Kennington Tube station and the other to the Oval. If PC Bone was taken out of the Underground system, he must have passed through one of those stations or the other, but neither unit found any trace of him, nor could they find any witnesses who had seen him.

'They carried out another search along the tracks overnight when the power was switched off. They took along a dog unit too. But still nothing. They'll be doing it again though, just to make sure they didn't miss anything.'

Simon was chafing his hands together impatiently and it was obvious that he could hardly wait to tell them what he had found out.

'I haven't completed all of my research yet, but guess what? I've discovered that there was another tunnel dug in 1893 on the east side of the Northern Line. Apparently the intention was to connect up Kennington with Peckham, but the tunnel was abandoned somewhere under Walworth as far as I can make out.'

'So why did they abandon it?' asked Jamila.

'Again, it looks as if it was turning out to be too expensive for the amount of traffic they estimated it was going to carry. Apart from that, it was causing too much subsidence to the houses directly above it, which was costing them an arm and a leg in compensation.'

'The search units didn't find this other tunnel though?'

'No. I expect it was bricked up when it was abandoned, but it might still be possible to get access to it somehow, like that tunnel under the carpet factory.'

'So long as it wasn't completely filled in it shouldn't be too hard to find,' said Jerry. 'We can use laser scanners, like we did when we went down the sewers. With any luck it won't stink so bad.'

'Now, then, take a look at this,' said Tosh. He switched on his laptop and turned it around so that both Jamila and Jerry could see it clearly. First he showed them picture after picture of the bones that had been found in the tunnel, scattered on the ground in front of the painting of the goat-headed man.

'These are all human bones, and from the various abrasions we found on them, we can tell that the bodies were dissected using a variety of knives and machetes. Most of the bones correspond with the cuts of flesh that were being barbecued in the shopping trolleys. So far, we've established from the skeletons that there were fourteen victims altogether, although one victim's head is still missing.

'Of course, the fact that all of these body parts were being barbecued is not in itself conclusive evidence that the perpetrators intended to eat them.'

'Then why bother to cut them all up into joints?' Jerry asked him. 'Why not just pile up the bodies and pour petrol all over them and cremate them?'

'Precisely,' said Tosh. 'And when we came to examine the bones, we could tell that the perpetrators almost certainly *did* have cannibalistic tendencies. Almost every bone had some remnants of raw flesh left on it, especially the forearms and the lower legs, but also the pelvis and the spinal column. Those remnants of flesh carry distinctive tooth marks – *human* tooth marks, not animals'. It looks as if the perpetrators butchered their victims and then gnawed away at any remaining bits of meat that they hadn't been able to cut off.'

Jamila looked at Jerry and said, 'Just like those who worshipped Balaa. But in the name of *whatever* god that you happen to worship – what kind of creatures can do such a thing?'

'I can't imagine, skip. And I don't think Sir Alex Ferguson would know either.'

'Sir Alex Ferguson? Is he your god?'

'Fergie? He's won more trophies than any other football manager, ever. Five FA Cups. Thirteen Premier League titles. Of course he's my god.'

9

The clouds were clearing away and a bleary sun was shining when they arrived at the South London Scout Centre.

'There,' said Elizabeth, as she opened the boot of the Seat so that Edward and John could lift out their sleeping bags and their rucksacks. 'It looks as if the rain's going to hold off. You should have a really good time.'

Duncan Wallace, their assistant Scout Leader, came across the wet grass with a wave of his hand and a cheery 'halloo!' He was no taller than Elizabeth, with cheeks as red as Braeburn apples, and a comb-over that had been stuck down with Brylcreem. He was wearing a short-sleeved teal shirt covered in badges and navy shorts, and he could easily have won a knobbly knees contest.

'Wonderful to see you two Willow boys again,' he said. 'Take your bags over to the Sunley Building and Peter will give you a groundsheet and a tent and show you where you can pitch it.'

'Thanks,' said Edward shyly. He was ten years old and John was eight. Both of them were pale and plump, although John was slightly plumper than Edward, and had curlier hair. They looked like cherubs from a painting by Raphael, even though they had no wings and both were dressed in scout uniforms with stripy scarves.

'Here, put your necker straight,' said Duncan Wallace with a kindly smile, tugging at John's lopsided scarf. 'Now off you trot.'

He watched the boys making their way to the main camp building, and then he turned to Elizabeth. 'How are they taking it?'

'Quite hard,' said Elizabeth. She was a small, dark-haired woman, quite pretty in a very English way, but she wore no make-up and her eyebrows were unplucked, and the simple black spotted dress she was wearing made her look older than thirty-seven.

'Well, I hope the next couple of days will take their minds off things,' said Duncan Wallace. 'We'll be keeping them very busy... they'll be making shoe-racks and lighting campfires and learning how to cook. A bit of astronomy too, if it's not too cloudy.'

'Edward seems to be more distressed than John,' said Elizabeth. 'He hasn't been sleeping and I caught him cutting his arm with Vivian's penknife. I'd be grateful if you'd keep a special eye on him.'

'Of course. It's understandable though, him feeling so upset. It hasn't been all that long now, has it?'

'Seven weeks. Seven weeks and two days, actually.'

Duncan Wallace reached out his hand as if he were going to give Elizabeth a reassuring pat on the back, but then he thought better of it, and lowered it again.

Elizabeth said, 'You have my mobile number, don't you, just in case?'

'Yes. Yes, I do. And will you be doing anything special while the boys are camping? It'll give you a bit of a break, won't it?'

Elizabeth turned to look at him. 'If you want to know the

truth, Duncan, it'll give me some time to cry. I need that more than anything else.'

With the help of an older scout, Edward and John pitched their circular blue tent at the side of the main field. It was sheltered by the sycamore trees that surrounded the centre, and next to a line of twelve other tents from the 34th Camberwell Scout Group.

'My name's Jaydon,' said the older scout. He was black and tall and skinny and very serious, and wore about half a dozen friendship bracelets. 'If there's anything you want, or anything you're not sure about, just go to the Ismay building and ask for me. We're having a yell and a sing-song at six o'clock round the campfire circle, and a barbecue with chicken legs and burgers and stuff. You're not vegan or nothing, are you?'

Edward and John both shook their heads.

'Is this your first time camping?' Jaydon asked them. 'You don't need to worry about nothing, honest. I'm only asking because you look a little shook, that's all. There's proper toilets and showers and all that. And I'll make sure you have a wicked time.'

'Thanks, we're okay,' said Edward.

Once Jaydon had gone, Edward and John unrolled their sleeping bags and unbuckled their rucksacks to take out their pyjamas.

'Do you think Daddy would mind us going camping?' asked John.

'Why would he mind?'

'Because we should be taking care of Mummy, shouldn't we? Not going off and having fun.'

'How can he mind? He's dead.'

'Yes, but if he was still alive.'

'If he was still alive then *he'd* be taking care of Mummy. And anyway, Mummy wanted us to go. She said it would do us good to do something normal.'

John was silent for a long time, and then he asked a question that he had never dared to ask before, in case their mother overheard him, or in case he couldn't stop himself from bursting into tears.

'Do you think it hurt?'

'What? When his car crashed?'

'I mean when it caught fire and he couldn't get out.'

'I don't know. I think he was probably knocked out and didn't feel anything.'

They were still sitting cross-legged in silence when Duncan Wallace's face suddenly appeared, peering at an angle into the porch of their tent.

'Hallo, you two Willow boys! All set up and raring to have some fun? We're just starting a game of seven-a-side footie and we could do with two more! Hubba-hubba!'

Edward looked at John and John looked back at Edward. Both of them had tears in their eyes. Edward wiped his eyes on the sleeve of his shirt and crouched his way out of the tent. He turned around and said, 'Come on, John. We can't go on feeling sad for ever.'

John stood up and the two of them went trotting after Duncan to the other side of the field, where several scouts were already shouting and whistling and kicking a football around.

It was dark by six o'clock. Edward and John put on their black puffa jackets and went to join all the other scouts sitting on the wooden benches around the campfire circle. The evening was chilly, but the fire was already well ablaze – eight or nine large oak logs, which had been lit with beech branches for kindling – and it was giving out a heat that flushed everybody's faces.

They started the evening with yells and songs so that everybody could let off steam and laugh. Songs like 'Banana Cheers' and 'Combination Underwear' and 'Great Green Gobs'.

'Great green gobs of greasy grimy gopher guts!' they all sang. 'Mutilated monkey meat and little birdie turdy feet!'

By the time they sang it for the third time, Edward and John were both singing at the tops of their voices and stamping their feet and smiling at each other, bright-eyed.

'Eagle eyeballs and camel snot! All these things were mixed in a pot! I lost my spoon so they gave me a straw!' they sang, and then joined in with the rest of the crowd to make loud sucking noises.

When they had finished singing they all queued up by the barbecue, and two adult leaders served out hamburgers and sausages and chicken legs.

'This is the best evening ever,' said John, biting at a burned sausage on a stick and holding a can of Tango Apple between his knees.

Edward was staring at the fire and wondering what it would feel like if he thrust his hand into it and held it there – whether he would feel the same pain that their father must have felt when he was trapped in his burning BMW.

'Yes,' he said distantly.

After they had eaten their sausages and hamburgers and chicken, every scout was given a pot of chocolate mousse and a plastic spoon. Edward stirred his mousse slowly, but John wolfed his down as fast as he could, and after he had emptied his pot he wiped his mouth with the back of his hand and said to Edward, 'I'm going to do my magic trick.'

'All right,' said Edward. 'Go on, then.' He was quite pleased in a big-brotherly way that John had cheered up so much. He only wished that he could feel the same.

John slid down his woggle and unwound his scarf from around his neck, and then he stood up and walked over to the campfire.

'Pay attention, everybody!' he called out. He held up his empty mousse pot in one hand and his scarf in the other. 'I'm going to show you some amazing magic!'

All the scouts stopped chattering and laughing, although one or two of them blew raspberries and one of them shouted out, 'What are you going to do? Disappear? That would do us all a favour!'

But John ignored the raspberries and the catcalls and waved his scarf from side to side, reciting his magic words, 'Wizardus, bizardus, spellus, macsmellus!'

He draped his scarf over the mousse pot, holding it up even higher. Then he recited more magic words: 'Pottus, splottus, vanishus, splanishus!'

With that, he whipped the scarf away with a flourish, and the mousse pot had disappeared. He shook the scarf and turned it this way and that, so that everybody could see it. There was a moment's silence, and then a few of the scouts whistled and clapped.

'So where is it?' one of them called out. 'Down your trousers? Up your bum?'

John tilted his head sideways, pressing one hand against his neck. As he did so, there was a sharp crackling sound, as if his spine were breaking. Then he straightened up, shook his head, and said, 'Oof! That's better!'

He lifted his left arm, and the mousse pot dropped out from his armpit, crushed flat. This time he was given loud applause and laughter.

When he sat down again, Edward patted him on the back and smiled. 'It was Daddy taught you that one, wasn't it? I wish he could have been here to see you do it.'

'I bet he's watching from somewhere.'

It was then that Duncan stood up and clapped his hands and announced that he was going to tell them a spooky story. They all shouted out, '*Wooooo!*'

'A brother and a sister went into the woods one day to pick *mushrooms*,' said Duncan, in a low, quavering voice. 'Unfortunately they got lost, and soon night began to fall. As they tried to find their way through the trees, they heard rustling noises, and growling, and they were sure they could see green eyes glowing in the dark.'

'*Woooooo!*' shouted the scouts, and burst out laughing.

'The brother and sister were really starting to panic when they saw lighted windows up ahead of them. It was a cottage, right in the middle of the woods, with smoke coming out of the chimney. They knocked on the door and a kind-looking man answered. They told him they were lost, so he invited them to come inside. He said that he and his wife would look after them until morning, when they could find their way home.

'The man's wife sat the two of them down in front of the fire and she fed them with tasty vegetable soup. When they grew tired, she made up two beds for them, and covered them with blankets. They could hear growling all around the cottage, and see yellow eyes peering into their bedroom between the curtains, but they knew they were safe and they soon nodded off and slept like potatoes.'

'Slept like *potatoes*?' several of the scouts called out.

'That's right,' Duncan retorted. 'Have you ever known a potato to open its eyes?'

The scouts all jeered and laughed even louder. Only Edward stayed quiet and serious, staring at the bonfire.

'The next morning the wife gave the brother and sister porridge for breakfast and then the husband pointed the way out of the woods. They hadn't been walking for more than ten minutes when they met their father and mother, who had come out searching for them. When they told their father and mother how the kindly couple had taken them in and looked after them, the mother frowned, and said, "Show me where their cottage is… we need to thank them."

'The brother and sister led them back, but when they reached the cottage all they could find was a ruin that must have been burned out years ago, because it was covered in ivy. Almost all that was left standing was the chimney stack. The mother said, "This was the cottage where I was born and brought up. Only two months after I left to go to college, there was a fire, and it was burned to the ground. Your grandfather and grandmother were found dead in their bed, nothing left of them but ashes and bones, but hugging each other."

'The brother and sister looked shocked. "So that nice couple who took us in last night – they were *ghosts*?"'

The instant Duncan said '*ghosts?*', two leaders jumped into the campfire circle, screaming. They were both wearing grey fright wigs and their faces were painted deathly white. One of them was dressed in pyjamas and the other was dressed in a nightgown, both of which had been scorched into tatters. They staggered around the fire like zombies, lurching up close to each group of scouts in turn, screaming and wiggling their fingers. The scouts screamed too, but only because they were joining in the fun.

When the leader in the scorched pyjamas approached Edward and John though, screaming at them, Edward stood up, his eyes wide and his fists tightly clenched. Without a word he walked quickly and stiffly out of the campfire circle and into the darkness of the main field, heading back toward their tent.

John stood up too, and ran after him; and Duncan came jogging after him too. They caught up with him just as he had reached the tent, and was about to duck inside.

'Edward?' said Duncan.

'I'm all right,' Edward replied, without looking at him.

'Are you sure? Has something upset you?'

'It was the burned man,' said John.

'I'm sorry. I don't understand.'

'When Daddy had his car crash, his car caught fire and he was stuck in it.'

'Oh my God, I didn't know that. I'm so sorry. If I'd known – I never would have arranged a story like that. Please. I knew that he had died in a car accident, but I didn't know any of the details.'

'It's all right,' said Edward, although his lower lip was trembling. 'It's like I said to John. We can't go on feeling sad for ever.'

Even though both of them were very tired, it took them a long time to go to sleep. They could hear the endless traffic on the main road that ran through Dulwich Common, and the rattling of trains, and the chattering and laughing of the other scouts.

'It was good though, wasn't it, apart from the story?' said John. 'And Akela did say sorry.'

'Well, they weren't to know,' said Edward. 'And you're not a cub anymore, so you don't have to call him Akela. You can call him Duncan.'

There was a long silence between them. Then John said, 'Do you think he can see us?'

'Who?'

'Daddy. Do you think he knows where we are?'

'He's dead, John. He was burned to death, and that means his eyeballs were fried. Of course he can't see us.'

'But when people are cremated their eyeballs get fried and they're supposed to be able to see us.'

'Why don't you stop asking stupid questions and go to sleep?'

'I just wanted to know if he can see us.'

'All right. Yes. He can see us. Does that make you happy?'

There was another long silence. John's sleeping bag rustled as he tried to make himself comfortable. Then, in a small miserable voice, 'I wish he was alive again.'

Edward didn't answer. He was lying on his back with tears sliding down each side of his face.

Eventually, well after midnight, they both fell asleep. The traffic had thinned out now and all the rest of the scouts had gone quiet. Now and again Edward murmured, because he was dreaming, and John breathed the way he always breathed when he was asleep, whistling softly through one nostril.

The sound of feet running softly across the grass outside didn't wake them up. But then there was a tearing noise, and the side of their tent was ripped wide open. Edward struggled to turn over and sit up, but he was too tightly zipped up in his sleeping bag and he couldn't find the catch. It was still dark, but not so dark that he couldn't see three hooded men aggressively wrenching the nylon fabric of their tent away from its frame.

'What are you *doing*?' he shrilled at them, but before he could shout out for help, one of them clamped a rough hand over his mouth and pinned him down to the ground with his knee. He felt one of his ribs crack, and a sharp jab of pain, as if he had been stabbed with a knitting needle.

John had woken up now, and was trying to wrestle himself out of his sleeping bag, but the fabric on the other side of the tent was torn right down to the ground, and a second man reached inside and stifled John's mouth with his hand. He dragged John's sleeping bag out onto the grass and lifted him up in his arms, as if he were a giant chrysalis.

Edward was pulled out too, and picked up. He kicked and squirmed, trying desperately to twist himself free, but he was still trapped within the confines of his sleeping bag and the man was far too strong for him.

The men didn't speak to them, although one of them growled and grunted and said something that sounded to Edward like '*yahada!*'.

They slung Edward and John over their shoulders and jogged across the main field and out through the gates of the scout centre. Both boys were bounced around uncomfortably inside their sleeping bags and they were too frightened and breathless to shout out. Five or six other men were waiting for them on Grange Lane, under the street lights, and when he twisted his head around Edward could see that most of them had hoods, so that their faces were hidden, and that they were all bundled up in thick coats and shawls.

The hooded men carried the boys along Grange Lane, and then along side streets and back alleyways and gardens until they reached a parade of shops. They turned down a narrow path with high brick walls on either side until they reached a dilapidated lean-to shed with a peeling black-painted door. One of the men wrenched open the door and they all crowded inside. There was a strong musty smell in there, like coal dust, as well as the body odour of the men themselves.

Before they closed the door behind them, two of the men lit candles. They growled to the other men and then they led the way down a steep and precarious flight of wooden steps, some of them rotten and some of them missing. The men who were carrying Edward and John held on to the handrail on the right-hand side so that they wouldn't lose their footing.

Both Edward and John had stopped struggling and both stayed limp and silent. Down here, in this pitch-black darkness, nobody would hear them but these men, whoever they were, and for whatever reason they had carried them off.

IO

'I'm cream-crackered,' said Jerry, taking off his leather jacket and hanging it up next to Jamila's fur-collared raincoat.

'How many years have I been stationed here in Tooting? You'd think I would have known by now how many Indian restaurants there are around here. There's bleeding *hundreds* of them! *Thousands!* That's what it felt like anyway. And every one of them wanted to give me a free curry. "Please, sir, have a balti, absolutely no charge whatsoever." If I'd taken them all up on it, I'd have been locked in the khazi for the next six weeks, I tell you.'

Jamila was sitting in front of her laptop, her silver-painted fingernails flying over the keys.

'Did you have any luck?' she asked him, without looking up. 'Had any of them heard of any cults that worship Balaa?'

'Only a couple of them had even *heard* of Balaa,' said Jerry, sitting down opposite her and loosening his tie. 'Most of the others thought I was asking about some spice.'

'Oh, yes, well, they would have done. Bala, that's a spice associated with the Hindu goddess of beauty, Parvathi. If you mix it with two other spices, ashoka and shatavari, you have a mixture that we call *tripura sundari*, or three times beautiful, and it is supposed to make women more attractive.'

'Pity my ex-wife never tried it.'

'I have heard no more from forensics,' Jamila told him. 'They have warned me that those remains were so badly burned it will probably take them a long time to make any kind of definite identification. Weeks, possibly, and that's if they ever can. There were fourteen victims altogether, but there has been no report of so many people going missing at once, so presumably they were abducted one or two at a time, at most.'

'That doesn't help us a lot, does it? As of last week, there were fifty-four thousand, three hundred and nine people missing in the Met Police area. Three thousand down on last year though, so we're making progress. I found two of them myself. Poor little kids abused by their dad, hiding in a garden shed in Furzedown.'

Jamila said, 'I asked DC Jeffries and DC Loizou to carry out a thorough search of the carpet factory and all around the surrounding area to see if they could find any of the victims' possessions. Wallets, handbags, clothing. Anything would have helped to identify them. But nothing. That makes me think that the carpet factory may not be the only location where this cult has been squatting.'

'Well, they took poor PC Bone off somewhere, didn't they? Perhaps we'll discover where they went if we can find this other Tube tunnel that Anorak was talking about.'

'His name is Simon.'

'It doesn't matter what his name is, he's still an anorak. But a useful anorak, I'll give you that.'

'I have already been talking with DCI Saunders. He is setting up a search team along with some tunnel engineers from a company called Mott MacDonald. They were involved in building Crossrail so if anybody can find that tunnel, I am sure that they can.'

'When do you want to go and see DC Malik's missus? Do you think we should take her some flowers?'

Jamila typed a few more lines, and then she said, 'We can go as soon as I have finished this report. I think you and I should also go and talk to PC Bone's parents. In fact, we should see them first. DS Bristow gave me an address.'

'They've already been told he's gone missing?'

'Yes, but we should give them some further reassurance that we are doing everything we can to find him. Apart from that, I would like to know something about his character and how he might be standing up to being abducted. It could make all the difference.'

'Not to mention losing his left hand. And having a bite taken out of it.'

'We still do not know for sure that it is his, Jerry, or if it was bitten before or after it was cut off. But your friend Tosh is fingerprinting it for us. I had hoped to hear from him by now.'

'He's the best, Tosh, but he's not the fastest. Tosh the Tortoise, we used to call him. But he always gets there in the end.'

Jerry sat back. It was late in the afternoon, and he kept thinking that he was hungry again. The trouble was that every time he thought of what he might eat, he pictured those shopping trolleys heaped up with blackened heads and charred human joints, and he couldn't forget what Jamila had told him about her aunt and the stillborn baby.

'Right, then,' he said, as Jamila closed her laptop. 'Let's go and see the Bones, as if we haven't seen enough bones already. Where do they live?'

'Streatham Wells. Sunnyhill Road, if you know where that is.'

'I do, as a matter of fact. I went out with a girl from Sunnyhill

Road once, longer ago than I care to remember. Her name was Marlene, would you believe. Half Indian, half something else. But a real looker. I mean, *phwoaar*! But she said I was boring, so that was that.'

They were putting on their coats when DCI Saunders unexpectedly appeared in the doorway. The expression on his face was even more grim than usual.

'Ah, you two off out? I was passing on my way back from Wimbledon Magistrates' Court and thought I'd drop in to see how things were shaping up.'

'I am afraid that it is too early to give you any definite news, sir,' said Jamila. 'We are still waiting to find out the identity of the victims. Once we know who they were and where they were taken from, we should have a better idea of *why*.'

'Okay, but I've got the bloody press office breathing down my neck like Puff the Magic Dragon, that's my immediate problem. Somehow the media have got wind that there's something majorly weird going on and they want to know why we won't tell them what it is.'

'Honestly, guv – I believe it can only hinder our investigation if we inform the media that we are trying to track down a cult that has killed fourteen people in order to cook them and eat them.'

'Well, I'm not saying it won't.'

'Yes, but you can imagine the lurid headlines and the tsunami of false information that would then come pouring in from every deranged or malicious person who has read those headlines. And you know that we will then be obliged to investigate every single piece of that false information, regardless of how ridiculous we think it is. It will squander hours and hours of our time, not to mention the cost. It will slow down our progress with this case almost to a standstill, and I believe this case is much more serious than any we have come across for a very long time, if ever.'

DCI Saunders went to the window and stared at his reflection. 'I hate this time of year, don't you, when it starts getting dark so early?'

Jerry and Jamila glanced at each other, as if to say, *is he all right?*

But then DCI Saunders turned around and said, 'As a matter of fact, Jamila, I happen to agree with you one hundred per cent. My budget's constrained enough as it is. Do you remember that case a couple of years ago – those five Somali immigrants in Brixton who were tortured and hung up from the ceiling of that warehouse? I led that case, and I can tell you that after it was splashed in the media, we were inundated with misleading and racist phone calls and tweets. *Inundated*. But just as you say, we had to look into them all, every one of them, and what a bloody waste of time that was. The public seem to think that we're just like the coppers they see on the telly, and what we do is some kind of TV series. They don't realise it's all real.'

He paused for a few moments. Then he said, 'I'll have to give the press office something though, because it's going to leak out anyway. Any ideas?'

'You could tell them that an unknown number of homeless people were squatting in this abandoned carpet factory, and that they started a fire,' Jamila suggested. 'Tell them that this led to some fatalities, and that we are still trying to verify the identity of those who lost their lives. That's all you have to say. It may not be the whole story but all of it is true.'

'But they'll want to know why we were keeping such a tight lid on it, won't they?'

'You could say that we didn't want to give out any details

until all the next of kin had been informed – you know, out of respect,' said Jerry. 'But for Christ's sake, guv, whatever you do, don't mention "barbecues" or "cannibals". Not in the same sentence, anyway.'

Sunnyhill Road was narrow, with small semi-detached houses on both sides, and lines of parked cars on both sides too, so that Jerry could only find a space a hundred yards away from the Bones' property. When he and Jamila walked up to the front gate, they could see that the living-room lights were on, and that somebody inside was watching television.

'You don't know how much I hate doing this,' said Jerry. 'When I joined the force I thought it was going to be one laugh after another.'

'Do you know what *my* instructor said to me, on my very first class? "Every day you will count yourself lucky if you have to deal with only one tragedy."'

They swung open the wrought-iron gate and went up to the front door and knocked. After a few moments a light was switched on in the hallway and they could see the fragmented outline of a woman behind the frosted-glass windows.

'Who is it?'

'Police, ma'am,' said Jamila. 'We have come about Nathan.'

The door was opened by a grey-haired woman in a droopy red cardigan and a flowery dress.

'It's not bad news, is it?'

'No, ma'am.' Jamila held up her ID card. 'Is it all right if we come in?'

'Of course. Don't worry about taking your shoes off.'

They stepped inside. The hallway was filled with the smell of recently fried sausages, which made Jerry feel like turning around and taking a deep breath of fresh air. Jamila glanced up at him and wrinkled up her nose, as if to say *I know*, and calm him down.

The woman led them into the living room, where a balding man in a maroon knitted waistcoat was sitting by the gas fire, one foot bandaged and propped up on a vinyl pouffe.

'Who's this, then?' he demanded.

'Police officers, Jack. Turn the telly off, will you? They've come about Nathan.'

'Have you found him? He's not dead, is he?'

'We haven't found him yet, sir, but there's no reason for us to believe that he's been fatally injured.'

'They told us he'd been taken hostage, but you don't know who by, or what for.'

'That's correct, sir. He was taking part in a major investigation in Lambeth when he was abducted by a person or persons unknown. We've heard nothing since, but DC Pardoe and I have come here to assure you that we're doing everything possible to find him and ensure that he comes to no harm.'

'Don't you have *no* idea at all where he is?' asked his mother.

'We are working on the assumption that he's still in the Lambeth area, or not too far away, anyhow. We have one or two leads but it's still too early to say for sure. What we wanted to ask you is how resilient he is – how you think he can cope with being held captive?'

'He's dead cool, as a rule,' said his father. 'Nothing ruffles him – nothing. He was one of the officers who tackled that terrorist on Westminster Bridge last year. The bloke had a machete and he was wearing one of them blow-yourself-up belts and everything. Nate just went straight up to him and collared him. Cool as a cucumber.'

'You have to admit that he's been a bit down in the past

couple of months, Jack,' his mother put in. 'Hardly surprising, because he lost his wife.'

'Yeah, very sad that,' said his father, shifting himself in his chair. 'Circular cancer.'

'*Cervical*,' his mother corrected him, and then said, 'Sheila, her name was. Sweet girl. Lovely. They'd only been married three years and they was planning on having their first baby. Hit poor Nathan really hard, I can tell you.'

'Hammer blow,' added his father.

'You believe though that he will stay calm under pressure?' asked Jamila. 'That can often increase a hostage's chance of survival. It gives them time to form a bond with their captors, and for their captors to see them as human beings and not as abstract enemies.'

'That gives us a bit of hope, then,' said his mother. 'I just can't understand why they would want to take him away like that. They haven't made no demands for money or nothing, have they?'

'Not yet, anyway.'

Jerry took in a breath of sausage-smelling air and thought, *maybe they haven't made any demands because they've got what they want already. Someone else to eat.*

They drove to Eglington Court, in Walworth. It was only five miles away, almost directly to the north, but the main road through the suburbs was congested with slow-moving traffic and it took them nearly three-quarters of an hour.

'I hate giving people hope about mispers,' said Jerry, as they sat behind a 315 bus on Brixton Hill, waiting for a long queue of passengers to climb aboard. 'I don't think I've ever given hope to anybody about a misper and then they've turned up alive. Not once.'

'I am almost certain that PC Bone is dead,' said Jamila quietly. 'Whether he has actually been eaten or not – well, only time will tell.'

'Sad about him losing his missus like that. At least they'll be together now, if you believe in that kind of thing.'

'I believe in Svarga, which is a kind of heaven, where you stay for a while and enjoy the rewards of having lived a good life before you are reincarnated. But I also believe in Naraka, which is hell. In fact, there are twenty-eight Narakas, like the Samghata, where you are smashed to a jelly between huge rocks, only to become whole once more, so that you can be smashed yet again, over and over, for hundreds of years.'

'Sounds a bit like another girl I used to go out with. Maureen, her name was, and she used to work at Tesco. Let's just say she wasn't exactly a lightweight.'

Jamila turned to Jerry and smiled. 'You know something, Jerry?'

'What?'

'You are good for me. You stop me taking myself too seriously.'

'You can't be serious in this job, skip. You'd go effing doolally.'

They arrived at Eglington Court, which was an L-shaped cul-de-sac overshadowed by three drab blocks of five-storey flats. A group of teenagers were sitting on a wall outside the entrance to DC Malik's flat, laughing and smoking weed. One of them gave them a mock salute and said 'hi!' as they passed, and Jerry said, 'That doesn't surprise me.'

DC Malik's flat was on the top floor, so they had to go up in the lift, which was covered in graffiti, one of which was *Satan Woz Here*.

'So – His Satanic Majesty got here before us,' said Jamila, and Jerry realised she was trying to show him that she could be flippant, like him.

They walked along a dimly lit corridor with a flickering fluorescent light until they reached number 517. Jerry rang the door buzzer and they waited until a woman's voice called out, 'Yes? Who is it?'

'Mrs Malik? DS Patel and DC Pardoe.'

The door was opened by a young woman in a black dress, wearing a black headscarf. She was pretty, but her eyes were swollen as if she had been crying.

Jamila held up her ID card but the young woman said, 'Yes. I remember you.'

'Really?'

'Yes, Chandran took me along to the news conference after that terrorist attack in Stockwell last year – you know, when all those people were run over. Come in. But please can you not make too much noise. I have only just managed to get our little boy to sleep.'

She took them into her living room, which was furnished with two crimson sofas piled with embroidered cushions, and three occasional tables crowded with family photographs and gilded figurines of Hindu gods and goddesses. Jerry could strongly smell patchouli perfume, and – more faintly – fenugreek.

'We've really come only to offer our condolences, Mrs Malik,' said Jamila. 'But we also want to assure you that we're doing everything possible to find out who killed your husband. Detective Pardoe and I have been attached to the MIT who are carrying out this investigation because we have specialist experience in this kind of incident.'

'Please – call me Nairiti. Can I offer you some tea, or coffee perhaps?'

'Thank you, no. We can't stay long but we'll keep you updated and if there's any help that you need, we'll make sure that you get it. Shopping, or babysitting, or just someone to talk to.'

'There is one thing that you could look into for me. When the officers came to tell me that Chandran had been killed, they brought me back his wallet and also his wedding ring, but they did not bring his hamsa necklace. It was very important to him, that necklace, so if you could please check to see if it was found.'

'Hamsa necklace, what's that?' asked Jerry.

'Many Hindus wear them, and other religions too,' said Jamila. 'It is a pendant in the shape of a hand, sometimes with a semi-precious stone in the middle. If it is worn with the fingers held upwards, it is to ward off the evil eye, Buri Nazar.'

'It was passed down Chandran's family, from great-grandfather to father to son, and they believed that it protected them from sickness and bad luck,' said Nairiti.

Didn't work very well for poor old Chandran, did it? thought Jerry, but he kept that thought to himself. DC Malik had been smashed up as badly as if he had been condemned to the Samghata.

'Do you have a picture of it, this hamsa?' asked Jamila.

Nairiti left the living room and came back with a photograph album. She found a page with a photograph of DC Malik bare-chested, with the hamsa clearly visible. Jamila took a picture of it with her iPhone. The hamsa was gold, with a turquoise set in the middle of it.

'How's your little boy taking it?' Jerry asked. 'Sometimes

kids don't show a lot of emotion when they lose their dad or their mum, but it's only because they don't really know how.'

'You are right,' said Nairiti. 'Today he sat all day with his phone in his hand, like when he plays his video games, but whenever I came into his room I could see that the screen was blank and he was simply staring at it.'

Jerry and Jamila stayed a little longer, because Nairiti wanted to show them photographs of DC Malik when they were married, and when he graduated from Hendon, and when he was presented with a certificate of commendation from the Royal Humane Society. By the time she closed the album, her eyes were almost blind with tears.

As they drove back to Tooting, Jerry said, 'That necklace... if the perp nicked it and he tries to pawn it, or flog it, that might give us a lead. We can send a picture to the National Pawnbrokers Association, and a few of the local fences.'

'It's interesting though,' said Jamila. 'Why would he take the hamsa and yet not take his wallet?'

'Good question. But you know as well as I do, skip – murderers move in mysterious ways.'

11

Edward and John were carried through a gloomy basement stacked with scores of chairs, and then out through a door that led to an echoing concrete stairwell.

Before he started climbing the stairs, the man who was carrying Edward heaved him from one shoulder to the other, and Edward was almost sick inside his sleeping bag. His mouth filled up with half-digested lumps of barbecued chicken but he managed to swallow them again.

As he was jiggled uncomfortably upwards, he counted three flights of stairs. There were narrow windows in the staircase and he glimpsed the street lights outside. Close behind him, he could hear the man who was carrying John. This man was snorting and panting with effort, but Edward couldn't see him. He wanted to shout out to John but his lungs were compressed so hard against the shoulder of the man who was carrying him that he could scarcely breathe.

When they reached the third floor, the two men carried the boys along a darkened corridor and into a large room lit by dozens of candles. They laid them down on the floor side by side, quite gently, and then stood back, their hands clasped, like worshippers who had brought an offering to a church.

Edward managed to tug down the zip at the side of his

sleeping bag, peel it apart and sit upright. John was lying on his back, trembling, and making no attempt to move.

'John?' said Edward, but John could only make a mewling sound.

Edward turned around. In the swivelling light of the candles he could see that they were surrounded by twenty or thirty men and women, all of them sitting cross-legged on the floor. They were staring back at him with glittering eyes – some of them grinning, with their teeth bared, others looking vacant, as if they were spaced out on drugs. They were shabbily dressed, some of them with wild tangled hair, others with hoods or scarves or floppy knitted beanies. Their faces were dirty and they smelled strongly of dried sweat and the mackerel odour of dried urine.

On the wall behind them Edward saw the painted image of a naked man with the head of a goat, his arms stretched wide, with rats and spiders and bristling wolves crowded all around him.

'Who are you?' Edward demanded. 'Why have you brought us here? What do you want?'

His voice was shrill and he was almost crying, but he tried to think how his father would have confronted this rabble. His father had never tolerated any nonsense from anybody, council officials or parking attendants or yobs making a nuisance of themselves outside the front of their house.

None of the men and women answered him, although some of them started to make a strange strangulated snarling sound, like dogs straining to be let off the leash.

'You can't keep us here! We're supposed to be at the scout camp! They'll wonder where we've gone and call the police!'

Still there was no response – only more snarling. Edward would have jumped up and tried to run for the door if it hadn't been for John, who was still lying in his sleeping bag, shivering with shock. He got up onto his knees though, and looked all around the room. It was then that he saw the skeletal remains of Jimmy and Cathy nailed to the wall, headless, but with their arms still intact. At first he couldn't grasp that these bones and arms were all that was left of two real people, but then he saw the tubular pile of small intestines that had slipped out of their butchers' hands and slithered to the floor, and the dark spatters of blood on the carpet.

He stood up, breathing hard, at a loss to know what he could do next. He could hardly believe that he wasn't still asleep in their tent, and that he wasn't having a nightmare. Yet the acrid smell of candle smoke and body odour that he was taking in with every breath told him that this was actually happening.

Without warning, all the men and women let out a shout, and scrambled to their feet. A grey-haired man with a broken nose entered the room. He was followed by two younger companions, one with ratty hair and the other with a lopsided Mohican. He looked over at Edward and John and nodded, and smiled, and then he turned back toward the open door and beckoned. A huge woman came limping in, and clapped her hands twice. She had two hats balanced on top of her head and she was wearing at least four layers of different coats and rugs, and a filthy mustard-coloured skirt. The man with the broken nose pointed toward Edward and John and she smiled too.

'Hed-*dah*!' the men and women chanted. 'Hed-*dah*!'

The large woman and the man with the broken nose came up to Edward and John. The man made a downward patting gesture with his hand, indicating to Edward that he should sit.

'Why have you brought us here?' Edward asked him. There

were tears running down his cheeks now, and he could hardly speak because he was so frightened.

The man said nothing, but repeated the patting gesture. Edward sat down on his sleeping bag, clutching himself as if he were cold. At the same time, two women came out of the crowd, one of them dressed in a grubby pink abaya and the other bare-legged and wearing nothing but a large green cable-knit sweater and a pair of black period pants. They tugged down the zip of John's sleeping bag and between them they lifted him up into a sitting position, making sympathetic humming sounds and stroking his scruffed-up hair.

John blinked at Edward and saw that he was crying, but Edward reached across and took hold of John's hand and squeezed it.

'It's all right, John. I don't know what they want. They won't say. But I don't think they're going to hurt us.'

John looked around the room, and then up at the large woman with two hats.

'Where are we?' he whispered. 'Who are these people?'

'I don't know. They don't seem to speak. I think all we can do is stay quiet and let them do what they want.'

'On the wall there. Is that real bones?'

'I think so. It's gross.'

'They're not going to do that to us, are they?'

The man with the broken nose beckoned again, and this time two men came up to Edward and John. One of them was emaciated, with enormous elf-like ears and a wispy white beard. The other was short and blocky and sweaty, with a cast in his eyes so that it was difficult to know where he was looking, and black stubble, and an underbite. The one with the beard was carrying a long glass bottle with a glass stopper in it, and the short one was carrying a yellow plastic cup.

Both men knelt down beside Edward and John, and the one with the beard pulled the stopper out of the test tube and poured some thin amber liquid into the cup. The short one held the cup out to Edward and repeatedly lifted his left hand up to his lips, indicating that Edward should take it and drink it.

Edward said, 'It's not poison, is it? I'm not drinking poison!'

The man with the broken nose closed his eyes and shook his head, as if to indicate that the last thing he would ever do is give them anything that would do them harm.

Edward took the cup and sniffed it. The liquid smelled like liquorice, but with a faintly menthol aroma too. It reminded him of the cough medicine that his mother had given him last Christmas, when he had the flu.

'Why do I have to drink this?' he asked, but neither the man with the broken nose nor the man with the beard would answer him. They simply stared at him expectantly. The woman with the two hats folded her arms as if she were prepared to wait for hours, if necessary. The rest of the men and women in the room shuffled their feet and some of them made that snarling noise, but only softly.

Edward sniffed the liquid again, and then he held the cup out and said, 'No. I'm not drinking it. I don't know what it is and I don't know why I should.'

The short man made no attempt to take the cup back. But then the man with the broken nose beckoned again, and the young man with the Mohican came forward and dropped down on his knees beside John. He slid a long carving knife out of a sheath inside his pants, and then he gripped John's hair in his left hand and pulled his head back sharply to expose his neck. He held the knife up to John's throat and turned to Edward, raising one eyebrow.

Not a single word had been spoken, but somehow that made the threat even more terrifying. The message was clear. *Drink, or watch your brother die, right in front of you.*

His hand shaking, Edward lifted the cup to his lips. He hesitated for a second, but then the young man in the tracksuit pulled John's head even further back and John said, *gah!* Edward drank. The liquid slipped down easily, and it wasn't at all unpleasant, although it had a dry aftertaste like cardboard.

He handed the cup back to the short man, and the man with the beard filled it up again. The young man with the Mohican released his grip on John's hair and stood up, sliding his knife back into its sheath. The short man held the cup out to John and made the same drinking gesture.

John looked anxiously at Edward, but Edward said, 'Go on. I don't know what it is but I don't think it's poison and it doesn't taste too bad.'

John took the cup and drank, his eyes still looking anxiously at Edward over the rim. He spluttered and coughed, but he managed to swallow all of the liquid and hand the cup back.

The man with the broken nose then repeated that patting gesture, and Edward realised that he wanted the two of them to lie down on top of their sleeping bags. He closed both his eyes too, and held his fingertips against his eyelids.

'I think he wants us to go to sleep,' said Edward.

'I'm not tired. I just want to get out of here and go home. That drink's made me feel funny.'

'We'll just have to be patient. If we do what they want, I don't think they'll hurt us.'

'That man pulled my hair and *that* hurt. And I thought he was going to cut my throat.'

'He only did it to scare us.'

'Well, it did. It *did* scare me. And I'm *still* scared.'

★ ★ ★

Edward was determined not to go to sleep, even though he kept his eyes closed. The man with the broken nose was prowling restlessly around the room, making grunting and growling noises to the men and women sitting on the floor, and he came back again and again to check on Edward and John, holding up a candle in front of their faces to see if they had dropped off yet.

'John,' Edward whispered, when he could hear that the man with the broken nose was on the opposite side of the room.

John didn't answer.

'*John!*'

There was still no answer so Edward opened his eyes. He saw that John was lying on his back, his mouth slightly open, and that he was fast asleep. He heard the man with the broken nose making his way back toward them, and so he quickly closed his eyes and pretended that he was asleep too.

When he opened his eyes again, he was sure that only a few minutes had passed, and yet it was daylight outside. It looked like one of those grey sunless days with no wind. He lifted his head cautiously and looked around. The men and women had all gone, and the room was empty except for him and the boy lying next to him, still asleep.

He had a vague idea that he should know who this boy was. He seemed familiar, and he was dressed in similar red-striped pyjamas, and the khaki padded mats on which they were both lying were identical. Yet Edward couldn't think of his name, or even a word for *what* he was.

He sat up. He had seen this room before, he was sure of it,

with its paintings, and with its two half-skeletons nailed to the wall. Yet he couldn't think when he had seen it, or how he had come to be sleeping in it.

He stood up and walked to the window. He tried to lean out but he knocked his forehead against the glass. He reached up and pressed his hand against it. There was nothing there, and yet the air felt solid.

He looked down and he was alarmed to see that the ground was so far below. Tiny people were walking up and down, and there were dozens of large boxlike objects sliding backwards and forwards. One of these boxlike objects was even larger than the others, and red, and he was sure that he could make out people actually sitting inside it.

When he raised his eyes, he saw a transparent boy floating in the air outside, and staring back at him. He jumped back in fright, but the boy jumped back too, and vanished.

Cautiously, he approached the window again, and the transparent boy reappeared. The two of them stared at each other for a long time. Edward wanted to ask him who he was, and how he could float in the air like that, but he couldn't think of any words. He knew there was a way of speaking, but all he could do was growl in the back of his throat.

He turned around. The other boy was awake now, and was sitting up and looking around. It was obvious that he was just as bewildered as Edward had been, and that he couldn't think where he was or what he was doing here.

He saw Edward and let out a squeaking sound, almost like a mouse. Edward crossed back toward the crumpled mats, but the boy jumped up and backed away to the wall where the two half-skeletons were pinned.

Edward wanted to say, 'It's all right. I'm not going to hurt you.' But again he couldn't think how to form the sounds that would tell the boy not to be frightened. Instead, he growled again, but tried to make the growling softer, and more reassuring.

The boy stayed where he was, glancing now and again at the severed arms and the vertebrae and the two pelvic girdles that were nailed to the wall beside him.

Edward growled again. He wanted to tell the boy who he was, and ask the boy who *he* was too. But he realised then that he simply didn't know anything about himself, not even his name.

The two of them were still standing looking at each other when the man with the broken nose came into the room. He was followed by his two younger companions, the one with the ratty hair and the one with the lopsided Mohican. Behind them came the large woman with two hats. This morning she was wearing a mangy fox-fur stole as well as her rugs.

The man with the broken nose came up to Edward, laid his hand on his shoulder and growled. To his surprise, Edward could mostly follow what he was saying to him.

'You're awake now. Did you sleep well?'

Edward cleared his throat and growled back, trying to convey how he felt.

'I don't know where I am. I don't know who I am.'

'You'll learn, little by little. You see? You can already speak to me.'

Edward pointed at John. 'This other boy? Who is he?'

'You don't know who he is either? He's your brother.'

'I don't understand. What is "brother"?'

'It means you came from the same man and the same woman.'

'I still don't understand.'

'Never mind. Like I say, you'll learn. But now we must give you names. You are the elder, right?'

Edward shrugged. He still had no idea of who he was, and how he could talk to this man in nothing but growls and grunts and understand almost everything that he was saying.

'You are the elder, so we will call you Erst. And your brother we can call Sek. My name is Faust, and she who speaks for the great one here is Hedda. As time goes by, you will learn the names of all of our tribe.'

Hedda came forward now, looming over Edward with her two wide-brimmed hats. Her fox-fur stole stared at him with only one beady eye.

'Welcome to our tribe, you two brothers, Erst and Sek. Today you will feed for the first time in honour of the great one. Then, tonight, you will go out and hunt for more food to eat in his name.'

She was wearing soft black gloves. She held out her right hand to Edward and her left hand to John. After a few seconds' hesitation the boys both took her hands and she drew them in close to her, beaming down at them with her moonlike face. Her clothes smelled of claustrophobic wardrobes, and mothballs. The boys looked back up at her, and then at each other. They still had no idea that they were Edward and John, or what they were doing here, or how long this nightmare might last.

12

Jamila was already in the office when Jerry arrived the next morning, with a cup of Starbucks coffee in one hand and a bacon roll in the other.

'You're up with the proverbial,' he told her.

'I went to see Chakshan Varma at the Muththumari Amman Temple. He had an early flight booked to Bangladesh so I had to see him before he left.'

'And?'

'He knew of Balaa, of course. But he had heard nothing about a cult that worships Balaa, not around this area – or anywhere, in fact, and he has contacts all over the country. He said that if there had been any hint of such a cult he would have heard about it. Balaa, after all, is the personification of pure evil. By comparison, Balaa makes Satan look like a mischievous child – those were his exact words.'

'So we may not be looking for a Balaa cult at all?' said Jerry, prising the lid off his coffee.

'I don't know. I still can't get over how much that painting on the wall looked like the picture in my aunt's house.'

'It could be just a coincidence. I mean, I'm not a what's-its-name, a theologist, but I do know that lots of different religions have demons that look like each other. And for some reason none of them are very fond of goats. Like there's Pan, isn't there, except that he's the other way round… body of a man, legs of a goat. Gives him that extra turn of speed when he's chasing nymphs round the forest.'

'Don't tell me. You've been googling religion and goats.'

'I have, yes. But it didn't tell me a lot that I didn't already know.'

Jerry took out his notebook and flipped over the pages. 'Apparently there was this goat-headed demon called Baphomet that the Knights Templar were supposed to have worshipped.'

'Yes, I have heard of Baphomet. He was half good and half evil. The same as most of us, I suppose.'

'And the pentagram – that's supposed to be based on the head of a goat – two pointy horns, two pointy ears and a sticky-outy chin. I never knew that before. And for some reason old Satan kept showing up at witches' sabbaths with a goat's head on. But I couldn't find a sausage about goat-worshippers being cannibals.'

'This could be a completely new cult that nobody has ever heard of. Like nobody had ever heard of the Manson Family until they started killing people. The search units will be continuing to look today for PC Bone, and to see if they can locate that abandoned Tube tunnel. Maybe they will find out more.'

'How about mispers? Are we making any progress with them?'

'Not really, but by yesterday evening I had managed to finish checking out nearly all the recent reports of missing persons in the Lambeth area, and before I left last night forensics sent me quite an interesting text, although I am not quite sure what to make of it. Most of the missing persons that have been reported are younger people – disaffected teenagers or drug addicts. But forensics told me that almost without exception, the victims in those shopping trolleys appear to be older – even elderly.'

'Really? That's a bit odd, isn't it? Like – if I was picking a human being to eat, I'd definitely go for somebody young and plump. I wouldn't like to be chewing on some old geezer who'd probably been smoking and drinking all his life and was chock-full of warfarin.'

'There are many mysteries to this, Jerry, and of course that is why they called for us.'

'You don't think it's anything *really* weird though, do you? I mean like that clothing virus we had to deal with, or those kids in the sewers? We're just dealing with a bunch of common-or-garden loonies here, aren't we?'

'I don't know, Jerry, any more than you do. We must try to think outside the box. First of all, I think we should go back to the carpet factory and reassess the scene. The CSIs are still combing through it, and maybe they have discovered something already that could help us, but are not aware of its significance. Apart from that, we could give them some encouragement. You saw the heaps of disgusting rubbish they are having to sort through.'

'Okay, but let me have some breakfast first. My stomach thinks that Linda's cut my throat.'

'You think that's a good idea? Maybe you should wait until we come back.'

'There speaks somebody who's never tried to eat a cold bacon roll.'

'Jerry, I have known many pigs in my life, but I have never eaten one, hot or cold.'

★ ★ ★

Three forensic vans were already parked outside the Royale carpet factory when they arrived, and when they went downstairs they found that seven technical experts were at work, rustling around the factory floor in their white Tyvek suits like ghosts.

The shopping trolleys filled with charcoal and human remains had been taken away to Lambeth Road so that they could be examined in the laboratories. The blankets and pillows and other bedding had gone too. Now four of the CSIs were painstakingly examining every inch of the walls and the floors with ultraviolet lamps, searching for bloodstains and fingerprints and other evidence that couldn't be seen under normal light. The other three were sorting through the heaps of rubbish that had been left under the windows by the squatters.

Three uniformed police constables were staying as far away from the rubbish as they could, and had opened up one of the windows to give themselves some fresh air.

Jamila and Jerry went up to the technicians sorting through the rubbish and watched them for a while as they separated plastic shopping bags filled with rotting vegetables and excrement from soggy sheets of corrugated cardboard and bottles half-filled with curdled milk and empty sardine tins.

'Looks like people wasn't *all* they ate,' said Jerry. 'Nothing like a varied diet, I suppose.'

Jamila peered down at the rubbish and said to one of the technicians, 'That tin of beans, that is Tesco own brand, and so is that pizza.'

'Yes,' said the technician, her voice muffled through her mask. 'Most of the packaging here comes from Tesco. Well – Kennington Tesco is only just across the road, so if you wanted to nip across and shoplift yourself something for lunch, you wouldn't have far to go.'

'They must have instore CCTV, so we will make sure we check that. Is there anything else here that might give us some clues to their behaviour? How many of them do you think there were?'

'It's not at all easy to say, but judging by the number of blankets we found on the shelves and all the discarded food packaging, I'd guess about a dozen at least. And then there's these... which we'll be taking back to the lab for DNA tests.'

The technician went over to a large blue plastic evidence bag and dragged out a damp white towel, heavily stained.

'We've salvaged eleven towels altogether. Some of them still had their ends knotted together so it looks as if they were used as sanitary pads. Some of them have been used as toilet paper... the same towel several times over, by the look of them.'

Jerry said quietly, so that only Jamila could hear him, 'Stay down, bacon roll.'

'They all have a name embroidered on them though, these towels,' said the technician, turning the towel over so that Jamila and Jerry could see it. 'Solace.'

'That would be the Solace Hotel Group, wouldn't it?' said Jamila. 'So it is highly likely that these towels came from one of their hotels. Probably stolen.'

'Well, that's a start, anyway,' said Jerry. 'I'll ask Edge to check all of their hotels – see if any of them missed that many towels all at once. I know your average guest tends to walk off with one or two – but if you were half-inching eleven you'd need a whole suitcase, wouldn't you?'

'Anything else?' asked Jamila, looking around the rubbish.

'We'll be able to give you literally hundreds of fingerprints and DNA samples.'

'I am quite sure you will. But first we have to make some arrests, so that we have somebody to compare them to.'

'Well, if we come across any more evidence like these towels—'

'Thank you. How are things going otherwise?'

'Ask Simon. I think they've just about wrapped everything up in the basement. There he is, talking to Marcia.'

'Is that him?' said Jerry. 'They all look the same to me, these CSIs. Invasion of the snowmen.'

Jamila and Jerry crossed over to Simon, who greeted them with a cheery salute.

'Ah, DS Patel – I was going to get in touch with you later today! One of the members of our railway enthusiasts' group tells me that he's pretty sure he's got a map somewhere of all the Underground tunnels that were excavated in the 1890s. It includes the ones that they abandoned because they didn't think they were going to be profitable. As soon as he's managed to dig it out I'll scan a copy and send it to you.'

'That could be most helpful,' said Jamila. 'Have you finished examining the basement now, and the tunnel?'

Simon gave her a blue-gloved thumbs up. 'We've photographed the whole tunnel as far as the blockage, as well as examining it with black light and infrared. We've taken casts of all the foot impressions and drag marks in the soil. On top of that we've labelled all the bones so that we can reconstruct exactly how they were laid out. You know – to see if it was just random, the way they were arranged, or whether there was some religious significance to it.'

'Excellent,' said Jamila. 'One of the reasons we've come

here this morning is to have another look at that painting on the wall.'

'Of course, yes. We've already dismantled all the lighting in the tunnel, but here – I'll give you a couple of torches.'

Simon handed each of them a large yellow plastic LED torch, and opened up the basement door for them. The main basement was still brightly illuminated, even though DC Malik's body had been removed and there were no forensic technicians working down there. They made their way between the long rolls of damp carpet to the hole in the wall, and shone their torches into the abandoned Tube tunnel. They could hear a Northern Line train rattling past in the distance.

'After you,' said Jamila, and Jerry climbed through the hole, turning around to give her a hand to follow him.

They stood in the darkness and shone their torches up at the goat-headed man. He seemed to be glaring at them as if he were angry at being disturbed.

'You know something, I could almost feel that we are dealing with aliens here,' said Jamila. 'People from either another planet or another time.'

'Don't say that. You're giving me the right willies.'

'But it strikes me as so strange that we have here a cult that seems to have a fully developed religion… a god or a demon to worship, and a ritual involving bones and eating people… and yet this is the first that we have heard of it. They might just as well have arrived on a flying saucer, or in a time machine.'

Jerry flicked his torch around the tunnel and then back up at the goat-headed man again. 'Do you still think he looks like Balaa?'

'In my aunt's picture, and in other pictures that I have seen of Balaa, he has red eyes, not yellow like he has here. Balaa is also holding a *panjmukh*, which is a five-headed spear. But otherwise this demon looks almost identical.'

'I only hope that this Balaa thing isn't leading us off in the wrong direction. For all we know this could be Old Nick, couldn't it, and these cannibals could be nothing more than a bunch of good old English Satanists. Maybe they've seen *The Silence of the Lambs* once too often. Nothing to do with Pakistani religion at all.'

'You could be right. But until we can find one of them, there is no way of telling.'

They were about to climb back through the hole in the wall when they heard another train passing at the end of the tunnel. Almost as soon as it had gone, they heard what sounded like two or three pairs of feet running toward them.

'Who the hell's that?' asked Jerry. 'I thought they said they'd finished down here.'

He shone his torch back down the tunnel. As he did so, three hooded men came into view around the curve. All three of them were wearing thick coats and scarves wrapped around their faces. One of them was holding up a hammer and the other two were swinging short lengths of scaffolding.

'*Hey! Back off!*' Jerry shouted at them.

The men took no notice but continued to come rushing toward them. Without breaking his stride the man with the hammer hit Jerry on the left shoulder, knocking him sideways but not knocking him down. One of the men swung his length of scaffolding at Jamila, although Jamila managed to duck down so that he missed her, and she kicked him hard between the legs.

'*Help!*' Jerry shouted. '*We need some help down here!*'

The man with the hammer hit him again, but this time Jerry managed to seize the shaft of the hammer and twist it clockwise so violently that the man lost his grip on it. Jerry punched him hard in his scarf-covered face and he was sure that he heard his nose crack.

As he took a step away, the second man with the scaffolding struck him so hard across his spine that he dropped down onto his knees. But Jamila, meanwhile, had kicked the man who was attacking her again and again, until he was doubled up and gasping, and she had wrenched his length of scaffolding away from him. Just as the second man was lifting his scaffolding to hit Jerry on the head, she swung the scaffolding and dealt him a blow on the side of his hood that made him stagger across to the wall.

All three men snarled and grunted and turned around to face Jamila and Jerry again, but before they could come any closer a blinding light shone into the tunnel through the hole from the basement. For a split second the men stood frozen, their eyes shining like diamonds as if they had been caught in a flash photograph.

'*Stay where you are! Don't move!*' a voice ordered them. The three officers who had been on security duty upstairs came scrambling into the tunnel, one after the other.

'*I said, stay where you are!*' the officer repeated, but the men had already started to run away. Two of the officers went after them, and they all disappeared around the curve in the tunnel. Even when they were out of sight, Jerry could hear them shouting and see their torches criss-crossing on the walls.

He slowly stood up, grimacing. Jamila came up to him and laid a hand on his shoulder. 'Are you all right, Jerry? Nothing is broken, is it?'

Jerry shook his head. 'I don't think so. Just bruised. Bloody well hurts though. You don't mind pushing me around in a wheelchair for the next few days, do you?'

'Will you be serious just for once? He hit you very hard on the back.'

'Tell me about it.'

'Who *were* those buggers?' asked the PC. 'We never saw them come down here, and we've been on duty since seven.'

'That's because they didn't come through the factory,' said Jerry. 'They came from out the tunnel. The same way they took PC Bone, I should think.'

'Come on, let's get you out of here,' said Jamila. 'I want you to go to St George's for a check-up, just to make sure that he didn't fracture any of your vertebrae.'

'Well, can you pick *that* up?' Jerry asked her, pointing to the hammer that he had twisted out of the hand of the man who had first attacked him. 'If that's not incriminating evidence I don't know what is.'

Jamila picked up the hammer and held it up. They could all see that it had a square head with deep-cut teeth – the same kind of hammer that had been used to smash DC Malik's skull.

'Crikey,' said the PC. 'You're dead lucky he didn't hit you on the bonce.'

Jerry took a limping step forward and winced. 'Nothing to do with luck, sunshine. Not when you've got a Krav Maga black belt for a sergeant.'

13

Edward and John tried to stay awake, but they both fell asleep again – Edward first this time, but John only minutes afterwards. Faust came into the room to look at them for a few moments, with an expression on his face that was almost paternal, but then Hedda called him with a shrill screech from another room, and he left them alone.

Edward dreamed that he was walking across a sloping field with his father. A strong wind was blowing so that huge white cumulus clouds were tumbling overhead, and thistles were nodding in the grass all around them like an approving crowd, but it meant that he could hardly hear what his father was saying to him.

At the end of the field he could see a narrow road lined on either side by dark yew hedges. On the other side of the hedges he could see orange flames leaping up, and as he and his father came closer he could see that it was a car burning.

'Dad! Dad! There's a car on fire!'

His father looked down at him. His face was silhouetted against the sky, so it was impossible for Edward to see if he was serious or smiling.

'I know, Teddy. It's my car. I'm in it.'

'What do you mean? How can you be in it? You're here!'

'Yes, Teddy. But this is now and that was then. I'm dead,

Teddy. I was burned to death. But that doesn't mean that we can't go for walks together, like we used to.'

Edward let out an anguished squeal, and woke up. He blinked at John lying next to him, and then he propped himself up on one elbow, and looked around. The goat-headed man was still staring down at him, and the skeletons of Jimmy and Cathy were still pinned to the opposite wall.

Edward bowed his head to the goat-headed man, the great one, and gave him a soft growl of respect. Even though he didn't know the man's name, he understood instinctively that he was the lord of everything. The lord of this world, and the world beneath it. Somehow Edward knew who he was, and where he had come from. He had risen from the darkness below their feet. The world of turmoil.

About Jimmy and Cathy's remains he was completely incurious, neither shocked nor disgusted. They were only bones, after all – no more interesting than the bones left over from carving a chicken. Their arms and their hands were still intact, their fingers curled, but they were spread wide in homage to the great one, as they should be.

He was still unsure about the boy lying next to him. Faust had assured him that he was his 'brother' and although he still couldn't grasp what that meant, he felt oddly protective toward him. He knew the boy's name was Sek, but that was all. He knew that his own name was Erst but he knew very little about himself either. He had no idea how he and Sek had arrived here or who Faust was, or why Hedda had seemed so delighted to see them. He couldn't stop himself from shivering a little when he thought about Hedda. She had spoken to them warmly, like an adoptive mother, but he had found her huge bulk overwhelming, and her warmth strangely threatening, and her smell had made him feel as if he couldn't breathe.

He climbed to his feet and bowed his head again to the goat-headed figure on the wall. Then he walked across to the window. The day was lighter now, although it had just begun to rain. He stood and watched in fascination as the raindrops speckled the glass. He couldn't believe how they clung suspended in mid-air, although he had already discovered that the air across the window frame was solid.

In the street below, people were hurrying backwards and forwards carrying enormous multicoloured mushrooms, and the boxes were still gliding along. Three large red boxes too, one after the other, filled with people. He found it fascinating, but perplexing at the same time. What were all these people doing, and where were they going? The strange thing was that they were all ignoring each other. None of them were fighting, and none of them were carrying weapons, only these enormous mushrooms, which they were holding up above their heads. None of them had animals with them either, except for three or four dogs. No cows, no goats, no sheep.

He stayed by the window for a while, but gradually his attention began to wander, and he started to think about the amber liquid that Faust had given him and Sek to drink. He couldn't remember how or when they had drunk it, but he licked his lips and he could almost taste it. He wasn't thirsty, but the thought of that liquid was giving him an itching feeling in his wrists and up his arms, as if scores of red ants were crawling up his sleeves. Perhaps if he drank a little more, his skin wouldn't feel so irritated.

He began to feel cold too, and shivery. If he could find Faust, perhaps he could persuade him to give him just one more cupful.

He turned around to find that Sek was standing close

behind him. Sek looked wretched in his red-striped pyjamas. He was shivering too, even more violently than Erst, and his face was white.

'I need some more of that drink,' he said, in his high, raspy growl.

Erst went up to him and laid his hand on his shoulder. It seemed completely natural, as if he had known him for ever.

'I need some too,' he told him. 'Let's go and find Faust.'

They made their way toward the door, but before they could reach it, Faust walked in, with his two younger companions close behind him.

'Ah! Good! You're both up! I was hoping you would be! It's feeding time!'

'We wondered if you had any more of that drink,' said Erst.

Faust gave him an odd, sly look. 'You mean that drink that you thought might be poison?'

'It isn't poison though, is it?'

'You really want some more?'

'We don't feel well... we're all cold and itchy and shivery.'

Faust looked round at his two companions, and both of them grinned, as if they knew exactly why Erst and Sek were feeling the way they were.

'Come on downstairs then,' said Faust. 'You can fill your bellies with food, and you can have some more of that drink to wash it down with. We have a name for it, that drink, by the way. We call it calla dew. Perhaps because it must have dropped down from heaven.'

Erst couldn't follow everything that Faust was saying. Some of his growls were too complicated. But he understood that he and Sek were being invited to come and have something to eat, and more importantly, that they would be given more of that amber drink. His teeth were beginning to chatter and he couldn't stop himself from scratching the back of his hands and his arms.

'We must find you some warm clothes too,' Faust told them, as he led them along the corridor. 'There are places where people leave children's clothes in doorways. I can send out Copf and Flecker to hunt for some for you. It will be cold soon and we can't light fires in every room in case the comelings see them.'

From the way that Faust clapped the two younger men on the shoulder, one after the other, Erst realised that Copf must be the one with the Mohican and Flecker must be the one with the long rats'-tail hair. The one called Flecker grinned at him with his two front teeth missing and stuck out the tip of his tongue, as if to say, *tasty! tasty!*

They went back down the same staircase that Erst and Sek had been carried up when they were brought here. The building echoed with loud banging noises and growling and weird distorted shouts, as if it were a menagerie for disturbed animals. When they reached the ground floor, Faust took them across a wide reception area with a rumpled blue carpet and through a pair of double swing doors.

Erst and Sek found themselves being ushered into a large kitchen, filled with smoke and almost hysterical laughter. It was lined with stainless-steel counters and hung with dozens of saucepans. A row of six ovens all had their doors wide open and were crammed with glowing charcoal briquettes, so that the heat they were giving out was almost unbearable. In the centre of the room stood a long stainless-steel table, and around this table were clustered the men and women who had been upstairs. They were shouting and growling and laughing and tearing with their hands at heaps of roasted flesh that had been piled up on the tabletop, as well as cabbages and swedes and potatoes, which had been scorched in the ovens until they were black.

At the head of the table, in her two wide-brimmed hats, sat Hedda. She was holding a human leg bone in both hands and gnawing off the last few scraps of it with her worn-down teeth.

'My new children!' she crowed, banging the bone on the tabletop. 'Bring them here, Faust, so that they can sit next to me and I can feed them!'

Faust jostled Erst and Sek through the crowd while Copf and Flecker dragged over two more folding chairs, and opened them out. Erst and Sek perched themselves uncomfortably on the edge of the chairs, one either side of Hedda, and she patted each of them on the head.

'My new children! What an exciting time we are all going to have together! What a chase! You have never chased opfer before, have you, my children!'

Erst didn't know what she was talking about, and shook his head. Sek sat with his head bowed and his hands clasped in his lap, shuddering.

Faust leaned over to Hedda and lifted his hand so that she could hear him over the noise. 'They need calla dew. Remember this was their first time, and they are only young.'

Hedda lifted up Sek's chin with her black-gloved hand. 'Of course. No wonder they look so white! My poor, poor children! Sclavin! *Sclavin!* Fetch two cups of calla dew for my children, as quick as you can!'

A girl of about fifteen or sixteen was standing close behind her. She had curly blonde hair tied up in rags instead of ribbons, a lumpy pink anorak stained with dirt, and grey woollen tights with gaping holes in the knees.

'Yes, Hedda,' she said, in a whispery, clogged-up growl. 'I go now, Hedda!'

The girl pushed her way out of the kitchen. When she had gone, Hedda reached across the table and picked up a dark red lump of meat, charred on one side, about the size and shape of a large bell pepper. She held it up in front of Sek first, but his head was still lowered and he didn't look at it, and so she showed it to Erst, almost touching the tip of his nose with it.

'Do you know what this is, little Erst?'

Erst shook his head again. His skin was feeling so itchy now that he could hardly sit still, and he felt like tearing off his pyjamas and scratching himself furiously all over.

'It's a woman's heart,' Hedda told him, staring at him with her pale, unblinking eyes. Their pupils were almost yellow, like crumpled cheese. 'This was what kept her alive. This was what allowed her to love the man in her life. This was what made her brave and also what made her weak.'

For the first time, Erst noticed that Hedda had a large mole on her upper lip, and he couldn't take his eyes off it. He couldn't clearly understand what she was trying to tell him, and in any case he wasn't really listening. His attention was fixed on her mole.

The girl called Sclavin returned, carrying a glass bottle and a plastic cup. She had a red bruise on her cheek as if somebody had hit her.

'For this child first,' said Hedda, and Sclavin poured Sek a cupful of the amber liquid. He drank it so thirstily that she had to hold the cup for him, or he would have spilled it. When he had finished it, he sat back in his chair, and looked across at Erst and licked his lips.

Sclavin filled a second cup for Erst, and he swallowed it with his hands trembling. Almost as soon as he had drunk it, though, a sense of deep relief flooded through him, and the itching that he had been feeling all over his skin subsided to a faint tingle, and gradually vanished altogether.

'There,' said Hedda, patting him on the head again. 'Do you feel better now? It's all gone, that jingle-jangle?'

Erst nodded. Somehow, he found Hedda easier to understand now that the itching had faded away. He could also understand some of the words that the men and women at the table were shouting to each other as they tore apart the ribs and triangular shoulder-bones and half-cooked vegetables. They were baiting each other about what they were going to do when they came back from their hunt this evening, especially to the women. 'I will make you swallow me,' growled one of the men to one of the women. 'Right down to the root.'

Hedda offered him the heart that she was holding. It was Cathy's heart. 'Here,' she said. 'Take a bite. It's a little hard to chew, but you'll like the taste.'

Erst smiled but shook his head.

Hedda's expression abruptly changed, and the tone of her voice changed too. 'I said, take a bite! You never refuse me. *Never!* That's the first thing you have to learn. I am the mother who speaks for the great one.

She paused, still holding out the heart and squeezing it rhythmically as if it were still beating, so that its juice dripped from between her fingers and onto the tabletop.

'If you say no to me, you little beggar, and you won't take a bite of this heart, I can just as easily take out *your* heart and feed it to your brother. I'm sure that *he* won't refuse me.'

She held the heart up to his lips, still squeezing it. There was a moment's pause, and when everybody in the kitchen saw what was happening, they fell silent.

Erst looked across at Sek, and Sek nodded. Erst bit into

the heart muscle and twisted his head sideways so that he could tug a piece away, and started to chew it. He chewed and chewed but he still couldn't manage to make any impression on it, even though Hedda was watching him and giving him small, encouraging growls. It was like chewing the flap of his school satchel.

Eventually, he managed to swallow it, almost choking himself. Hedda poured him half a cupful of calla dew and offered it to him.

'There,' she said, as he gratefully drank it. 'My brave boy. Now you're *my* son and nobody else's.'

A frizzy-haired young woman sitting close to Hedda tore off choice pieces of meat from the pile on the table and passed them down to Erst and Sek, as well as ripping off scorched cabbage leaves for them. After swallowing that rubbery piece of heart, Erst was hesitant to try any more, but when he took a bite of chest meat, with a crackling skin and a congealed layer of fat, he found that it was easy to chew and full of flavour. It tasted like gammon, only stronger. There was a nipple on one of the pieces that the woman gave him, with hairs sticking out of it, but once he had tugged out the hairs he thought it was even tastier than the flesh around it, like a maraschino cherry on top of a cake.

Sek hardly spoke because he was so absorbed in eating a tubular length of flesh that had been fried until it was covered in bubbles, and crunched when he bit into it.

After they had all eaten, Faust and Copf and Flecker took the boys up to the first floor. Here, they entered a vast gloomy room with chairs stacked on either side of it and a stage at one end. The women were settling down cross-legged on the carpet and picking up clothes that they had been sewing, while some of the men were lighting fires in metal buckets. Other men went up to the walls and carried on painting them with pictures of dogs and cats and birds and strange orange creatures that looked like demons, with bat-like wings and goggling eyes.

'Everybody must work,' said Faust. 'Tonight we will hunt so everybody must be ready.'

'Do we have to work too?' asked Erst.

Faust led them over to a group of women who were sitting in a circle. They were all winding cords around their elbows and knotting them together.

'You can help these women today. Tomorrow the men will take you out and show you how we gather everything else we need, apart from opfer.'

Two of the women shifted themselves sideways so that Erst and Sek could sit down between them. Faust patted them both on the shoulder and growled, 'I will see you later. We will be going out hunting at the seventh dark.'

The women all smiled at Erst and Sek, apart from one old woman who looked as if she had never smiled in her life. There were seven of them, of various ages. Among them were two pretty black girls in shiny blue anoraks who looked like twins, a bosomy young woman who appeared to have made up her eyes with a black felt-tip pen, and a petite middle-aged woman in a faded brown dress who reminded Erst of some woman he knew.

'Here, this is simple to do,' said a plump woman in a grubby white roll-neck sweater. She gave each of them a handful of greasy lengths of string, about a metre long. She picked up a handful herself, fastened them at one end and then started to plait them together. In the middle of the plait she tied a large knot. When she had finished she held it up so that Erst and Sek could see what she had done.

'What is it?' asked Sek, frowning.

The woman leaned over and looped it around his neck, with the knot over his Adam's apple, like a garrotte. She pulled it tight, so that he coughed. 'See? For when you go out hunting.'

14

Jamila and Jerry had to wait over an hour in the A & E department of St George's Hospital before Jerry could be examined. He kept insisting that Jamila could leave him there because he knew that she wanted to go back to her flat in Redbridge and change, but she insisted on staying.

'Jerry – I have to make sure that you are fit for duty.'

'Really, skip? I reckon you just want a cup of coffee and an hour off so that you can read *Hello!*'

She looked at him and smiled and he couldn't be sure if it was affectionate, this smile, or simply tolerant. He gave her a quick non-committal smile back.

Eventually he was seen by a harassed woman doctor with thinning ginger hair who asked him to take off his shirt so that she could feel his spine. She manipulated his vertebrae one after the other and her probing was so painful that he couldn't help sucking in his breath.

At last she told him, 'You have a nasty contusion, but nothing's fractured or misplaced. I'll prescribe you some ibuprofen for now, but if you experience any severe pain in your back in the next week or so, you should go to see your GP. Have you caught the man who did this to you?'

'When we do, I'm going to crush his kneecaps, I can tell you.'

'If you do manage to arrest him, detective, please resist the temptation to hurt him. We're hard-pressed enough as it is, and we'll still have to treat him, whatever he's done to you.'

He drove Jamila to Tooting Broadway so that she could take the Tube to Redbridge, and then he went back to the police station. He found Edge in his office, talking on his phone and walking up and down as he talked.

'Okay, thanks, yes,' said Edge, and then he put down his phone and said, 'Jerry! I heard what happened to you and DS Patel. Are you all right?'

'A bit bruised and battered, but I'll live. What's the SP?'

Edge held up his phone again. 'That was the last of the Solace group. They own nine hotels altogether in the Greater London area. According to them, their guests nick anything that isn't nailed down – towels and bathrobes and pillows. Some of them even walk off with the tellies. Honestly, mate – I don't know why they don't call them "burglars" instead of "guests". But none of their hotels say that they've lost eleven towels all at once.'

'Oh, okay. Maybe they were taken a few at a time. Or else they were lifted from the hotel laundry.'

'I thought of that, and I got in touch with SunFresh cleaners in Wallington. They handle all of Solace's sheets and towels, but they said their system is really secure and they're not missing anything. Well, one or two random pillowcases, but not that many towels.'

Jerry sat down at his desk, wincing, and switched on his PC. He scrolled through the latest missing persons bulletins to see if there were any reports that fourteen elderly men and women had disappeared.

An eighty-seven-year-old man with dementia had gone

shopping for cat food in Streatham two days ago and still not returned, but he was the only senior citizen in the list. Apart from him, a young married couple had left St Anselm's Church in Kennington yesterday afternoon and not been seen since, leaving their car with its doors open in the church car park. Two Boy Scouts had also gone missing, brothers aged eight and ten. They had vanished overnight from the South London Scout Centre, taking their sleeping bags with them and leaving their tent in tatters.

The disappearances of both the married couple and the two Boy Scouts were being treated as possible abductions, although no communications or ransom demands had been received about either of them.

'How about the search units looking for PC Bone?' Jerry asked Edge. 'Any word? That train-spotter CSI – what's his name, Simon – he says he knows somebody who has maps of the Tube tunnels that were dug back in Victorian times but never put into service.'

'That could be handy. So far the search units haven't found even a sniff of PC Bone.'

'Poor bastard. Lost his missus only a couple of months ago too.'

Jerry stood up and was just about to go down to the canteen when his computer warbled. It was a Skype call from Tosh Brinkley at the Metropolitan Police Forensic Science Laboratory in Lambeth Road. Tosh was sitting in his laboratory with a Bunsen burner flickering on one side of him and a half-eaten sausage roll lying on the other.

'Jerry? Glad I caught you. Couple of updates.'

'Good. Haven't got a tip for Cheltenham, have you? Every time I bet on a horse it drops dead after the first furlong.'

'Wandering Minstrel in the four-fifteen. But we've identified that severed hand. And more than that, we've identified who bit it.'

'You're kidding.'

'No, mate. It's the wonders of DNA. The hand is definitely PC Nathan Bone's. It was severed with a machete or something similar. We verified it with hair samples that we took from his cap. Whoever bit him left distinct tooth marks on his hand, but more importantly they left saliva.'

'Do you know, Tosh, sometimes I can't decide whether I envy you your job or not. At least you don't get clobbered with scaffolding poles like I just did.'

'Yes, I heard from Edge that you'd been in the wars again. Nothing too serious, I hope? Good, good. But let me tell you about this saliva. It's a match for a serial offender called Connor Greene. He's been nabbed countless times for shoplifting and burglary and vehicle theft, mostly mopeds. He's homeless, of no fixed address, and he sleeps rough around the Lambeth and Kennington areas, although in February he spent a few nights at the Thames Reach shelter.'

Tosh held up a photograph of a young man in his early twenties with a shaved head, slightly protuberant blue eyes and a receding chin.

'He's done a couple of short stretches in Wandsworth nick too. According to his records he has a low IQ but he was reasonably well behaved and on both occasions he was allowed out early on parole.'

'If he's reasonably well behaved, how come he abducted a PC, cut off his hand and then took a bite out of it? And what if it was him who killed Malik? Whoever did that was a total nutjob.'

'Nutjob's putting it mildly. More like a stark staring psycho. But that bushing hammer arrived here at the lab about half an hour ago for fingerprinting and DNA. If it *was* Greene who killed Malik, we should be able to tell you for certain within an hour or two.'

'Great. All we have to do then is find the bugger.'

'I've another update too,' said Tosh. 'It came through this morning from Dr Sylvia Wardle. She's easily one of our best forensic chemists. She's been analysing paint samples from the picture on the wall of that Underground tunnel.'

'Oh, you mean that devil or whatever it is?'

'That's the one. The bloke with the head like a goat. According to her, the paint's made by a German company called Spektrum and it's one of the best oil colours on the market. But here's the thing. At the moment it's only available in the UK at branches of WH Smith. They bought up a load of gift sets at a discounted price in time for Christmas.'

Jerry frowned. 'Spektrum oil paint? That was one of the art supplies that big smelly twonk in the dress was trying to steal from WH Smith at the Tandem Centre.'

'That's right,' said Tosh. 'We did a fingerprint check here on a couple of the gift boxes, to match them with his knife. That's why I thought I'd mention it to you.'

'The manager told me that some of those same oil paints were stolen before, about three weeks previous. I wonder if there's a connection. You know – maybe the big smelly twonk's a member of this cult that's been killing people and cooking them. The three blokes who attacked me and DS Patel – they all looked like members of the great unwashed.'

'Maybe you should ask him.'

'I could try, but up until now he hasn't said a dicky bird. He was supposed to be having a psychiatric examination sometime today, to see if he's fit to plead. If he's not fit, I reckon he's off to Broadmoor.'

'You never know. Sometimes these psychotic types suddenly get the urge to boast about what they've done, don't they? Tell him he's the greatest painter since Leonardo da Vinci. That might get him talking.'

When he went downstairs to the custody suite, Jerry found DS Bristow talking to Dr Helen Masefield, the criminal psychologist. Sergeant Miller was there too, along with a burly uniformed officer who had obviously been called in to give them extra security.

Jerry had worked with Dr Masefield several times before, when it was obvious that an offender was suffering from some kind of mental disorder. A year ago she had helped him to coax a confession out of a Pakistani husband who had thrown his wife and three children from the balcony of their fifth-floor flat because he believed they had been possessed by the spirit of his dead uncle.

She was a small woman, only two inches over five feet, with wavy brunette hair and wide-apart eyes and she was wearing a smart grey suit. She always put Jerry in mind of Jackie Kennedy, despite speaking with a distinctive northern accent.

'Ah, Jerry! How's the Lambeth job coming on?' asked DS Bristow. 'You know Dr Masefield, don't you?'

Normally, DS Bristow had a descriptive nickname for almost every major investigation, such as 'the catalytic converter caper' or 'the scrap metal scam', and this one might have been 'the cannibals' cookout'. In this case, though, New Scotland Yard had imposed a strict embargo on openly discussing any of the details, in the event that the media got wind of any suggestion that people had been killed to be eaten.

'Early days yet, skip,' said Jerry. 'Early days.'

'DC Pardoe... good to see you,' said Dr Masefield. 'DS Bristow tells me you arrested this particular offender.'

'Arrested *and* deodorised him for you. Believe me, he was the smelliest melt I've ever had the misfortune to pull in, bar none.'

'DS Bristow tells me he hasn't spoken to you at any time?'

'No. Not a word. But forensics have just told me that there could be a link between him and the investigation I'm working on with DS Patel. That's why I've come down here now, to see if I can get him to talk. It seems like he was trying to steal the same kind of paint that was used by the gang we're looking for.'

'Excuse me? The same kind of *paint*? What on earth have they been doing with paint?'

'Painting a life-size picture of the Devil on a tunnel wall. We're guessing they're some kind of religious cult.'

DS Bristow said, 'A brief came by this morning to interview King Kong in there and see if he was fit to plead.'

'And?'

'He still wouldn't speak, or couldn't. But ever since breakfast he hasn't been a well boy, and he seems to be getting progressively worse. He brought up his porridge and he's sweating like a pig and he's got the hippy-hippy shakes. That's one of the reasons we called for Dr Masefield.'

'I've just been into his cell,' said Dr Masefield. 'He turned his head to look at me, so he's conscious, but it's obvious that he's having severe muscular spasms, and that he's in considerable pain. In my opinion, he's suffering from acute opioid withdrawal.'

'You mean he's coming down off drugs? So is it worth trying to ask him any questions? Suppose we dangle a hypodermic full of heroin in front of his nose? Do you think he might open up then?'

'DC Pardoe, that would be totally unethical. I couldn't condone that.'

'You wouldn't have to know about it. And I'm only asking theoretically. Keith? We've got plenty of drug paraphernalia in the evidence cupboard, haven't we?'

'I was suggesting to DS Bristow that we should call for a doctor to give him a dose of methadone,' said Dr Masefield. 'That would at least relieve his withdrawal symptoms.'

'Well, you're the expert. But while he's under stress, it's possible that we might be able to persuade him to talk to us, don't you think, even if we don't tempt him with a shot of the hard stuff? I'd like to ask him about the oil paint, if nothing else. I mean – if I can establish a connection with the cult we're looking into, that would be a start.'

'I don't suppose there's any harm in you trying. But we still need to call for a doctor, and then send him off to a secure hospital unit for a detox.'

'I'll give that Dr Lemmon a bell,' said DS Bristow. 'Meanwhile – you're welcome to have a crack at him, Jerry, but I don't think you'll get much out of him. Make sure he doesn't whack you one like he did the last time, although I think he's too sick for that.'

Sergeant Miller peered into the spyhole in the cell door to make sure that the man was lying on his bunk, and then he unlocked the door and pushed it open. The burly PC went in first, and Jerry followed, with Dr Masefield staying close behind him.

The man was lying with his back to them. His grey tracksuit trousers were stained with a dark patch where he had wet himself, and the cell was filled with an acidic smell of vomit.

Jerry went up to the side of the bunk and said, 'Hallo! Any chance of a chat? Specifically about oil paints? Can you hear me? Oil paints? Like – was it you who painted that geezer with the head of a goat, down in that tunnel?'

The man made a growling noise but kept his back turned. He was shivering, and even though he was handcuffed, he was holding his hands up to cover his face.

'Is that why you wanted to nick those paints from WH Smith's?' Jerry persisted. 'You wanted to paint some more of those devils, or whatever they are?'

The man growled again, and gave a convulsive shudder. The burly PC leaned over him, laying a hand on his shoulder to turn him over, but then he suddenly stood up straight again.

'What's the matter?' Jerry asked him.

'There's blood.'

'Blood? Let's have a look, then. What's he gone and done to himself?'

The PC took hold of the man's shoulder again, and rolled him onto his back. The man was still quaking, but he didn't resist. When he saw him, Jerry breathed, 'Gordon Bennett,' and Dr Masefield gasped out, 'Oh, my God!'

The man had gouged both of his eyes out of their sockets, and they were dangling down onto his cheeks, bloodshot and expressionless, like a doll's eyes. One was staring at Jerry and the other was staring at the wall.

The man's face and neck were smothered in blood. Not only had he pulled out his eyes, it appeared that he had bitten large lumps of muscle out of both of his hands, in the same way that PC Bone's hand had been bitten. There was no sign on his chest or on his bunk of the lumps that he had bitten; Jerry could only guess that he had chewed them and swallowed them.

'*Keith!*' Jerry shouted to the custody sergeant. 'Paramedics! Like, *pronto*! And fetch us the keys to these hooks! And the first-aid kit!'

He made a grab for the man's arms, intending to get Sergeant Miller to unlock his handcuffs so that he could wrap his bleeding hands in bandages. But the man wrenched his arms away, turned his head to face the wall again, and pulled at his right eye so hard that the optic nerve snapped. Without any hesitation, he pushed his detached eyeball into his mouth, and bit it. Clear fluid burst out from between his lips and mingled with the blood on his chin.

Both Jerry and the PC tried to seize the man's arms again, but he was too quick for them. He tugged his left eyeball free and pushed that into his mouth too. They distinctly heard it pop as he bit it. Then he turned back to face them. His two eye sockets were both empty now, with stringy optic nerves hanging out of them, and he was shivering even more violently than he had been before, but the way he was chewing was almost triumphant. *There – I've blinded myself and you couldn't stop me!*

Dr Masefield said, in a ghostly voice, 'I've *never* – not in the whole of my career – I've seen self-harm – patients cutting themselves – but – you'll have to excuse me—'

She clamped her hand over her mouth and hurried out of the cell door, bumping into Sergeant Miller as he came hurrying in with the first-aid kit.

'Sorry,' he told her, and then he saw the man on the bunk.

All he could say was, 'Christ on a bicycle, Jerry. I mean, Christ on a fucking bicycle.'

15

Erst and Sek were both lying silently on their sleeping bags when Flecker came into the room and said, 'Come on, you two. Time to stir your stumps.'

Erst sat up. 'Where are we going?'

'Hunting for opfers. They won't come to us, will they, so we have to go out and look for them.'

Erst looked toward the window. 'It's dark outside.'

'All the better. We don't want them to see us, do we?'

Sek sat up too. 'I don't feel well. I feel dizzy. Do I have to go?'

'You'll feel worse if you don't,' said Flecker. He nodded toward the goat-headed man on the wall. 'Those who don't hunt don't get to eat, and if you don't eat you'll make the great one angry. Believe me, you don't want to make the great one angry. He'll demand *you* for a sacrifice too. Do you want *your* head cut off and roasted, so that your brother can eat your brain?'

Erst stood up and said, 'Come on, Sek. We should go.' He still didn't quite understand why he felt so protective toward Sek, but he knew that he didn't want him to come to any harm, and even if he wasn't squeamish about eating the flesh of other people, he didn't want to find himself eating Sek.

They followed Flecker down the staircase. The evening was

chilly, but one of the women had given them warm clothing to put on over their pyjamas. Erst was almost drowned in a bronze puffa jacket that was two sizes too large for him, so that his sleeves appeared to be empty, while Sek wore a thick green fisherman's sweater that almost came up to his nostrils. Both of them wore baggy second-hand jeans with frayed hems, and dirty second-hand trainers.

Flecker led them right down to the basement. Faust and Copf and all the rest of the men were assembled here, growling and shuffling their feet. A few of them were swinging hammers or cricket bats or short lengths of scaffolding, although most of them were holding only the hand-woven garrottes that Erst and Sek had been helping the women to weave together, and were spinning them around in the air.

The basement was eerily lit by handmade torches made out of tightly twisted pillowcases soaked in cooking oil. Shadows danced around the walls as if the men were being entertained by the ghosts of their former selves, or the spirits that they would one day become.

Flecker ushered Erst and Sek to the centre of the crowd, up to Faust, and Faust laid his hands on their shoulders, gripping them tight. He gave them both an affectionate shake, as if they were his pet puppies.

'Our new sons are joining us tonight!' he declared, and the men all roared in approval. Erst could understand almost everything that Faust was saying now, although some of his more guttural growls still sounded like a foreign language, especially when he grew excited.

'We will show the comelings who is going to multiply! We will show them who is going to take over the world!'

Erst couldn't think what a 'comeling' was, but the men roared again, more aggressively this time. Then, with Faust taking the lead and Flecker and Copf holding up torches on either side, they all made for the far end of the basement, where a cavernous hole had been knocked through the wall. They climbed over a heap of broken concrete into the darkness of a tunnel. Faust turned around to give Erst a helping hand, while one of the men picked up Sek under his arm and lifted him clear over the rubble.

After they had covered about a kilometre they turned left into a narrow brick-lined passageway, so that they had to walk in single file, and Erst covered his nose and his mouth with his sleeve so that he wouldn't have to breathe in the smoke from the cooking-oil torches. Eventually, though, they all stopped, and he saw Faust pulling aside five timbers that had been nailed together to form a makeshift door. A dim light entered the passageway, and the men who were carrying torches dropped them onto the ground and stamped them out.

On the other side of the opening, the passageway joined up with a main Underground railway tunnel. Faust peered out into the tunnel, holding up his hand for all the men to be quiet, so that he could hear if any distant trains were approaching.

After a few moments he said, 'Come on, everybody,' but before he stepped out into the main tunnel he turned around to Erst and Sek and added, 'It's not so dangerous at this time of night. Not so many trains. But whatever you do, don't touch any of the rails, especially the middle rail or the outside rail. You will die instantly if you do. We learned that the hard way.'

He went ahead, his boots crunching on the aggregate and one hand trailing against the left-hand wall so that he could keep his balance and stay well away from the track. Erst and Sek followed close behind him, and Erst saw that the light was coming from a station platform, about fifty metres off to their left. When Faust reached the station platform, the boys climbed up after him. Only a few people were waiting there – three young men who were laughing and horsing around as if they had drunk too much, and two women with scarves on their heads who looked like cleaners. Looking around, Erst could see that there were circular signs on the walls with the station's name on them, and he knew that those signs could tell him where they were, but he was unable to read them. It was the same with the posters. He could understand the pictures but not the words.

The passengers on the platform took no notice of Faust and his men at first, but when more of them began to climb up onto the platform and start walking quickly toward them, the three young men stopped laughing and the two women took a few steps backwards.

Faust bellowed, '*The woman on the left, in the red! The man in the brown leather jacket!*'

Erst had understood what he had called out, but to the five passengers he must have sounded as if he were barking like an angry dog. His men started to run forward, and before the passengers realised what was happening, one of them had wound a braided garrotte around the neck of the cleaner that he had pointed out, and two more had seized the arms of the young man in the brown leather jacket, while a third had come up behind him and wound a garrotte around his neck too.

The two other young men shouted and tried to pull Faust's men away from their friend, but they were roughly dragged aside and pinned against the curving station wall. The other cleaner started to scream, but another of Faust's men slapped her hard across the cheeks, twice, and then forced her to lie face down on one of the wooden benches.

Faust looked up at the indicator board. 'Now – let's *go*!' he growled. 'And we must be quick! We have only four fingers before the next train comes to crush us!' He held up one hand with his thumb folded back to show his men how much time they had left.

The cleaner and the young man were frogmarched back along the platform, both of them half-strangled. Meanwhile, Erst and Sek had been left by themselves while Flecker and Copf had joined the other men in seizing their two victims and keeping the other passengers at bay. Now the boys could only follow the hurrying crowd of men, confused and worried that they would be left behind.

They were less than halfway along the platform when Erst heard a man behind him shouting, '*Hey! You lot! Stop!*' He turned around and saw a police officer in a yellow high-vis jacket running toward him, with a brindled Alsatian tugging at its lead. Five more police officers came tumbling out of the passage behind him.

Faust must have seen what was happening because he screamed out, '*Erst! Sek! Faster!*'

The dog handler bent down to unfasten his Alsatian's lead and the dog came tearing toward them. It sprang up and seized the sleeve of Sek's sweater in its teeth, shaking him violently from side to side so that Sek stumbled and fell over.

Erst snatched the Alsatian's collar in both hands and pulled it up and away from Sek as hard as he could. The dog released its grip on Sek's sweater and twisted itself around to bite at him. He tried to push it off but it jumped up and knocked him over backwards onto the platform. His head hit the concrete paving slabs and for a split second he blacked out.

The next thing he knew he was being hauled to his feet by one of the police officers, who held on tightly to the hood of his puffa jacket. Tiny white stars were prickling in front of his eyes, but through the stars he could see Sek being dragged away by two of Faust's men. They swung Sek bodily off the end of the platform into the arms of another man who was standing in the tunnel, and then all of them disappeared into the darkness.

The dog handler and the rest of the officers went clattering along the platform after them, but before they could climb down into the tunnel the officer who was holding Erst shouted out, '*Matty!* Leave them, Matty! There's too many of them and the track's still live! At least we know where they're going now!'

He paused for breath, and then he said, 'Khan – give them a shout down at the Oval and tell them there's a mob of around twenty heading their way, so they'll urgently need some backup. We'll have to stay here in case the buggers turn around and try to make their way back!'

He waited for a few moments, until he was sure that one of his officers had sent the message through to the search party down at the Oval station, and then he looked down at Erst.

'My name's Sergeant Bryan. What's your name, sonny?'

Erst could understand him, but when he tried to answer he found that he could only growl.

'I said, what's your name?' Sergeant Bryan repeated. 'What are you, a fucking dog?'

Erst closed his eyes and tried to think how he could say 'Edward'. He took a deep breath and contracted his throat muscles and managed to come out with 'Eh!'

'Eh? What kind of a name is that?'

'Dahwoo. *Dahwoo!* Eh-*dahwoo!*'

'I think we'd better take you to the nick and have a bit of a chat with you there, sonny. God knows what you're doing with that bunch of animals.'

Sergeant Bryan turned around to the officer standing close

behind him. 'Matty… give that DS Patel a bell, would you, and give her the heads-up? She's going to love us. But Smiley told us that if we come across anything down here that could be connected with that sect she's looking for, we need to inform her immediately, day or night, and if that mob wasn't a sect then I don't know what it was. Tell her we'll take this lad to Tooting and she can meet us there.'

His fellow officers were talking now to the cleaner whose friend had been garrotted and taken away, and the other two young men.

'Who *were* these people?' asked the cleaner, in a Polish accent, wiping tears from her eyes. 'What will they do to her? They will not hurt her, will they? Her name is Ola nska. Her family is still in Poznań. What can I tell them?'

'Don't know, love,' said one of the officers. 'We're as mystified as you are, to tell you the truth. They just seem to come out of nowhere, these people. We don't have a clue who they are or what they're after. But don't you worry. We'll do everything we can to find your friend and get her back safe. I can promise you that.'

It was 1:30 in the morning before Sergeant Bryan and two of his officers brought Erst to Tooting police station. By then he was shivering and he was beginning to feel that itching sensation again, all the way up his arms and down his back. He would have done anything for another cupful of that calla dew that Faust had given them.

He was led into the custody suite, where two PCs took off his puffa jacket. They raised their eyebrows when they discovered that he was wearing nothing underneath his jacket and his jeans but red-striped pyjamas. They searched his pockets but found nothing except for a tube of Smarties that one of Hedda's women had given him.

'Not exactly armed and dangerous,' said one of the officers. Then they took him to the reception desk where he was asked again what his name was, and where he lived, and how the officers could contact his parents.

'Eh-dah-woo,' he managed to repeat.

'Edward? Is that what you're trying to tell us?'

Edward nodded, scratching his forearms. Then he said, 'Scow cam.'

'Scow cam?'

Edward lifted both hands and described a triangular tent-like shape in the air. 'Scow cam.'

'Oh! Scout camp!' said the desk sergeant. 'This must be one of the lads gone missing from the Scout Centre in Dulwich! Is that where you've come from? Dulwich Scout Camp? Hang on, let me rustle up your details!'

He tapped away at his keyboard with two fingers, and then he said, 'Here we are... Edward and John Willow. Reported missing last night from the South London Scout Centre. Is that *you*, son? Edward Willow? Yes? So where's your brother, John?'

Edward shook his head. He wanted to say that John had been taken away down the tunnel by Faust and his men, but he was trembling too violently now and he found it impossible to speak, either in words or growls. He was swallowed up by darkness and his knees gave way, and it was only because the PCs standing on either side of him caught his elbows that he didn't pitch onto the floor.

'Get him onto a bed and I'll call for a bus,' said the desk sergeant. 'It looks to me like he's been smoking something. Bloody hell – don't know what the world's coming to, when even the Boy Scouts are off their nuts. "Be prepared", that's their motto, isn't it? Too right! Be prepared to sing some songs round the campfire, smoke some spice and shuffle around like a zombie.'

One of the PCs carried Edward through to an empty cell, his arms and his legs dangling like a newborn gazelle, and laid him down on the bunk. The night duty officer stood in the doorway and watched as the PC levered off his worn-out trainers and covered him with a thin brown blanket.

'Keep an eye on him, won't you?' the PC asked him. 'We think he's OD'd on something and we don't want him doing what that fat geezer did, do we, and pulling out his peepers?'

16

It was still dark when Jamila and Jerry arrived at the police station, but they found that Edward had been seen by paramedics only twenty minutes before, and that they had taken him off to St George's Hospital.

Sergeant Bryan was waiting for them though, sitting in the canteen with a mug of tea and an early breakfast of beans on toast. He was a big man with tiny eyes like nail heads and a prickly shaved head.

'We was doing a quick repeat search of Kennington station,' he told them. 'To be honest with you, we didn't expect to find nothing down there. We couldn't believe it when we come out onto the northbound platform and there's a whole gang of these buggers hauling this woman and this young bloke away.'

'But apart from that one boy, they all escaped down the tunnel?'

'We was under strict instructions not to enter the tunnels while the tracks was still live. But we contacted the second search unit down at the Oval, and they arranged for the power to be switched off, so that they could intercept the offenders before they could find a way out of the system. Our unit stayed at Kennington in the event of the offenders doubling back on themselves.'

'But? The second unit didn't find them?'

Sergeant Bryan shrugged. 'Not a trace. But then we hadn't taken the Kennington Loop into account. That's a loop line that doubles around and connects the southbound track with the northbound track, so that trains heading out of London can turn around if they need to and head back to Charing Cross. I reckon that instead of them carrying on down the tunnel toward the Oval, this mob walked the wrong way around the loop and escaped out of the other side of the station. Highly risky thing to do, especially if a train's coming the other way, but it seems like they got away with it.'

'They obviously have a very comprehensive knowledge of the Underground,' said Jamila. 'How many of them would you estimate there were?'

'I'd say somewhere between fifteen and twenty. Plus those two boys. They're all on CCTV. Scruffy-looking bastards, all of them.'

'We'll be going up to the control room to have a look in a minute,' said Jerry. 'Do you know who they abducted?'

Sergeant Bryan took out his smartphone and scrolled down until he found his notes. 'A young bloke called Derek Feather, twenty-two years old, works for Atlas Travel Agents in Lambeth, and a woman called Aleksandra Rucinska, thirty-five, works for Streatham Office Cleaners. She's a Polish national who's only been in England for seven months.'

'Have their next of kin been informed?'

'Derek Feather's, yes. He lives with his aunt and uncle in Southwark. We have a contact number for Aleksandra Rucinska in Poznań, in Poland, which we've rung, but we haven't been able to get an answer. We'll be letting the Polish Embassy know when they open in the morning.'

'What about the boy?'

'He was in a proper state but we were able to identify him

as one of two brothers who went missing from the South London Scout campsite in the middle of the night before last – Edward and John Willow. His mother's been informed and the last I heard she was on her way to St George's.'

'We will be going to see him too,' said Jamila. 'Did the paramedics give you any idea of what was wrong with him?'

'They thought the same as us. Opioid overdose. Pupils contracted, shallow breathing, slow heart rate, arms and legs floppy.'

'Overdose? How old is he?

Sergeant Bryan checked his smartphone again. 'Ten. They get younger and younger, don't they? Before we know it they'll be mixing fentanyl in with their Farley's rusks.'

Edward was lying upstairs in the intensive care ward at St George's, with his mother sitting beside him. His face was white and there were dark rings around his eyes, but at least his eyes were open and when Jamila and Jerry came into the ward he turned his head to see them. His mother, Elizabeth, looked up too.

'Mrs Willow?' said Jamila. 'And you're Edward? I'm Detective Sergeant Patel and this is Detective Constable Pardoe. How are you feeling, Edward?'

Edward gave an odd nasal snort and growled, opening and closing his mouth as if he were trying to tell them something but couldn't think of the right words.

'He can't speak,' said Elizabeth. 'He fell over and knocked his head when the police caught him. I don't know if that has anything to do with it. They've given him a brain scan but they can't see any sign of bruising.'

Edward growled again, and managed to say, '*ohn... ohn...*'

'I think he's talking about his younger brother, John,' Elizabeth told them. 'You don't have any news of John, do you?'

'No, sorry, 'fraid not,' Jerry told her. 'We've sent out three more search units though, and they've all got tracker dogs with them, so I reckon we've a fair chance of finding him.'

'*Ohn,*' Edward repeated, even more urgently. Then, '*ess-ess-ess—*'

Elizabeth squeezed Edward's hands and said, 'Try, darling, *try*! What is it you want to tell us?'

'Ess-ess-*Sek*!' Edward managed to spit out.

Jamila and Jerry looked at each other. 'Sek? What does that mean?'

'*Ohn,*' Edward insisted, waving his hands from side to side. '*Ohn – Sek.*' He was becoming increasingly frustrated at his inability to explain what he meant. His eyes welled up with tears and he began to make sad blubbing sounds.

'I'm sure he's desperate to tell us something about John, but I can't think what,' said Elizabeth, taking out a tissue to dab at his cheeks.

A doctor in a long white lab coat appeared around the corner, accompanied by the IC ward sister and three young students. The doctor was Indian, tall and elegant, with rimless glasses and a beard that was clipped into a spade shape.

'This is Dr Seshadri,' said the ward sister. 'Doctor – this is Detective Sergeant Patel and Detective Constable Pardoe.'

'How do you do,' said Dr Seshadri, in a cultured drawl. 'I have been told of the circumstances under which this unfortunate young man was discovered.'

'We gather you've given him a brain scan,' said Jerry.

'Yes, and fortunately he appears to have suffered no injury to his brain. However, I have just been given the results of his blood tests, and they are extremely interesting, to say the least. Perhaps we can go over here, out of earshot. We don't know if he can understand us. We certainly can't understand *him*, although we are hoping that his inability to express himself is only temporary.'

The ward sister stayed with Edward while Elizabeth joined Jamila and Jerry over by the window overlooking the car park. It was raining outside and tiny people were hurrying to and fro, like a Lowry painting.

Dr Seshadri held up a clipboard with a printout on it. 'Your son is O positive, Mrs Willow, which is the most common blood type. His blood counts are all healthy – red blood cells and white blood cells and platelets. But he has traces in his blood of a strong opiate, which we estimate was given to him about twelve hours ago.'

'Do you know what it was?' asked Jamila. 'Oxycodone, or something like that?'

'We haven't yet been able to work out for sure what it is, although we know that it contains a morphinane alkaloid like heroin. It binds to specific opiate receptors in the brain and affects brain function. Unlike heroin, though, it appears to have a suppressive effect on the way that the brain works. In other words, it makes it more difficult for your brain to function at an elevated level instead of giving you a high.'

'And is that why Edward's finding it so hard to speak to us?' asked Elizabeth.

'It certainly seems like it, Mrs Willow. But whatever this opiate is, it contains at least two substances that we have never come across before, and which we're still trying to analyse.'

'He *will* recover though?'

'As I said before, we're keeping our fingers crossed that his condition is only temporary. Normally, it takes anything from three to five days for somebody to come completely down from heroin, although you might still find traces of it in their hair and their nails for up to a year afterwards. But we won't really know how long the effects of this particular opioid will last until Edward recovers.'

'He's not in any pain, is he?' asked Jamila.

'No. He was shivering and itching when he was brought here, which is typical of addicts when they come off heroin abruptly, but we're giving him measured doses of buprenorphine to relieve his withdrawal symptoms.'

'One of these days, somebody's going to invent a drug that I can pronounce,' said Jerry.

'Sorry,' said Dr Seshadri. 'You probably know it as Suboxone.'

Jamila took out her card. 'This is our contact number, doctor. As soon as you have some idea of what this drug contains, and especially where it might have come from, please let us know.'

They went back to Edward's bedside. Edward was drinking orange juice through a straw and he looked more relaxed. In the tilted bed next to him, an elderly man with hollow cheeks was groaning as if he were suffering unbearable pain and two women were stroking his hands and silently weeping, but Edward didn't seem to find this biblical scenario at all disturbing. Jerry guessed that his Suboxone tablets were keeping him calm.

'Sometimes I feel that God is out to punish us, me and the boys,' said Elizabeth. 'Don't ask me what we've done to upset Him, but this has been the worst year in the whole of our lives.'

'Really?' Jamila asked her. 'What has happened, apart from this?'

'I lost my husband in a car accident only seven weeks ago. The boys lost their father.'

'I am so sorry for you. I hardly know what to say.'

Elizabeth looked at Edward and tried to smile, to show him that everything was going to be all right.

'Please find my John for me, that's all I ask,' she said to Jamila and Jerry. Her eyes were red but she wasn't crying. Jerry guessed that she had probably run out of tears.

As they drove back through the rain to Tooting police station, Jerry said, 'I don't know if it's just a coincidence.'

'What?'

'Well, that PC Bone, he'd just lost his wife. And now these two lads Edward and John, their dad died only a couple of months ago.'

'So what are you suggesting? Everybody loses people they love. It is not as if it is something unusual. My grandmother passed away in May.'

'I don't know. It was a thought, that's all.'

'Put it behind your ear for later. Right now, I have done enough thinking for one day.'

17

Hedda was waiting for them, sitting cross-legged on the floor underneath the painting of the goat-headed man. She was wearing a tatty grey shawl and two wide-brimmed hats, which kept her face in shadow. The men all crowded into the room and gathered around her, pushing Derek Feather and Aleksandra Rucinska up in front of her to show her the opfers that they had managed to bring back from their hunting expedition.

'*Two?*' she demanded. 'Is this all? How long do you think these two will last us?'

Faust stepped forward. 'The hunt was going well. But then the comelings arrived, without any warning, and they had a dog. We had to escape before we could go up into the street to catch any more. Please, don't be angry. When the darkness returns we can go out hunting again.'

'Hey, do you mind telling us exactly what the hell is going on here?' said Derek Feather, in a trembling voice. 'Who are you people, and what do you want?'

'You have to let us go!' shrilled Aleksandra Rucinska. 'You cannot keep us here!'

Hedda ignored them, looking around at her assembled men. 'You disappoint me,' she growled. 'You truly disappoint me. You were scared off by a dog and a few comelings?'

'We were not afraid of them, Hedda, but you know what could happen if they find us here. It would not be a few comelings, it would be many, and they would capture us all, like they captured Kittel when he went to find paints. We must thank the great one that Kittel must have kept his silence.'

Hedda was looking around from one man to another while he spoke, her eyes glittering beneath the shadow of her hats like a wolf hiding in a cave.

'I can see Sek there,' she said at last. 'But where is Erst?'

Faust took a deep breath. 'That is what I was going to tell you. Sadly, the comelings caught him.'

There was a long silence. All the men in the room shuffled their feet uneasily, and two or three of them coughed.

Hedda heaved herself up from the floor in her ragged grey shawl.

'*What!*' she screeched, once she had struggled to her feet. '*What!* You allowed the comelings to take one of my new sons! How do you think our tribe will flourish unless we bring in young blood? Why didn't you let them take one of *you* instead? Copf – you were supposed to be taking care of Erst, weren't you? And *you*, Flecker! You ran away like a terrified rat and allowed the comelings to rob us of our future?'

Both Copf and Flecker held out their hands. Flecker dropped onto his knees.

'It was so quick, Hedda. The comelings came running in and their dog went for Erst as fast as a bolt of lightning and there was nothing we could do.'

Hedda stalked up to them. Copf dropped onto his knees too, and they both looked up at her with their hands pressed together in prayer.

'There *is* something you can do,' she said. Her voice had dropped now, to a hoarse and threatening whisper. 'You can make amends for losing Erst. You can make amends for all of your hunting party here, coming back with only two opfers.'

'I beg you, Hedda – in the name of Ba-Abla.'

'*What*? You dare to speak his name? You – you miserable creature who has let him down so badly? *You dare to speak his name?*'

'Please. We'll find you another son. We'll go out tonight, back to the camp, and fetch you another.'

Hedda stalked up and down in front of them, swirling her shawl in rage.

'No, you won't. You'll make amends here and now. Faust – nail them all to the wall. They won't make much of a feast but it'll be better than nothing.'

Flecker let out a terrible howl like a run-over dog and Copf threw himself flat on the floor, clutching at the hem of Hedda's mustard-coloured skirt in supplication. She kicked him away, one foot after the other, and then she stamped with her worn-down boots on his hands, again and again, until the bones of his fingers crackled.

'You're crazy!' Derek Feather cried out. He was panicking now. 'You've got to let us go! You're all bloody crazy!'

'*Let us go! Let us go!*' screamed Aleksandra Rucinska. To them, the shouting between Hedda and Copf had sounded like nothing but animals snarling at each other.

Again, Hedda ignored them. She gave Copf one more kick, and spat at him, and then she limped out of the room, with the brims of her two hats waving like ravens' wings. When she had gone, Faust turned to his men and said, 'You heard Hedda. Get to work.'

Flecker scrambled up and tried to make a run for the door, but three other men caught his tracksuit and threw him onto the floor, kneeling on his back to pin him down. Two other men seized hold of Copf and forced him to lie flat beside him. Then, between them, five others dragged Derek Feather and Aleksandra Rucinska across to the wall that was painted with the image of the goat-headed man, and pushed them down until they were kneeling in front of him.

'Tell the great one how pleased you are that you can give everything you have in his honour,' said Faust, his voice still thick and growly, but speaking in words that they could understand. 'Tell him that your whole life has been leading up to this moment when you can sacrifice yourselves for his greater glory. From the day you were born, you were chosen to be his opfers.'

Aleksandra began to sob, her shoulders shaking, while Derek could only say 'no, no, no, I don't believe this', over and over again.

At least half a dozen men gathered around them and started to pull off their clothes. They both struggled and kicked, but it was hopeless. On the other side of the room, more men were stripping Flecker and Copf. The two of them lay as limp as if they were dead already. They knew that any resistance would be futile, and that they would risk having their arms and their legs broken. They would be suffering pain enough in only a few minutes from now.

While the four victims were having all their clothes wrestled off them, three women came into the room, one of them pushing a shopping trolley with a squeaking wheel. They were followed by a thickset man in a donkey jacket, carrying a claw hammer. They went up to the wall where the remains of Jimmy and Cathy were still pinned, and the man stepped up and used his claw hammer to lever the nails from the palms of their hands and their elbows. Once they were freed, he handed Jimmy and Cathy's decomposing arms back to the women, who dropped them into the shopping trolley. Then he twisted their pelvic girdles away from the wall as if they were two steering wheels and passed those back too.

One of the women wiped down the plaster with a damp grey dishcloth and then she turned to the men in the room and said, 'There! All ready for you to make your offering to the great one.'

Derek Feather and Aleksandra Rucinska were lifted up bodily by two men each, and pressed with their backs against the wall. Derek was thin and white-skinned with a hairy crucifix on his narrow chest, while Aleksandra had pendulous breasts, a plump belly and thighs rippled with cellulite. She was still sobbing, but shaking her head from side to side as if she were trying to shake herself awake so that this wouldn't be happening.

'*You can't do this!*' Derek screamed. '*You cannot do this!*'

Faust didn't even turn round to look at Derek and Aleksandra. He was too busy watching Flecker and Copf being carried up to the wall next to them, their knees sagging and their feet trailing along the floor. They too had their backs pressed against the plaster, but then Faust made a circling gesture with his finger to the eight men who were holding them, and growled something that sounded to Derek like '*cough oobah*'.

The men turned Flecker and Copf upside down, with their heads downwards and their feet upwards and their legs splayed. Faust growled again and the man in the donkey jacket handed him his hammer and all the nails that he had pulled out. Without hesitation, Faust went up to Copf, positioned the point of one of the nails up against his left ankle, and then with three hard blows hammered it in between his tibia and his talus bones. Copf screamed, but almost choked on his own saliva.

Faust next nailed his right ankle to the wall, so that the four men who were keeping him up could let go of him and stand back, leaving him hanging.

'*You're crazy! You're all out of your fucking minds!*' Derek screamed at them.

Faust stepped across to Flecker. As he approached him he looked down at the floor in revulsion, because Flecker had vomited in fear. His nostrils were clogged and his eyelashes were stuck together and pale strings of puke were dangling down among his long tangled hair.

Faust tilted his head sideways to give him a disapproving stare. '*Ugh*, Flecker!' he snarled. 'That won't do much to sharpen our appetites, will it?'

He didn't wait for Flecker to try and answer him. He stood up straight and dug the point of another nail into Flecker's left ankle and banged it into the wall. Then, by way of showing his disgust, he twisted Flecker's right foot sideways and drove the next nail through his heel bone, which took five hammer blows so hard that they cracked the plaster. Flecker gagged and brought up even more vomit and Faust flapped his hand at him dismissively.

'I thought you were a drowfganger, not a baby.'

He turned then to Aleksandra, monotonously tapping the head of the hammer against the nails that he was holding in the palm of his hand.

'Look at the size of you,' he grinned. 'The great one will be very pleased with you. And you have nothing to cry about, do you? Eh? I'll bet money that you've been trying to lose weight for years. Now you're going to lose it all... every bit of it.'

Aleksandra had stopped sobbing and now she was breathing deeply, as if she had been running all the way here.

'*Jesteś demonem!*' she panted. '*Kiedy umrzesz, pójdziesz do piekła! Będziesz palił się i palił na zawsze!*'

'If only I knew what you were babbling on about,' said Faust. He stopped tapping at the nails and dropped all but one of them into his jacket pocket.

'I say you are demon! I say you will go to hell and burn and burn for ever!'

'You are right. I probably *will* go to hell. But the great one will take care of me in hell, and give me everything I want. Money, music. The finest suits to wear. Women whenever I want them, babies to eat.'

The man who was holding Aleksandra's right hand up against the wall turned his head away. Faust dug the point of the nail into her palm and gave it three hefty blows with the hammer. Aleksandra closed her eyes tight and bit her lip but made no sound at all.

Faust nailed her elbows and her knees to the wall and then he turned to Derek.

'You bastard,' Derek whispered. 'You utter bastard.'

'Well, that's very perceptive of you, my friend,' said Faust. 'As it happens, I never knew my father.'

He nailed Derek's hands and elbows and knees to the wall, and with every bang of his hammer Derek let out a shout of pain.

When all four of his victims were spreadeagled against the plaster, Faust raised both of his hands. The men in the room had been joined by the women, and several of them were already holding up carving knives and tenon saws in eager anticipation of the butchery that was going to follow.

'During this darkness, when we went to hunt for opfers, we had to call off our hunt,' Faust told them. 'Perhaps we should have shown more courage, although I still believe it would have been a terrible risk for our tribe if all or any of us had been caught by the comelings. Still – we have these two opfers, and we have Copf and Flecker, whose cowardice allowed Erst to be snatched away from us. Their flesh is all that we are able to offer the great one tonight, but we can promise him faithfully that when the darkness next returns, we will go out again and fetch him more.'

The men and women let out a defiant roar, and flourished their knives and saws, and stamped their feet in a complicated shuffle that sounded like a train gathering speed.

Faust weaved his way between them to stand in front of the painting of the goat-headed man. 'Oh great one,' he said, speaking in growls. 'Please accept this offering – this flesh, these lives, these spirits. What *we* eat nourishes you, because we are yours, and yours alone, and always will be yours, until time is turned on its head and we start our journey back to the days when you were triumphant.'

The men and women let out another roar, and stamped their feet in one thunderous drum roll.

Faust pointed to the four naked victims nailed to the wall and said, 'Right! Let the carving begin.'

18

Chrissie the postgirl was trundling her trolley along Meeting House Lane in Peckham when she saw thick grey smoke drifting across the street about five hundred metres up ahead of her. As she neared the source of the smoke, five or six people in anoraks and hooded coats came hurrying across the road. They disappeared up the alley opposite, which ran behind a block of flats.

She began to push her trolley faster, and as she did so, more people came running across the road, at least fifteen of them, all of them wearing thick coats or bundled up in blankets. Some of them had bulging rucksacks slung across their shoulders, while others were carrying shopping bags. One young woman was even holding a red cocker spaniel under one arm and a gingery mongrel under the other. They all disappeared up the alley too.

When Chrissie reached the corner of the street, she saw that the smoke was billowing out of the ground-floor windows of the Charles Babbage Primary School. The school was a three-storey Victorian brick building that had been closed over two years ago, and was awaiting demolition and redevelopment. Chrissie knew that it was occupied by squatters because she had seen them several times coming out of the gate at the side of the school, which was supposed to be padlocked.

She took out her phone and prodded out 999. While she was telling the operator that the Charles Babbage school was on fire, a man came out of the house next to her, and then other people began to appear from the houses further along the street.

'I've called the fire brigade myself,' the man told her. He had a tiny moustache and a droopy green cardigan. 'I'm worried there might be somebody left inside.'

'You don't want to be going in there to find out, bro,' a tall black man advised him. 'Not unless you want to be roasted. That's well alight.'

'I'll take a butcher's in through the windows, anyway, just to make sure.'

He went in through the side gate, which had been left wide open, and Chrissie and the tall man followed him. The smoke was pouring out of a broken skylight, and when they looked into the windows next to it, all they could see was darkness, with an occasional tongue of orange flame licking up.

'I can't *see* nobody,' said the man with the tiny moustache, leaning close to the window and shielding his eyes with his hand. 'In fact, I can't see bugger all.'

'I think they must all have got out,' said Chrissie. 'I saw at least twenty of them running up Willowdene. They had all their bags with them and everything.'

The man with the tiny moustache touched the window and yelped out, '*Yow!* Shit! That's effing hot already!' He shook his hand furiously and blew on his fingertips. 'If there *is* anybody still in there, I don't fancy their chances!'

As soon as he had said that, though, they saw what looked like a pillar of flames approaching the window through the smoke. It came closer and closer, slowly and unsteadily, but it was only when it was less than a metre away from the inside of the window that they realised what it was. A woman, on fire, her long hair rising off the top of her head in a fan of flame, her face shrivelling up and her eyes already blind. If she had been wearing any clothes, they had all been burned off her.

'Holy Jesus,' said the tall man.

The burning woman bumped into the window and then dropped sideways, out of sight, although occasional flames from her body continued to flicker up over the sill. Chrissie and the tall man and the man with the tiny moustache all looked at each other in shock, knowing that there was nothing they could have done to save her.

At that moment they heard the honking of sirens as two fire engines came speeding up Meeting House Lane.

'Bloody hell,' said the man with the tiny moustache. 'I'm going to have nightmares about this for the rest of me natural life.'

Jerry found a parking space fifty metres up Naylor Road and then he and Jamila walked back to the school. Both fire engines were still there with their lights flashing and they had been joined by an ambulance and three squad cars from Peckham police station. Although the fire had been put out, an acrid smell of smoke was still lingering in the air.

They made their way through the small crowd of sightseers who were being held back behind a police tape. PC Berners recognised them immediately and lifted the tape so that they could duck underneath it.

'DCI Walters is inside,' he told them. 'Didn't think arson was up your street, you two. Thought you was into all that creepy stuff.'

He waggled his fingers as if he were trying to scare them and said, '*Wooooo!*'

'Leave it out, you melt,' said Jerry, and followed Jamila in through the side gate.

All the downstairs windows were now smashed and the school playground was flooded and had been turned into a snake pit of fire hoses. Firefighters were tramping in and out of the front door and Jamila and Jerry recognised one of them as Station Officer Johnson from Peckham. He was wearing a white station officer's helmet and talking seriously on his phone. He reminded Jerry so much of Karl Malden that it was only because Karl Malden was long dead and SO Johnson spoke with an Essex accent that he knew for certain that it wasn't really him.

'Ah, Detective Sergeant...' he began, when he had finished his phone conversation. He had obviously remembered their faces but forgotten their names.

'Patel,' said Jamila. 'DS Patel. And DC Pardoe. We were told there was at least one casualty.'

'Yes, I'm afraid so. A woman, but we only know that because she was seen by witnesses during the early stages of the fire.'

'So she's badly burned?'

'More like cremated. Apart from ashes and bones, there's not a lot left.'

'Well, they will be sending a forensic anthropologist from Lambeth Road,' said Jamila. 'I expect her orthodontics will tell us who she is, even if there are no other individuating characteristics.'

'Any idea how it started?' asked Jerry, nodding toward the school.

'Apparently the building's been occupied for some months

now by squatters. It looks like the main blaze was started in what used to be the assembly hall. There's a garden fire pit in there... you know, like a metal basket for burning leaves and weeds and other rubbish. It was filled up with charcoal briquettes.'

Jamila and Jerry exchanged meaningful looks. Neither of them needed to mention the shopping trolleys at the Royale carpet factory.

'This fire though, this was a bloody inferno by the look of it,' said Jerry. 'How do charcoal briquettes start something like this? It takes me half an hour to get my barbecue hot enough to grill a couple of hot dogs, let alone burn down a school.'

'Whoever started this fire obviously had the same problem,' SO Johnson told him. 'There's a melted petrol can lying on the floor next to the fire pit, and so the logical conclusion is that they splashed it all over the charcoal to try and get it going. Maybe they were drunk, or high, or maybe they simply dropped the can and the petrol went everywhere. But it would have been like an incendiary bomb going off. The fire investigator should be able to tell us, when he shows up.'

Even as he was speaking, a red van with a yellow stripe on it pulled up close behind one of the fire engines. The lettering on its side read LFB for London Fire Brigade, and Fire Investigation Unit.

'Speak of the devil,' said SO Johnson.

'Is it safe to go inside and take a look?' asked Jamila.

'Yes. In fact, DCI Walters is in there already, with a couple more officers.'

Jamila and Jerry stepped over the fire hoses and went in through the school's main door. The walls were streaked with smoke and there was rubbish strewn all over the floor. It was the same kind of rubbish they had seen at the Royale carpet factory – sardine tins and empty milk bottles and filthy towels.

A small reception area led into the assembly hall where the fire had started. There were two uniformed police officers standing by the bay window, guarding the blackened remains of the woman who had burned to death. SO Johnson had been right: there was little left of her except for ashes, and her skeleton. She had her back turned, so that they could see her shoulder blades and her spine. One bony arm was still raised, as if she had been trying to reach up to the windowsill.

DCI Walters and two other detectives from Peckham were standing around the fire pit, talking in low voices.

'Ah,' said DCI Walters, as Jamila and Jerry entered the assembly hall. 'The dynamic duo who rush in where angels fear to tread.'

He was the senior officer for the area's Major Investigation Team. Even in his baggy grey raincoat he looked thin, and stooped. His receding black hair was combed straight back from his forehead, and he had a large complicated nose, like an eagle.

'You're looking well, Jamila,' he remarked, although his eyes were not on her, but ceaselessly roaming around the assembly hall, as if he thought he had somehow missed something important. 'How's life up in sunny Redbridge?'

Jamila wasn't entirely sure how to take that. If by 'sunny' he meant that most of the ethnic population had the appearance of being tanned, then he was being subtly racist.

Before she had the chance to answer, though, he turned to Jerry.

'I saw the report on that coke bust in Streatham last month. Good work, that. Good work. Excellent, in fact.'

'It wasn't just me, guv. There were five of us on it. DS

Bristow should take most of the credit. He knew the geezer who knew the geezer who knew when the stuff was going to be shipped.'

'You shouldn't be so modest, Jerry. You'll never get yourself promoted by being modest. Anyhow, I thought it would be a good idea for you to come here and check out the scene of this fire. I'd say that it has distinct connections with that investigation in Lambeth you're working on. Do you have a name for it yet?'

'Not yet. I was thinking of "Operation Scary Goat", to tell you the truth, but I don't think DCI Saunders would go for it.'

'I don't suppose the press office would either. But I have to say that it's not altogether inappropriate. Wait until you see this.'

He beckoned Jamila and Jerry to follow him, and together they left the assembly hall and walked along a short corridor. He opened a door that still had a tarnished brass plaque on it reading STAFF ROOM. Inside, the room was empty of furniture except for three old Parker Knoll armchairs, which had been stacked one on top of the other in one corner. On the parquet floor, however, there was an elaborate pattern of human bones – arm bones, leg bones, collarbones, ribs and vertebrae. A row of eight skulls were lined up along the skirting board, and on the wall above the skulls, the attenuated figure of a naked man had been painted in oils, almost twice life-size, a naked man with an erect penis and the head of a goat. His arms were spread wide like the Christ crucified, but the gleam in his yellow eyes was anything but divine.

Jerry and Jamila entered the room and circled carefully around the pattern of bones. Jerry sniffed. Apart from the mustiness of a room that hadn't had a window opened since the school closed down, he could smell oil paint and something that reminded him of the menthol cigarettes he used to smoke in the days when he smoked, and had a cold.

Jamila pointed to the bones. 'Look, Jerry. The way that they have all been arranged, it is almost the same as the way the bones were laid out in that Tube tunnel, under the carpet factory. It must be some kind of symbol. Like a pentagram, perhaps. Or the wheel of Dharma.'

'It's the same mob though, no doubt about it,' said Jerry. 'It's that same goat-headed bloke, whoever he is.'

'You don't think it's Satan, then?' asked DCI Walters.

'It could well be,' said Jamila. 'Satan has taken many forms in many different cultures. But from the behaviour of this cult, or sect, or whatever it is, I am not at all sure.'

'You might as well know that I've been given a confidential need-to-know briefing about the cannibalism,' DCI Walters told her. 'I'm wondering if this is what they were trying to do here, before the petrol spilled and it all went pear-shaped. Isn't there some religious expert you could consult, and find out who this goat man is?'

'I am sure there are many religious experts who would have an opinion on his identity,' said Jamila. 'But we need hard evidence, not superstition. Facts, not faith. When I was growing up, I saw so much cruelty and injustice done in the name of religion that I do not trust any man who purports to speak on behalf of whichever god he worships. To me, it does not matter who they are. Vicar, priest, mufti, rabbi, hazzan, ayatollah. I believe none of them.'

DCI Walters looked quite shocked. At first he couldn't think how to respond, but as they walked back to the assembly hall, he said, 'What do you do for Christmas, then? Not very much, I don't suppose.'

★ ★ ★

Jamila and Jerry stayed at the school until the crime scene investigators arrived. They stood at a discreet distance and watched while the forensic pathologist carried out a preliminary examination of the woman's burned body. After he had taken dozens of photographs, he wrapped her skull in cotton wool and bubble wrap. Then, with the help of another forensic expert, he carefully lifted her bones and ashes onto a vinyl sheet and lowered them into a cardboard coffin.

The pathologist swept the floor beneath the window for any debris that had been left behind, especially for any of the woman's teeth that may have become dislodged. He bagged and labelled all of these remains so that he could take them back to the laboratory to sift through them.

On the other side of the assembly hall, Tosh Brinkley was supervising the team who were taking samples from the fire pit and the petrol can. They were also lifting fingerprints and DNA from the doorknobs and all the surrounding panelling, as well as footprints from the floor. They had even been filling test tubes with water from the school's lavatories.

'Here we are again, Tosh,' said Jerry. 'Happy as can be.'

Jamila said, 'Have you inspected the other room yet? The staff room? What do you make of it?'

Tosh shook his head. 'Unbelievable. It definitely looks like the same lot that barbecued all those people at the carpet factory, doesn't it? But come and take another look. I've been counting.'

They went back to the staff room, with its painting of the yellow-eyed goat-headed man and the bones arranged in a pattern on the floor.

'Do you know how many people they must have killed to produce this many bones?' said Tosh. 'There's eight skulls, yes, but there's at least three dozen tibias. That adds up to eighteen victims, at least. You're looking at a massacre here, in this one room alone. And there's still flesh on some of the bones, with what appear to be tooth marks.'

Jamila and Jerry stared down at the bones for a long time, in silence. Then Jerry said, 'Now we know what happens to all those mispers who disappear and don't ever get heard of again. It was fifty-five thousand last year, from London alone. Fifty-five thousand! I bet a fair proportion of them ended up here, or in that carpet factory, and got noshed.'

Outside the school, they found the two Peckham detectives questioning Chrissie the postgirl and the two neighbours who had witnessed the woman on fire. Chrissie was pale and shivering and hugging herself, and both of the neighbours also looked seriously shaken.

Another man was standing there too, short and fat, wearing a tweed hat with a pheasant's feather in it and a sheepskin jacket.

'This is Councillor George Broome, from Southwark Council,' said one of the detectives. 'He tells us that the council have been aware for some time that there were a number of homeless individuals squatting in the school. And this young lady saw approximately twenty of them running away soon after the fire started.'

'They went off in that direction, behind the flats,' said the other detective. 'There's plenty of CCTV around so we should be able to track where they went.'

'They looked like homeless people,' Chrissie told them.

'All shabby, you know, and carrying shopping bags. And even dogs.'

'Why did the council allow them to squat there?' asked Jamila.

Councillor Broome held out his chubby little hands as if he were appealing to a court of law. 'We simply don't have the facilities to shelter that many homeless people, that's why. The council's running desperately short of funds, especially since traditional benefits were replaced with universal credit, and so long as we received no complaints about the squat, it made sense to allow them to stay there.'

'Same as Lambeth Council, isn't it, with the carpet factory,' said Jerry. 'If you don't have the budget, turn a blind eye. Waste of space, that homeless lot, anyway. They'd only spend any money you gave them on Carlsberg Special Brew and crack, wouldn't they?'

Councillor Broome frowned at Jerry as if he couldn't decide if Jerry was joking or not. Jamila was tempted to tell him that a woman had been burned to death in this school, and an unknown number of victims had been ritually murdered here and probably eaten. Then he would understand.

Instead, she turned to Jerry and said, 'I think that is all you and I need to know for now. Detectives – you will make sure that you get in touch with us, won't you, the minute you get some results from the CCTV? We need to catch these people before they can set up another squat.'

Jerry drove them back through Tulse Hill to Tooting. They hardly spoke. They both knew that the key to this investigation was discovering what this cult was, and how widespread it had become, and who was behind it. Yet so far they had made almost no positive progress. Five separate search parties had still failed to track them down in the Underground tunnels, even with dog teams and the assistance of Mott MacDonald, the tunnel engineers. Only one cult member had been arrested, and he had blinded and mutilated himself, and had refused to speak, even if he were capable of it. One possible victim had been rescued, Edward, but he too seemed to be incapable of saying anything coherent.

As they turned into the station car park, though, Jerry said, 'I have an idea. Maybe that Edward can't talk, but supposing we give him a pad and a pencil and ask him to *draw* what happened to him? It doesn't matter if he's not Picasso... maybe he'll be able to give us some visual clues. You know – where these people are, and who they are. It's worth a shot.'

'Good idea,' said Jamila. 'I have been thinking too about DC Malik's hamsa necklace.'

'We haven't heard from any pawnbrokers, have we? I reckon it could have simply snapped off when he was attacked.'

'I am not so sure. The forensic team gave that basement such a thorough going-over.'

'Well, yes. But you have to admit that it was a right dog's dinner down there. All those rolls of carpet and machinery and stuff. You could have lost your granny in there and not found her for a fortnight.'

Jerry opened the station door for her and they climbed the stairs to their office. Edge was sitting in there, his nose so close to the screen of his laptop that it looked as if he needed glasses. He lifted one hand in salute.

'Maybe Malik's killer just took a fancy to that necklace, and kept it,' said Jerry.

'Of course, yes, that is one possibility. But I cannot help asking myself why that was *all* he took, and why he beat Malik with such incredible ferocity. I mean, his killer *smashed* him, didn't he, and ripped him open. Was he provoked, because Malik was wearing a hamsa? After all, the hamsa is worn to protect its wearer from the evil eye.'

'I can't say I know a lot about the evil eye, to be honest with you. I know my mum used to give it to my dad if he left the toilet seat up.'

'Almost every religion believes in the evil eye, in some form or another,' said Jamila. 'In Pakistan, if somebody pays you a compliment – about the beauty of your daughter, for instance – you will say "*Masha'Allah*", which means "God wills it". That is in case they are jealous and giving her the evil eye, and you say it to shield her from any harm. We call the evil eye *Nazar*.'

'All right,' said Jerry, taking off his jacket and sitting down. 'So how does that help us?'

'I have read that some cults use the evil eye to injure their enemies, or to bring them everlasting bad luck, or to hypnotise their victims while they rob them or rape them. Sometimes even to kill them. So it might go to motive. It could be that Malik's killer pulled off his hamsa out of anger, or revenge, or *fear*, even, in the same way that a Muslim might have pulled the crucifix from a crusader.'

'Okay. But I'm still not sure where you're going with this.'

'Jerry – if we can identify a cult who not only worship a devil with the head of a goat and practise cannibalism, but believe that they possess the power of the evil eye, that might give us some idea of who they are and where to find them.'

Edge had been listening to Jamila, and he looked up from his laptop and raised his eyebrows.

'I don't know,' said Jerry. 'That all sounds a bit too—'

'Esoteric?' Jamila challenged him. 'Speculative?'

'Those weren't exactly the words that I was going to use, but yes, if you like. I was actually going to say "clutching at straws".'

19

Sek spent the whole morning snuggled up in his sleeping bag in a small side room. He was woken up two or three times by banging and shouting outside in the corridor, but not by nightmares. Earlier, he had watched as Derek and Aleksandra and Copf and Flecker were nailed to the wall, and then beheaded, and butchered down to their bones, leaving only their outstretched arms, but he had found their gradual dismemberment fascinating, rather than frightening.

He had never realised that when you slit the human stomach open, such slippery heaps of intestines would come tumbling out, as if you had discovered a nest of giant worms. He found it hard to believe that inside his own body he had the same wriggly intestines, as well as a liver and kidneys and bagpipe lungs.

While he was watching, a young woman had made her way to the back of the crowd where he was sitting, and sat down next to him. She had a pale oval face and thinly plucked eyebrows, and her long brown hair was hanging down in dirty, complicated braids. She was wearing a puffy crimson dress that looked as if it had been tacked together out of a quilted bedspread.

'Sek?' she had purred, in the back of her throat. 'My name is Laurel Eye.'

He had looked up at her, and seen that her left eye was pale green, but that she was missing her right eye, and it had been replaced by plain bottle-green glass.

'Now that Erst has been taken away, Hedda has asked me to take care of you,' she told him. 'Come along with me now. I'll take you to see Apo, so that you can have another cup of calla dew.'

'When is Erst coming back?' Sek had asked her.

Laurel Eye had shaken her head so that her braids swung. 'We don't know. Perhaps never. The comelings will probably kill him and eat him.'

'I miss him. I want him back.'

'Well, you never know. Perhaps he will be lucky, and escape.'

Sek had stood up, and Laurel Eye had taken his hand and led him through the crowd and along the corridor. They had climbed the stairs to the next floor, and then along another corridor until they reached a door at the very end. Laurel Eye had knocked and called out that it was her, and that she had brought Sek with her.

A young woman with short-cropped blonde hair and a floor-length dress had opened the door for them. She was so emaciated that she was almost transparent, like a ghost. The bearded man who had given Erst and Sek their first drink of calla dew had been sitting at a dressing table. More than a hundred small glass bottles were clustered on top of the dressing table next to him, each about the size of a test tube, with a glass stopper in it, and each filled with the same amber liquid.

'I am sorry to hear about your brother, Sek,' the bearded man had told him. His voice was very deep, and even growlier than most. 'But here – let me give you another cup of calla dew. That will make you feel calmer. You will need at least three or four cups a day for the first few days... then only once a day, although there may be times when bad things happen and you feel the need for more.'

'What's in it?' Sek had asked him, as the bearded man opened up one of the bottles and poured the liquid into the yellow plastic cup.

'Ha! Ha! I wish I knew. I'm trying to find out, believe you me. If I knew, it would make me the master of the whole world.'

Sek had drunk the calla dew, and coughed, and handed back the empty cup, and then Laurel Eye had led him downstairs to the side room so that he could sleep.

When he finally woke up, and it was daylight, he stayed in his sleeping bag staring at the wall. The inside of his head felt as if it were filled with murky water, like a pond, and that his thoughts were like fragments of broken crockery that somebody was dropping into it. He was conscious that he ought to know who he was, and where he was, and how he had come to be lying here, but the pieces seemed to float to the bottom of the pond and none of them fitted together or made any sense.

He was hungry and his bladder was so full that it ached, yet he made no attempt to climb out of his sleeping bag because he had no idea what he was supposed to do next.

He heard a clock chiming somewhere far away, again and again, although he didn't know how to count. While it was still chiming, Laurel Eye came into the room in her puffy crimson dress and bent down to smile at him.

'Sek? You awake? Come downstairs for something to eat.'

She tugged down the zip of his sleeping bag and folded it back for him so that he could roll himself out of it.

'How did you sleep? Did you dream?'

He stood up, clutching himself. 'I really need to pee.'

'Then pee. Go in the corner.'

He went over to the opposite side of the room, lifted his sweater and opened his jeans and urinated a seemingly endless stream against the wall. Laurel Eye waited for him impatiently. 'What in the name of the great one did you drink last night? The river? Is there any water left for the boats to sail on?'

He finished at last and followed her out of the room. 'What's a "river"?'

'Water that moves. You will see it one night when we go out hunting for opfers.'

The kitchen was crowded with at least thirty men and women. Only three of the six ovens were open but it was still suffocatingly hot, like a ship's boiler room, and the air was thick with smoke and the smell of charred flesh. Hedda was sitting at the head of the table with Faust beside her. She was gnawing on a curved rib and talking loudly with her mouth full. Faust was holding the right lobe of a human liver in both hands and taking repeated bites out of it, saying nothing as he chewed, but occasionally spitting out bits of ligament.

As before, when Erst and Sek had first eaten here, the middle of the table was heaped with roasted meat and vegetables, but today there was much less red meat, and it had been supplemented by piles of spongy white tripe and brains that had been cut into quarters. There were several pigeons too, and two magpies, all of which had been roughly plucked and seared on a hotplate, still with their heads and wings on.

Laurel Eye led Sek to the head of the table and a serious-looking Chinese woman who was sitting next to Hedda shifted herself to one side so that Sek and Laurel Eye could take her place.

'My child – my only remaining child!' purred Hedda. She wrapped her arm around his shoulders and hugged him so hard against her rough sour-smelling shawl that he thought his ribs were going to crack.

'So sad that we have lost your brother, Erst! But soon – soon we will find more children, and our tribe will grow greater, and we will make you all fit and healthy, so that you can fight any comeling! Here – take one of these ribs! This is the meat from the two opfers we caught when poor Erst was taken from us! Eat them out of revenge! Eat them to get strong!'

Sek took the rib and started to nibble the flesh from it. From one end he bit off a lump of fat, and for a split second he remembered that he hated fat, and that it made him feel sick. When he started to masticate it, though, he found that he actually liked it, even though it was so rubbery that it squeaked between his teeth. The only trouble was that it took him so long to chew it that his jaw started to ache and in the end he swallowed it whole.

'Every mouthful takes you closer to being a man, young Sek,' said Hedda, winking at him. Her chin was shiny with grease and a small blob of brain was clinging to the side of her mouth. She wiped it away with the back of her left hand, and it was then that Sek saw she had only two fingers and a thumb on that hand, and that her nails were all purple, as if they were bruised.

'What happened to your fingers?' he asked her.

She pushed her hand into her coat pocket to hide it. 'My dog had them,' she told him. 'He was a pit bull terrier. My guard dog, in those days when I was out on the streets. Hammer, his name was. Of course, you don't know what a "hammer" is yet, do you? But one night a friend of mine got drunk and kicked Hammer because he was lying in his way. Hammer went for him – nearly tore off his trousers. I shouted at Hammer to stop, and smacked him across the head, but then he went for me too, and bit off my fingers. Poor old Hammer.'

'What happened to him?' asked Sek, using his fingernail to prise a bit of gristle from between his teeth.

'Hammer? He was run over by a lorry. Well, you'll find out what a "lorry" is when you go out on the streets. Squashed flat as a pancake. Served him right, I suppose, but I still miss him. Oh, look, listen – we're in for some music now.'

A pretty young mixed-race girl with a huge puffball of frizzy hair and an oversized Fair Isle sweater had climbed barefoot onto the far end of the table. The men and women all roared their approval and drummed so hard on the table that the meat and bones and charred root vegetables bounced up and down.

The girl lifted a slender white recorder to her lips. It looked as if it had been made out of a human leg bone, with holes drilled into it. She started to play a thin, sad tune, and all the men and women in the kitchen joined in, humming the same tune, linking their arms, and swaying from side to side. Sek noticed that Hedda stayed silent, and sat completely still, her eyes flicking from one person to another, as if she were checking that each one of them was genuinely carried away by the music, and not pretending.

Next to Sek, Laurel Eye was humming, and swaying, and after a while she caught hold of Sek's arm and made him sway with her. He found that he was enjoying himself, and once the girl on the table had repeated the tune three or four times, he could hum along too. For some reason, the swaying and the humming gave him a sensation of sitting outside, around a fire – not the scout campfire, but another fire, much fiercer, with trees and branches stacked up into a tall crackling pyramid.

He could feel that he was in the open air, under a cloudy night sky, with mountains all around. It was so real that when the girl stopped playing, it took him a moment to realise that he was back in the hot, crowded kitchen, sitting between Laurel Eye and Hedda, in front of a table strewn with roasted human remains and vegetables.

He looked at Laurel Eye and said, 'I feel – I feel like two people. I feel like me, but then I feel like another me. I don't know which me I am.'

'It's the calla dew,' Laurel Eye told him, tossing her braids back over her shoulder. 'After a few days, don't worry, you will feel like only one person.'

'But which one?'

Hedda had been listening, and she put her arm around him again, and squeezed him. 'You will be my child and my child only. That is all you have to know.'

The girl on the table whistled another tune, faster and happier than the first one, and everybody drummed in time. Sek clapped too, feeling even more excited than before. When the girl had finished and climbed down from the table, he said to Hedda, 'I can do some magic.'

'Magic?' she smiled. 'Did you say "magic"? I don't believe you.'

'I can. I promise you.'

'Go on, then, child. Show us.'

The Chinese woman had been drinking from a white polystyrene coffee cup. Sek reached over and picked it up, tipping out the last of her water. To Laurel Eye, he said, 'Can I borrow your scarf?'

Laurel Eye shrugged, pulled off her silky brown nylon scarf and handed it to him. He stood up and walked down to the far end of the kitchen. Once he had taken off his dirty trainers, he used a chair to climb up onto the table and stand where the girl with the flute had been standing.

Hedda spread out her arms and shouted out, 'Sek has boasted to me that he can work magic! Let us see if he is as good as his word!'

There was more laughter and more drumming on the table. Sek held up the coffee cup and showed it to the men and women sitting around him.

'You see this cup? I will now make this cup vanish!' he announced. He knew that he was supposed to recite some magic words, but he couldn't remember what they were, so he made some up. 'Cup, cup, have no fear! I can make you disappear!'

He covered the cup with Laurel Eye's scarf, and then he shouted out, 'Go, cup, go! Out of sight! Don't come back until it's night!'

With a flourish, he waved the scarf in the air, so that it made a snapping sound, and the cup had gone.

He smiled, and bowed. He had hoped for laughter and applause from the men and women in the kitchen, but he had not anticipated what happened next. Every one of them stared at him in silence. Some of them had their mouths open, and he saw half-chewed food drop from one man's mouth onto the table.

Then, one after another, they pushed back their chairs and knelt down on the floor, covering their heads with their hands. The only person who remained seated was Hedda, and even she had her hands pressed together.

After a few moments' silence, she beckoned to him. He jumped awkwardly down from the table and walked back to her. As she passed the kneeling men and women, each of them growled in a way that sounded like '*got it*'.

He sat down next to Hedda. Even Laurel Eye was kneeling on the floor with one hand on top of her head. She too whispered, '*Got it.*'

'I did not know that you could work miracles,' said Hedda.

Sek blinked and shifted awkwardly in his chair. He didn't know what she meant, and apart from that, he had to reach behind him so that he could take the coffee cup out from underneath his arm, crush it flat without making too much of a crackling noise, lift his sweater and push it down the back of his jeans. He was not sure why, but he suspected that if Hedda realised that the disappearing cup was nothing but a trick, she would feel that he had made a fool of her in front of her people, and punish him.

'From now on, you will come with me wherever I go, and you can have whatever you want,' said Hedda. 'And we must give you a new name. We will call you Sowber Sek.'

She looked around the kitchen. Everybody was still kneeling, with their hands on their heads.

'You can tell them to rise, if you wish it,' she said.

Sek stood up. He was even more excited than before. Did all these people actually believe that he was a real magician?

'You can all get up now,' he told them. 'Get up and finish your food.'

'Sowber Sek!' Hedda announced, as everybody took their places again, with a loud scraping of chairs.

'*Sowber Sek!*' they chorused, and thumped the table with their fists. '*Got it!*'

20

Jerry put down the phone and said, 'Now it seems like we might be getting somewhere.'

Jamila looked up from her laptop. 'Who was that?'

'Jimmy from Wandsworth nick. His search team went back to Kennington station early this morning while the power was still switched off. They found a small blocked-up door that they'd missed before, and there's a passage behind it that leads through to another one of those abandoned Tube tunnels. The problem is that it's like a bloody maze down there. He said it's going to take them a fair amount of time to search through all of them, even with those tunnel engineers giving them a hand.'

'What about that Simon? Has his train-spotting friend found his map of the Underground yet?'

'Anorak? No, I haven't heard from him. I'll give him a bell and see if he's had any joy. But according to Jimmy, it's not just a question of locating the tunnels. Some of them have half collapsed because the brickwork was never completed, so they're pretty dangerous, and some of them are flooded.'

'All the same, this cult know their way around.'

'That's another problem that Jimmy mentioned. He said they brought in three search dogs from Nine Elms – two Alsatians and a Lab – but none of them picked up a scent. In fact, it was more like they *did* pick up a scent but they didn't want to follow it. It was almost as if they were scared to.'

'Search dogs? *Scared?* I have never heard of that before.'

'Me neither. But he said that when they rescued that Edward, one of the dogs went on the attack like he'd never seen a search dog go for anyone. His handler said afterwards that he only got hyper-aggressive like that when he was frightened.'

Jerry picked up his cup of coffee, sipped it, and grimaced, because it had gone stone cold. 'I don't know. This whole thing is so weird. How did a whole cult spring up without us even catching a sniff of it? Especially a cult that fucking eats people.'

Jamila sat back. 'Do you know what I was thinking? That councillor we talked to, he may have given us the answer to that. All the cult members that we have come across so far have been homeless people. And apart from one or two charities, like the Salvation Army and Centrepoint, we ignore homeless people. Perhaps they have found a way now of getting together and fighting back.'

'Oh, come on! By kidnapping people and *cooking* them?'

'Perhaps their god demands it. Perhaps he is like the goddess Kali. When she fought the evil demon Raktabija she wounded him, so that he bled. Every drop of his blood turned into a clone of him before it fell to the ground, but Kali devoured every one of them. How do you defeat your enemies, both spiritually and physically, body and soul? You eat them.'

'I don't know,' said Jerry. 'I just think it's gone beyond bonkers. Listen – do you want another cuppa? And you like those Bahlsen biscuits, don't you? Those chocolate ones?'

'Don't tempt me. I am trying my best to lose weight.'

'What? You don't need to, skip. You look fine as you are.'

Before Jamila could answer him, though, there was a knock

at their open door. It was Tosh Brinkley, clutching a briefcase and looking slightly out of breath.

'Bloody hell! When are you going to get your lift repaired?'

'Never, probably,' said Jerry. 'They'll be selling this station soon and we'll all be moving to Wimbledon. The Met's boracic, just like everybody else. How's tricks? You got any updates for us?'

'I have, yes, and since I have to go up to the Kremlin I thought I'd drop in and brief you in person.'

He dragged over a chair and sat down, opening up his briefcase and taking out a printed report.

'That bushing hammer, yes, that *did* have Connor Greene's fingerprints and DNA on the handle. On the face of the hammerhead we also found DC Malik's DNA, so the evidence that it was Connor Greene who killed him is fairly conclusive, I'd say.'

'He'd better pray that I don't collar him first, I can tell you,' said Jerry. 'I'll give him the orthodontic treatment of a lifetime.'

Tosh took out a second report. 'We've also completed our analysis of the faecal samples we took from the Royale carpet factory. They all contain traces of an opioid that we've never come across before. It would appear to be highly addictive, like heroin or crack cocaine, but it has other unusual components, which we're still testing. One of them appears to have the specific ability to alter the functions of Broca's area. That's the part of the left temporal lobe of the human brain that controls speech.'

'Maybe that's why that twonk who ate his eyeballs couldn't speak,' said Jerry. 'And that young Edward, he was having trouble speaking too. His doctor at St George's told us that they'd found some kind of unknown opioid in his blood, so I reckon you and him need to compare notes.'

'Dr Seshadri,' said Jamila, and wrote down the name and number for him.

Tosh said, 'There's one more thing, which may be important and it may not.' He picked up his phone and scrolled through his photographs. When he had found what he was looking for, he held it up so that Jamila and Jerry could see it, but to both of them it appeared to be nothing more than crudely printed numbers on a dark brown background – A-7632.

'We had to enhance this chemically, because the skin was so badly burned.'

'That's skin?'

'Yes, we took it from the arm of one of the victims found in the shopping trolleys. I told you before that all the victims appeared to have been elderly. This number is a tattoo, and it corresponds with the tattoos given to female Jewish prisoners at Auschwitz.'

'You're joking,' said Jerry.

'No. And we know it was Auschwitz because that was the only concentration camp where prisoners got tattooed.'

'That means we should be able to identify her,' said Jamila. 'I know that several online archives have records of Holocaust survivors – Jewish Heritage, for one. If we can discover who she was, it could possibly help us to find out who all the other victims were.'

'Ironic, isn't it?' said Tosh. 'Or tragic, rather. You know what "holocaust" means, don't you? It's Greek for "sacrifice by fire". This poor woman escaped one holocaust and over seventy years later she got herself murdered in another.'

Jamila said, 'I will get on to Jewish Heritage right away. Jerry – do you want to chase up your friends at Peckham and see if they have any results from the CCTV yet? We really need to know what has happened to all those people who ran away from that fire. Where did they all go to? Where are they now?'

'You got it, skip. Tosh – thanks for bringing us up to speed. And if you happen to bump into DCI Mellors when you're up at the Kremlin, can you tell him hallo from me, and happy Christmas, and I still think he's a total prick.'

Jamila spent almost an hour in front of her laptop, scrolling through the records of the Jewish Heritage archive.

At last, she said, 'There. Incredible. I think I've found her.'

Jerry was still on the phone. He was waiting for DC Mike Brown from Peckham to tell him if they had found any helpful CCTV footage of the homeless people running away from the Charles Babbage school fire.

'Are you talking?' Jamila asked him.

'No. I think he's forgotten about me and gone off for his tea.'

Jamila stood up and came over with the notes that she had scribbled on her pad.

'According to the archive, the woman's name was Betina Fredanov. She was a Romanian Jew who was sent to Auschwitz in 1943, and tattooed with the number A-7632. Tosh was right. It was only at Auschwitz that the Nazis tattooed their prisoners, and then they only tattooed those prisoners who were considered fit enough to work – not those who were sent to be gassed.'

'God almighty. Doesn't bear thinking about it, does it? But she survived.'

'Yes. And it seems that she was lucky, in a way, if you can call it luck. After the Soviet army liberated Auschwitz, she spent about three months at a rehabilitation centre for

Holocaust survivors in Katowice, about thirty-five kilometres north of the concentration camp. It was set up by a Russian military doctor, Major Mikhail Kamenev.

'According to the archive, this Major Kamenev was something of a saint. He treated hundreds of concentration camp survivors for typhus and other illnesses, and he helped them gradually to restore their health. Many of them were so malnourished that when they tried to eat solid food, it killed them. Once Betina had recovered from typhus, and she was strong enough, she returned to her home town – which was Braşov, in Romania.'

'Okay,' said Jerry. 'But what was she doing here, now, in England, and was there any special motive why *she* was being barbecued? Was it anything to do with her being a Holocaust survivor or was she picked out at random? And, like, who were all the other people she was being barbecued with?'

'That, of course, is what we still have to find out.'

'Tosh said they were all elderly, so it sounds to me as if they could have been a group of some sort. A club, or a society, or maybe just friends. There has to be a reason they were chosen. Like I said before, if you were going to order a meal in a restaurant, you wouldn't ask for a steak from an eighty-five-year-old cow, would you?'

'I will contact the Romanian police, and see if they can find out for us why Betina had come here to the UK. Maybe she had emigrated here. She must have friends or relatives in her home town who know.'

At that moment, DC Brown picked up his phone and said, 'Jerry? It's Mike. Sorry to keep you so long, mate. We've been over the CCTV footage again and again, just to make sure we haven't missed anything.'

'So what's the score?'

'They all ran down an alley called Willowdene, and then between some blocks of flats called Pinedene. Then they ran into that massive building site right next to our nick where they're putting up all those new flats. The site itself isn't covered by CCTV, so we lost them. The nutty thing is though that there's no sign of them running out the other side. The site's main gate is right on the Queen's Road, but they didn't come out there. Even if they'd exited by one of its two side gates, they still would have been picked up by the security cameras on the front of the nick. But they weren't, so they couldn't have done.'

'You've searched the site?'

'Of course. There wasn't a lot of work going on there today, because they were waiting for several loads of Belgian facing bricks that were held up at Dover. But we talked to the foreman, and he gave us what you might call a guided tour. No trace of those homeless people anywhere. It beats me, mate. It really does. It was like they'd simply vanished into thin air – like, *poof*!'

'You're absolutely sure there was no place where they could have hidden? Like, in the Portaloos or somewhere?'

'Positive. There were only five portable toilets so where are you going to hide twenty-three homeless people and two dogs? That's how many there were. Twenty-three. And two dogs.'

'So where do you think they went?'

'I haven't an effing clue. But we've put out a BOLO and we'll be interviewing other homeless people to see if they recognise them.'

Jerry put his phone down. 'Well?' asked Jamila.

'They disappeared. Totally disappeared. You remember that building site next to the Peckham nick? Mike says they broke in there and that was the last they saw of them.'

He paused, and then he said, 'You know something? I'm seriously beginning to think that there could well be some spooky supernatural force at work here. Something like your aunt's devil, Baloo.'

'Balaa. Baloo is the bear in *The Jungle Book*.'

'Baloo, Balaa, whatever. I wouldn't fancy meeting either of them on a dark night, I can tell you.'

21

When Jerry came down the stairs to the station's reception area that evening, zipping up his jacket, he found Linda waiting for him.

'Linda! How long have you been here?' He nodded toward the desk. 'You should have asked John to call me and I would have come down.'

Linda stood up. She was hugging herself in her bobbly blue wool coat and she looked pale and upset. She was a small woman, 'five feet and a bus ticket' according to Edge. Her long dark hair was usually tied back in a ponytail and her make-up was usually perfect, but now her hair was tangled and her mascara was blotchy, and it was obvious that she had been crying.

Jerry put his arms around her and held her close. He could smell the Flowerbomb perfume he had bought her for her birthday last month.

'What's wrong, sweetheart? It's not your dad, is it?'

She nodded, and sniffed. 'He passed away at lunchtime. Yesterday they thought he might be getting a bit better, but during the night he took a turn for the worse. My sister June was there too, but he never regained consciousness so he didn't know.'

'Why didn't you call me?'

'I knew you were all tied up with this really important case. I didn't want to disturb you.'

'You should have done. There's nothing in my life at the moment that's more important than you.'

Jerry had told Linda that he and Jamila were investigating a serious homicide, although he had said nothing about a cult, or cannibalism. He hadn't wanted to upset her, and in any case those details were still tightly under wraps. Even the media had been kept ignorant of everything that had been discovered at the Royale carpet factory. Nor had they been told that the fire at the Charles Babbage school had probably been started when a woman was about to be murdered and roasted.

'Come on,' said Jerry. 'Let's get you home and you can have a stiff drink and a shower. That's unless you want to go back to yours.'

'No, no. I want to carry on staying with you. Especially tonight.'

'Right, let's go. It's not raining, is it?'

'No. It was earlier, but it's stopped now.'

They stopped on the station's front steps. Jerry took out a silver packet of Sterling cigarettes and handed her one, and they both lit up. Then, both blowing smoke, they walked arm in arm toward the main road junction of Amen Corner.

Jerry had moved three months ago to an upstairs flat in a terraced house in Crowborough Road, which was less than five minutes' walk from the station. It was £50 a month cheaper than his previous flat, and his only complaint was that his landlady, Nora, who lived downstairs, was almost stone deaf. She always turned up the volume on her television so loud that it made the water in his fish tank ripple. Fortunately, she went to bed at eight, or shortly after.

'Who's going to be making all the funeral arrangements?' asked Jerry.

'June's sorting everything out. The will, and all that. She's a legal secretary, so she's better at that kind of thing than me.'

'You run a charity shop.'

'Yes, but I have to sort through dead people's clothes every day. I don't want to sort through Dad's.'

They waited at the corner for the crossing lights to change. As they were standing there, Jerry noticed a bearded man hunched in the doorway of the estate agents on the opposite side of the road. He was wearing a black balaclava and he was covered by a blanket and a waterproof groundsheet. A brown-and-white Jack Russell terrier was lying next to him.

It appeared to Jerry that this man had caught sight of them too, because he suddenly climbed to his feet, dropping his blanket and his groundsheet onto the still wet pavement. He took three or four steps out of the doorway, facing in their direction, and then he stopped, his arms spread out and his head lifted. It looked as if he were breathing in deep lungfuls of exhaust-laden air. His terrier also stood up, and shook itself.

The pedestrian lights changed to green and Jerry and Linda crossed over Amen Corner. As they reached Southcroft Road, where they would have to turn right to get to Crowborough Road, Jerry looked back and saw that the man had bundled his blanket and his groundsheet into the doorway and that he and his terrier were crossing over Amen Corner too.

Was he following them? Jerry was tempted to wait until he had caught up with them, and confront him. But Linda was tugging at his arm and he decided that she had suffered more than enough distress for one day, without having to witness a face-off with some bearded vagrant.

When they reached Crowborough Road, Jerry looked back once again. The man and his terrier were standing on the corner of Southcroft Road, quite still. Maybe he wasn't following them, after all. Yet Jerry still felt uneasy about the way in which he had scrambled to his feet as soon as he had seen them at the traffic lights.

They dropped their half-smoked cigarettes into the gutter and then he opened the front door of number 15 and they went inside. Nora didn't allow smoking because her late husband had been a chain-smoker and died of throat cancer. The hallway, as usual, was as hot as the tropics, with Nora's capes and cardigans hanging on a coat stand like a drooping palm tree. Her living-room door was half open, with the television turned up to deafening.

'You all right, Nora?' Jerry shouted, putting his head around the door.

'Oh, is that you, Jerry? Yes, thanks. Listen – I was going to tell you, I'll be having a kipper for me tea, so if there's a bit of a fishy smell coming up the stairs, don't worry about it. I've got some floral spray if it gets too much.'

'Right, okay, love.'

Jerry and Linda climbed the stairs to Jerry's flat, which had a large living room, a kitchenette, a bedroom and a bathroom. The living room was decorated with pink striped wallpaper and hung with prints of landscapes by Constable and Jack Vettriano's painting of two people dancing on a beach while their butler and their maid held umbrellas over their heads. Jerry detested it, mostly because his ex-wife, Nancy, had adored it.

Linda took off her coat and laid it over the back of one of the armchairs, with her scarf draped on top of it. Jerry poured them both a large Scotch.

'Here's to your dad,' he said, raising his glass. 'At least he's not suffering anymore.'

'You never would have known that he was suffering,' said Linda, tucking up her feet on the sofa. She was wearing a black roll-neck sweater and the gold wolf's-head medallion that Jerry had given her for her birthday. 'He was such a quiet man. Never said much. Never complained. I'd see him staring out the window sometimes into the garden looking sad and I'd wonder what he was thinking about. Too late to ask him now.'

She sipped her whisky, puckering her lips to stop herself from sobbing, but she couldn't stop the tears that rolled down her cheeks. Jerry pulled a tissue out of the box, sat down beside her and dabbed her face for her.

'I'm not going to tell you that time's the great healer, because it isn't. It never gets better. My mum died when she was only sixty-four and it still hurts as much now as it did the day she left us. You learn to live with it, that's all.'

Linda attempted a smile. 'That's one thing I love about you, Jer. No matter how bad I feel, you always manage to make me feel a little bit worse.'

They could hear the muffled sound of Nora's television through the carpet, so Jerry put on his CD of relaxing classical music. After a day of blood and shouting at work, he liked to lie back and listen to Albinoni's Adagio in G minor, and other soothing tracks.

'Do you want anything to eat?' he asked Linda.

'No thanks. I couldn't. Don't let me stop you though.'

'I might have something later. I think I'll wait until Nora's cooked her kipper.'

Jerry was getting up to pour himself a refill when he heard a loud bang, as if somebody had collided with the front door downstairs. This was followed almost at once by a splintering crash, and then by Nora shouting, and then screaming.

'What the *hell*?' said Jerry.

He opened the living-room door and went out onto the landing. The front door had been broken off its hinges and was lying on its side in the hallway with its crescent glass window shattered. Two men were standing next to it, one wearing a hooded brown duffel coat and the other a black padded jacket. Both of them had scarves wrapped around their faces, so that only their eyes showed.

Jerry shouted, 'I'm a police officer! Get out of here, now! I've called for backup!'

He heard Nora screaming again, so he started to bound down the stairs. Before he had reached the bottom, though, the man in the black padded jacket mounted the first three stairs and seized Jerry's sleeves. He used Jerry's own momentum to pull him down the rest of the flight, slamming his back against the newel post, and then kicking his legs from under him. Snarling like a rabid dog, he pushed Jerry so hard that he fell backwards over the front door and hit his head against the skirting board. The man in the brown duffel coat then grabbed hold of his arms and dragged him out onto the garden path. He kicked him in the ribs again and again, and then kicked him twice in the face. He finished up by rolling him over, off the path and into the small paved front garden. After giving him a last hard kick in the back, he growled at him fiercely as if he were warning him to stay where he was.

Jerry lay bruised and winded. The last kick had hit him exactly where he had been struck by the scaffolding pole, and he felt as if he had been electrocuted, so that every nerve in his body was crackling with pain. When he opened his swollen eyes, he saw that a plastic gnome was smiling at him. He touched the bridge of his nose but it didn't feel as if it were broken.

Grunting, he tried to turn himself over. As he shifted himself onto his back, he saw the man in the black padded jacket coming out of the house. The man was hunched over, because he was carrying a leg under each arm, and as he came out further, Jerry saw that the man in the brown duffel coat was behind him, and that between them they were carrying Linda.

'*Stop!*' he shouted, even though his ribs hurt so much that he could barely breathe. '*Stop, you bastards! Put her down!*'

The two men took no notice, shuffling past him and carrying Linda out through the front gate. She was silent, and Jerry saw that her arm was swinging loosely, which meant that they must have knocked her out, or worse.

He managed to climb up onto his knees and reach for the windowsill so that he could haul himself up onto his feet. But he was still kneeling when a third man appeared out of the house – the bearded man who had followed them from Amen Corner. His terrier was with him too.

'Bring her back,' Jerry croaked at him. 'I don't know what you're up to, but I'll have you for assault and abduction, and you'll be banged up for years.'

The man snarled at him again, took one step forward, and kicked him in the stomach. Jerry doubled up and knelt with his forehead pressed against the wet terracotta paving tiles. He heard the man snarl again, and then walk away, with his terrier pattering after him.

Biting his lip to suppress the pain, Jerry managed at last to climb to his feet. He went out of the gate and looked down Crowborough Road, but the three men and Linda had gone.

He limped back into the house, stumbling over the broken front door. Nora's living-room door was wide open now, and her television was still blaring. She had been watching *Michael McIntyre's The Wheel*, and the audience was roaring with laughter.

'Nora?' he called out. 'Nora, are you okay?'

There was no answer, so he stepped into the room. The first thing he saw was the diagonal streaks of blood across the yellow tiled fireplace. Looking around, he saw blood spattered across the flowery wallpaper over the couch. There were even fine drops of blood on the ceiling.

He found Nora behind the door, lying on her back with her arms crossed over her pullover and her grey pleated skirt lifted to expose her pink support stockings. Her head was smashed so that her face was flat and unrecognisable and her brains had squirted out of the splits in her skull and become tangled in her thin white hair.

Jerry stood staring at her for a few moments, breathing slowly, trying to keep the ham roll that he had eaten for lunch where it belonged, down inside his bruised stomach. Then he turned around and mounted the stairs as quickly as he could, to find his phone.

22

Sek was woken up by the sounds of screaming and snarling and doors banging from somewhere downstairs. He sat up and listened. He felt strangely detached from reality, as if he were floating six inches off the floor. After he had eaten, Apo had given him another cupful of calla dew, and he had slid down into unconsciousness almost at once. He could only suppose that one of the tribe had carried him upstairs and tucked him into his sleeping bag. It was growing dark outside and five night lights were flickering in the opposite corner of the room, in the pattern of a pentagram.

He climbed out of his sleeping bag and went to the door to see if he could find out what all the noise was about. As he started to walk along the corridor to the staircase, Laurel Eye came up the stairs. She had twisted her coarse brown braids into a tall pyramid on top of her head.

'Oh! You're awake!'

'All that screaming woke me up. What's going on?'

'You don't have to worry about it. But don't go down there. Some of the men are fighting.'

'What are they fighting about? I should tell them to stop. I'm Sowber Sek now. They have to do what I tell them.'

'*I* know you're Sowber Sek and Hedda knows that, and so

do the rest of our tribe. But some people from another tribe have arrived and they don't yet know who you are.'

'But why are they fighting?'

'I'm not sure. I think they want to stay here but Hedda says they can't. There isn't enough room and there isn't nearly enough for everybody to eat.'

'There are *lots* of empty rooms,' said Sek. 'And Faust sent two girls out, didn't he, to the food place, to bring back vegetables and milk and bread? And when it gets dark we'll be going out again, won't we, to bring in more opfers? If there's more of us that need feeding we'll just have to catch more of them.'

'Yes, but Hedda doesn't want this tribe here. I don't think she likes Mody – he's their chief. And she says that if they come to join us, the comelings are much more likely to find out that we're living here.'

'They're going to find us anyway if they carry on making all that noise. I'm going down.'

Laurel Eye caught Sek's sleeve. 'No, Sek. You're only a boy and you could get hurt. I'm supposed to look after you.'

Sek pulled her hand away. 'I'm not just Sek, I'm Sowber Sek. And I can look after myself.'

He started on his way downstairs, with Laurel Eye following close behind him. The screaming and the banging had stopped now, but he could still hear growling and snarling and arguing.

When he reached the reception area, he found that it was crowded on one side with Hedda's tribe, some of them carrying hammers and sticks, and on the other side by at least twenty men and women he had never seen before, although they were dressed in much the same way, in hooded duffel coats and puffa jackets. There was a strong smell in the air of body odour and dried urine and smoke.

Hedda was standing in the middle of the reception area. Facing her was a short bald man with a bushy grey beard and a belly so huge that he had only been able to fasten the toggles of his brown duffel coat halfway down. A man was lying at their feet with his arms and his legs spread out. His face was smothered in blood, but Sek recognised him as Apo, who handed out the calla dew. His eyes were wide open but they were staring at nothing.

On Hedda's right-hand side, two of her men were holding the arms of a tall, thin, spidery man with near-together eyes and protruding teeth. He was trying everything he could to free himself, kicking his legs in a gallop and then tilting himself violently backwards, but another of Hedda's men came up with a kitchen knife and prodded his waterproof jacket with it, and gave him two or three threatening grunts, and after that he kept still.

The crowd of Hedda's people all shuffled back when Sek appeared, to give him space to walk up to Hedda. Some of them reverentially placed one hand on top of their heads, and some of them murmured, '*Got it, got it.*'

Sek approached Hedda and the fat bearded man. He looked down at Apo and saw that one side of his forehead had a semi-circular dent, as if he had been hit with a scaffolding pole. There was no doubt that he was dead.

'What's going on?' he asked.

'There's been a fight, Sowber Sek,' said Hedda. She pointed to the tall, thin spidery man. 'This piece of excrement was demanding that Apo give calla dew to all of these people, but Apo said he wouldn't. He lost his temper and hit Apo and killed him.'

'The calla dew isn't yours alone,' protested the fat bearded man. 'It's high time you shared it out more fairly. All of my people are always suffering because you're so tight-fisted with it.'

'That's because it can't last for ever,' Hedda retorted. 'If I let you have as much as you want, it would be gone in a few weeks or even days and then what would you do? And like the morons you are, you have killed the only one among us who could have worked out how to make us more.'

'We still need somewhere to stay, and food to eat. At least until we can find ourselves another shelter.'

Hedda put her arm around Sek's shoulders – not in the way that she had first hugged him, like her own child, but gently, and respectfully, as if she were holding a saint.

'Sowber Sek, this is Mody, and these are Mody's people. They have arrived here without warning and demanded that we take them in and look after them. We all used to live together but Mody always wanted different rules, and more food, and more calla dew. So in the end they went off to live in another place. We kept supplying them with calla dew, but only if they brought us an opfer in return for every cupful.'

She turned back to Mody and said, 'Mody, this is Sowber Sek. He has shown us that he is the "got it".'

'Why have you come here?' asked Sek. 'What's happened to your other place?'

'It was all burned to ashes in a fire,' said Mody. 'We were forced to leave and now we've lost everything – not that we had much to lose. But our muster has gone, and that took us over a year to put together.'

'Your muster?' asked Sek. 'What's that?'

'Never mind,' Hedda interrupted. 'This member of Mody's tribe has murdered our Apo and that means that our whole future is threatened. As I said, the calla dew won't last for ever, and here's Mody and his ragged gang of fools, complaining that we don't let them have enough.'

'After the stress of that fire, Hedda, we desperately need some now,' said Mody. 'Look at Sabina, with her dogs. She's shaking like a tambourine.'

'So where are your opfers?' Hedda demanded. 'You know what the price is, for each cup of calla dew.'

'How could we catch opfers when we were running for our lives? In the name of the great one, Hedda, have some pity. If you take us in now, and give us calla dew, I promise you that we will go out tomorrow and fetch you all that you ask for, and more.'

'I am not a believer in promises,' said Hedda. 'I can't count how many people have made me promises, ever since I was a young girl, and where did I end up? Raped more times than I can remember, hungry, abandoned, and living on the street. It was calla dew that saved me, and so I will never give it away lightly, and for nothing.'

She turned around to the tall, spidery man. 'We can start with him. As a punishment for murdering Apo, and as an opfer.'

'What? That's Biro! He and me, we've been together for more than ten years! We're like brothers! He lost his temper, that's all! His mind and his body, they're crying out for calla dew! All of us are crying out for it!'

'Mody, I don't care. If you want to show me that when you make a promise you can keep a promise, then give us your friend here to prove it. There's not too much meat on him, is there, but it's better to have a marrowbone to suck than nothing at all.'

Biro struggled again, but Hedda's two men held on to him. 'I didn't mean it!' he shouted, in a ragged voice. 'I didn't mean to hurt him! But when I asked him for calla dew he told me to go and fuck myself and turned his back! It wasn't even *me* that hit him! It was my need! It was my *need*, Mody, it was my *need*!'

Hedda lowered her head so that her face disappeared into the shadow cast by the brims of her hats. Without looking up, she said, 'You can't have calla dew without an opfer, Mody. At least one opfer. What do you think, Sowber Sek? Do we punish this Biro for killing Apo and eat him for our supper tonight, or do we forgive him and let him go free?'

Laurel Eye came up and stood at Sek's side, holding up a candle. The candlelight gave Sek a more cherubic appearance than usual, with his plump face and his curly blond hair and his sweater two sizes too large for him. Laurel Eye said nothing, although her bottle-green glass eye was reflecting the candlelight and winking at him, as if to suggest that *you have the power now, Sek. You may be no more than eight years old, but you have the power of life or death.*

Sek felt that power rising inside him. It was the most wonderful sensation that he had ever experienced. He felt strong, and grown-up. In fact, he felt invincible. He was more than a boy who could work magic that made everybody bow down before him. He felt that he was a living instrument of the goat-headed god – a high priest in a religion that was twenty times older than Christianity. In a way, he was a god himself.

'Well?' said Hedda, her face still invisible. 'Do we spare him, or eat him?'

Mody dropped to his knees and clung on to the hem of Sek's droopy sweater. 'Please,' he begged.

Sek remembered a film he had seen about Roman gladiators. He didn't know where or when he had seen it. He might even have actually been there in the arena, in person. But he recalled clearly that Caesar had turned down his thumb to indicate that a defeated man should die.

He went up to Biro, looked him in the eye, and smiled. Biro gave him a nervous smile in return. Then Sek raised his right hand and turned down his thumb, like Caesar.

'You're *supper*,' he whispered.

At once, Biro was forced down onto his knees. The man with the kitchen knife promptly came up behind him, reached around, and sliced his throat so deeply that his head dropped back as if it were on a hinge. Blood spouted up into the air, spattering Mody, who was still kneeling down next to him. Mody held up both of his bloody hands and let out a long, wavering howl of despair. Almost all of his men and women cried out too, and the young woman called Sabina fell sideways onto the floor and lay there shaking and trembling, with her two dogs circling around her and whining in distress.

Hedda groaned and lifted her head up so that Sek could see her doll-like face. To him, she appeared to be bright-eyed with glee, but if he had known about orgasms, he would have recognised her reaction to Biro's execution for what it was.

That evening, the kitchen was crowded. Hedda's people sat on one side of the table and Mody's people sat on the other. All six of the ovens were open, so the heat was intense. There was very little roasted meat, apart from two ribcages that had been split into four, and four legs, and a heap of intestines that had been chopped up and mixed with carrots and swedes. The girls that Faust had sent out to the Tesco supermarket had shoplifted five French loaves and these had been sliced and toasted and thinly spread with fish paste.

Hedda and Mody sat at the head of the table, with Sek sitting between them. That afternoon, three of the women had gone out to Kennington Park and cut branches from a laurel hedge, which they had plaited together to form a crown for him, so that he looked like a miniature emperor.

A few members of Hedda's tribe and Mody's tribe were talking among themselves, but most of them were staring at each other across the table with suspicion and hostility. Mody's people had always been more passionately devoted to the goat-headed great one than Hedda's, and they had insisted on singing a long prayer of thanks before they started eating, while Hedda's people were already twisting off ribs and cramming squares of scorched intestine into their mouths with their fingers.

Mody himself sat hunched over a bowl of soup made from potatoes and the shredded meat of human feet, which had one of the strongest flavours, seasoned with thyme.

'We'll need at least six opfers to feed this crowd,' said Hedda.

'You don't have to tell me,' said Mody. 'I've made you a promise and I'll keep my promise.'

'But when you bring them back you must take the utmost care not to be seen. I mean it. Look at all the people we have here now. The comelings have already found Hiker's place at the old carpet factory. If they discover us here, it would be a disaster.'

'If they find us we'll just have to fight back,' Sek declared. 'We'll have to kill more of them. Then they'll leave us alone.'

'Oh, you really think so?' said Mody, putting down his spoon. 'That shows how much you don't know about life, little boy. The comelings didn't care if we lived or died when we were out on the streets, even though we weren't doing them any harm. We call them comelings, but do you honestly believe that they'll be frightened to take their revenge on us if we start to kill more?'

'You should never speak to Sowber Sek that way,' Hedda admonished him. 'He's quite capable of making you disappear into thin air, or ordering you to be turned into tomorrow's breakfast. And speaking of that, here's your chance to show me that you *do* keep your word.'

One of Hedda's women came away from the ovens, carrying a wooden chopping board. She was a wide-hipped woman, with a red headscarf wrapped around her sweat-studded forehead. Although she was so hot, she was smiling triumphantly. Balanced on top of the chopping board was Biro's head, his hair frizzled, his face charred black, with cracks in his cheeks where his scarlet flesh showed through. The heat of the oven had popped both of his eyes and his lips were shrivelled into a tight circle as if he were saying '*oh!*' in dismay.

Hedda slid Mody's soup bowl to one side, and the wide-hipped woman set down the chopping board in front of Mody so that Biro was facing him.

'There,' she said. 'Your friend for you. Not a rare friend, I grant you, but medium rare!'

With that, she gave a wheezing laugh, and took out a knife and fork from her apron pocket, setting them down on the table for him.

Mody stared at Biro's blackened features for a long time, and Sek saw that there were tears glistening in his eyes.

'Go on, Mody,' said Hedda. 'You've had only a little soup so far. You have to keep up your strength. *And* your promise.'

'I can't,' Mody told her, shaking his head. 'I knew him for so long. We did so much together. He always helped me out when times were bad, and most of the time, the times were terrible. I couldn't have made it without him.'

'Do *you* want to be cooked, the same as him?' said Sek.

Mody turned around to face him. 'So you think you're a *Sowber*, do you?' he sneered. 'Well, I think you're nothing but a snotty-nosed kid who's full of himself – not a "got it". Make me disappear, can you? Go on, then! *Make* me disappear! Or *prove* to me, here and now, that you're a Sowber, because I don't believe for one moment that you are!'

Everybody at the table went quiet, and Sek heard two or three of them sucking in their breath. He looked round at Hedda, expecting her to support him and tell Mody not to speak to him with such disrespect. But Hedda simply shrugged and said, 'Show him, Sowber Sek. Make him eat his words – and then his friend.'

Sek was taken aback, and started to feel panicky. There were no polystyrene cups on the table, so he couldn't perform his cup-disappearing trick. Anyway, they had all seen that one already, and if he botched it they would realise at once that he wasn't a real magician. He still found it hard to believe that they had been so impressed by it in the first place.

He knew only one other trick – a trick that he had always found difficult, because his hands were so small. But the kitchen was badly lit, even though twenty or thirty candles were flickering on the shelves around the walls, and so there was a reasonable chance that nobody would see how he was doing it, even if he fumbled.

'Your spoon,' he said to Mody, doing his best to sound challenging. 'Can you bend it with your bare hands?'

'*What?*' said Mody.

Sek took the spoon out of Mody's soup bowl and handed it to him. 'Go on,' he said. 'Bend it.'

Mody took the spoon in both hands. He tried hard to bend it, gritting his teeth, but it was stainless steel, with a thick handle, and after grunting and snorting he finally gave up, and handed it back. Some of his tribe laughed nervously, but when he turned around to glare at them, they fell silent.

Sek held the spoon in his right fist, so that only the bowl was visible. He made it appear that he had all his fingers clamped around the handle, but in fact he only had his little finger hooked around its neck. He then placed his left fist on top of his right fist, again giving the impression that he was holding the whole length of the spoon's handle in it. He pressed the bowl down against the tabletop, gradually lifting his fists so that it looked as if he were bending up the handle at an acute angle, and grimacing with pretended effort. In reality, hidden by his fists, the handle was still lying flat.

All of the men and women around the table stared at him in awe. He held his fists in the same position for a few moments, and then he lowered them again, with another grimace. As a finale, he twisted the spoon around and held it up with a flourish so that everybody could see that he had straightened it again.

'There, Mody!' said Hedda gleefully. 'What more proof do you need? Sowber or not Sowber?'

Mody sat back. Everybody else in the kitchen had dropped onto their knees and placed one hand on top of their heads. He hesitated, and then he too placed his hand on top of his shining bald head.

'You are indeed the "got it",' he said. 'I'm sorry that I didn't believe you – truly sorry. I hope you can find it in your heart to forgive me.'

Sek dropped the spoon back into the empty soup bowl. 'Go on,' he said. 'Your friend is there waiting for you. Eat up.'

Mody picked up his fork. He took several steadying breaths and then he dug the tines into Biro's blackened cheek, just below his left eye socket. He twisted off a small lump of crusty flesh, and then he put it into his mouth and started to chew it.

'How does he taste?' Hedda asked him. 'Does he taste sweet, like revenge?'

Mody shook his head. His eyes were filled with tears again, and they dropped down and sparkled in his beard.

Sek smiled and lifted his hands, indicating that everybody in the kitchen should resume their seats and continue eating.

'This is the new time!' he announced, in a clear, choirboy voice. 'This is the time of Sowber Sek. From now on, every day will be magic!'

23

Linda opened her eyes and saw that she was lying on her side on a gritty red carpet. She had a brain-splitting headache, and when she reached up and gingerly touched the back of her head, she felt a lump so sore that she sucked in her breath.

She eased herself up into a sitting position, and looked around her, although she found it difficult to focus. It was still dark, but there was enough light from the street lamps outside for her to see that she was in a bare grey-painted room, with the ghostly outlines on the walls of pictures that had once hung there. There was a smell of dust and stale cigarette smoke, and a faint unpleasant odour of something else, like rotten chicken.

When she moved her legs, she saw that both seams of her dark blue velvet dress had been ripped apart, almost up to her hips, and everything came back to her. The front door being smashed open, and Jerry going down to see who had broken in. Then two masked men thundering up the stairs and bursting into Jerry's flat, and grabbing hold of her. One of them must have hit her on the head, but she didn't remember that. She blinked, and blinked, but her vision was still blurred.

She managed to stand up and hobble to the window. Below her was a car park, which had no cars in it, but two skips filled with chipboard panels and broken bricks and sodden mattresses. Judging by the rooftops of the houses all around the car park, she guessed that she was up on the third or fourth floor of whatever building she was in. In one of the houses, she could see a family sitting around a kitchen table. The mundane sight of them having their supper made her feel completely detached from reality, as if she were a princess in a Grimm's fairy tale, trapped in a tower. Her head was still throbbing and she almost fainted, so that she had to hold on to the windowsill and close her eyes and take several deep breaths to stop herself from collapsing.

God, where am I? She opened her eyes again and turned around and limped her way back across the room. There was a door on one side, and when she opened it she saw a washbasin and a shower cubicle. *This must be a hotel. An abandoned hotel. But why did those men bring me here? What did they want from me? And where are they?*

Next to the main door there was a built-in wardrobe with empty hangers and a crumpled laundry bag. On the door handle, a cardboard notice said *Do Not Disturb*. Very cautiously, she opened the door and looked out. The corridor outside was in darkness, but from somewhere down below she could hear shouting and whistling and what sounded like dogs growling at each other.

She took one step outside, but then a sharp snarling sound right behind her made her jump. A man in a black T-shirt appeared out of the darkness and without a word he seized her arm and started to pull her roughly along the corridor.

'Let go of me!' she screamed at him. 'Let go of me! What do you want?'

The man took no notice. He was bald and burly with tattooed arms and far too strong for her to resist. He continued to drag her along the corridor until they reached a staircase, and then he didn't hesitate for a moment but began to pull her downstairs. She kept stumbling because it was too dark to see the stairs, but the man held on to the banister with one hand so that he could heave her back upright whenever she lost her footing.

He manhandled her down two flights of stairs and then along another corridor. At the end of the corridor he pushed her into a large room that was lit by scores of candles. This room was crowded with at least forty men and women, all wearing thick coats and jackets, many of them hooded. Some of them were lying down asleep, but most were sitting up cross-legged and smoking and growling to each other. The smell of unwashed bodies was overwhelming.

On the right-hand wall, Linda saw an eerie painted figure of a naked man with the head of a goat. Underneath this figure, three people were sitting – a fiftyish man with a broken nose, a woman with two broad-brimmed hats on, one on top of the other, and a young curly-headed boy in a baggy green sweater. The boy looked as if he were only about eight or nine years old, and yet he was smoking a cigarette.

From the way that all the other people in the room were sitting in a reverential semi-circle around these three, it appeared to Linda that they were in command. The burly man pulled her up in front of them, and then released his grip on her arm.

'Who are you?' Linda demanded. Her throat was so constricted that she could barely swallow but she tried her best to sound angry, rather than afraid. 'Why have you brought me here? Let me tell you – my boyfriend's a police officer. He'll be after you before you know it, and then you'll be sorry.'

The woman with the two hats looked her up and down

and made a growling sound in the back of her throat. Her growls were complicated, and she sounded to Linda as if she were saying something, although she couldn't make out what it was. The man with the broken nose plainly understood her, however, because he stood up and beckoned to an Arabic-looking man in a pointed hood who was sitting on the other side of the room.

The Arabic man got to his feet and stepped through the crowd toward them. As he reached Linda, another young man and a young woman in a headscarf both stood up and took hold of her upper arms.

'Get off me!' she snapped at them. 'I said – get *off* me! Let me go!' But they gripped her even tighter, and when she turned to glare at them, they both gave her benign, vapid, flower-power smiles in return, as if they were high.

The Arabic man lifted up the front of his dirty khaki jacket and drew out a hammer that was hanging in a loop on his belt. Then he reached into his pocket and brought out a handful of long steel nails.

The man with the broken nose nodded toward the wall on the opposite side of the room, and growled, and then drew his index finger across his throat. Linda turned her head. She could see that the wall was chaotically splattered with reddish-brown stains, as if somebody had smashed half a dozen bottles of burgundy wine up against it, which had run right down to the skirting board. Not only was the wall stained, it was pockmarked all over with holes in the plaster, where nails had been driven in and later pulled out.

The young man and the young woman pulled Linda backwards until her shoulders were pressed against the wall. Then the man with the broken nose came up to her, with the Arabic man close behind him.

'Who are you?' Linda asked him. 'What are you going to do to me?'

The man with the broken nose turned around and pointed to the goat-headed figure on the opposite wall, and then turned back with his teeth bared – not grinning, but tightly clenched, as if that explained everything. The Arabic man held out the hammer for him, and he took it in his right hand, and then held out his left hand, palm upward, for a nail.

The young woman who was holding Linda's left arm lifted it up, and forced her hand flat against the plaster. The man with the broken nose then dug the point of a nail into her wrist. Linda let out an '*ah!*' of pain, and looked into his eyes in desperation, searching for the slightest hint of compassion. All she could see was glittering indifference, as if his eyes were two glossy beetles.

He raised the hammer and filled his lungs with a deep intake of breath. He was about to strike when the curly-headed boy shouted out, although to Linda he sounded just like a puppy barking.

The man with the broken nose hesitated. Linda could see from the movement of his jaw that he was grinding his teeth. There was a long moment when he kept the point of the nail digging into her wrist and the hammer raised, and then he slowly let out his breath through his nostrils and stepped back.

The young man and the young woman who were holding Linda's arms both released her, and they stepped back too. The man with the broken nose handed back the hammer and the nail to the Arabic man, and folded his arms. The expression on his face was a mixture of resignation and tightly suppressed anger.

The curly-haired boy was coming across the room toward Linda, still holding his half-smoked cigarette. He was smiling, almost beatifically, like a child in some religious painting. He held out his hand to her and gave two or three little yapping noises.

'I don't understand you,' said Linda. 'Please... I don't understand what you're trying to say and I don't know why you've brought me here. I just want to get out of here and go home.'

Taking her hand, the curly-haired boy led her across the room to where the woman with two hats was sitting. The woman with two hats looked almost as angry as the man with the broken nose, but she gave Linda an odd, irritated smile.

'What do you *want* from me?' Linda asked the boy. 'Can't you just let me go?'

The boy pressed the back of her hand against his cheek and said, with obvious difficulty, 'Muh... *muh*... thuh... *thuh*...'

'*What?*' said Linda. She whipped her hand away and stared at him in horror.

'Muh... thuh,' he repeated, and took hold of her hand again. '*Muh*... *thuh*.'

'My God,' she said. 'I'm not your mother!'

The woman with the two hats patted the floor, and beckoned, and it was clear that she was expecting Linda to sit down next to her. Kneeling close behind her was a girl with brown hair braided into a high conical point, and one bottle-green eye. She beckoned too, with both hands, but much more enthusiastically.

Linda turned around. The man with the broken nose was staring at her, his arms still folded, making no attempt to look anything but cheated. The young man and the young woman who had pressed Linda against the wall were standing on either side of him, with odd simpering expressions on their faces. Since she seemed to have been given the choice between pretending that she was the mother of this yapping curly-haired boy or being nailed to the wall, Linda could see that she had no alternative but to sit down, and go along with whatever these people wanted her to do.

She knelt down awkwardly beside the woman with two hats. The boy sat close beside her, taking hold of her hand yet again and looking up at her with adoration.

My God, he really does believe that I'm his mother. But if he hadn't stopped them, what would they have done to me? Nailed me to the wall, and then what? This is like some terrible illogical dream, in which nothing makes any sense. Who are these people, and why do they only speak in grunts and growls and snarls, like animals?

She could focus more clearly now, but she still had a splitting headache and she couldn't stop herself from trembling all over, partly with cold but mostly with fear. She badly needed the toilet too, but she couldn't think how to ask, or what would happen if she did.

The woman with two hats laid a hand on her shoulder. She was wearing black angora gloves and Linda felt as if a large hairy spider had settled on her back. When she flinched, the woman glanced at her, but didn't smile, and then she waved her hand toward a short blocky man sitting on the opposite side of the room, with his back against the curtains. She let out a series of growls, which sounded as if they could have been instructions, and the man nodded, and stood up, and disappeared out of the door.

Now, suddenly, one of the women sitting in the middle of the floor started to slap her thighs and sing. The rest of the men and women joined in, some of them clapping and some of them beating against the floor and the walls with their fists. The curly-haired boy crushed out his cigarette against the sole of his trainer and joined in, singing in a strange warbling falsetto.

Linda had never heard any song like it. It was a combination of humming and howling and ululating, interspersed with short, urgent screams. She didn't know why, but it unsettled her badly, and for some reason that she couldn't understand she felt impelled to turn around and look at the goat-headed man painted on the wall behind her. She almost felt that if they carried on singing like this, he was going to come alive and step down from the wall and into the room among them. She squeezed her thighs together but she couldn't stop herself from shivering, and out of sheer fright she wet herself a little.

The curly-haired boy squeezed her hand and said, 'Muh – *thuh*!' and his eyes were bright with delight.

Gradually, the singing died down, and the clapping became quieter, until it sounded no louder than water lapping against a dockside. The short blocky man came back into the room, carrying a glass bottle filled with some amber liquid and a yellow plastic cup hooked around his little finger. He came over to Linda and the woman with two hats and knelt down in front of them.

'Muh-muh,' the boy repeated, and made a drinking gesture. 'What?'

The boy let out another of his puppy-like yaps, and gestured again. The short blocky man took the stopper out of the bottle and half-filled the cup. He passed it to the boy and the boy held it out for Linda.

Linda took it and sniffed it. 'You want me to drink this? What is it?'

'Cah – *cahju*.'

'I don't understand you. What's "cahju"?'

The woman with two hats dropped her black spidery glove

onto Linda's shoulder again, and nodded toward the man with the broken nose. Then she too made a drinking gesture. There was no mistaking the look in her eyes. *Drink, or I will give you back to be nailed to the wall, mother or no mother.*

Linda took the cup and lifted it to her lips. She hesitated for a moment, and then she tipped her head back and drained it. At once, the woman who had started the singing let out a high, warbling howl, and clapped her hands, and everybody else in the room started howling and screaming and clapping their hands too.

Linda smiled, and then pressed the side of her hand against her lips as if she were wiping them. What the celebrating crowd were unable to see was that she had managed to hold most of the liquid in her cheeks without swallowing it, and spat it down the sleeve of her dress.

'Muh – *thuh*!' said the curly-haired boy, and he was so pleased that there were tears in his eyes. He reached out and hugged her, and she stroked his sticky curls, even though she gladly could have shaken him violently, backwards and forwards, like a puppet, until his head fell off.

24

When Jamila came into the IC unit the next morning, Edward had just finished his breakfast, two Weetabix and a mug of warm milk. Dr Seshadri was there too, frowning at a clipboard, while a nurse was rolling up Edward's sleeve so that she could check his blood pressure. Edward was still pale, and he still had dark circles under his eyes, but he was sitting up and he appeared to be much less distracted than he had the day before.

'Ah, good day to you, detective sergeant,' said Dr Seshadri. 'Our patient here is making good progress, I am happy to tell you. We're not out of the woods yet. He is still suffering withdrawal symptoms from the opioid that he was given, but Suboxone is helping him to tolerate them.'

'Can he speak yet?' asked Jamila, giving Edward a smile and a finger-wave.

'A little improvement, but he is still incapable of expressing himself clearly. He seems to know what he wants to say to us, but for some reason his brain simply refuses to form the words for him.'

'And how about the drug? Have you worked out yet what's in it?'

'Not completely. I am hoping that the laboratory will be able to give me some further information later today, or maybe tomorrow. They have been co-operating very closely with your forensic people in Lambeth so I think we can be confident that we have the best minds working on it.

'So far they have told me that apart from the morphinane alkaloid that suppresses brain function, the drug appears to contain a chemical that resembles harmine, which as you probably know is a very powerful hallucinogen. Harmine is derived in the Middle East from the husks of Syrian rue and other plants.'

'So Edward here could have been hallucinating?'

'The effect of the opioid has certainly been to affect his perception of the world around him, and his ability to understand who he is or where he is. For instance, he *recognises* his mother but he still doesn't seem to understand their relationship.'

'Is it all right for me to talk to him?'

'Of course. Any communication can only be helpful.'

The nurse had finished taking Edward's blood pressure, so Jamila drew up a chair and sat down next to his bed. Edward smiled and made a low purring sound in the back of his throat.

'How are you feeling, Edward?' Jamila asked him.

'*Erst*,' Edward whispered, and pointed to his chest.

'Erst? I don't know what you're trying to tell me. What does "Erst" mean?'

Edward pointed repeatedly at his chest and repeated, '*Erst! Erst!*'

'Sorry, I still don't understand you,' said Jamila. 'But look, I've fetched you this sketchbook, and these coloured pens. Maybe you can *draw* what you mean.'

She lifted up the canvas bag that she had brought in with her, and took out a drawing pad and a box of Crayolas. Jerry had bought them in the same WH Smith store at the Tandem

Centre where the man in the dress had been arrested. Edward growled again as Jamila opened the pad and set it down on the blanket in front of him, on top of his knees.

Jamila then bent back the lid of the box of Crayolas, exposing the tops of the crayons, and held it up.

'Go on, take one,' she coaxed him. 'Draw me an Erst.'

Dr Seshadri was standing well back, but watching with intense interest. Jamila guessed that he was waiting to see if Edward recognised what the crayons were, and if he knew what he was supposed to do with them.

Edward reached out for the row of different-coloured crayons, but hesitated, wiggling his fingers over them as if he couldn't decide what to do next.

'Go on,' Jamila urged him gently. 'Draw me an Erst.'

Edward looked at her and gave her a strangely dreamy smile. Then he picked out a dark brown crayon, tugged off its lid and started to draw. Jamila turned around to Dr Seshadri and gave him a thumbs up

'This is *most* interesting,' said Dr Seshadri, coming up close behind Jamila's chair so that he could see what Edward was drawing. 'Even if some of his brain functions have been suppressed, such as his ability to talk, it seems that other functions are working perfectly well. Whatever substances he has been given, they are highly selective in their effects.'

He gave a rueful grin. 'I almost wish I had some to administer to my more garrulous colleagues.'

'Well, you and me both,' said Jamila. 'I think it is what my partner would call "shutting their yaps".'

She could see now that Edward was drawing a boy. Once he had finished the outline, he picked out a yellow crayon and gave the boy curly blond hair, like his own. Then he chose a red crayon and drew vertical stripes on him, like his own red-striped pyjamas. He had still been wearing those pyjamas underneath his jacket and his jeans when he was brought here to St George's.

He held up the drawing pad and growled, '*Erst.*'

'So Erst is you,' said Jamila. But before she could ask him anything further, Edward lowered the pad onto his knees again and started to draw another boy. This boy looked almost the same, with curly blond hair and red-striped pyjamas, but he was smaller.

'Sek,' he growled, stabbing at the picture with his finger. '*Ohn.*'

'That's your brother, John? Okay. But you call him Sek. You're Erst and he's Sek.'

The nurse who was writing down the results of Edward's blood pressure test looked up from her sloping table. 'You know, that sounds so much like "first" and "second" in German. *Erste* and *sek.*'

'You speak German?' Jamila asked her.

'I am Polish, but I come from Szczecin, which is very close to the German border. All my life I hear a lot of German speaking.'

'Well, that is interesting – *German*. But why would Edward call himself and his brother "first" and "second" in German?'

'They could have been given those names by the people who abducted them and drugged them,' said Dr Seshadri. 'Over the years I have treated numerous addicts who had completely forgotten their own names and could only remember the nicknames by which their fellow addicts had known them. One elderly man insisted that his name was Roberta, although he could never explain why.'

'So Edward and his brother could have been kidnapped by Germans? That doesn't make a lot of sense.'

'Look,' said Dr Seshadri. 'See what else he is drawing.'

Edward had picked out a black crayon and now he was carefully outlining a tall figure, at least three times the height of the picture he had drawn of himself. It was a naked man, with a large erect penis. Instead of a man's head, though, it had the head of a goat, with horns.

'What is *that*?' breathed Dr Seshadri, but Jamila recognised it immediately. It was almost identical to the figure that was painted on the Tube tunnel wall under the Royale carpet factory. However, she said nothing. Edward was still drawing, with the tip of his tongue clenched between his teeth in concentration, and she didn't want to put him off.

When he had finished outlining the goat-headed man, Edward coloured his body orange and his eyes yellow. He sat back for a moment, apparently satisfied with what he had drawn, and then he placed his left hand on top of his head, among his curls, and growled, '*Ba-Abla*.'

Jamila still said nothing, even though 'Ba-Abla' sounded so much like 'Balaa'. Most likely it was nothing more than a coincidence.

Edward carried on drawing. He was totally engrossed now, and he didn't turn to Jamila again to show her what he was doing, or to seek her approval. He finished embellishing the goat-headed man with triangular tattoos and prickly-looking pubic hair. Then he started to draw a large figure that could have been a man or a woman. The figure was wearing an open coat, so that Jamila could see that he or she was dressed in layers, with a jacket and a cardigan and another sweater underneath, and underneath all of those layers, a knee-length orange dress. Its most distinctive feature though was that it was wearing two black hats, like a Stetson and a fedora, one perched on top of the other.

After he had given this figure a pair of black boots, Edward carefully tucked the crayon back in its box and then dropped back onto his pillows.

'Is that it?' Jamila asked him, picking up the drawing pad.

Edward nodded, his eyes half-closed. It seemed that all that drawing had exhausted him.

'Can you tell me who this is? This person here, with the two hats on?'

Edward shook his head.

'This is Erst and this is Sek and this is Ba-Abla. Can you not just give me a name?'

At that moment, Edward's mother, Elizabeth, appeared. The shoulders of her coat were still sparkling with raindrops.

'What's going on? What's that you've got there? You haven't been tiring him out, have you?'

Jamila stood up and held up the drawing pad. 'Edward has been doing a few sketches for us, Mrs Willow. That is all. He still cannot speak, so my partner suggested that he might be able to draw us some pictures of the people who kidnapped him and his brother. Rather like a police artist's impression.'

Elizabeth peered at the figures that Edward had drawn. 'That's ridiculous. Those are like something out of a pantomime.'

'They are quite bizarre, I admit. But it was worth a try.'

'I hope you didn't tire him out, that's all. He's been through enough. Why aren't you out looking for John?'

'We are, ma'am, believe me. Every officer has a description of him and we are searching every location where he could possibly have been taken, and a few more besides.'

Elizabeth sat down on the chair. She took hold of Edward's hand and then she burst into tears.

'I thought that it would help them to get over their father, going to scout camp. I can't believe this has happened. If only I had kept them at home.'

Jamila said, 'Mrs Willow – you should not blame yourself. This was not your fault. Edward is going to get better very soon. Dr Seshadri and his team here will see to that. And we are doing everything we possibly can to find John for you. Please do not get yourself upset. Everything will turn out well, I promise you.'

Edward looked up from his bed and gave Jamila the weakest of waves. Jamila blew him a kiss in return. Dr Seshadri joined her as she walked along the corridor to the lifts.

'Do you truly believe that you will find his brother?' he asked her.

'I have not yet had my breakfast, Dr Seshadri. And you know what the White Queen said, in *Alice*.'

'I'm sorry, detective. You have me there. I was brought up only on stories about jogis and magic monkeys.'

'The White Queen said that she could believe six impossible things before breakfast. Well, I can too.'

When she returned to the station, Jamila found Jerry in their office, standing by the open window, smoking. She hated the smell of tobacco smoke but she knew how worried he was, and what he had been going through lately, and so she said nothing. As soon as she came in, though, he dropped his cigarette into the car park below and closed the window.

'Any news?' she asked him.

He turned around and she saw that he had a crimson bruise underneath his right eye.

'Nothing so far,' he told her. 'There was one witness sighting through the window of McDonald's. They confirmed that there were three of them, and two of them were carrying Linda between them. The witness assumed she was drunk, or ill.'

'But nobody else saw them?'

'Nobody that we've been able to find, anyhow. It was half five, remember, so people were more interested in getting home than three blokes carrying a woman who looked like she was pissed.'

He sat down in front of his laptop. Jamila came up behind him and laid her hand on his shoulder.

'Are you okay?' she asked him.

'Bit battered, that's all. But worried sick about Linda.'

'Do you have any idea why they picked on her?'

'I have no idea at all. She's a looker, yes, but there are loads of pretty girls around. There's that teacher training college up the road and there's some smashers there. But it was like this homeless geezer took one look at her and something clicked and he came straight after her.'

'Have you had any forensic report back yet about your landlady?'

'Only that she was probably hit in the head with a hammer, and then picked up by her ankles and thrown around her sitting room like some fucking rag doll. Tosh is in charge of the team that's looking into that and he's promised to get back to me soonest.'

'I'm so sorry about your Linda, Jerry. I am praying that she is safely returned to you.'

'Thanks. As if she hasn't been through enough. She lost her dad only yesterday. Pneumonia. She was in bits about it.'

Jamila laid her canvas bag down on her desk. 'What was that you said before, about all of the missing persons being bereaved?'

'It was only a thought. Probably just a coincidence.'

'But now we have three of them – PC Bone and that Willow boy and Linda, and every one of them had recently lost somebody close to them.'

'I don't know. Maybe that means something and then again maybe it doesn't. How did you get on with young Edward? Did he draw anything for you?'

Jamila took out the drawing pad and opened it to the page where Edward had drawn himself, his brother John, the goat-headed man and the figure wearing two wide-brimmed hats.

'That taller boy, that's him. He calls himself Erst and his brother Sek. There was a Polish nurse in the ICU and she reckoned "Erst" and "Sek" is German for "first" and "second".'

'*German?* What's that about, then? I thought we'd left the EU.'

'Don't ask me, Jerry.'

'He's drawn that devil too, or whatever it is. Jesus.'

'He called it "Ba-Abla", and after he had drawn it he put his hand on his head as if he was worshipping it.'

'"Ba-Abla"? Sounds a bit like "Balaa", doesn't it?'

'That's what I thought. But I didn't want to jump to any conclusions. If the people who took him were German, why would they be worshipping a Pakistani demon? Or some version of him.'

'Search me, skip. All I can think about right now is Linda. If those bastards lay a single finger on her, and I catch up with them – I mean it, they'll wish we hadn't abolished hanging.'

Edge came into the office, eating a Greggs sausage roll. He was wearing a new North Face jacket, navy blue with a hood.

'Well, I must say that you are looking very smart now, Edge,' said Jamila.

'I should bloody well hope so. Ninety-eight notes this cost me. Any updates on Linda, Jer?'

'No. These people – it seems like they can just disappear. One minute somebody sees them carrying Linda along the street, the next minute there's no sign of them. They're like bloody magicians.'

Edge took off his jacket and came up to Jamila's desk, still chewing on his sausage roll. He looked down at Edward's drawings and said, 'What's these, then?'

Jamila told him and he chewed and nodded, but then he said, 'What's *she* got to do with it?'

'Who?'

'Baggy Nell. That fat bird with the two hats on.'

'Baggy Nell? Is that her name? So you know her?'

'Know her? I should say so. I ran into her nearly every other day when I was stationed up at Kennington nick. She was always hanging around that Tibetan Peace Garden in the grounds of the Imperial War Museum, sleeping rough and making a nuisance of herself. She was like a kind of a Fagin, you know, running a whole gang of homeless kids who went out shoplifting.'

'You're joking,' said Jerry, standing up again and taking a closer look at the drawing pad. 'So it could be *her* that's organising all these abductions.'

'Wouldn't surprise me, mate. She was a toughie, I can tell you. Smelled like a kipper smoker on his day off too. As far as I know she used to be married to some racehorse trainer, and she was quite well off. But he got himself killed in a helicopter crash at Aintree and she ended up broke and a bit bonkers and living on the streets.'

He picked up the drawing pad and shook his head. 'Well, well, Baggy Nell. Never thought I'd ever see that old munter again.'

'I think it's worth going up to Kennington and asking a few rough sleepers if they know where she is now,' Jerry suggested. 'You want to come, Edge? You know the territory.'

'Sure. I've just got a couple of calls to make and then I'll be with you.'

Jamila said, 'I'll stay here for now. I need to chase up the Romanian police about Betina Fredanov. I also want to do some more research into this demon or devil or whatever it is, this Ba-Abla. The connection with Balaa appears to be so strong. It looks so much like him, the name is so similar, and now we have the strongest evidence that the Willow boys were taken by the same group of people or cult or whatever they are.'

'I've just got my fingers crossed it wasn't them who took Linda,' said Jerry. 'I mean, apart from the fact that she'd just lost her dad, it was the way that our landlady was killed. Her head smashed in, exactly like poor old Malik.'

Jamila gently patted his hand. 'We will find her, Jerry. Don't worry.'

Jerry grimaced, and shrugged, and then took his jacket down from the coat stand. 'Whenever you're ready, Edge, I'll meet you outside. I've got a sudden craving for another fag.'

25

Jerry and Edge found four rough sleepers huddled under blankets in the Tibetan Peace Garden, three men and a woman. They were sheltering next to an abstract stone sculpture on the north side of the garden, which represented the element of fire.

All three men had bushy beards and the woman had the wildest ginger hair that Jerry had ever seen. They were smoking and passing round a bottle of McKendrick's whisky, which was about the cheapest Scotch on the market, even supposing they had paid for it.

It had stopped raining and the skies had cleared, but even though a dazzling sun was shining the temperature had dropped sharply and a keen north-east breeze was blowing. It was forecast to drop even further during the night, down to minus four or five.

Jerry and Edge made their way around the circular bronze plaque that stood in the centre of the garden. 'Hey, Bry!' Edge called out. 'How's tricks?'

'Well, fuck me,' said one of the men, wiping his mouth and handing the whisky bottle to the woman. 'If it ain't Bobby the bobby. Ain't seen you in donkey's. What you been up to, then, you old bastard? Still making a bleeding nuisance of yourself, are you?'

'I'm stationed down at Tooting now,' Edge told him. He pointed to the fire sculpture. 'Sitting next to the fire to warm yourselves up, are you?'

'Oh, still Mister Comedian! Going a bit bald though, ain't you, Bobby? That's funny!'

'How's Martin? Ever get that bricklaying job, did he?'

'Martin? No, mate. He snuffed it last Christmas. Got himself pissed as arseholes and fell off Lambeth Bridge into the river. Fell, or jumped. He always used to say that he'd been a champion swimmer when he was at school, but you know – it's not a great idea to go swimming in the Thames in a Crombie overcoat after five pints of Skol and a bottle of Smirnoff.'

'This is Jerry Pardoe, by the way,' said Edge. 'Him and me, we've come out looking for Baggy Nell. You seen her lately?'

'Baggy Nell?' said Bry, shaking his head. 'Ain't seen her for about as long as I ain't seen you. Not that I'm complaining. Right fucking cow.'

'Yeah, right fucking cow,' repeated one of the other men, blowing out smoke. 'And pen and ink, or what? Smell on her, she could knock you unconscious from half a mile away.'

'*I* seen her,' put in the woman.

'Really?' said Jerry. 'When, and where?'

'I seen her about a month ago. Haven't got a cough on you, have you?'

'Yeah, sure,' said Jerry. He took out his packet of cigarettes and gave her three. She put one in her mouth and the other two behind her ears, buried in her curls. Jerry gave her a light and she inhaled deeply.

'I seen her coming out the Hercules. It looked like she was having a barney with somebody inside. Screaming her head off, she was. "You don't know who I am, do you?", that's what she was screaming. "You don't know who I am, do you?" Like, over and over.'

Although the woman pronounced it 'Her-kewls', Jerry knew that she meant the pub on the corner of Hercules Road and Westminster Bridge Road, which was only a minute's drive away from the Tibetan Peace Garden.

'That's well weird though, for Baggy Nell to be shouting that out to anybody,' Edge remarked. 'Everybody from here to the Elephant knows Baggy Nell. I'll bet even the Archbishop of Canterbury knows Baggy Nell. Bet he sits there in Lambeth Palace and smells her every time she walks past. You know, like holds his nose and says "Jesus!"'

'If that was only a month ago, that means she could still be around here somewhere,' said Jerry. 'Any idea where, love? There's a homeless shelter just down the road, isn't there?'

'Sorry, haven't a clue,' the woman told him. 'I don't think she's staying at the shelter. I've got a couple of friends there and they would have told me.'

'She used to have a whole gang around her,' said Edge. 'That's why we came here first. Any of them still around? That bloke with the stutter, what was his name? And that bloke with only one arm?'

'Oh, you mean Perper Pete? I remember the geezer with only one arm but I never knew his name.'

'Lefty Brogan,' put in one of the other men. 'We called him Lefty because it was his left arm what was missing. He used to work for the council trimming trees but he had a bit of an altercation with a chainsaw.'

'Ain't seen none of that lot lately, to tell you the truth,' said Bry. 'In fact, come to think of it, I ain't seen none of them since Baggy Nell disappeared.'

'So it could be that they all went off somewhere together?' asked Jerry. 'But you don't have any clue where?'

The four of them all shook their heads. Bry said, 'Ain't got another spare fag on you, have you, mate?'

Jerry took out the whole packet of Sterling and tossed them to him.

'Cheers, mate,' said Bry. 'If we see Baggy Nell or any of her motley lot we'll give you a bell. And that's a promise.'

'Do you want my number?' Edge asked him.

'Got it already, mate. Nine-nine-nine, ain't it?'

As they walked back to their car, Jerry said, 'Let's take a stroll up to the Hercules, shall we? Maybe the landlord or one of the regulars knows where Baggy Nell's hiding herself these days.'

'Sounds like a plan,' said Edge. 'Might even force myself to have a pint while we're at it. All in the line of duty, of course.'

They had reached the corner of Lambeth Road when Jerry's phone warbled. It was Jamila, and she sounded urgent.

'Jerry – where are you? We have just received an emergency call from DS Gurmani, who is attending the funeral of DC Malik at the Lambeth Cemetery.'

'Oh, yeah?'

'About fifteen minutes ago, when the funeral party was gathered around the grave, they were openly attacked by approximately twenty men, and these men attempted to abduct at least five of the mourners.'

'*What?* Right in broad daylight? You're joking, aren't you?'

'No. Two of the mourners managed to pull themselves free, but the men dragged the other three away. The thing is, though, that when they tried to take them out through the cemetery gates, some late arrivals to the funeral turned up – all police officers from Waltham Forest, where DC Malik used to be stationed. The men couldn't get out of the cemetery, so they retreated into the chapel, taking the three mourners with them, and barricaded themselves inside.'

'So what's the SP now?'

'They're still inside, holding the mourners as hostages. But why I'm calling you is because DS Gurmani described them as looking like vagrants, or rough sleepers.'

'So you think—?'

'I don't know. There's no way of telling for sure. But that is the situation as it stands, and I am going to the cemetery myself right now. How soon can you join me?'

'Well, like, twenty minutes, maybe less. Edge and me are in Kennington, just round the corner from where Kennington nick used to be.'

'I'll meet you at the cemetery. Drive safely.'

As he put away his phone, Jerry saw that Edge was staring at him like a dog that knows it's not going to be taken for a walk after all.

'It's a shout, isn't it? So, goodbye pint. And I even had my lips curled, ready.'

They ran back to their car, climbed in, and sped off down Kennington Road. Edge took the wheel, which allowed Jerry to keep in constant touch with Jamila. He swerved through the slow-moving traffic at over sixty miles an hour, so that they were followed by a barrage of furious horn-blowing from other drivers.

'How about we switch on the blues and twos?' Jerry suggested.

Edge shook his head. 'No. Drivers are so bloody thick these days. They hear your siren behind them or they see your blue lights flashing in their rear-view mirror and what do they do?

They stop dead, that's what they do, or they pull out in front of you. Better to weave in and out, mate. Better to weave in and out.'

It was six miles to Lambeth Cemetery but it took them only seven minutes. A line of squad cars and police vans were parked already along Blackshaw Road, outside the cemetery. Edge pulled in behind them and yanked on the handbrake.

'You know something, Edge, you're a maniac,' said Jerry, as they made their way through the side gate into the cemetery. 'You're going to get yourself arrested one day, driving like that.'

'Got you here, didn't I? Didn't shit yourself, did you? Well, then.'

About thirty police officers were surrounding the small gothic chapel that stood in the middle of the cemetery grounds, including armed response officers dressed in black, holding Heckler & Koch carbines, and three MIT detectives. Looking around, Jerry could see several newspaper and TV reporters that he knew, with their cameramen, although they were being held well back by the cemetery's main entrance.

Jamila was standing under a leafless tree, talking to DCI Saunders and DS Bristow and a tall Pakistani in a black suit, who he guessed was DS Gurmani.

'Bit of a stand-off, sir, by the look of it,' said Jerry, as he came across the lawn to join them.

'We're playing it by ear, Pardoe,' said DCI Saunders. 'Playing it by ear.'

'Kamran has told me that one of the hostages is Nairiti Malik,' said Jamila.

'Oh, shit. Do we have any idea who they are, these hostage-takers, or what they want?'

'I am sure they must belong to the same cult as that man

who ate his eyes, and those kidnappers who took Edward and John Willow. A specialist officer has tried to communicate with them through the door of the chapel. He could hear them, but they answered only by growling and barking. He said it was like trying to have a conversation with animals.'

Jerry said, 'They're not armed though, are they, as far as you know? Can't we just break the door down?'

'Daren't risk it,' put in DS Bristow. 'According to Kamran here, some of the assailants were carrying garrottes, which they wound around the necks of the three hostages they abducted. So like DCI Saunders says, it has to be softly, softly, catchee monkey. You can see those doors there. Solid bloody oak. Even if we use an enforcer, they'll hear us as soon as we start boshing away and that'll give them enough time to choke the hostages before we can gain access. There's a smaller door, at the back of the chapel, but that's solid too.'

'What's the plan, then?'

'I've called Tooting Motor Recovery. They should be here any minute. We can wrap chains round the door handles and use their tow truck to pull them right off their hinges.'

'That's good thinking, guv. Very creative.'

'Well, it would have taken half an hour to get a police recovery vehicle here from Charlton, and we don't know how much time we have.'

'You're right, guv. If this lot is even half as bonkers as that bloke who smashed poor old Malik to bits and hit me with a hammer down in that tunnel, or that bloke who noshed his own eyes, for that matter – bloody anything could happen.'

They were still talking when the tow truck drove in through the main gate. It was bright yellow, with 'Tooting Tow' emblazoned in red on the side. Two uniformed officers guided it across the lawns and then beckoned it to reverse into the chapel's portico until its rear bumper was less than two metres away from the doors. The driver jumped down from his cab and lifted two heavy chains from the back, which he handed to one of the officers.

'Perhaps I should try to get through to them again, before we tear off the doors,' said Jamila. 'There might be a chance that they will agree to surrender peacefully. I mean, they must realise that there is no way out for them.'

DCI Saunders pulled a face. 'I suppose it *could* be worth having a shot at it.'

He turned to DS Gurmani. 'What's your feeling about it? When they first attacked you, what kind of mental state would you say they were in? Were they screaming and shouting, or did they seem quite controlled?'

'They made no sound at all,' said DS Gurmani. 'We were standing around the grave watching Babar's body being turned toward Mecca, twelve of us, when they came running across the grass in complete silence. They wound belts or garrottes around the necks of five of the mourners, and I think they would have taken more of us, if we had let them. Two of us managed to pull off their garrottes and fight them off, and the rest of us did our best to free those three that they were taking away, but there were too many of them, and some of them were armed with hammers and knives and what looked like lead pipes.'

'But they seemed quite calm?' asked Jamila.

'Yes, they did. That made it all the more frightening in a way. I might be mistaken, but I would say that they were under the influence of special k or crystal meth or something like that. I remember we had to break up a rave in Streatham once. About thirty young kids had taken over an empty office building, and they were the same. Totally chilled out. Almost like they were walking in their sleep.'

'Let me try to get through to them,' said Jamila. 'Jerry – do you want to come with me?'

Jerry followed her up to the chapel doors. The armed response officers had already wound the chains around the handles and fastened them to the tow truck's crane. The tow truck's engine was running so Jamila went back to the cab and asked the driver to switch it off, so that she could hear any response that she might get from the hostage-takers.

The cemetery was suddenly silent. The sun had gone down now, behind the spidery branches of the trees that surrounded it, so that it was growing dark. Jamila knocked on one of the doors and called out, 'Inside there! In the chapel! Can you hear me?'

There was no answer, so she knocked again. 'I am a police officer! I am asking you to come out of there so that you can tell us why you have taken these people hostage, and what you want! We are prepared to talk to you!'

Again, there was no answer. She turned to Jerry and shrugged.

'It is possible that they have been worshipping a Pakistani devil. Maybe they understand Pashto.'

'No harm in giving it a go, skip.'

Jamila knocked again, harder this time, and then shouted in Pashto.

For a few seconds, there was no response, but then they heard a woman scream, 'Save us! Get us out of here! Please! They're going to—!'

The woman stopped screaming abruptly, and they heard a fierce snarling sound, more like an angry lion leaping onto its prey than a human.

'*Stop!*' Jamila shouted, banging on the door with both fists. '*Leave her alone, or Ba-Abla will punish you!*'

Instantly, they heard more screaming and crashing sounds like furniture being tipped over, as well as agonised howling. There were four or five heavy thumps against the doors, as if people were colliding with them, or trying to force them open.

Jamila called out to the tow truck driver, 'Go! Go! Go *now*!'

The driver started up his engine with a rumble and the truck jerked forward, so that the chains clanked and then tightened. Inside the chapel, the screaming and howling was growing even more hysterical, and one of the small windows next to the doorway was smashed.

'*Go!*' Jamila shouted.

The truck jolted forward again, and then again, its exhaust bellowing. With a hideous creak and a splintering sound, the chapel doors were ripped off their hinges and fell flat onto the paving stones. The tow truck driver dragged them away, bouncing over the grass, and as he did so he switched on his floodlight. What Jamila and Jerry saw inside the chapel was like a medieval painting of hell.

The hostage-takers came staggering out of the chapel like zombies, their arms held out in front of them. There were around twenty of them, as DS Gurmani had described, and they were stumbling and bumping into each other and three or four of them tripped on the steps outside the chapel entrance and dropped to their knees.

Every one of them was blind. Some of them had streams of blood running down their faces, as if they had been stabbed in the eyes. Others had eyeballs dangling on their cheeks. They had other injuries too – criss-cross cuts on the palms of their hands, cuts across their throats and the sides of their necks, ears hanging by a thread as if they had tried to slice them off.

Apart from being blind, almost all of them were smothered in blood, and Jerry could see that at least three of them were gnawing at their hands, in the same way that the oil-paint thief had chewed at himself, and PC Bone's hand had been bitten.

'*Down on the ground!*' ordered the specialist firearms officer, stalking toward them with his carbine raised. '*All of you! Face down! Flat on the floor!*'

The hostage-takers ignored him, and kept on shambling out across the lawn.

'*Down on the ground!*' the SFO shouted at them, yet again, and this time he was almost screaming.

'It is no use!' Jamila called out. 'They cannot see you and they cannot understand what you are telling them!'

'*Tasers!*' the SFO shouted. He unhooked his own Taser and fired it at the nearest hostage-taker, who fell onto the grass, shuddering as if he were having an epileptic fit. More officers came running up and tasered the rest of the hostage-takers. Two of them had to be tasered twice, and one three times, but eventually they all dropped onto the ground. Officers rolled them all over and handcuffed them behind their backs. They lay there like a shoal of beached porpoises, some of them snuffling and growling, but most of them silent.

DCI Saunders came up to Jamila and Jerry. 'I've contacted the ambulance service to pick up this lot and take them across the road to St George's. There's no point in trying to get any sense out of them now. That's assuming that we ever will.'

'But where is Nairiti Malik, and the other two hostages?' asked Jamila, frowning at all the figures lying on the grass. 'I cannot see them in the chapel and I do not see them here.'

'They must still be inside somewhere,' said Jerry. With that, he crossed over to the chapel portico and went up the steps into the vestibule. Jamila was right. There was no sign of the hostages in here, only a small figure of Christ hanging on the cross and a bulletin board with bloodstained notices pinned all over it. It smelled like churches in there, but there was another smell too, which the hostage-takers had left behind them, a mixture of body odour and menthol.

'Nairiti? You there?' Jerry shouted. Jamila was right behind him now, with DC Gurmani and two armed response officers.

He pushed open the heavy double doors into the main chapel, which was in darkness, but one of the armed officers immediately switched on a flashlight, and flicked it around the pews and along the aisle and up to the altar. It was then that Jerry saw three dark figures hanging on the wall on the gospel side.

'Bloody hell,' he said. 'There, mate, off to your left.'

The armed officer shone his flashlight onto the figures. All three of them were dressed in black – two women in burkas, and a man in a black suit. Three paintings of the stations of the cross had been taken down from the wall and were now lying with their frames broken on the floor. The three hostages had been hooked up in their place, with their garrottes wound around the nails that had held the pictures. Their feet were no more than fifteen centimetres off the floor, but that was enough for them to be slowly strangled.

'For Christ's sake, get them down!' Jerry shouted. He vaulted over three rows of pews and took hold of the hips of one of the women. He heaved her up as high as he could, grunting with effort, and when he heaved her up a second time the garrotte around her neck was lifted from the nail and she dropped heavily into his arms.

The armed response officer had taken a hassock from one of the pews. He had stood on it so that he could reach up to cut the garrotte of the man in the suit, before sliding him down the wall to lie on the floor. DS Gurmani, meanwhile, had grasped the second woman and taken her weight until the armed response officer could drag over the hassock, climb up onto it, and cut her down too.

Jerry carefully laid the woman that he had lifted down on the nearest pew, with one of her arms hanging down. The armed response officer handed him his Swiss army knife and even though the garrotte had bitten deep into the woman's neck he managed to work his finger underneath it, and then saw through it.

He bent his head down over her, and listened. He couldn't hear her breathing, but when he placed his fingertips against her carotid artery he was sure that he could feel a faint pulse.

Jamila was close behind him. 'Is she dead?' she asked.

'She might have a chance. Do you want to give her CPR?'

He stood up and Jamila knelt down beside the pew, pulling up the woman's burka and starting to compress her chest. After thirty compressions, she breathed into her mouth.

Jerry looked round at DS Gurmani and the armed response officer. Neither of them were attempting to revive the man or the other woman, who were lying on the floor face to face, staring at each other sightlessly.

DS Gurmani shook his head. 'They are both gone. This poor woman. The garrotte has almost cut off her head.'

Suddenly, all the lights in the chapel were switched on. DCI Saunders came marching in, accompanied by DS Bristow and the specialist firearms officer.

The woman on the pew let out a gasp, and then another gasp, and opened her eyes. Jerry looked down and saw that it was Nairiti Malik. Her lips were blue and her eyes were bloodshot, but she was alive.

DCI Saunders made his way between the pews and saw

Nairiti and the two bodies lying on the floor. For several long heartbeats he said nothing.

At last he turned to DS Gurmani. 'I assume you can put names to these deceased,' he said grimly.

'Yes, sir. This gentleman is an old friend of my family, Faisal Wazir, and this young lady is a cousin of DC Malik, Babra Kasi.'

'How old is she? Or *was* she, rather?'

'Twenty-two, sir. Just had her twenty-second birthday.'

'Twenty-two, that's tragic,' said DCI Saunders. 'I know what they call me behind my back. They say that I haven't got a sense of humour. Well, this is why.'

Jerry walked out of the chapel and stood in the portico, looking at all the scruffy blinded men lying handcuffed on the lawn, their faces and their hands smothered in blood. Already in the distance he could hear the scribbling of ambulance sirens.

Even in the middle of all this chaos, he could think about nothing else but Linda, and pray that the men who had abducted her had not belonged to the same murderous cult.

26

It was nearly a quarter to ten before Jamila and Jerry and Edge managed to return to Tooting police station.

After the last ambulance had left the cemetery grounds, the three of them had driven to St George's Hospital. They had made sure that every one of the hostage-takers would be under twenty-four-hour police guard, and then they had given a briefing to the medical staff who would be treating them for their self-inflicted injuries. They had warned both doctors and nurses that their patients were potentially violent, and spoke only in unintelligible growls.

Jerry had then called Tosh and asked him to send a forensic team to take photographs of the hostage-takers, as well as finger-prints and DNA samples. Once they had recovered sufficiently, each of them would be assessed by a police psychiatrist to see if they needed to be sent to Broadmoor or Rampton or some other secure hospital for dangerous mental patients.

DCI Saunders had remarked sourly that the way they barked and snarled, they would be better off in Battersea Dogs Home.

Back at the station, Jerry hung up his leather jacket and flopped down into his chair. 'I'd kill for a drink. And a smoke too. And I gave all my fags to those thirteen amps in the Peace Garden.'

'Nobby down on the desk, he smokes,' said Edge. 'He'll let you have one.'

'No, mate, I ought to be giving it up. It was only Linda got me back on it. She said it would steady my nerves so that I didn't lose my rag when I was talking to Nancy. God, I hope Linda's okay.'

Jamila had been tapping away at her laptop. 'I have some messages,' she said.

'Nothing about Linda?'

'No, I am afraid not. But I have been sent a message from the Romanian police in Braşov. They say that they have located relatives of Betina Fredanov, and that one of her cousins has told them why she was here in England. She had come here to attend the funeral of Mikhail Kamenev – that Russian major who had taken care of her and so many other concentration camp survivors at the end of the war.'

'His funeral was being held *here*, in England?'

'According to them, he had come to live here in the UK in the mid-1950s. They did not explain why. But her friends said that Betina Fredanov had arranged to meet up at his funeral with several other Holocaust survivors in honour of his memory.'

'Did they know how many other survivors she was meeting, or what any of their names were?'

'No, or at least they did not say, although I can ask them. But they all came from central European countries like Romania and Poland and the Czech Republic, which is why they have not been reported missing here in England.'

'We've got *his* name though, haven't we, this Russian major's,' said Edge. 'We can find out all his details from his death certificate, where he lived and where his funeral was held. There must be somebody at the church or the crematorium who can give us a lead. You know, how many mourners there were, and where they were staying while they were here in England. I'll get on to it.'

'*Mourners*,' said Jerry. 'More bloody mourners! This is looking less and less like some kind of weird coincidence.'

'I have another message,' said Jamila, and now she sounded even more concerned. 'Those skulls and bones that were lying on the floor of that school in Peckham... it seems as if the way they were laid out was not haphazard. They were not simply thrown down. One of the forensic team has sent me a diagram that she has traced from the photographs of them. Come and see.'

Jerry went over to her desk and peered at the screen of her laptop. The forensic artist had drawn a wheel with six spokes. Between each spoke was an elaborate pattern of squares and triangles and parallel lines.

'Look at me,' said Jamila, holding up both hands. 'I am shaking!'

'Why? What does it mean?'

'It is similar to a Kalachakra mandala in Buddhism, only it is far older than that, and has a different meaning.'

'What's a Kalachaka-whatsit when it's at home?'

'It is a wheel of time. It is where certain gods live. But *this* wheel, this is almost the same as the wheel that hung in my aunt's house, over the picture of Balaa. This wheel is the way through to the shadow world, where you lived before birth and where you will go when you die. And it is also the way through to *this* world for Balaa himself.'

Jerry stood looking at the wheel in silence for a while, frowning. Then he said, 'You know what this means, don't you? Even if this Balaa is only imaginary?'

'Of course. It means that the squatters who killed and

roasted Betina Fredanov and her friends in the carpet factory belong to the same cult as the squatters who were living in the Charles Babbage school in Peckham. Both groups of squatters worship Balaa.'

'And those loonies at the cemetery,' said Jerry. 'They pulled out their eyes and bit their hands and growled – just like that fat bastard we collared for stabbing an assistant in WH Smith. All right, maybe it was only a fluke that the oil paint he was trying to nick was the same make as the paint that was used for that picture of Balaa. But don't tell me they don't all belong to the same bunch of weirdos.'

Jamila held up the sketch pad with its drawings by Edward Willow. 'And of course, here is Balaa yet again. Wherever they took young Edward and his brother, he must have seen an image of Balaa.'

'And Baggy Nell too, in the smelly flesh,' put in Edge.

Jamila sat back. 'I have tried from the beginning not to jump to conclusions about this, since we have so little concrete evidence. But let us sum up what we know now. This cult are definitely worshippers of Balaa. They are abducting innocent people, murdering them and eating them. This is exactly what Balaa demands of his disciples. And if young Edward and that offender who ate his own eyes are anything to go by, they are all high on some drug that forensics have not yet completely been able to analyse.

'It looks as if this cult has many more followers than was first apparent. They occupied two squats – one at the Royale carpet factory and the other at the Charles Babbage school – but where did they go when they were forced to leave those? There must be at least one other squat somewhere. Perhaps there are more.

'There is one thing we know for sure: they use those

abandoned Tube tunnels to make their way around this part of London without being seen. We have been searching those tunnels, but so far without much luck.'

'Well, they haven't been used for more than a hundred years, have they?' said Jerry. 'Some of them are flooded and some of them have fallen in, because they never got around to bricking them.'

'You never know,' said Jamila. 'There may be ways around the tunnels that look impassable. We could really use that old map that forensic officer Simon was talking about. As soon as possible, in fact. You can tell him it is urgent.'

Edge stifled a yawn. 'Another thing that's urgent. I could do with some kip. I've been up since five.'

'We all could,' said Jamila. 'You too, Jerry. I know how worried you are about Linda, but you won't be fit for much tomorrow if you don't get some sleep.'

'Take a couple of Nytol,' said Edge. 'They're good, they are. Every time I take those I dream that I've won the lottery.'

'You haven't though, have you?'

'You're having a Turkish, aren't you? You think I'd still be working here if I had? I'd be sitting on the beach in the Maldives, mate, sipping a pornstar martini.'

It was too late for him to buy any sleeping pills, but when he returned to his flat Jerry poured himself a large glass of Scotch whisky. The front door had been hung back on its hinges and a sheet of plywood fitted over its broken window, but the door to Nora's living room was still closed, with yellow police tapes stuck across it.

Jerry stood in the middle of his own living room sipping Scotch and staring at himself in the mirror over the blocked-up fireplace. He thought he was looking battered and tired. Linda's blue wool coat was still lying over the back of the armchair where she had left it. He picked it up and held the collar up to his nostrils and took a deep breath. It smelled of the Flowerbomb perfume that he had given her, and it smelled of her.

He took his glass of whisky into the bathroom and set it down on the shelf next to his toothbrush. Then he undressed, kicking his clothes into the corridor outside the bathroom door, and stepped into the shower. When he turned on the tap, he shouted out loud. The water was freezing because Nora had not been at home to turn on the heater. He washed himself frantically quickly and then jumped out of the shower, shivering, and grabbed a towel. That was damp too, because the towel rail was cold.

Once he was nearly dry, he struggled into his grey tracksuit, because it would be warmer than pyjamas. He sat in his armchair with his glass of whisky and switched on the television. Almost as soon as Sky News had come on, though, his phone warbled.

'Jerry, mate. It's Tosh. Sorry to ring you so late but I couldn't get through to DS Patel and I thought you'd want to know this asap. By the way, any news of your Linda?'

'Not so far. I've still got my fingers crossed they haven't hurt her.'

'Well, I'm thinking of you, mate. Meanwhile, we've taken photographs of all those weirdos who blinded themselves, as well as lifting their dabs and taking samples of their DNA.'

'Don't tell me. They're Martians.'

'Not as exciting as that. But quite exciting. We compared their pictures with the CCTV footage of those squatters who were running away from that burning school in Peckham. Eleven of them matched. The others probably match too, but they stabbed themselves several times in the face as well as putting their eyes out, so their features are well messed up. We may have to rely on their dabs to ID them. But those eleven, no question at all.'

'Well, that doesn't surprise me. DS Patel and me and Edge, we were talking about them this evening. All the evidence we've managed to collect so far points to them belonging to the same cult, or branches of the same cult. They all worship this demon Balaa, and Balaa expects them to abduct people and kill them and eat them. DS Patel knows a whole lot more about it than I do. But it looks like we're definitely dealing with a whole bunch of cannibals. It's enough to turn you vegan, I tell you.'

'There's one more thing, Jerry,' Tosh told him. 'The doctors took blood and urine samples from all twenty of them. Their early results show that they're intoxicated with the same opioid that boy Edward Willow had in his system – the one that we've been analysing too, at Lambeth Road. We know that it affects their speech, and some cognitive functions, but they've also isolated an ingredient similar to burundanga.'

'Burundanga! Of course! Why didn't I think of it before? What the hell is burundanga?'

'You know about scopolamine.'

'Scopolamine? Sure. We've had two cases involving scopolamine in the past six months. Turns you into a zombie, almost. The burglar or the rapist blows a bit of scopolamine powder up your schnok and then you do whatever you're told. It's stronger than date-rape drugs like Rohypnol, because you remember absolutely nothing about it afterwards. One poor cow in Streatham gave away all her jewellery to some twonk and emptied her bank account too, but try as she might, she simply couldn't recall doing it.'

'That's right. Burundanga is an extract of a South American plant called brugmansia and it contains very high levels of scopolamine. They call it the Devil's Breath.'

'What – a bit like mine after twenty fags and a biryani?'

'More than likely. But they call it that because it makes you obey whatever a demon wants you to do. Or a criminal, of course. And it also affects acetylcholine in your brain, which is a neurotransmitter essential to your remembering things. Whether they've been snorting it voluntarily or not, the drug that this bunch have been taking contains something that has much the same effect as burundanga.'

'So how are they being treated?' asked Jerry. 'They've had the Willow boy on Suboxone, and it looks like he's gradually getting over it.'

'I believe they're giving them the same,' said Tosh. 'We'll just have to wait and see if they've suffered any brain damage. It takes only ten milligrams of the Devil's Breath to put you into a coma and kill you.'

'Right, Tosh, thanks for the update. I think we're getting a lot closer to cracking this one. Now I really must catch some zees. I'm knackered.'

'Before you go, mate, there's one other thing. Three of the weirdos were in the same room together, and when we were taking their pictures and fingerprints they didn't stop growling to each other. My assistant Nolwazi, she's African, and she reckoned that all that growling isn't growling at all, it's a proper language. It reminded her of some language they speak in Africa, like Xhosa.'

'So all we have to do is find somebody who can speak Weirdo, and we'll know what they're saying to each other?'

'Well, that's just what I was thinking. And would you believe that I happen to know a professor of linguistics who teaches at the School of Oriental and African Studies in Bloomsbury. My daughter Sally's doing a three-year course in Chinese there, don't ask me why. But I can arrange for this professor to come down to St George's tomorrow morning and have a listen to this growling and see if it makes any sense.'

'Okay. Brilliant. If we can just find out where all these weirdos are hiding themselves, that's really going to move this case forward.'

'I'll give you a bell in the morning,' said Tosh. 'Get yourself some shut-eye, mate. I totally understand how worried you must be about Linda, but you know what they say.'

'Oh, sure. Life's a shit and then you die. Then they throw dirt in your face. Then the worms eat you. But just be grateful it happens in that order.'

27

The next morning was foggy and grey, so that when Jerry walked down to the station, the high street looked as if it were populated by a company of ghosts.

Before he had gone to bed, he had texted Jamila to give her an outline of what Tosh had told him. He had received no reply, so he had guessed that she must have switched off her phone already and gone to sleep.

He had thought that his anxiety about Linda would keep him awake, but only a few minutes after he had switched off his bedside lamp he had dropped into a deep and dreamless sleep. He had slept until a quarter to seven, and after he had woken up he had lain on his back for a while staring up at the ceiling, his arms spread wide, feeling as if he had spent the night swimming across a wide dark lake.

Tosh had called him shortly after nine to tell him that he had arranged for the linguistics professor to come down to St George's at half past twelve. 'Professor Walmsley. You'll like her.'

'Oh. He's a she?'

'Come on, Jerry. You know as well as I do that women are ten times brainier than men.'

When he came into the office, Jerry found that Jamila was

still eating her breakfast bakarkhani, a flatbread, which she was spreading thickly with cottage cheese.

'I have just finished reading your text again,' she said, with her mouth full. 'I am sorry that I did not reply to you last night. I was exhausted.'

'You and me both, skip. But I have a good feeling about today. If this linguistics professor can tell us what these weirdos are burbling on about, we might be able to find their den and beard them in it.'

'Do you know, I often wonder how we can work so well together. Sometimes I can hardly understand a word that you are saying.'

'Neither can I, to be honest with you. Have you heard any more from Romania?'

'No. But Edge was in earlier, and he told me that he has found out where that Russian major was cremated. It was at Honor Oak Cemetery in East Dulwich and the service was conducted by the parish priest from St Thomas More Roman Catholic church. Edge is going over there tomorrow morning to talk to him, to see if he can find out the names of the mourners and where they were staying while they were here in England.'

Jerry sat down and peeled the lid off the coffee he had bought on the way into the station.

'Are you okay?' Jamila asked him.

Jerry stared at his cappuccino as if he half expected to see a face appear in the foam.

'Not really. Now I can understand how people feel when somebody goes missing. It's one thing to know what's happened to them, even if they've thrown themselves under a train. But when they've just disappeared and you don't know whether they're alive or dead...'

Jamila stood up and came across to Jerry's desk. She placed her hands on his shoulders and simply stood there for a while, saying nothing. Jerry took hold of one of her hands and said, 'Thanks. I'm trying to be optimistic, but it isn't easy.'

Jamila started to say something, but she was interrupted by a knock at their open door. It was Simon, the forensic examiner, and he was carrying two cardboard postal tubes under his arm.

'I'm not disturbing you folks, am I? I went to the desk downstairs but they said I could come straight up.'

'No, come in,' said Jamila. 'Have you brought us what I hope you have brought us?'

Simon held up the postal tubes. 'The map, yes! My friend Nick Goggins found it at last, and you'll never guess where he found it! In his greenhouse, under a whole lot of plant pots! It's a bit stained, so that's why I've fetched it in person. I was thinking of scanning it but I didn't think it would come out too clearly.'

'Here,' said Jerry. He stood up and went across to Edge's desk, clearing aside the clutter of notebooks and empty coffee cups and Greggs sausage roll wrappers.

Simon carefully slid the map out of one of the postal tubes and unrolled it, spreading it out on the desk. Its ink was faded and its paper had turned yellow, and where it had been repeatedly folded it had worn almost right through. It had been marked with eight brown circles by the plant pots that had been resting on it, and spots where the plants had been watered, but despite that, it was still possible to make out the lines of the Underground tunnels that radiated under Lambeth and Kennington and Camberwell like a spider's web.

The map was headed *City & South London Railway, Proposed Extensions, May 1890.*

Simon smoothed out the map as reverently as if it were one of the Dead Sea scrolls. 'When this was drawn, the C&SLR only had six stations and a little over three miles of track, running from the City to Stockwell under the River Thames. But they were a very progressive company. Very experimental. They were the first to use electric-powered trains, and eventually they built twenty-two stations, stretching all the way from Camden Town in north London to Morden in the south.'

'There's a lot more than twenty-two here,' said Jerry.

'Yes, and that's the point. They started to excavate some of the tunnels but never got round to completing them. The trouble was, they ran out of money. Their trains were always packed. "Padded cells", their passengers called them, because of their high-backed seats and how small the carriages had to be built to go through the tunnels. But their fares were low because that was all people could afford in those days and digging the tunnels cost an absolute fortune.

'What I've done is, I've drawn an overlay, so that you can see which tunnels were finished and which were started but never completed. I've done it on a map of London as it is now, because there are buildings today standing in places which in 1890 used to be fields. It was always cheaper for the tunnels to be routed under open spaces because the C&SLR wouldn't have to pay compensation to homeowners whose houses had subsided when the tunnels were dug underneath them.'

Simon gave the second postal tube a shake, and out dropped a thick sheet of clear plastic, on which a black-and-white map of London had been printed. He had marked existing Tube tunnels in green and unused tunnels in red. He laid the plastic sheet on top of the paper map, and Jamila and Jerry could see at once that there were at least a dozen tunnels that had been started but never finished, or finished but never brought into service.

'At least half of these tunnels I was unaware of myself,' said Simon. 'And I always prided myself on being something of an expert on anything to do with railways.'

'It's unbelievable,' said Jerry. 'Underneath Lambeth and Kennington and Walworth – it's like a bloody rabbit warren down there. Eat your heart out, Watership Down.'

Jamila said, 'We need to get a copy of this urgently to Sergeant Bryan and the rest of the search teams who have been looking for PC Bone. They have been having incredible difficulty locating all of the tunnels, even with dogs. Sergeant Bryan said the dogs seem to be very nervous when they are taken down those tunnels, for some reason.'

She looked across at Jerry. She could have mentioned Linda as well as PC Bone, but they had no firm evidence yet that the men who had taken her belonged to the cult that worshipped Balaa.

'Look where *this* tunnel runs,' said Jerry, pointing to the map. 'It branches off from the Northern Line only half a mile south of Tooting Broadway station, underneath Blackshaw Road. Right past Lambeth Cemetery. I wouldn't mind betting that's how those weirdos got there.'

'You could very well be right,' said Jamila. 'But what we need to find out is where they started out. Just look at this map. They could have come from anywhere within a ten-mile radius.'

'Well, if this linguistics professor is any good, maybe we'll be able to ask them. Or beat it out of them, if they don't want to tell us.'

★ ★ ★

Tosh was waiting for them in the reception area of St George's, as well as his assistant Nolwazi and Professor Walmsley.

Nolwazi turned out to be a tall, slender Nigerian woman but her beaded plaits were the only concession to her ethnicity. She was wearing a formal grey suit with a white turtleneck sweater underneath it, so that she looked more like a head teacher or a tax inspector than a forensic examiner.

As for Professor Walmsley, Jerry guessed that she was only three inches over five feet. She had a sharp brunette bob and high cheekbones and sapphire-blue eyes and she was bundled up in a thick quilted Zara coat. Jerry thought she was almost film-star attractive, but she didn't smile when they came in through the doors and she stood back with an air of authority about her, as if she had little time for idiots.

Jamila held out her hand. 'Thank you so much for coming to assist us, professor. I expect Mr Brinkley here has told you how critical it is for us to be able to question these men, and try to get some answers out of them?'

'Every language can be understood,' Professor Walmsley told her sharply, with a slight Ulster accent. 'We can understand what birds and animals are saying to each other. Even trees can speak, in a way.'

'*Trees?*' said Jerry. 'What do they have to say to each other?'

Professor Walmsley looked at him as if he were the slowest student in her class. 'Supposing there's a forest fire. Trees give off vibrations through the soil to communicate panic. And when they're cut down, they cry out.'

'Oh. Right. Next time I go to the park, I'll have a listen.'

Professor Walmsley ignored him. 'Nolwazi here has given me some idea of what these men sound like, and she says that it resembles some African languages. But we'll see. The first step is to identify some speech patterns.'

'Dr Seshadri's waiting for us upstairs,' said Tosh. 'He's picked the bloke who's making the most progress.'

A uniformed police officer was standing beside the lift, and when they went up to the second floor, they saw more officers sitting on plastic chairs in the corridor, one outside each room. Every door was open, and as they passed by, Jerry could see the blinded men lying in bed in hospital gowns, with white gauze dressings over their eyes. They were all connected to intravenous drips. The officers who were guarding them gave Jamila and Jerry a nod of recognition and one or two 'all right?'s.

They reached the room at the end of the corridor where Dr Seshadri was waiting for them. On the bed lay a man with a brambly grey beard and a huge rounded belly. His bare feet protruded from underneath his blanket and his blackened nails were so long that they curled over the ends of his toes. Like all the other blinded men, his eyes were covered by a thick pad of gauze.

'His physical condition is extremely poor,' said Dr Seshadri. 'He has alcoholic cirrhosis of the liver, as well as polycystic kidney disease and severe eczema. I would say it is almost certain that he has been sleeping rough for a number of years. But he's responding well to Suboxone, better than most of his companions. Several of them are still comatose.'

Professor Walmsley approached the bed. 'Has he been speaking? Or trying to speak?'

'He's been growling, if that's what you mean, and making some grunting noises. Nothing that makes any sense.'

'Is he awake now? He's not moving.'

Dr Seshadri went around to the other side of the bed and took hold of the man's hand. The man immediately pulled it away, and snarled.

'Yes, he's awake.'

Professor Walmsley turned to Jamila and Jerry. 'I might be wrong, but I think I know already what the problem is.'

She took a digital voice recorder out of her pocket and then she unzipped her quilted coat. Jerry stepped forward and helped her to take it off. Underneath, she was wearing a clinging knee-length dress of purple wool, with a large gold medallion around her neck.

She approached the bed again and said to the man, 'Can you hear me? You're in safe hands now. We're going to take good care of you.'

The man growled in the back of his throat. Professor Walmsley held up the voice recorder and inclined her head so that she could hear him more clearly.

'What's your name?' she asked him. 'Try to tell me your name.'

He hesitated for a long time, licking his lips and repeatedly swallowing. Then he blurted out '*Moh.*'

'Moe? Is that your name?'

The man shook his head. '*Moh – dee.*'

'Moe Dee?'

Now the man nodded.

'Where have you been staying, Moe Dee? Can you tell me that?'

Once more the man hesitated, and swallowed, but when he eventually spoke, it was only a long slurring growl.

'I'm sorry, Moe Dee. I didn't understand that. Can you try again?'

The man took several deep breaths, and started to say '*Keh – keh,*' but he couldn't manage any more than that, and lapsed again into growling.

Professor Walmsley said, 'He knows what it is that I'm asking him, there's no question of that. So he understands

English. But obviously this opioid has affected his ability to speak in English, although he knows what he wants to say, and he's trying his best to come out with it.'

'It was exactly the same with young Edward Willow,' said Jamila.

'This *growling* though. I'm sure that Nolwazi's right, and it *is* a language. I distinctly heard three repeated sounds that could have been consonants, rather like the clicks in that African language Khoisan. But I think it sounds as if he's growling only because he's speaking extremely slowly.'

She held up her voice recorder. 'I'm going to see if I can get him to growl a bit more, and then play it back at different speeds. I don't think it's English, but I may be able to identify if it's a known language. Even if it isn't, I should be able to work out what he's saying because he's doing his best to answer my questions.'

She turned back to the man who called himself Moe Dee and said, 'Where did you sleep the night before last? Was it outside, or in a shelter?'

Moe Dee let out a long stream of guttural grunts, some so high they were almost squeaky, and some very breathy and low.

'All right,' said Professor Walmsley. 'And why did you go to the cemetery and abduct those people? Did you know them? Where were you going to take them?'

Moe Dee started to say, 'Heh – heh –', but he had to pause for breath, and swallow two or three times, before he eventually came out with an explosive, '*Dah!*'

'I'm sorry,' Professor Walmsley told him. 'I still can't understand what you're trying to say.'

Moe Dee bunched up his fists and beat them against his blanket in frustration, again and again.

'Heh – *dah*! Heh – *dah*!' Now he was almost hysterical.

'*Header*? Is that it?'

Moe Dee shook his head and groaned. But before Professor Walmsley could ask him another question, there was a loud crash from somewhere downstairs, and then an echoing scream, followed by more crashing and the sound of breaking glass.

Jerry said, 'What the hell's that? Sounds like there's a war going on!'

He went out into the corridor, with Jamila close behind him. All the officers who had been sitting on guard had now stood up.

'What is going on?' Jamila called out.

'Don't know, sarge. We're just going down to take a butcher's.'

There was another scream, and then a clattering sound like feet running upstairs. The officers were only halfway along the corridor when seven or eight men in hooded jackets appeared at the top of the staircase and started rushing toward them. They were snarling ferociously and brandishing hammers and spanners and lengths of metal pipe.

'*Jesus*,' said Jerry. He started toward them but Jamila grabbed his arm.

'No,' she told him.

The officers were armed with expandable batons, but they had no chance to take them out before the hooded men attacked them in a frenzy, beating them down to the floor again and again and then kicking their heads and stamping on their chests. Blood sprayed up the walls and dripped down the windows.

'Inside – *now*!' ordered Jamila. 'Lock the door and barricade it!'

Dr Seshadri had also come out to see what was going on,

and she pushed him back so hard that he stumbled into Tosh, and Tosh in turn stumbled into Professor Walmsley. Jamila went in after them and immediately took out her phone to call for urgent reinforcements.

Before he stepped back into the room, Jerry saw that more hooded men had come charging up the stairs. Two of them had already gone into the first door along the corridor and were dragging out the blinded man who had been lying in there. He was growling loudly, and it looked to Jerry as if he were trying to wrestle himself free.

'*Jerry!*' snapped Jamila, and so he went back inside, closed the door and locked it. He knocked the phone and the flask of water from the top of Moe Dee's bedside table and then Tosh helped him to slide the table across to the door and wedge it under the handle.

They could hear more banging along the corridor outside, and more growling. Moe Dee started to growl too.

'Shut your cakehole, will you?' Jerry hissed at him. 'We don't want them to know that you're in here!'

Moe Dee growled even more loudly, as if he were calling out to the hooded men for help, and he struggled to sit up. Jerry pushed him back down flat. Then he loosened his tie, yanked it off, and wound it around the back of Moe Dee's head, tying it into a tight knot between his teeth, so that the loudest sound he could make was an angry gargle.

'There you are. Tooting United Cricket Club. That should keep you quiet. They haven't won a match all season.'

The door handle was turned, and then furiously rattled, and then the door was shaken by a heavy thump, as if one of the hooded men had rammed his shoulder against it. There was a moment's pause, and then another thump, and another, and then it sounded as if they were kicking it.

Moe Dee tried to sit up again, whining and gargling, but Jerry forced him back against his pillow.

'Stay there and keep schtum, all right, chumly? I don't want to have to sit on you. You're too fucking fat.'

After a while the kicking and the thumping stopped, and the footsteps and the growling faded away. Jamila and Jerry and Tosh and Nolwazi and Professor Walmsley and Dr Seshadri all looked from one to the other in silence. Somewhere in the distance they could hear police sirens, gradually growing louder.

Two or three minutes went past, and then Jamila said, 'It's probably safe to take a look outside now, don't you think?'

Jerry was just about to answer when the door handle was turned again, and there was a rapping at the door.

'Oh my God,' said Professor Walmsley, clutching her pendant.

'Police,' called a voice. 'Everybody all right in there?'

Jerry pulled back the bedside table and unlocked the door. Standing outside were three armed officers in full riot gear.

'We are all fine,' said Jamila. 'But those poor men out in the corridor—'

'Let's get you out of here,' said one of the armed officers. 'We're closing off this whole wing for now.'

'One of you should stay here to guard *him*,' said Jamila, nodding toward Moe Dee.

'Yes, will do. But it looks like he's the only one left.'

'*What?*'

'They've all been sprung out of here, by the looks of it. Nineteen of them, weren't there?'

They followed the armed officers along the corridor. Doctors and nurses had already hurried upstairs from A & E and were bending over the bloodied bodies of the officers who had been beaten by the hooded men. A nurse was giving one of the officers CPR, but it was obvious from the grim looks on the faces of the doctors that the rest of the men had been killed.

Every door along the corridor was wide open, so that Jamila and Jerry could see inside every room. Every bed was empty, with the intravenous drip stands tipped over onto the floor.

Down in reception, they saw that the glass front doors had been shattered and glittering splinters were scattered all over the carpet, so that their shoes crunched. The two receptionists were both being tended by nurses, and one of them had a bloodstained bandage wrapped around her head.

As they walked out into the car park, they saw DCI Saunders talking to the leader of the armed response team. He was looking even grimmer than usual.

'Ah, the dynamic duo,' he said, as they approached. 'You're not hurt at all, are you? I was worried about you two, I must say. And Brinkley, you're okay? I'm afraid I don't know this lady.'

'Professor Walmsley, she's a linguistics expert from the University of London. She came here to see if she could work out what these offenders are talking about, when they growl.'

Professor Walmsley took out her voice recorder and held it up. 'I have a few minutes of growling on here. There might be enough for me to interpret it. If not, I could always come back if that's possible and question that Moe Dee at greater length.'

Jerry clapped his hand against his shirt and said, 'Shit. I left my tie wrapped around his gob.'

'You'd better go and rescue it, then,' said DCI Saunders. 'I suppose we can be thankful that there's at least one of the buggers left. The rest of them have all been spirited away.'

'Spirited away?' asked Jamila. 'What does that mean?'

'At least half a dozen witnesses saw them running into Blackshaw Road toward the cemetery but after that they literally disappeared into thin air. There's CCTV all around the hospital so your people will be scanning through that, won't they, Brinkley?'

Jerry turned to Jamila. 'I'll bet you a thousand to one they went down that Tube line. That's how they managed to disappear. We need to get a search team together asap and see if we can find the way in.'

As they were talking, a Sky TV van turned into the car park, followed by a car that Jerry knew belonged to a BBC news reporter.

'Uh-oh,' said DCI Saunders. 'Here come the media. What can I tell them that doesn't sound like I've totally lost my marbles?'

As the Sky News reporter was climbing out of the van, Dr Seshadri stepped out of the broken glass doors and came hurrying toward them.

'Officers! I have some bad news! That boy Edward Willow – he has been taken too!'

28

Laurel Eye shook Sowber Sek's shoulder and said, 'Wake up! They're fetching Mody's men back!'

Although it was not yet three o'clock in the afternoon, Sek had been given another cupful of calla dew and he had been sleeping deeply. He opened his eyes and yawned and then he sat up. Linda was standing by the window, staring at the fog, which had still not yet cleared.

'Muh-*muh*,' he growled, and climbed to his feet. He crossed the room and curled his arms around Linda's waist, looking up at her and smiling. He growled some more, although she couldn't understand that he was saying, 'I'm so happy you came to find me. Now we can all be a tribe – you and me and Laurel Eye and Hedda.'

Linda tried to give him a smile back, and ruffled his hair, even though she felt like shoving him away. He smelled like the whole room smelled, and his eyes were glassy and unfocused. She had seen the short blocky man pouring out more of that amber liquid for him, and she was sure that it must be some kind of mind-altering drug.

'We've brought back Mody and his men,' he growled at her.

Linda nodded, trying to convince him that she knew what he was saying.

'Mody and his men were supposed to catch us lots of opfers

to pay for their calla dew, but they messed it up and got caught by the comelings. They pulled out their eyes like they were supposed to, but the comelings took them into their healing house. Never mind. We've brought them all back now and they can pay the price.'

Linda nodded again. Sek continued to look up at her, as if he expected her to answer him, or to ask him what was going to happen next, but she stayed silent.

He unwrapped his arms from her waist, took hold of her hand, and started to tug her toward the door. 'Come on. We can watch them being nailed to the wall, the same way that they almost nailed *you* to the wall! We'll be having a feast tonight!'

He led her along the corridor, down the stairs, and into the candlelit room with the painting of the goat-headed man on the wall. It was crowded and noisy, with all the men and women growling at once. At one end of the room, Mody's men were sitting cross-legged on the floor, wearing nothing but their blue-spotted hospital gowns, some of them spattered with blood. Most of the nineteen still had their gauze bandages over their eyes, but three of them had lost their bandages and their eye sockets were soggy and hollow. In the left-hand corner, next to the wall that had been pockmarked all over by nails, Edward was kneeling, looking frightened and confused.

As soon as Sek came into the room with Laurel Eye, Edward jumped up and frantically waved both arms. '*John!*' he called out. 'Iss me! Iss *me*, John! Eh – *duh*!'

He began to step carefully between the blinded men toward Sek, but before he could reach him, two of Hedda's hooded men jostled through the crowd to intercept him. They seized his arms and pressed him back against the wall.

'*John!*' Edward shouted. 'John! Iss *me*, John! Eh – Eh – *Edward*!'

Sek frowned at him but it was clear that he didn't recognise him and he looked away. Edward struggled and twisted and started to cry, but the two men kept him pinned against the wall and wouldn't let him go.

'John!' he sobbed. 'Iss *me*!'

Jerry had told Linda about Edward and John, and anyway she could see from their faces and their blond curly hair that they were brothers. She turned to Sek and gave him an appealing look, but she was afraid to say anything because she knew that he wouldn't understand her, and he might realise that she wasn't under the influence of that amber liquid. Not only that, she was terrified by all the rough hooded men in the room, and she was frightened that if she upset Sek, he might change his mind and have her nailed to the wall, whether he believed that she was his mother or not.

Sek didn't even acknowledge her, because Hedda and Faust had walked in through the door. All of the men and women in the room roared a raucous greeting to her, and stamped their feet, and clapped. Hedda gave them a queenly wave, and nodded, and then she went over to the blinded men and stood in front of them, her arms folded in triumph.

'You see what happens when you anger the great one,' she said. 'You have to return to the shadows in which you were hiding before you were born, like the frightened animals that you are. You have done that. You have blinded yourselves and returned to the shadows. But now you have to surrender your whole bodies as opfers, to make up for the opfers that you failed to bring back to nourish us all.'

She paced backwards and forwards, occasionally leaning forward to stare at one of the blinded men more closely. Once or twice she contemptuously flicked their chins or the tips of their noses with her jagged fingernails.

After a while, though, she stood up straight, with her forehead furrowed.

'Where – where is *Mody*?' she demanded.

A young man with spiky hair stepped forward. 'Mody wasn't there,' he told her.

'What do you mean, he wasn't there? He *must* have been there! If he blinded himself, where else would they have taken him?'

'If he was there, Hedda, we couldn't find him.'

'But Mody is their leader! It was Mody who defied me! I don't care about any of this riff-raff! They're good for eating, and that's all they're good for! I want Mody! I want Mody killed and roasted and I want to eat Mody's cock on the end of a skewer!'

She worked herself up into such a rage that she stormed up and down, slapping the blinded men hard across the face and pushing some of them over.

'We could go back out and try to look for him again,' the young man told her nervously. 'It won't be easy though. The comelings will be watching out for us now. And anyhow, they've probably taken him away by now to some other healing house, so that we can't find him.'

Hedda clenched her fists and let out a harsh scream of fury and frustration. Then she turned to Sek.

'Where is he, Sowber Sek? Where have they taken Mody? You have the gift of magic, you must know!'

Sek gave an unexpected shiver. He glanced across at Edward, who still had tears sliding down his cheeks. Sek vaguely recognised him but he couldn't think where he had seen him before.

'Erm... I'm not sure,' he told Hedda.

'What do you mean, you're not sure? You can make solid objects disappear, can't you? You can bend spoons and then unbend them, with nothing but the power of your mind! What's so difficult about finding out where Mody has gone? He's big enough!'

'I can find him, yes, Hedda. But the comelings will be hiding him, and so it might take quite a long time. I'll have to use a finding spell, and it's very complicated. I'll have to say all these special finding words and draw a special finding map.'

Hedda was gradually calming down, but her nostrils were still flaring and her two hats had tilted so far back that they had almost dropped off, exposing her greasy iron-grey widow's peak.

'Very well,' she said, and patted his shoulder. 'It wasn't my intention to insult you, Sowber Sek. I apologise. I wouldn't want you to use your magic against *me*, would I? But how long do you think this finding spell is going to take? I want these men all prepared *together*, and cooked in our ovens together, as a special feast to earn the great one's forgiveness. But it needs to be all of them, every one, especially Mody. He's their leader. He's the father of their tribe. A sacrifice would mean nothing without Mody. The great one would feel as if we were mocking him.'

Sek said, 'I'm not sure how long it's going to take. But I'll try to say the magic words and draw the magic map as quickly as I can.'

'Will you be able to find Mody before the sixth dark?'

Sek glanced at Edward again, but Edward was staring in resignation down at the floor and he couldn't catch his eye. Sek had a feeling that in some strange way this boy might be able to help him. Yet he felt no particular sympathy for him. If Ba-Abla demanded that he should be dismembered and cooked and eaten like all of these blinded men sitting on the floor, so what? There was nothing Sek could do about it. In fact, he thought that this boy would probably taste much better than these hairy-legged men with bunions on their feet and bandages over their eyes.

He reached out and took hold of Linda's hand. 'Hedda wants me to find Mody. She says that until we catch him and bring him here we can't hold the feast to say sorry to the great one.'

Linda looked at him blankly. As far as she was concerned, he had said nothing intelligible. He had only growled and wuffled at her like a puppy that wants to be taken for a walk. She tried a variety of expressions – smiling and nodding and then trying to appear worried, in the hope that one of these expressions would be an appropriate response to what he had said.

'Let's go back upstairs,' Sek suggested. He gave Hedda a reassuring look, as if everything was under control, and then he turned back to Linda and said loudly, 'You can help me to say all the words of the finding spell, and draw the map.'

Linda stayed where she was, still completely baffled by the noises he was making. Sek pulled at her hand, but before he could lead her out of the room, Hedda said, 'Wait, woman!' and stepped forward to confront Linda, drawing her shawl tightly around her shoulders like a judge.

'Sek believes that you are his mother,' she challenged her. 'I know that you cannot be his real birth mother, but he is the Sowber Sek and he may choose any woman in the world to be his mother, if he so wishes it. But tell me, woman, what's your name, and where do you come from? My men who fetched you here said you were grieving, and that was why you caught their attention. Who are you grieving for?'

Hedda's growling and sniffing and teeth-sucking meant nothing to Linda, and all she could do was stare back at her.

'Did you understand what I just asked you?' Hedda demanded. She leaned in so close toward Linda that the hard felted brims of her two hats knocked against Linda's forehead, and with every word she spat right into her face. Linda took a step back but then Hedda took another step forward, as if they were dancing a tango. Linda stepped back again but this time she bumped into the wall. When she twisted her head around she saw that the figure of the man with the head of a goat was glaring down at her with his yellow eyes. She was trapped between an aggressive harridan and a painted devil.

Hedda snarled at her, 'You don't *understand* me, do you? You're still a comeling!' She stood simmering for a moment, but then she relaxed and laid her hand gently and respectfully on Sek's shoulder.

'Sowber Sek – for some reason your mother isn't one of us – at least not yet. She was given the calla dew, wasn't she? I saw it myself. But it seems as if it didn't work. So – we must give her another cupful! You can't have a mother who doesn't understand a word you say! How can she help you to find Mody when she doesn't even know that you're looking for him?'

Sek said, 'Honest, Hedda – I didn't know. I thought that she was shy, that's all, and that's why she didn't speak. But – yes – fetch more calla dew. Then we can work the finding spell together.'

Hedda looked around the room. 'Stammer!' she called out, in a rasping voice, and the blocky man stood up from the back of the crowd and waved his hand. 'Stammer – fetch more calla dew! Quick! Go and get it now!'

Stammer waved his hand again and elbowed his way out

of the room. Linda could only guess where he was going, and why Hedda was standing in front of her and Sek and preventing them from walking out, although her guess was that Hedda had realised that she couldn't understand what they were saying.

Hedda stayed where she was, but turned around to the crowd and slapped her black gloves together and called out, 'There's no need for us to wait! *Faust!* Let's start to nail these failures to the walls! At least the great one will know that we're serious about preparing a feast for him!'

As soon as she said that, the eighteen blinded men all moaned in chorus, and some of them started to climb to their feet, stumbling and clinging on to each other to try and keep their balance. But Hedda's men pushed them roughly back down onto the carpet, and Faust came forward with his hammer.

Linda could only watch in horror as the first of the blinded men was lifted up and his hospital gown ripped off him. Naked, he was dragged over to the pockmarked wall, and his arms forcibly spreadeagled. He was so bony and undernourished that his ribs looked like a birdcage.

She couldn't stop herself from shuddering when Faust knocked the first nail into the palm of the man's right hand, and the man let out a warbling shriek of pain. She knew how close she had come to being nailed to the wall herself. Only Sek's delusion about her being his mother had saved her, and she was still apprehensive that he might suddenly recognise that she wasn't.

The blinded man shrieked over and over again as Faust nailed his left hand to the wall, and then his elbows, and then his kneecaps.

Faust held out his hand for more nails, and called out,

'*Next!*' and as another man was lifted up and his hospital gown torn off him, the blinded men all moaned again like a classroom of terrified children. One of them shouted hoarsely, 'We may not be your tribe, Hedda, but we're your brothers! How can you do this to us? You're supposed to care for us, not kill us! The great one will punish you for this!'

'Oh, you think so?' Hedda barked back at him. 'If the great one is going to punish anyone, it's *you*, for your dismal failure! *You* were supposed to take care of *us*! You were supposed to go out and bring back enough opfers for us to feed on, and to worship the great one too!'

The man who had shouted climbed up onto his knees and blindly shook his fist in her direction. 'The great one loves his own people! *All* of them! He would be furious if he knew what you were doing to us! We've already atoned for our failure! We've returned to the shadows! Isn't that enough?'

'I *know* you,' said Hedda. 'You're Craggen, aren't you – Mody's favourite bum-sniffer? You used to be a Catholic priest, didn't you, before they threw you out of your church for messing around with choirboys? That's how you ended up homeless, on the streets, wasn't it? Well, you listen to me, Craggen, this tribe obeys the rules of *my* religion, not yours. I speak for the great one, and if *your* God ever says anything at all of any value, He squeaks only like a mouse.'

Craggen stood up. 'Yes, Hedda, the great one expects obedience. But he doesn't expect you to use his name to satisfy your own greed. He doesn't expect you to distort his commandments because you've worked up such a lust for human flesh. It didn't start like this, did it, when you first started taking calla dew? Don't blame the great one because you've developed such a hunger for eating people. That's like blaming the Pope because you've developed a hunger for wealth.'

Hedda contemptuously flapped the wings of her shawl, like a swan landing. She pointed at Craggen and snapped, 'Nail him to the wall! Faust, do you hear me! Nail him to the wall!'

Three of her men seized Craggen and ripped off his hospital gown. He collapsed onto the floor, pressing his hands together like a martyr in prayer, but not shouting out nor saying a word. The men dragged him across the floor and lifted him up against the wall beside the door.

Linda looked away as Faust nailed his hands and his elbows and his knees to the wall, but as she turned back she saw him driving a nail through one of his testicles. Hedda let out a slow, creaking laugh.

It was then that Stammer came back into the room, with a plastic cup and a bottle of amber liquid. Hedda beckoned him over, and said to Linda, 'Here – drink some of this. You will understand then what we are saying to you, and you will be able to speak to us. You will be properly part of the tribe.'

Linda turned to Sek, but he simply smiled and nodded and gave a gruff little noise that sounded like encouragement.

Stammer poured out half a cupful of calla dew and held it out to her. She hesitated, but during every second she hesitated the sounds of hammering and screaming continued, and if anything convinced her that she had no alternative but to drink it, those sounds did. She took the cup in both hands, trying to keep them from shaking. Hedda was staring at her and Sek was staring at her and Stammer was wiping his nose with the back of his hand.

She drank the calla dew, all in one gulp. At first it had quite a pleasant liquorice flavour, but as she handed the empty cup back she began to taste metal, and some acidic chemical.

'Now you need to sleep for a while, so that the calla dew can creep into your mind and change you into one of us,' said Hedda, although Linda still thought that she was growling. 'Sek – take her back to your room. Laurel Eye, you go with them and make sure that she settles down to sleep. The sooner she understands us, the sooner she can help Sowber Sek to find Mody.'

She looked around. Between the door and the end of the room, where all their previous victims had been nailed, the wall was now completely taken up with eight of Mody's blind and naked men, with their arms spread wide. Faust was now pinning another man onto the wall beside the window.

'Faust! You won't have enough wall for them all!' Hedda called out to him.

Faust banged the last nail into a young black man's kneecap. 'Don't worry!' he called back, standing up straight and swinging his hammer like a bandmaster's baton. 'There's plenty of space on the floor!'

Linda could hear a singing noise in her ears and she was beginning to feel strangely detached from all the hooded and smelly men and women who were crowding around her, as if she were dreaming about them. Apart from the hammering and the screaming there was a constant undertone of growling and the rustling of padded nylon jackets as they circulated around the room and rubbed up against each other.

She swayed, and closed her eyes. Laurel Eye took hold of her arm and said to Sek, 'Come on, we need to take Muh-muh upstairs. She'll feel better when she's had some sleep.'

Linda took one staggering step forward. '*Jerry*,' she whispered.

'What?' said Sek. 'What does "Jerry" mean?'

★ ★ ★

She was woken up by a high voice, singing. It was a song like no other song she had ever heard before, rising up and dipping down like a wind blowing through a valley. Yet she managed to catch some of the words, and she lay for a while watching the candlelight flickering on the ceiling, trying to follow what the singer was saying.

'You walked off... into the shadows... you walked off... you never turned around...'

She sat up. It was Laurel Eye who was singing. She was sitting on the floor opposite Sek, who was leaning with his back against the wall, picking his nose and smoking a cigarette at the same time.

'You vanished... into the shadows... into the darkness... which way did you go?'

As soon as she saw that Linda was awake, Laurel Eye stopped singing, and smiled, and said, 'Aha! Welcome back! You must have been having a nightmare, the way you were shouting!'

'Was I?' said Linda. 'Where am I?'

'In your bedroom, with me and your wonderful magical son Sowber Sek.'

Linda blinked at Sek. His blond curly hair was sticky and tangled and smoke was leaking out of both of his nostrils.

'You're my son?' she said. 'I didn't even know I had a son. I didn't know I had any children, boys or girls.'

Sek stood up and came across the room to plonk himself down on the mattress next to her. He grinned and pressed his cheek against her shoulder and said, 'Mummy. You're only saying that to tease me.'

'He believes that you're his mother,' said Laurel Eye. 'He's the Sowber Sek, so who are we to deny it?'

'He's the Sowber Sek?' said Linda. She actually knew that 'Sowber' meant 'Magic' and that 'Sek' meant 'Second'. 'But he's so young!'

'You don't need to be grown up to work magic, do you? I've seen babies coming straight out of the womb and striking men dead.'

Linda carefully but firmly loosened Sek's grip on her arm and stood up. She crossed over to the desk first because her attention had been caught by the candle burning, and she found it fascinating. After a few moments she reached out and tried to pick up the flame, but she immediately said, 'Ahh!' and whipped her hand away.

'It's hot!'

Laurel Eye got up too, and stood next to her. 'I'm sorry, that's my fault. I should have warned you. There are some things that you won't remember from the time before you took the calla dew, like this candle.'

'Is that what it's called? A "candle"? Have I seen one before?'

Laurel Eye stroked Linda's cheek. 'Some things you won't have forgotten, and some things you'll know more about than you did before. But most of the things that you don't remember will come back to you, little by little, or else you'll learn about them all over again. We need candles because it doesn't matter if it's dark outside or if it's light, we have to keep the curtains drawn in the front windows in case the comelings see us.'

Linda nodded. She knew that 'comelings' was a word for 'weaklings', although she couldn't imagine why they should be afraid of weaklings.

She bent down to look at the candle more closely, and as she did so she caught sight of her reflection in the mirror at the back of the desk. She reached out beside her and tightly gripped Laurel Eye's hand.

'Who's that?' she whispered. 'There's a woman looking at me through that hole.'

Laurel Eye tapped the mirror with her knuckle. 'That's you. This is what we call a self-see. It looks like there's two candles, doesn't it, but there's only one. And it looks like there's two of you, and two of me, but there's only one of each of us. And – look behind you – there's another Sek!'

Linda stared at herself for a long time in the mirror. 'Is that really me?'

'Yes.'

'But I have candles in my eyes.'

'Yes. Your eyes are self-sees too.'

'It's nearly the ninth dark,' Sek piped up. 'We should go down and see if they've finished the nailing. And it'll be time to eat soon. Not that we'll have much to eat tonight, because of Mody.'

'You're right,' said Laurel Eye. 'Are you ready to come downstairs, Muh-muh?'

'Are you really going to call me that?'

'You're Sek's mother. What else should we call you?'

Linda thought hard. She was sure that she had a name. She could imagine it. But it was like a tune that she had forgotten, and even when it came to tunes she could only think of the song that Laurel Eye had been singing.

'You walked off... into the shadows... you walked off... you never turned around...'

'I'm so thirsty,' she said, as she followed Sek and Laurel Eye along the corridor to the staircase. 'This place is so dusty and I must have been sleeping with my mouth open because it's all gone down my throat.'

They could hear the tribe shouting and singing, even from two floors up.

'Don't worry,' Laurel Eye assured her. 'The women went out this afternoon to gather bread and milk and vegetables and drinks. There won't be much opfer meat but there'll be plenty of everything else.'

When they walked into the room with the great one painted on the wall, the noise was deafening. The men and women of the tribe were dancing around with bottles of wine and gin and some of them were already so drunk that they had fallen, laughing, onto the floor. One woman was leaning against the wall at the end of the room, splattering yellow vomit beneath the bare feet of one of the blinded men who was nailed there.

Linda was pushed into the centre of the room, so she could see that every other wall was taken up with eleven of Mody's blinded men, all nailed up in a row with their arms held out wide. The remaining eight had been nailed to the floor underneath the window, and Hedda was circling around them, with a half-empty bottle of vodka in one hand and a cigar in the other. Every now and then she swung one of her worn-down boots and gave them a vicious kick in their ribs or the side of their head.

'Sowber Sek!' she called out. 'Come and see the failures! And Muh-muh! You're awake! Can you follow what I'm saying now, woman?'

Hedda had drunk so much vodka that she was lurching as she paced around and slurring her words, but Linda found that she could clearly understand her. She vaguely remembered having seen Hedda earlier, before she had fallen asleep, but she hadn't realised then how impressive she was, how commanding, with her two wide-brimmed hats perched on top of her head, and her shawl, and her layers of coats and jackets and sweaters. She was the voice of the great one, after all, the one who could hear Ba-Abla murmuring in the shadows, so that she could tell the tribe what Ba-Abla advised, and what Ba-Abla demanded.

'See these drivelling failures? Hedda repeated, taking a swig from her bottle of vodka and then trying to puff at her cigar, although it had gone out.

Linda went to join her, and looked down at the naked men nailed to the carpet. All of the bandages had been torn off their faces, so their eyes were nothing but sagging holes. She found the sight of their flaccid penises quite arousing, an arousal that was heightened by the fact that she could stare at them for as long as she wanted, but none of them could see her.

Sek called, 'Muh-muh! Muh-muh!' and beckoned her.

He was standing in the corner of the room, jiggling up and down with excitement. Lying at his feet, nailed to the carpet, was Edward. He was unconscious, his lips pale blue, and he was breathing only in tiny gasps.

When she first saw him, Linda had a wave of feeling that she couldn't qualify. For some reason she felt that she wanted to pull out the nails that were keeping his hands and knees stuck to the floor, and pick him up, and carry him away in her arms. Almost at once, though, that feeling faded away like a distant train whistle, and she saw how jubilant Sek was. She gave him a hug, lifting him off his feet.

'He's going to be mine – all mine!' Sek told her, as she put him down. 'He's going to be my dinner tomorrow, when we find Mody! I'm going to eat his crunchy ears!'

Linda's mind was still a jumble, but she suddenly remembered something serious. Over the singing and shouting, she leaned close to Sek and said, 'We have to find Mody first, Sek! If we don't find Mody, they're going to be eating us!'

29

Jerry couldn't sleep that night. He was exhausted, and he lay on his crumpled bed too tired to get up and make himself a cup of tea. He couldn't stop thinking about Linda, and seeing pictures of her in his mind's eye laughing as she ran across Tooting Bec Common, or sitting on the sofa by the fire, her knees drawn up, the tip of her tongue between her teeth, painting her toenails. The fire had been reflected in her eyes like two candle flames.

Occasionally, cars drove up Crowborough Road, and he saw their headlights swivel across the ceiling. Apart from Linda, it was painful for him to think of Nora too, and the way in which she had been killed downstairs in her living room. How can an elderly widow have lived a quiet and harmless life, taking care of her husband and bringing up three children, eventually to settle down with her crochet and her television and her weekly bingo club, only to be smashed and beaten and crushed to death against the walls of her own house?

He wondered if Linda were dead now too, and if she had been killed with the same brutality. It was beginning to seem increasingly likely that she had been abducted by the same gang of homeless squatters who had taken PC Bone and murdered DC Malik and incinerated that poor woman at the Charles Babbage school in Peckham, as well as taking hostages at Lambeth Cemetery. If it had been them, he had to doubt if there was anything but the slimmest chance of her still being alive.

Jerry was not one for crying. The last time he had been forced to wipe his eyes was when his father had died of prostate cancer five years ago at the Royal Marsden Hospital. But as he lay in bed thinking of Linda and what might have happened to her, he felt a cold tear slide from each eye and onto the pillow.

He couldn't even pray to God to protect her. He had seen too much violence and too much cruelty in his nine years as a detective to believe that there could possibly be a God. What kind of a God allows millions of his worshippers to die of pandemics, and his beloved only son to be nailed to a cross?

He managed to doze off for about an hour as it began to grow light. When he woke up, he could hear the rain gurgling in the gutter outside his window. He swung himself out of bed and went through to his kitchenette to fill up his kettle. He suddenly remembered that he had forgotten to feed his ryukin goldfish. He had christened it Quasimodo because ryukins have hunched backs.

'It's God's fault, isn't it, Quaz?' he said, as he sprinkled dried flakes onto the surface of his fish tank, and the ryukin rose to nibble at them. 'He didn't make man and the Devil of equal strength.'

That was Jerry's favourite quote, from *The Hunchback of Nôtre Dame*. In fact, it was the only quote he could remember from school. The only other quote he remembered came from

The Sweeney, that 1970s' TV police series. 'If you're going to get hitched, make sure it's either a 9 or a 3. A stunner or a shitter.'

He was about to pour himself a mug of tea when his phone rang. It was Jamila, and she sounded as tired as he felt.

'Jerry? I've had a call from Professor Walmsley. Tosh passed her on to me.'

'Bit bloody early, isn't it? What time is it?'

'Half past seven. But she told me she's been up all night, working on that recording from Moe Dee.'

'Can't say I've had that much kip myself. Did she get anywhere with it?'

'Apparently, yes. She told me that she listened to it again and again at different speeds, and then she suddenly had a Damascene moment.'

'Oh yeah? What's one of them, then? Like the menopause?'

'A moment of sudden enlightenment, Jerry. Like Saul on the road to Damascus.'

'Sorry, you know me. I'm not very biblical. What was it, this moment?'

'When she played the recording back at a very slow speed, she could distinctly hear elements and phrases of two separate languages. These homeless people seem to have their own dialect – but she said it's not at all like Cockney or Shelta, the Irish traveller language. It hasn't been developed by the homeless people themselves for their own protection, over the years, like those two languages.'

'Don't tell me there's a night school, where you can go and learn growling.'

'No. Professor Walmsley is almost sure that it is down to the opioid that these people have been taking. Tosh and Dr Seshadri both agree that it affects the speech centres in their brains, but Professor Walmsley believes it is rather like a chemical version of Google Translate. She admits that she needs to make more recordings to support her theory, but she seems very confident about it.'

'So all that wuffing and barking, that all makes some kind of sense?'

'It does if you've taken a dose of this particular drug, and you can listen at a third of the normal speed.'

'These two languages – does she have any idea what they are?'

'She said that she could only hazard a guess at the main language. It was a highly educated guess, of course, because she is an expert in evolutionary linguistics. But she thinks that its roots date almost as far back as the Stone Age, from forty-three thousand BC or even before – a language called Pre-Indo-European. What really surprised her, though, was that apart from that, she thought she picked up quite a few phrases and words in modern German. And not just "Erst" and "Sek" either.'

'So these buggers *are* German, just like we thought they might be. But that still doesn't explain them talking like cavemen and worshipping some Pakistani devil, does it?'

'Listen – Professor Walmsley wants to make more recordings of this Moe Dee character, so that she can build up a decent vocabulary. If she does that, we should be able to persuade him to tell us where the rest of those homeless people are hiding out. That woman with two hats, for example, that Edward Willow drew for us.'

'Baggy Nell? I'm almost glad I didn't have a decent night's sleep last night. I would have had nightmares about her.' He paused, and then he said, 'I hope to God that Edward's all right.'

'I thought you were not biblical.'

'I'm not. But who else can I pray to? Ronald McDonald?'

'Anyway,' said Jamila. 'I have agreed that we should go to St George's at eleven-thirty and meet up with Professor Walmsley. DCI Saunders has arranged for Moe Dee to be moved to a room next to the ophthalmic ward in the Lanesborough Wing and he has an armed guard.'

'Okay. I'll meet you there. You don't have any of those kheema patties left, do you? Fetch a few along if you do. I know I'll be starving by lunchtime.'

Jerry hung up. He stood for a long time watching his ryukin nibbling its fish food. He was doing everything he could to act normally, as if he were in charge of everything, like a detective should be. Instead, he felt like a helpless passenger on a roller coaster, whirling and dipping and spinning, not strapped in, and only just managing to cling on.

He picked up Linda's scarf from where she had left it draped over the back of the armchair, and pressed it to his nose so that he could smell her.

'Linda,' he whispered. But the only response was a pigeon landing with a scrabbling sound on the gutter outside the living-room window, and starting its repetitive mating call.

Dr Seshadri met Jamila and Jerry and Professor Walmsley when they arrived at the Lanesborough Wing and he showed them up to Moe Dee's room on the second floor.

'His general health remains poor,' he told them, as they went up in the lift. 'Apart from that, though, his system seems to be recovering from the effects of that opioid reasonably quickly – much faster than that unfortunate boy Edward Willow. It could be down to his much greater body mass. Is there any news of Edward, by the way, or any of the other patients who were taken away?'

Jerry shook his head. 'Not a sausage, I'm afraid. But we're hoping that this joker may be able to tip us off where they are.'

When they entered the room, they found Moe Dee sitting up in bed and looking far healthier than he had the previous day. He had been washed and his beard had been trimmed and a fresh gauze dressing had been taped over his eyes. A half-eaten ham sandwich lay on a plate on his bedside table, as well as an empty salt-and-vinegar crisp packet.

As they pulled up chairs and sat around his bed, he jerked his head from side to side and blurted out, 'Who's that?'

Professor Walmsley looked across the bed at Jamila and Jerry and raised an eyebrow, as if to say, *how about that – he's speaking in English!*

'Moe Dee, this is Professor Walmsley,' she said, taking out her voice recorder. 'Do you recognise my voice? I came to talk to you yesterday. I would like to talk to you some more today.'

Moe Dee gave a long and complicated growl. However, he seemed to know that Professor Walmsley wouldn't be able to understand what he was trying to tell her, because after he had finished growling he concentrated hard and managed to say, 'Muh – my – muh – my – *peep* – uhl.'

'Your people, is that who you mean?'

'Muh – my – *tribe.*'

'Your tribe, very well. I get that. You want to know what's happened to your tribe?'

Moe Dee nodded. 'Hed – dah. Hed – dah took muh – *peep* – uhl.'

'Hedda? Is that the name of a woman?'

Moe Dee raised his left hand and placed it on top of his

bald head. Then he raised his right hand and placed it on top of his left.

'You're covering your head,' frowned Professor Walmsley. 'What does that tell me?'

'Tuh – tuh – *too!*' Moe Dee exclaimed. Then he took another quick breath and said, '*Hah!*'

'I'm sorry, I still don't know what you're getting at.'

'Hass! Too hass! Hedda – too hass!'

'He means *hats*!' said Jamila, clapping her hands. 'Two *hats*! He's talking about that woman with two hats that Edward drew!'

'Baggy Nell,' said Jerry. 'That's who sprung his partners in crime. Baggy bloody Nell. Where's she hiding out, mate? Can you understand me? Baggy Nell or Hedda or whatever she calls herself – where's she hiding out? Come on – don't try to kid us you don't know where she is!'

Moe Dee was becoming flustered now, and started flapping his arms around as if he were trying to swat away a swarm of bluebottles.

'Calm down!' Professor Walmsley told him, taking hold of one of his hands. 'Moe Dee, calm down!'

To Jerry, she said, 'Don't press him too hard, detective, please. He's been under enormous psychological stress. He may not have been suicidal but he's blinded himself. We won't make progress unless we take this very easy. One step at a time.'

Professor Walmsley gave Moe Dee a drink of water and gradually he relaxed.

'Now,' she said. 'You've told me that Hedda took your tribe. Are you *pleased* that she came to rescue them? And are you sorry that they didn't take you? You were shouting out to them yesterday, after all.'

Moe Dee shook his head but he was still too emotional to find the words to answer her in English, and so he gave her a lengthy series of growls and grunts. Professor Walmsley held up her voice recorder so that she could play it all back later at a slower speed, but even Jerry could get the gist of what he was saying. It didn't take a genius to see that Moe Dee was angry, and frightened, and vengeful. When he had shouted out to Hedda's men yesterday, he had probably been telling them to go away and leave him and his tribe alone, so that they could recover from their self-inflicted blindness. They had given their eyesight, what more did these people want?

Moe Dee rested back on his pillow for a few minutes, while Professor Walmsley played back some of what he had said. As far as Jerry was concerned, it sounded no more intelligible at half speed than it did when Moe Dee was talking quickly – nothing but long, slurring growls and occasional yaps. But it must have made some kind of sense to Professor Walmsley, because she was furiously jotting down notes while she listened to it.

'Hoh,' said Moe Dee at last, when he had rested. 'Hoh – *dell*.'

Professor Walmsley looked up, her ball pen poised. 'Say that again, Moe Dee. Slowly.'

'Hoh – dell. Keh – keh—nung – dun. Hoh – dell.'

'I believe he's trying to say "hotel",' said Professor Walmsley. 'He's already been describing a place where travellers stop for the night, but of course in pre-Neolithic language they had no word for "hotel".'

'So what's "Keh – keh – nung – dun"?'

'I think he means Kennington,' said Jamila. 'A hotel in Kennington, that is what he is telling us about. That is where this Hedda and her tribe must be hiding. It makes sense. It is halfway between Lambeth, where those Holocaust survivors were found, and Peckham, where that school burned down. And a hotel would be able to accommodate a considerable number of homeless people.'

Jerry snapped his fingers. 'The Duchy Hotel! I think that used to be a Solace hotel before they sold it off! That's where those towels could have come from!'

'Are you sure?' asked Dr Seshadri. 'I thought that the Duchy Hotel had been demolished a couple of years ago.'

'Well, it was a right dump, I'll give you that. But I don't know whether it's been knocked down or not.'

'I have driven past the place where it used to be, several times. When the traffic on the main road is bad, I use it as a shortcut on my way to St Thomas' Hospital. There is nothing there now but a very high wall covered in graffiti. If the hotel *is* still there, it is not possible to see it from the road. But I believe I read somewhere that it was demolished to make room for a new housing estate.'

Jerry turned to Moe Dee. 'This hotel you're trying to tell us about. Is it the Duchy?'

Moe Dee nodded and made more growling noises.

'So maybe they haven't knocked it down yet – or not all of it, anyhow! We can soon check that out. Bloody hell – me and Edge were only up at the War Museum yesterday, and that's just across the road from there. We could have taken a butcher's for ourselves.'

Professor Walmsley said to Moe Dee, 'You're telling us that if we go to this Duchy Hotel in Kennington we'll be able to rescue your people, is that it?'

Moe Dee frantically shook his head, and clung to the sleeve of Professor Walmsley's dress.

'No – no – *no!*' he begged her, and his mouth was dragged

down in a howl of anguish. 'No – you go – you go – Hed-dah – Hed-dah—'

He was lost for words now, but he stuck out the index finger of his right hand to simulate a knife blade and made a slicing gesture across his Adam's apple with it.

Professor Walmsley said, 'He's telling me that if we attempt to rescue his people, Hedda will cut their throats.'

Moe Dee tugged at her sleeve again. He mimicked that he was cutting his stomach open, and then he cupped both hands to pretend that his intestines were sliding out of him, and he was doing his best to catch them.

'Bloody hell,' said Jerry.

Moe Dee continued to cling on to Professor Walmsley's sleeve and began to growl at her again. This time he spoke quickly, and in a soft tone that sounded deadly serious. She recorded everything he said, and when he had finished and settled himself down again, she played it all back.

'What does he say?' asked Jamila. 'That sounded to me like a warning of some kind.'

'You're right,' Professor Walmsley told her. 'I haven't been able to catch all of it, but the essence of it is that if we try to break into the hotel, Hedda will order the immediate killing of everybody in there, including her own people. She will do that because their god demands it. If they fail as hunter-gatherers, their god expects them to blind themselves. Moe Dee calls that "returning to the shadows".

'The men are expected to go out every day and every night and bring back human victims to feed their people and to honour their god. Moe Dee had a German word for those. He called them "opfers". In German, *Ein Opfer* is a sacrifice.'

'Him and his mob made a right dog's dinner of that Lambeth Cemetery job,' said Jerry. 'That must be why they poked their eyes out. But what's this about killing the whole bloody lot of them?'

'That part of what he said I understood very clearly. Should Hedda be convinced that she and her people are surrounded by overwhelming odds, and that there is no hope of them defeating their enemy or escaping, she will order their mass killing.'

Professor Walmsley turned back to Moe Dee. 'How many people would you say are hiding in that hotel?'

She held up the fingers of both hands to emphasise what she was asking him. In return, Moe Dee held up the fingers of both hands seven times, and then the fingers of one hand once.

'Seventy-five,' said Jamila. 'Not quite Jonestown, as cult suicides go, but still quite a massacre. If those people really *are* in that hotel, we will have to plan this operation with extreme caution.'

Moe Dee lifted a hand to acknowledge that he had understood her, and had appreciated what she had said.

Jerry went up close to his bedside. 'When you could still see, mate, you didn't happen to clock a young woman in that hotel, did you? Dark brown hair, blue velvet dress?'

Moe Dee growled and shook his head. Professor Walmsley said, 'He's not too sure. It was very crowded in there. "Gedranger", is what he called it. The German word for a scrum or a crush is *Gedränge*.'

Jerry reached into the pocket of his jacket and pulled out Linda's scarf. He held it in front of Moe Dee's face and said, 'Have a sniff of this. Is there a young woman in that hotel who smells like this?'

Moe Dee took hold of Jerry's hand so that he could draw the scarf nearer to his nose. He took several deep breaths, held them, and then he said, 'Yeh – *yeh*,' and nodded. Flowerbomb perfume was sweet, with a distinctive smell of bergamot, but it was expensive and not many young women wore it.

'So it *was* those bastards who snatched her,' said Jerry. He couldn't stop his voice from shaking. 'I wouldn't be surprised if they've been responsible for just about every missing person who's been reported this year. Human bloody sacrifices, Jesus.'

'Now we know where she might be, Jerry, we will do everything we can to get your Linda back for you,' said Jamila.

'If she's still alive. If these bastards haven't killed her and eaten her.'

'If she's still alive, Jerry, yes.'

Jerry gave Moe Dee a hard shove in the chest. 'You bastards. You inhuman bloody bastards. What did you do with your eyes, eh? Eat them, did you? I wish you hadn't. I wish you'd left them in. Then I could have had the pleasure of poking them out for you.'

Moe Dee pressed his hands together as if he were begging Jerry's forgiveness.

'Noh me,' he managed to say, with a great deal of effort.

'Oh, not you? Then who was it, if it wasn't you? You melt!'

Moe Dee turned to where he thought Professor Walmsley was sitting, although by now she had stood up and crossed over to the other side of the room.

'Noh me,' he repeated. '*Calla dew!*' and he lifted his hand to his mouth as if he were drinking from a cup. He did this twice, and then he tapped his forehead.

'Calla Dew?' said Jerry. 'Who's Calla Dew?'

But Moe Dee shook his head vigorously and lifted up his imaginary cup one more time.

'I believe he is trying to tell us that "calla dew" is a drink,' said Dr Seshadri. 'Perhaps it is the name of the opioid that he has been taking. It could be that he is tapping his forehead to indicate that this drink affected his thinking.'

Now Moe Dee nodded again.

'I was right, then,' said Dr Seshadri. 'But I can't say that I've ever heard of an opioid called "calla dew". It's not a chemical name that I've ever heard of, nor a generic name, nor a brand name. It's not a street name, either, like monkey or greenies.'

Professor Walmsley approached Moe Dee's bed again. 'Say it again, Moe Dee. Say "calla dew". Say it slowly.'

'Cah-ladge-ew,' said Moe Dee.

'And again,' she coaxed him, tilting her head to one side so that she could hear him more clearly. 'And again.'

At last she said, 'I don't think he's saying "calla *dew*" – not like the morning dew that you get on the grass, anyway. I think they're both words that have an Urdu root, like quite a lot of the words he uses. They have their origin in this Pre-Indo-European language that I've been telling you about. I think he's telling us that a drink called "kala jadu" affected his brain.'

'So what's that, then?' asked Jerry. 'Does that mean anything?'

'Very definitely,' said Professor Walmsley. 'In Urdu, *kala jadu* means "black magic".'

30

Now Jamila and Jerry acted quickly. They climbed into Jerry's Toyota and he drove them as fast as he could to Kennington, weaving in and out of the traffic and running red lights whenever he had to. While he was driving, Jamila called DCI Saunders and brought him up to date on everything that they had managed to find out from Moe Dee.

'How trustworthy is he, this Moe Dee?' asked DCI Saunders. 'He hasn't been leading you up the garden path, has he? What if this hotel no longer exists?'

'Then we will have wasted an hour of our time and several litres of petrol, sir. But I have a strong feeling that he was telling us the truth. This Hedda woman has made him incredibly angry, and we believe that he would do almost anything to have his revenge.'

'All right, then. Keep me up to speed, won't you? If he was right about her being prepared to kill all of her followers, this is going to be a very tricky one, and no mistake. We came in for enough bad publicity last week from that one lunatic in Walworth who shot himself when we went to collar him. But seventy-five! You can imagine the front page of the *Sun*! It doesn't bear thinking about!'

'How did Smiley take it?' Jerry asked, as he turned into Black Prince Road.

'Oh, his usual jolly self. Look – this must be it. This high metal fence.'

Jerry turned into a long narrow side road. On the left stood a terrace of red-brick Victorian houses. On the opposite side, running the entire length of the road, was a grey steel security hoarding. It was covered in graffiti – tags and cartoons and wildstyle lettering. A huge grinning skull had been stencilled near to the centre of the hoarding with the caption 'Death Lives Here'.

They parked and went up to the hoarding. It was at least three metres high, so it was impossible to see over the top of it. Not only that, it had no gaps or boltholes in it, and it had been fitted with steel skirting so nobody would be able to see underneath it.

Two of the panels could obviously be opened for access to the demolition site, but they were both closed and padlocked, and there was a notice on them 'Toogood Developments, Trespassers Will Be Prosecuted'.

Jamila sat back in the car and opened her laptop. She logged onto Zoom and checked the latest satellite pictures of Kennington.

'Yes, Jerry – look. Some of the site has been cleared, but the main part of the hotel building is still standing. Of course, this shows only the roof, so it is impossible to tell if anybody could live in it.'

She enlarged the image as much as she could and peered at it closely. 'We can try calling these Toogood Developments. If they fail to answer, I am sure that the District Ward Officer can tell us if the hotel still has walls and windows, and if there is anybody squatting in it. Or somebody at Lambeth Council must know.'

Jerry was thinking of parking his car close up to the

hoarding and climbing up onto the roof. But he was just about to open the driver's door when an elderly woman appeared from one of the houses opposite, with a shopping basket on wheels and a panting Labrador. He went across and held up his ID. 'Excuse me, love. Police.'

'I thought that was all settled,' the woman quavered.

'Sorry, what?'

'I went back to the newsagents and paid for those sweets. I was only being forgetful.'

'No, it's not about that, love. I was wondering about the old Duchy Hotel – whether they've knocked out the windows.'

'Oh. Yes. No. They knocked down the whole of the *side* part, the very old part. But they haven't knocked down any of the new part yet. It's still got windows in it, yes. They were supposed to be leaving that part and tarting it up so that they could turn it into offices. Or flats. I'm not sure which. I don't think anybody's quite sure which. They seem to keep changing their minds. I wish they'd hurry up and get on with it, that's all. I hate that fence. The last thing you want is a skull staring at you through your sitting-room window day and night, especially when you're my age.'

Jerry glanced up at her house. 'I suppose you can see the Duchy out your bedroom window. What's left of it, anyway.'

'Just the top two floors of it, yes.'

'Do you ever see any people moving around in there? Or lights?'

The elderly woman shook her head. 'I don't think there's anybody *living* there. But then all the curtains are drawn, so I couldn't really say for sure.'

'Do you ever see people going in and out of the building site?'

'No. It's always locked. And that fence goes all the way

around. I know that because my friend lives in Dolby Road and she's got the fence at the end of her garden. She hates it as much as I do.'

'All right, then,' said Jerry. 'Thanks, love. You've been a great help.'

The elderly woman tugged at her Labrador's lead, and then she said, 'Is there something going on there, in the Duchy? Like drugs or something?'

'Nothing for you to worry about. But if you *do* see anything – even if it's only a light at one of the windows – do you want to give me a bell? Here's my number.'

He went back to join Jamila.

'What's left of the hotel has still got windows, that's what she said. And curtains too.'

'Really? It is easily large enough to accommodate seventy-five squatters.'

'I was thinking of climbing up on the car roof so that I could cop a vada over the fence, but I'm dead nervous about any one of them catching sight of us. I could have asked that old dear if I could take a butcher's out of her bedroom window, but you never know who might happen to be looking this way.'

'We could call in the air service. A helicopter would have thermal imaging, and that would tell us for certain if there are squatters inside.'

'Too risky, skip. What if those twonks hear a chopper overhead and get all antsy about it? I was thinking myself that maybe we could use a drone to scout the place out, but then there's a good chance that they'll see it or hear it. If that Moe Dee wasn't stringing us a line, they could well start topping themselves. Linda's in there, skip, and I can't risk the slightest chance of that.'

Jamila was frowning at the grinning skull, almost as if she

were daring it to wink at her. 'Very well, Jerry. Fair enough. You are quite right to be extra cautious. Let us go back to the station and plan this out properly. I would like to take another look at that map of the Tube tunnels that our friend Simon gave us. I also want to contact the developers and the council planning department and the DWO at Lambeth.

'If we are going to break into this part of the hotel, we will need to know what condition it is in, and we will need a detailed floor plan. We must know where all the doors are, and all the stairs. If there are squatters in there, we must not give them the time to kill themselves. Not a second.'

Back at the station, Jerry unfolded a copy that he had made of the frail old Tube tunnel map, and laid the plastic sheet on top of it.

'There,' said Jamila. They could see at once that sometime in the 1890s a tunnel had been excavated from the Northern Line at Kennington underneath Black Prince Road. It looked as if the railway company's original intention had been to connect it up with Vauxhall main-line station, about a mile due west, but after less than half a mile they had abandoned it. Even so, it had reached as far as the Duchy Hotel, and it ran directly beneath the hotel's cellars.

'Look at this,' said Jerry, and ran his finger down the network of tunnels, some in daily use by trains but some unfinished. He traced a path directly from the Duchy Hotel to Lambeth Cemetery. 'I was right, wasn't I? A million to one Moe Dee's mob went through all these tunnels to get to the cemetery. And that mob who turned up at St George's to grab them and take them away – I'll bet they used the same route.'

Jamila had been watching him, although she was on the

phone at the same time. She kept trying different numbers, and eventually she managed to get through to the District Ward Officer for Lambeth and to Lambeth Council's planning department.

When she eventually put the phone down, she said, 'Your old lady was correct. The older part of the Duchy was built in 1856 and it was in a poor state of repair, so the council granted planning permission for it to be demolished. A large extension was built in 1922 and that is the part that they have left standing. The council granted permission for it to be converted into a combination of offices and flats.

'Two years ago, though, the developers went bankrupt and work came to a halt. The council are still looking for somebody to take the project on. It is all rather complicated, according to the council, because Kennington is owned by the Prince of Wales as part of the Duchy of Cornwall, which is why the hotel was called the Duchy.'

'Did the DWO know if there were any squatters in it?'

'He said that he was not aware of any, but he was very evasive and he gave me the feeling that he had never looked into the site to find out. It was the same with the council planning department. They said the site was secure and could only be inspected by appointment.'

Jerry looked down at the Tube tunnel map. 'So the hotel's pretty much intact, and it's almost certain that this Baggy Nell or Hedda or whatever she calls herself is hiding in there with her gang of cannibals. And my Linda could be in there too. And that poor little Edward kid. What the hell do we do now?'

'The council are emailing me a copy of the drawings that were submitted as part of Toogood's planning application. As soon as we receive that, we need to sit down with DCI

Saunders and DS Bristow and an armed response unit and decide how we are going to break into that hotel without any loss of life.'

'Jesus. There's seventy-five of the buggers. It's going to take a bloody army to nick all that lot in about ten seconds flat.'

Jerry was still studying the Tube tunnel map when a soft voice said, 'Hello? Jamila? Jerry?'

He looked up and saw Nairiti Malik. Apart from her purple headscarf, he could see that a thick pink bandage was wrapped around her throat. She had her son with her, a shy-looking boy of about six or seven years old, with his mother's huge dark eyes.

'Nairiti,' said Jamila. 'How are you? And this is—?'

'Kalmesh,' she said. Her voice was hoarse, as if she had a cold. 'He said he wanted to come and help you catch the terrible people who murdered his father.'

'I'm afraid to say that we haven't caught them yet, Kalmesh,' said Jerry. 'But we have a good idea who they are, and where they are. It's just that we have to go a bit careful because they're a bunch of very bad men, and we don't want anybody else to get hurt, the way your dad was.'

Kalmesh came forward, holding up a small brown cotton bag.

'I know the men are very bad. I have this for you, to keep you safe when you catch them.'

He handed the bag to Jerry, and Nairiti smiled and nodded and said, 'Open it. It is not an antique, like Chandran's, but it still has the same power. The men who killed him took his away, so that he would no longer be protected. But this one will shield you from Buri Nazar, the evil eye, if you keep it close to you.'

Jerry loosened the bag's drawstring and shook out a hamsa

necklace, with a silver hand and a small garnet set between the fingers.

'Thank you, Kalmesh,' said Jerry. 'I'm touched. I think I'm going to need all the protection I can get.'

He fastened the hamsa around his neck and showed it to Jamila.

Nairiti said, 'I would have brought one for you too, Jamila, but when you came to visit me I saw that you were already wearing a ring to protect yourself against the evil eye.'

Jamila held up her hand to show her blue Murano glass ring. 'Yes. I am not superstitious, but it seems to have kept me safe so far. A man came running at me with a machete once, but I held up my ring and he tripped over and hit his head and almost knocked himself out. He may just have been clumsy but I like to think that it was the power of Kali that saved me.'

'How are you coping, Nairiti?' Jerry asked her.

'I take every day as it dawns. My sister is staying with us at the moment and she is a great comfort. She lost her husband too, last year, so she understands when to speak to me and when to be silent.'

Nairiti and Kalmesh had only just left when Edge appeared, his tie askew, looking exhausted. He dropped himself down at his desk and blew out his cheeks.

'Bloody traffic,' he complained. 'I got stuck in bloody Streatham High Road for nearly half an hour. It's only six miles to Dulwich. I could have walked it quicker.'

'Did you see the priest?' Jamila asked him.

'Oh, yes. I saw him all right. And he nearly did my head in. Wouldn't stop rabbiting. Talk about using a hundred and ninety-eight words when one would have done it. He was still rabbiting when I was driving away. He's probably still rabbiting now.'

'But did he tell you anything useful?'

Edge took out his voice recorder. 'It's all on here, skipper. But I can give you a summary if you don't feel like sitting through three hours of waffle.'

'Go on, then. Let us hear the summary.'

'The reason he was living in England, this Russian geezer, this Major Kamenev, he'd been a bit of a double agent during the 1950s. You know, James Bond stuff. When his bosses in Moscow got wind of what he'd been up to, he did a bunk and came over here. Even changed his name to Rodney Miller.'

'That's funny,' Jerry put in. 'I knew a Rodney Miller at school. Right plonker too. But he always came top in maths.'

Edge rolled his eyes up impatiently. 'Don't interrupt me, Jer. I don't want to forget any of this. Major Kamenev went to mass at St Thomas More church every Sunday, and he helped out with a lot of their charity activities – you know, fêtes and whist drives and that sort of thing. When this new parish priest came to join the church, he made really good friends with him, partly because he's Polish and he could understand Russian. Don't ask me what his name is, it's got a lot of zeds in it.'

'We can look it up,' said Jamila. 'Carry on.'

'Last Christmas, Major Kamenev found out that he had cancer and his doctor only gave him about six or seven months to live. He went to this Polish priest and made a long confession about things that he'd done during the war. He told him that he'd treated dozens of survivors from the concentration camps, and nursed them back to health, and that after the war he'd stayed in touch with quite a few of them.

'He said that when he died, he wanted the priest to invite any survivors who were still living to come to his funeral. After the funeral, the priest should read out his confession. He thought he had a duty to let them know that he hadn't been any kind of saint. He'd only treated them so well because the Russians had found out that the Nazis had been using some of their prisoners at Auschwitz as guinea pigs for this new kind of chemical. He'd been ordered to find out exactly what this chemical was composed of, and see if he could make some of it himself.

'All he knew about this chemical was that it could totally zonk your brain. It could turn the clock back on your human evolution. A couple of doses and you ended up as thick as your average caveman – or caveperson, I should say, shouldn't I? The Nazis had thought that if they could find a way to spread it around Britain, they'd have a whole nation full of savages who would do whatever they were told.'

'That is incredible,' said Jamila. 'This could well be why Moe Dee and all the rest of them speak that Stone Age language. This opioid that they have been taking – it could be the same chemical that the Nazis invented, or some drug with a similar effect, anyway. They use German words too!'

'Ah, but there's more, skipper,' said Edge. 'The priest told the survivors that Major Kamenev was sorry that he had never told them the truth, but there was something that he hadn't wanted them to find out until he was brown bread. The chemical not only turned you into a caveperson, it had an ingredient a bit like LSD that made you believe in a Stone Age god. I mean, really believe that he was really real. You know, like some nutters think they've really seen Jesus?

'The Nazis had thought it was important for the British people still to have some kind of religion. You know, to keep them in order, even when they were thick as shit. But they hadn't wanted them to go on worshipping the Christian God, because Christians believe that every life is sacred. The Nazis had wanted them to worship a god who told them to top any one of their number who was too ill or too old to work, or who didn't pull their weight, or who caused any kind of aggro. Not only that, this god also expected his worshippers to show them how much they loved him every now and then by killing and eating another human being.

'What Major Kamenev had never told these survivors was that he had followed the Nazi experiments to the letter. He had made all of them do what the Nazis had made them do, and eat human flesh. Not that he had to top anybody. They had a surfeit of dead bodies knocking around in those days.'

'Bloody hell. What was their reaction, these survivors? Did the priest tell you?'

'Are you joking? He only spent about half an hour telling me about it. He said they were devastated. It was like somebody had dropped a bomb on them. The trouble was, they'd all been so grateful to Major Kamenev for saving their lives. Ever since the end of the war, they had believed that the sun shone out of his arse. They all had his photograph stuck up on their walls at home, and whenever they went to the synagogue they all said prayers of thanks to God for sending Major Kamenev to save them.'

'Did the priest have any idea that they had all been murdered?'

'No. But of course we haven't released their names yet, have we, or any details of how they died. He said that after the service they had three minicabs waiting for them outside and that was the last he saw of them.'

'Ubers?'

'He didn't know. But I'll check with Uber and any other cab companies around that area.'

'Yes, do that. We need to know where they all went after that, and how they were all caught and killed.'

'I'm wondering again if it all comes back to them being mourners,' said Jerry. 'Maybe there's something about mourners that these cannibals can *smell*. It's like when Linda and me were walking back to my flat, this homeless bloke suddenly jumped up as if he was sniffing the wind.'

Jamila's laptop pinged.

'That should be the plan of the Duchy Hotel,' she said. 'Now we need to meet with DCI Saunders and work out a plan of attack.'

'Come on, Edge,' said Jerry, zipping up his jacket. 'We'll fill you in on the way.'

'What? Not even time for a cuppa?'

'Not even time to draw breath, mate. Not even time to draw breath.'

31

Once they had found DS Bristow and brought him up to date, they all drove over to Walworth police station to meet up with DCI Saunders. Thirty uniformed officers had been assembled, and after twenty minutes, five officers from the armed response unit arrived, and they could start to discuss how they were going to attack the Duchy Hotel with minimum loss of life.

'There's too many bloody unknowns, that's the trouble,' said Jerry.

'Exactly,' said Jamila. 'From what Moe Dee has told us, there is obviously access to the hotel's cellars through this abandoned Tube tunnel. The problem is that this access does not appear in the plan of the hotel that I have received from the council's planning department. There is no way of telling if it is wide or narrow, or if the squatters have a way of closing it off, or if they keep a twenty-four hour watch on it.'

'That's right,' Jerry added. 'We could send the AFOs charging in there but they could find that they're stuck in the cellar and can't get any further.'

'And this is not like most siege situations,' said DCI Saunders. 'We can't use flashbangs or tear gas. From what this Moe Dee fellow says, they're going to start slaughtering themselves as soon as they realise that we're breaking in. Personally, I couldn't care less, but the publicity would be appalling, and there are one or two innocent individuals among them.'

'Glad you appreciate that, guv,' said Jerry. 'As it happens, I have an idea that might work. Supposing I dress myself up as a squatter and sneak into the hotel sometime tonight when most of this Hedda's mob are spark out. If they really are as thick as cavemen, perhaps they won't realise that I'm not actually one of them. Once I'm inside, I can give you an idea of how many there are and where they're all located.

'If I'm armed, I might be able to stop this Hedda from giving the order for them to kill themselves. And I might be able to rescue my Linda and those Willow boys – always supposing they're still alive.'

DCI Saunders nodded in approval. 'That's not a bad plan, Pardoe. Not a bad plan at all, although I can see a couple of snags. You could run into trouble if the Tube tunnel's somehow blocked off, or if like DS Patel says it's constantly guarded. And if these squatters twig that you're an imposter, I can't say I fancy your chances much. They duffed you up before, didn't they? And of course there's also the risk that they're going to realise that you're the advance party, as it were, and that we're going to be coming in after you. They might start to do themselves in before we can stop them.'

'If anybody knows how to get into the hotel without attracting attention, surely Moe Dee must,' said Jamila. 'If we agree that DC Pardoe should disguise himself as a squatter, then we can go and ask Moe Dee what he thinks his chances are.'

'Like I say, it's not a bad plan, even if it isn't foolproof,' said DCI Saunders. He turned to the armed response officers. 'What do you think, gents?'

'Can't say I'm over-excited about DC Pardoe carrying a

weapon,' said the leading AFO. 'I seem to remember him on the range at Limehouse once. He hit everybody's target except his own.'

'I've had a bit more practice since then,' Jerry retorted. 'Besides, what are you worried about? You're all wearing bulletproof vests.'

Jamila called Professor Walmsley at London University, only to find out that she was already back at St George's, recording more of Moe Dee's Stone Age speech patterns.

When Jamila and Jerry arrived at the hospital, Moe Dee was sitting in an armchair beside his bed with his head tilted back, holding a mug of tea, while Professor Walmsley was busy scribbling notes on a large legal pad.

'You should really have informed us that you were intending to talk to Moe Dee again,' said Jamila sharply.

'I'm sorry, DS Patel. But Dr Seshadri was more than happy to let me come back. He believes that this questioning is excellent therapy. The more Moe Dee talks, the sooner he will be able to converse in proper English again. But before he forgets all his Pre-Indo-European vocabulary, I wanted to record as much of it as I possibly could. You do realise that nobody has heard it spoken since about ten thousand BC?'

Jamila and Jerry sat down. 'Has he told you any more about the squatters in the Duchy Hotel?' asked Jamila.

'Not much. We've mostly been talking about his past life and how he came to be homeless. He's known this woman with two hats for quite a few years – the one who now calls herself Hedda.'

'Baggy Nell,' put in Jerry.

'Yes, that's what he said she used to be called. After work

stopped on the Duchy Hotel, she moved in there with some of her friends and it wasn't long afterwards that he came to join her. That's when she first gave him some of this drink he calls "calla dew".

'More and more homeless people came to live in the hotel, and in the end there were far too many, so Moe Dee and about twenty others moved out to that abandoned school in Peckham. But they were still addicted to calla dew and so they kept in contact with Hedda and paid her the price she asked for every dose.'

'And the price was—?'

'Opfers. Sacrifices. People they snatched off the streets and who were given up as offerings to their god. Hedda had always been a gang leader and now she had set herself up as a kind of high priestess for this god. But you're never supposed to speak his name out loud.'

Jerry said, 'Moe Dee, can you hear me, mate?'

Moe Dee nodded. 'Yesh. I cuh – I can hear you.'

'You see?' said Professor Walmsley. 'His English is already much better. From my point of view it's a pity, because I want to hear so much more of his Pre-Indo-European.'

'I want to get into the Duchy to rescue your friends, Moe Dee. Do you understand me?'

'Yesh. Yesh,' said Moe Dee, and then he growled.

'There's an old Tube tunnel that connects up with the Duchy's cellar. Is it always open? Is it easy to get into?'

Moe Dee spoke very laboriously, half in English and half in Stone Age growling, with Professor Walmsley translating for him. He explained that the hole between the hotel cellar and the unfinished Tube tunnel was never blocked up, and never guarded. Hedda's tribe were confident that nobody would ever find it.

'He says that Hedda's tribe believe the great one will always keep them hidden and keep them safe.'

'The great one being that geezer with the goat's head and the massive stonker?'

'If I understand him correctly, he says that the great one is furious with Hedda and her tribe for taking his people out of the hospital. They had already blinded themselves to show him how sorry they were for failing to bring him any opfers. He didn't expect them to sacrifice their lives as well as their sight.'

'How does he know that the great one's so pissed off?' asked Jerry.

Professor Walmsley had another growling conversation with Moe Dee. Interspersed between the growls, Jamila and Jerry could hear 'call him' and 'bones' and a German word that sounded like '*Fleischwerdung*'.

Professor Walmsley made some more notes, and then she said, 'I'm not sure about this, but I think he told me that he can actually talk to the great one, and that the great one talks back to him. That's how he knows how angry he is.'

'Oh, really?'

'Some evangelists claim that God speaks to them, Jerry,' said Jamila. 'It's no different.'

'The great one has a goat's head, skip. It depends if you can understand goatinese.'

'Moe Dee says that the great one can help you to enter the Duchy Hotel without being noticed. The great one will give you the power to save his people and for you to arrest Hedda and her tribe.'

'So how's he going to do that?'

'He asks if the painting of the great one and the bones that were laid at the great one's feet are still in the tunnel under the carpet factory.'

'Yes,' said Jamila. 'That is still an active crime scene. They have not been disturbed.'

'Good. Because the bones are in a special pattern and he can use that pattern to bring the great one through from the shadow world. That's what he says, anyway.'

'The wheel of time,' said Jamila. 'It is the same pattern that we found on the floor of the Charles Babbage school. Like a Kalachakra mandala.'

'He's jerking our chain,' said Jerry. 'Isn't he? Or isn't he?'

Jamila was silent for a few moments. Then she said to Moe Dee, 'You are talking about bringing Balaa out of the darkness. Is that it?'

Moe Dee jolted in his chair as if somebody had come running across the room and kicked it, and he tipped his mug into his lap. He jumped up, blindly pulling out his hospital gown to stop the hot tea from scalding his thighs.

'Doh – dohn – *don't shpeak – don't shpeak hish name*!'

Jerry stood up and pushed the call button for a nurse. He waited beside Moe Dee, holding his arm to keep him steady, but at the same time he was looking at Jamila.

'Maybe we *should* let him have a shot at bringing this great one to life. Like, why not? You remember that Adeliza Friendship. She wasn't supposed to be real, was she? But there she was.'

'Jerry, we are not talking about some witch. Adeliza Friendship was nothing more than a resonance from another time, even if she did have supernatural power. We are talking about a *god* here. A demon. We are talking about the devil who kept my aunt in thrall for most of her adult life. We are talking about—' Jamila's lips formed the name *Balaa*, but she didn't say it out loud.

'If he's that powerful, skip, perhaps there's an outside

possibility that he can actually help us. I mean, he's well narked at Hedda and her mob, isn't he? I don't really believe that Moe Dee here can bring him to life, but you know me. I'll try anything once, especially if there's a chance that it's going to make life a bit cushtier.'

The ward sister and a nurse came in, followed by Dr Seshadri.

'Is everything all right?' asked Dr Seshadri. 'What is going on here?'

'Slight accident with a hot mug of Rosie Lee, that's all,' said Jerry. 'But maybe you can get Moe Dee here dressed in some street clothes. We need to take him out for a while to give us a hand with our investigation.'

'You want to take him out? I'm not sure I can allow that. He's not in a fit condition.'

'This is critical, doctor,' Jamila told him. 'We will take good care of him. He will have myself and other police officers to protect him, and we will bring him back as soon as we can. But we are hoping that he can help us to find his friends and bring them back here to continue their treatment.'

'I don't see how a blind man can be of any help to you,' said Dr Seshadri.

'For what he's going to be doing for us, doc, he won't need his mincers,' Jerry told him.

'Do I have any choice in the matter?'

'No, quite frankly. We're only asking you because we're really polite.'

They drove back to Walworth police station, taking Moe Dee and Professor Walmsley with them. The nurses had found Moe Dee a thick black roll-neck sweater and a pair of baggy jeans and a duffel coat that he could just about manage to fasten up over his belly.

They held a further briefing with DCI Saunders and the assembled officers, and decided that Jerry should enter the hotel at 0100 hours, when they hoped that most of Hedda's tribe would be asleep. The firearms officers would wait in the Tube tunnel for a signal from Jerry that they could come storming in after him, and the rest of the officers would follow, armed with Tasers and batons and pepper sprays.

Jamila would remain with Moe Dee and Professor Walmsley and three uniformed officers in the tunnel next to the basement of the Royale carpet factory. There, using the wheel of bones, Jamila would help Moe Dee to perform the ritual that would supposedly bring Balaa out of the shadows and into the real world. She was sceptical that he could do it, but she had seen for herself the influence that Balaa had exerted over her aunt, and she had learned during her career as a police officer how dangerous it can be to question other people's beliefs. If Moe Dee thought that he could bring Balaa to life, then by all means let him try. Jamila thought that he might be able to rouse some supernatural power, even if it wasn't Balaa.

A young woman officer came into the briefing room holding up a filthy bronze puffa jacket as if it were a dead dog.

'DC Pardoe?' she said. 'This is for you. I was told you wanted it stinky. Is this stinky enough?'

'Whoa, yes,' said Jerry. 'Where'd you find it? Stuffed down the back of the khazi?'

He took off his leather jacket and shucked on the puffa jacket, raising the hood and then pulling it halfway down over his face.

'How do I look?' he asked the assembled officers.

'A considerable improvement, Pardoe,' said DS Bristow. 'Don't know why you don't wear it all the time.'

They went over their plan again and again. Although Moe Dee couldn't see the hotel layout for himself, he was able to describe the location of the main room where the squatters' victims were nailed to the wall, and where the kitchens were, and which bedrooms were occupied. If anything went wrong, and the squatters started to kill each other, the officers would rush them, force them into separate rooms, and Taser as many as they could.

'I'm looking for the minimum loss of life possible,' said DCI Saunders. 'But if it comes to a choice between you and them, I don't expect you to hesitate. It takes up to three months to train a police officer and it costs twelve thousand nine hundred pounds. It takes no time at all to make somebody homeless and it costs bugger all to look after them. So there's no contest.'

At midnight, they left for the Royale carpet factory, parking all the way along Mountford Place. Inside the building it was dark and dusty and echoing with nearly forty footsteps. As they walked across the factory floor to the basement door, Jerry thought that he could still detect the lingering smell of roasted corpses, but he told himself that it was only his imagination.

They made their way through the basement between the rolls of musty carpet and then stepped into the Tube tunnel. Most of the officers headed past the painting of Balaa and disappeared into the darkness with their flashlights dancing. Three of them remained – two holding Moe Dee between them and the third setting up LED lamps all around the pattern of bones on the tunnel floor.

Jamila was gazing into Balaa's yellow eyes as Jerry came up to her.

'You going to be all right, skip?' he asked her.

'Of course. I very much doubt that our friend here will really come to life.'

'Like you say, though, something or other might pop up, even if it's not—'

He was about to say 'Balaa' but he suddenly realised that Moe Dee was close behind him.

'—chummy here.'

Jamila laid her hand lightly on his shoulder. 'Please be careful, Jerry. These people are extremely dangerous. I know that you are determined to rescue Linda, but I beg you not to take any unnecessary risks.'

'You know me, skip. They don't call me Mr Precautious for nothing.'

He looked at his watch. 'I'd better get going. We can walk down the middle of the main-line tunnel now the trains have stopped running and the power's been switched off, but it's going to take us at least twenty minutes to get there.'

'Jerry,' said Jamila, and her eyes were glistening in the dazzling light from the LED lamps.

'What?' he said. He was sure that she was going to ask him to kiss her.

She sniffed her fingers and said, 'That jacket – it really does smell awful.'

'Oh. Well, I have to make them believe that I'm a genuine homeless person, don't I? I'll catch you later.'

'Make sure that you do, Jerry. I'm holding you to that.'

32

Once Jerry had jogged off to catch up with the rest of the officers, Jamila turned to Moe Dee and said, 'Well? We're ready. Detective Pardoe is on his way to the Duchy Hotel, and he should be there in about twenty minutes to half an hour.'

Moe Dee growled, and Professor Walmsley glanced up at the painting of Balaa with obvious trepidation. 'He's telling us that we should kneel in a circle around these bones.'

They all knelt, even the officers who were guarding Moe Dee. Jamila looked across at them and shrugged, as if to say, *Don't worry, nothing's going to happen – at least I don't think anything's going to happen. We're only doing this to make sure that we've got every option covered.*

Moe Dee started to clap his hands in a complicated rhythm, although so softly that his clapping was barely audible. He swayed from side to side, and sang in a high-pitched growl that was almost falsetto.

'He's calling for his god to wake up and come out of the darkness,' Professor Walmsley translated, in a whisper. 'He calls him "lord of the shadows". He's asking him to come out of the darkness where people live before they enjoy their brief time on Earth, and where they return when that brief time is over.'

Moe Dee went on singing and growling. It was only for

another three or four minutes, but to Jamila it seemed endless, particularly since she was kneeling on several sharp lumps of aggregate.

'Jesus,' said one of the police officers. 'He sounds like my cat when she's on heat.'

Moe Dee let out a piercing shriek, which made them all jump, and slapped his hands together over his head.

'*Greywun!*' he shouted, which Jamila took to mean 'great one!' '*Greywun riiiiise up! Greywun!*' Then he carried on clapping.

Not only did her knees hurt, but Jamila was beginning to feel tight-chested and claustrophobic down here in this tunnel, even though it was so brightly lit, and she was coming to the conclusion that she should call off this whole pointless performance. There was no sign of Balaa making an appearance, or any other kind of supernatural manifestation. Moe Dee had clearly been stringing them along for some reason – either that, or he was certifiably insane.

Jamila was almost prepared to think that she was as mad as he was, kneeling in this abandoned Tube tunnel next to a scattering of human bones, and expecting some Stone Age demon to step out of the shadows.

Moe Dee was still clapping, and now he began to growl deep in the back of his throat, as if he were pretending to be a motorboat.

Jamila said, 'That's it, Moe Dee. This clearly isn't working. I think we should call it a night. What do you think, professor?'

Professor Walmsley said nothing, but stared at her blankly.

'Professor? Tell Moe Dee to stop. Tell him his god has not appeared, so we are going to take him back to the hospital.'

Still Professor Walmsley kept on staring at her. She turned to the three officers, but they were staring at her equally blankly.

She tried to stand up, but her knees refused to unbend and she felt totally paralysed. When she opened her mouth to ask Professor Walmsley and the officers if they felt paralysed too, she found that her lips were numb, and she was unable to speak.

Now Moe Dee was whirling both hands around, as if he were inciting a crowd to riot. He whirled them faster and faster, and gradually the LED lights began to dim. Their brightness shrank away until they looked like nothing more than orange glow-worms, and then they died out altogether and the tunnel was plunged into absolute darkness.

Jamila felt a fear that she had never felt before. She had been threatened when she was a young girl in Pakistan, and scores of times in her police career, but on those occasions she had been able to hit back, or run away. Here, in the utter blackness of this Tube tunnel, she was totally frozen. If anything appeared, she would be unable to escape from it, or fight it off.

Moe Dee suddenly stopped singing and growling and clapping his hands. The only sound that Jamila could hear now was the faint draught blowing through the tunnel. Because it was a Sunday night there were no Tube trains running, and because the tunnel was so deep underground she could hear no traffic. Neither she nor Professor Walmsley nor the three officers could speak to each other.

Several minutes went past. Jamila closed her eyes and tried to calm herself, even though she was having trouble breathing. After a while she heard a sound like a heavy blanket being dragged slowly across the aggregate, and then rattling over the bones. As it came closer, she thought she could hear somebody inhaling and exhaling, but with a creaking noise, like an old pair of leather bellows.

She opened her eyes. The tunnel was still overwhelmed in darkness, but she could see a pair of yellow eyes about three metres from the floor. They had rectangular slit pupils, like a goat.

She couldn't move. She couldn't cry out. All she could do was watch as the eyes came nearer, and seemed to hang suspended in the darkness right above her, with their pupils occasionally swivelling from side to side.

She heard a crunch, and for a few seconds the eyes were obscured. She realised that one of them must have stood up, probably Moe Dee. The next thing she heard was feet walking away down the tunnel, with that blanket-dragging sound following after them.

At least ten minutes passed. Then, gradually, she began to feel her knees again, and as sensation returned to her legs and then her arms and at last her lips, the LED lights brightened and the tunnel was lit up.

Jamila stared at Professor Walmsley and the three officers. They all looked as shocked as she was. Moe Dee had gone.

'Don't tell me he fucking did it,' said one of the officers.

'If he did not, then tell me what those eyes were,' Jamila retorted, trying to keep her voice from shaking. 'You must have seen those eyes, and heard that sound like somebody walking right past us.'

She looked up at the painting of Balaa. That was still there, leering down from the tunnel wall. It was not the painting that had come to life. But *something* had come out of the shadows, something that breathed and made a dragging noise, and that something had gleaming yellow eyes like Balaa.

Jamila stood up and switched on her r/t so that she could tell Jerry what had happened. She also wanted to warn him that Moe Dee and this yellow-eyed creature had set off in his direction. Perhaps they weren't following him. Perhaps they simply intended to escape down one of the myriad Tube tunnels and disappear for good. Jerry still needed to be alerted.

Her r/t crackled and hissed but she was unable to get a signal. The three officers tried their radios, but they couldn't get a signal either.

'Right,' said Jamila. 'One of you needs to go back up and advise DCI Saunders that Moe Dee has managed to raise some kind of spirit or another, and that they have both got away. Moe Dee is blind, of course, but the spirit must be guiding him.'

'Smiley's going to think we've gone doolally,' said one of the officers.

'It does not matter what he thinks. You saw those yellow eyes for yourself, and you can tell him that.'

'What are you going to do, skipper?' asked another officer.

'Me? I am going after Moe Dee, and I want two of you to come with me. Professor – you should leave us now and I will contact you later. Please do not mention what you have seen here to anybody – not to any of your colleagues and above all not to the media.'

'But if that *is* Balaa – could be highly risky, couldn't it, going after him?'

'If it *is* him, yes. It could be the most dangerous thing that I have ever done. But I was trained to wait until the danger was all over before I asked myself questions like that.'

Jamila and the two officers hurried along the tunnel until they reached the blockage where Jerry had found PC Bone's hand. They scrambled up the heap of crumbled clay soil and aggregate and dropped down into the main Northern Line Underground tunnel.

The officers shone their flashlights left and right, along the shining rails, but there was no sign of Moe Dee in either direction.

'If he went south, then he will be no threat to DC Pardoe or the rest of the team,' said Jamila. 'If he went north, though, they need to be warned. So let us go north.'

They ran along the tracks with an odd side-to-side gait so that they would avoid tripping over the sleepers or the white ceramic pots that held up the third rail. It took them over ten minutes to reach the junction with the abandoned tunnel that led off toward the Duchy Hotel, by which time all three of them were out of breath and beginning to stumble. Jamila had thought about shouting out a warning to Jerry, but then she decided that it would alert Moe Dee that they were following.

They had only run about two hundred metres into the abandoned tunnel when Jamila found that her feet were feeling numb and that her lungs were filling up, almost as if she were suffering from pneumonia. One of the officers behind her started to cough, and the other one gasped out, 'Christ, I can't breathe.' Although this tunnel had no sleepers or rails to impede them, they slowed down and stopped, and then sank down to their knees. Jamila wanted to tell the officers to shine their flashlights as far up ahead as they could, but her lips and her tongue were paralysed, as they had been before. All she could do was kneel there, squeaking for breath.

There was nothing up ahead but total blackness – not even the flashlights of the armed response team and all the other officers who were supposed to be backing up Jerry, even though there were so many of them. The tunnel had only the slightest curve to it, so she couldn't imagine how she was unable to see them.

Her head was throbbing and she was feeling close to collapse, and so she leaned her shoulder against the tunnel wall. For no more than a split second, she was sure that she saw the two yellow goat's eyes turning around to stare back at her out of the darkness, but then they were gone.

Jerry, she said silently, inside her head. *Jerry, please do not let it get you, whatever it is.*

33

It was less than fifteen minutes earlier that Jerry had arrived at the hole that was broken through from the Tube tunnel into the cellars of the Duchy Hotel.

Neither he nor the thirty officers lined up behind him said a word, although their boots shuffled and their black protective vests all rustled against each other. They had only three dim flashlights switched on and now they kept them pointed downwards to the tunnel floor, so that even if there was anybody keeping watch inside the cellars, they wouldn't be seen.

Jerry had a small penlight himself, taped inside his sleeve. Apart from that, and his radio transmitter, he was carrying a Sig-Sauer P238 in the right-hand pocket of his jacket, a small compact automatic that weighed only fifteen ounces but which could fire six .38 bullets in quick succession.

His left-hand pocket was crammed with three cans of Carlsberg Special Brew, to give him the authentic homeless look.

He gave the leading AFO the thumbs up, and then he clambered over the broken bricks into the cellars. The first cellar was small, only about two metres square, with a door in it, and he realised that it must have been a cupboard. He pressed his ear against the door, but he could hear no voices or footsteps, so he carefully eased it open. He found himself in the main cellar, and a quick flick around with his penlight showed him that there were concrete steps on the opposite side, which had to lead up to the hotel itself. An assortment of junk was heaped up around the cellar walls – old bedsteads, a bicycle with only one wheel, aluminium beer kegs, a broken lamp, and a reception desk with a jagged hole in the front, as if somebody had kicked it in a temper.

On the left side of the cellar there was a brick archway, dangling with cobwebs, and when he shone his penlight through it, Jerry could see a large cast-iron boiler, rusted and covered in dust. On the far side of the boiler, the wall had partially collapsed, and there was nothing beyond it but a dark void.

He was about to cross the cellar when he heard a door opening, and voices, and somebody starting to come down the steps. Although he was reasonably confident that he could pass himself off as a squatter, they might ask what he was doing down here all alone, and lift his hood to take a look at his face, and realise that he wasn't really one of them. He hurriedly tiptoed over to the damaged reception desk and crouched down behind it, although he could still see most of the cellar through the hole in the front of it.

Two people came down the staircase, a man and a woman. The man was carrying a paraffin lamp, so that the cellar was lit up with a swivelling light. He was middle-aged, grey-haired, in a ripped green sweater and baggy jeans. The woman was brunette, with a frayed tartan overcoat hung loosely over her shoulders. She was carrying a green plastic shopping basket that looked as if it had been lifted from a supermarket.

As the man put his arm round the woman's waist to guide her toward the archway, he pulled her coat back, and Jerry could see that underneath it she was wearing a dark blue velvet dress. It was split all the way up to her hip, and he caught a flash of bare thigh.

She turned to say something to the man, and Jerry saw that she was Linda.

For an instant, he was tempted to spring to his feet and shout out to her, but then he thought, hold on, she's probably just playing along with this bloke to keep herself safe, and if I let him know that I'm here, he's going to warn all the rest of the squatters and this whole bloody plan's going to go tits up.

He heard the man growl something to the woman, and he saw Linda lift the basket and growl something back.

He felt a cold sensation sliding down his back. *Linda's growling like him, for Christ's sake.* They must have given her some of that opioid, that 'calla dew' or whatever Moe Dee called it. She's not playing along. She's been drugged. Shit. That's going to make it ten times more difficult to get her out of here.

Jerry stayed where he was, squatting down behind the reception desk. He saw Linda and the man go through the archway together and then step through the broken wall beyond it. There, the man's lamp illuminated what looked like a tall black metal pillar, crusted with rust. The pillar had a rectangular opening in its side, and hanging out of the opening Jerry could see fluffy yellow lagging, like the insulation that plumbers wrap around hot-water pipes.

The man growled to Linda again, and then he started to tear back the lagging and slide out long glass phials with shining amber liquid inside. He placed each one of the phials carefully into Linda's shopping basket, at least twenty of them, until the basket was half full. Then he growled again, and Linda growled something back to him, and the two of them climbed back into the boiler room.

Jerry tried to get a good look at Linda as she crossed the cellar floor. She was staring straight ahead, with no expression on her face at all, one hand holding the basket and the other clutching the collar of her coat to stop it from slipping off her shoulders. He had never seen her so emotionless, ever. Usually, she was laughing or crying or smiling or frowning. As she made her way to the cellar steps her eyes were unblinking and blank, as if she had been concussed.

He waited until he had heard the two of them reach the top of the steps and close the door behind them. Then he switched on his r/t and told the leading armed officer that he had been delayed in the cellars for a few minutes, but he was now going to make his way up into the hotel.

'Roger, Squat,' replied the AFO. Jerry had thought the operational nickname was funny when he had first thought of it, but now he was beginning to wish that he had called himself something more serious.

Before he climbed up the steps, he went through the archway and shone his penlight at the rusty black pillar. He couldn't work out what it was. It rose from floor to ceiling, tilted at a slight angle, like a leaning tower of Pisa made of corroded metal. A curved piece of steel was lying on the floor next to it, and that must have covered the opening before somebody prised it off.

He climbed through the broken wall to examine the pillar more closely. He wished he had a more powerful flashlight, but he could see that the interior of the pillar was completely stuffed with yellow asbestos lagging. When he reached inside, he could feel that the lagging was thickly wrapped around countless glass phials of amber liquid. Whole wads of asbestos had been ripped apart, so dozens of phials had already been removed, but he guessed that there must still be hundreds in there, maybe thousands.

He took two steps back and shone his penlight upwards. The ceiling was partly brick and partly compacted mud, but now he realised what the pillar actually was. It had four fins at the top, mostly buried in the mud but still visible. It was a bomb. It was massive, and Jerry guessed that it weighed at least two and a half tons. Judging by how corroded it was, it must have been dropped during the Blitz on London in the Second World War. It had penetrated the cellar but, like so many other unexploded bombs, its impact had thrown up a geyser of rubble and debris and mud that had swallowed it up.

Not that *this* huge bomb had ever been intended to explode. Jerry stared up at its fins and slowly shook his head. As bizarre as this investigation had been from the beginning, he couldn't believe how its logic was now fitting together. They had learned from the late Soviet major that the Nazis had experimented on concentration camp prisoners to create a drug that would reduce the IQ of anybody who took it to the level of a Stone Age cave dweller. And here this drug actually was. It looked certain that the Nazis had managed to perfect it, and manufacture it, and drop it on London during an air raid.

He couldn't think how they had expected to spread the drug around, but they must have had some plan. Maybe they had expected bomb disposal officers to open up the bomb and try the drug and then share it with anybody with whom they came into contact.

In any case, it was likely that Baggy Nell or Hedda or whatever she called herself had found the bomb when she took over the hotel, and drunk the calla dew, and given it to all her homeless friends to drink. Seventy-five years after the war, she had created what the Nazis had tried to create, but failed – a tribe of subservient cannibals.

Jerry switched on his r/t again, so that he could pass on to DCI Saunders what he had found, but all he heard was a steady hissing noise, interspersed with a thick, intermittent crackle. He switched it off and on again, but he was still unable to get through. Maybe the signal was being blocked by the walls of the cellar. He just prayed that he would be able to make contact once he had gone upstairs to mingle with the squatters.

He climbed the steps and opened the door that led to the hotel reception area with its rumpled blue carpet. He could hear singing and laughing coming from an open door on the opposite side of the reception area, as well as a clattering sound. Tugging his hood even further down over his face, and hunching his shoulders, he crossed over to the door and quickly glanced inside. He saw that it was a large kitchen, and although it was so late, it was still crowded, so he ducked back almost immediately in case anybody saw him.

He need not have worried, because everybody in the kitchen was too busy drinking and growling and tearing flesh from the heap of charred meat that was lying on the table in front of them. He waited for a few seconds and then he looked again. The kitchen was like a Breughel painting of some unholy bacchanalia. It was lit all around by scores of flickering candles, and the doors of its six ovens were all wide open. Every oven was filled up with white-hot charcoal briquettes, with human arms and legs and ribcages sizzling inside them. In one oven Jerry could see three heads, their hair burned off and their faces blackened, grinning as if this was the most hilarious thing that had ever happened to them.

The heat was intense. It was so hot that most of the squatters had taken off their jackets and their sweaters and dropped them onto the floor. Several of the men had stripped to the waist, and two of the women too. Their skin was dead white and grubby and melted fat was smothering their chins and sliding in runnels down their chests.

At the head of the table, Jerry saw Baggy Nell, or Hedda, with her two hats, although she had kept her coat on and her shawl wrapped around her shoulders. Sitting on her left was curly-headed John, in his red-striped pyjamas, with a one-eyed girl close beside him, wearing nothing but a dirty sleeveless vest. Sitting on her right was the grey-haired man who had been down in the cellars, and Jerry could see now that he had an S-shaped broken nose. Next to him sat Linda. She had shaken off her tartan coat and now she was sitting with both elbows on the table, gnawing at a human clavicle, her eyes closed as if this was the most delicious thing she had ever eaten.

Jerry noticed that there was no sign of Edward, even down the far end of the table.

The singing and the growling was almost deafening, but suddenly John climbed up onto his chair, waving a half-chewed rib in one hand, and shrilled something at the top of his voice, and when he did everybody stopped singing to listen. Jerry couldn't understand a word of what he was screaming, but when he had finished, and sat down, the whole company roared out approval, and banged the table with their fists, so that a whole roasted swede rolled onto the floor.

Jerry was still watching the feasting when a fat bearded squatter pushed past him into the kitchen, growling what sounded like an apology. Jerry raised one hand and grunted back.

Now was the time for him to take a look around the rest of the hotel. He counted thirty or forty of Hedda's tribe in the kitchen. He needed to see how many more were squatting upstairs, and whether they were asleep or awake. He tried again to get a signal on his r/t but again he heard nothing but hissing. Once he had assessed how many squatters in total the police team were up against, and where they were all located, it looked as if he would have to go back down to the Tube tunnel to brief them in person.

He started to mount the stairs from the reception area to the first floor. When he was only halfway up, another two bulky squatters in anoraks came hurrying down. They were growling through their beards to each other, and they growled at him as they passed him. Again, he gave a grunt in reply, and hoped that he wasn't saying something in Stone Age language that would give him away, but the staircase was so dark he doubted if they would have recognised that he was a stranger.

When he reached the landing, he began to hear groaning, and then a desperate, tremulous wailing, like cats in pain. The groaning and wailing grew louder as he made his way along the corridor. Ahead of him he could see an open door and a large dimly lit room. There were other rooms on either side of the corridor, most with their doors closed, but three of them had been left ajar, and inside he could make out squatters lying on mattresses and folded blankets, all asleep. He tried to do a body count, but the rooms were so dark that it was almost impossible to tell how many squatters were huddled inside them.

In contrast to the furnace-like kitchen, this upstairs corridor was numbingly cold, and instead of roasting flesh it smelled strongly of sour perspiration and dried urine and stale tobacco. Jerry thought that Stone Age cave dwellers would not have smoked, but God knew how many packets of cigarettes these squatters must be getting through every day.

The groaning and wailing kept on and on, and when he entered the large room at the end of the corridor, he stopped dead. He could hardly believe what he was seeing.

The room was lit by only three or four guttering night lights, which were lined up on the floor underneath a painting of the goat-headed demon with the yellow eyes. All around the remaining three walls, and on the floor, naked men were nailed with their arms held out wide. Some were painfully thin, some were paunchy, most of them were badly bruised. There must have been around twenty of them altogether, although five of them had already been butchered – their heads sawn off, their ribs levered away and all their hearts and lungs and intestines emptied out. There was nothing left of them nailed to the wall but their arms and their spines and their pelvises, with a few ragged strips of red flesh hanging off them.

The men who had yet to be cut apart were all blind, with empty eye sockets. Jerry recognised one or two of them as Moe Dee's men, who had been abducted from St George's Hospital.

He stepped slowly into the centre of the room. He could see that more than half of the men were either unconscious or dead, their heads hanging down and faeces sliding down the wall between their legs. Being blind, though, the few who were still alive and conscious seemed to be unaware that he had come into the room, and they carried on moaning and wailing. Even if they had sensed his presence, they would have assumed that he was another one of Hedda's tribe, and that would have only added to their desperation. They would have thought it was their turn next to be dismembered.

Jerry tried his r/t once more, but now it was completely dead. He saw that there were several tools lying on the floor beside the night lights, two saws and a crowbar and a claw hammer, as well as a scattering of bloodstained scalpels. For a moment he thought that he ought to start going around the room, pulling all the nails out of all these men's hands and elbows and knees, but he quickly realised that would take far too long, and one of Hedda's tribe could come in at any moment and catch him at it. Apart from that, the men would drop down heavily onto the floor, and that could easily make their conditions worse. What they needed was experienced paramedics, and urgently.

He turned toward the window, to check if any of the men who were nailed to the floor were still alive. That end of the room was partly in shadow, behind the open door, and it was only when he stepped nearer to the window that he saw Edward, lying next to the wall.

'Bloody hell, Edward,' he breathed, and knelt down beside him to see if he was breathing. Edward's bare skin was chilly and his face was white, but when Jerry pressed his fingertips against his neck he could feel his pulse. He stood up immediately and went back to pick up the claw hammer. He could give Edward CPR but the best option was to get him out of here.

As carefully as he could, he eased out the nails that were pinning Edward to the floor, even though he heard his left kneecap crunch as the head of the hammer pressed against it. Once the last nail was out, he dropped the hammer and picked Edward up, hoisting him over his shoulder in a fireman's lift, with his arms hanging down his back. All this time, the groaning and wailing around the room had continued, and he was sure that the man lying next to Edward had let out a death rattle in the back of his throat.

'Let's go and fetch your brother, and my Linda, and get the hell out of here,' said Jerry, under his breath. He jogged along the corridor, ignoring the open doors and the sleeping squatters inside. Now that he had seen what Hedda's tribe had done to Moe Dee's men, his idea about storming the hotel had completely changed. Sod Smiley's instruction about causing 'the minimum loss of life possible'. These people were primitive-minded, sadistic, homicidal maniacs, even if their brains had been twisted by some eighty-year-old Nazi drug.

He carried Edward down the stairs to the reception area and laid him gently on the carpet, close to the doorway that led to the cellars. Edward shivered and let out a whisper, but he didn't open his eyes. He needed warming up and medical attention, and quickly.

The laughter and singing from the kitchen was even louder than it had been before. Jerry reached into his pocket for his automatic pistol, thumbed off the safety catch, and then walked in. He kept his head down and swaggered from side to side as he walked, as if he were slightly drunk. Although he was the only one in the kitchen who was still wearing an outdoor coat, apart from Hedda, nobody took any notice of him. They were all too busy eating and drinking and singing this weird warbling song. He glimpsed one man cramming a handful of slimy brains into his mouth, and spluttering some of them out through his fingers as he tried to join in the chorus at the same time.

Jerry went past the open ovens and around the head of the table. When he reached Linda, he laid his hand on her shoulder and she turned to look up at him.

'Linda,' he said, keeping his voice down, but bending close to her ear so that she could hear him. 'We're getting out of here, now.'

Linda stared at him blankly. He could tell that she didn't recognise him, and that she hadn't been able to understand what he had said to her.

'Come on, girl, we're going,' he told her, and he thrust his hands forcibly under her armpits and lifted her up off her chair. She stood up, confused, still not realising who he was, and her chair tipped backwards and clattered onto the floor. Hedda and John and the man with the S-shaped nose looked around, and Hedda let out a snarl that sounded to Jerry like 'what's going on?' It was clear that even she didn't realise immediately that Jerry wasn't one of her tribe, even though she must have seen that he was clean-shaven.

John said something too, in his puppy-bark. It sounded like '*Muh-muh!*' Once Jerry had pushed Linda in the direction of the door, he reached around behind Hedda's back and grabbed the sleeve of John's pyjamas.

'Come along, mate, you're coming too. Enough of this cannibal malarkey.'

John tried to pull his arm out of his sleeve, but Jerry dragged him off his chair. Giving Linda another hard shove, he shouted, '*Go!* Do you hear me? We're getting out of here, *now!*'

The man with the S-shaped nose let out a harsh, angry roar, and stood up. Everybody in the kitchen stopped singing and stared at the struggle at the head of the table in bewilderment. Jerry pushed Linda again, and she stumbled past the open ovens toward the door. As much as anything else, he was relying on the squatters' bovine Stone Age mentality, and their unquestioning obedience. He reckoned that if he shouted loudly enough, and with enough authority, he might be able to drag Linda and John out of the kitchen before the squatters understood that he was not one of them, after all.

But the man with the S-shaped nose was obviously quicker on the uptake than all the rest. He reached across the bone-strewn table and picked up a long carving knife. He roared again, even louder, and even more harshly, and he came stalking toward Jerry with the knife held up.

Jerry stopped, although he didn't release his grip on John's sleeve. John tried to kick his ankles with his laceless trainers, but Jerry gave him a hard sideways kick back.

The man with the S-shaped nose gave a low, threatening growl, and spun the knife around and around, as if he were threatening to cut Jerry's stomach open. Jerry was surging with adrenaline, but he couldn't help thinking of the scene in *Indiana Jones* in which an Arabic swordsman threatens Indy with a display of elaborate swordsmanship but Indy simply shoots him.

He tugged his automatic out of his jacket pocket, pointed it at the man's chest, and fired twice. The two loud bangs made his ears sing, and the man stared back at him in stupefaction. For almost three heartbeats, Jerry thought that the shots were going to have no effect at all, but then the carving knife slipped out of the man's fingers, and he pitched sideways into the table before falling on his back onto the floor, with a shower of half-eaten bones and burned vegetables dropping down on top of him.

Hedda screamed out, '*Stammer!*' and a bulky bald man with a beard climbed up onto his chair and started to walk across the top of the table toward Jerry, kicking meat and cabbages out of his way. Jerry gave John a hard shake to stop him from struggling, and then fired two shots at this man too. He hit him once in the chest and once in the groin, and the man dipped and bowed as if he were performing a *saludo* from a folk dance and then rolled off the table into the laps of two bare-breasted women who were sitting on the opposite side.

John started to fling himself from side to side and screech at Jerry in defiance, but Jerry thrust his automatic back into his pocket and slapped him hard across the face, twice. Then he turned around again and gave Linda another shove. She had been standing behind him, completely confused, not knowing who he was or why he was trying to force her out of the door.

John was crying now. Hedda let out another scream and started to march toward Jerry, her face distorted with rage. He pulled out his automatic again, and pointed it at her, and shouted, 'Freeze! Do you hear me? *Freeze!* I don't want to shoot you but I will!'

She ignored him, and continued to storm closer, roughly pushing her bemused fellow squatters out of her way, the brims of her two hats flapping up and down like the wings of some predatory raven.

Jerry squeezed the trigger of his automatic but it simply clicked. He squeezed it again, but it had jammed. Hedda crossed over to the ovens, picked up a coal shovel, and pushed it with a sharp crunch into one of the open oven doors. She shovelled out a glowing heap of charcoal briquettes and then she faced Jerry again, holding them up in front of her with both hands. The air wavered above the white-hot briquettes so that her doll-like features appeared to be melting.

She shuffled closer and closer. Jerry backed away, but then he bumped into Linda, who was still standing in the doorway, uncertain what to do.

Hedda waved the shovel threateningly up and down, and

hissed some words that Jerry was sure were an out-and-out ultimatum. *Let the boy go or I'll throw these all over you.*

'Back off, Baggy Nell!' Jerry snapped at her. 'This is all finished! Do you understand what I'm saying? This is the end of it, all this Stone Age crap!'

Hedda continued to edge closer. Although she was too far away for Jerry to be able to kick the shovel out of her hands, he could actually feel the heat radiating from it. John had stopped crying but he was whimpering and snivelling now, and Jerry guessed that he was even more apprehensive than he himself.

'I told you to back off!' he repeated. 'This is all going nowhere at all! You're only making things worse for yourself! How long do you think you're going to be spending in Bronzefield nick after this?'

Hedda started to swing the shovel slowly to the left, keeping it level, but it was clear that she fully intended to hurl the shimmering charcoal at him.

'*Balaa!*' she hissed at him. '*Balaa!*'

It was the name of the demon that inspired Jerry to do what he did next. If Hedda saw herself as the avenging representative of Balaa, the great one, then there was a chance that she would fear what Balaa feared, just as much. And why had DC Malik's hamsa necklace been torn off his body by whoever had smashed him to death? Nothing else had been taken from him, only that.

Jerry fumbled inside his jacket and yanked out the silver hamsa necklace, with its orange garnet and its upraised fingers. He held it up in front of Hedda and said again, 'Back off, do you hear me? Balaa can't touch me and if you're his slag then neither can you! Back off, Baggy Nell! You hear me?'

He could hear that his voice sounded shaky and strained,

as if he had a bad cold. He had no idea if the hamsa could really ward off an evil spirit like Balaa. But in the other cases that he and Jamila had worked on together, he had witnessed supernatural powers so extraordinary that he was prepared to put his faith in it. Nairiti had believed in the hamsa, after all, enough to make a special point of giving it to him for his protection.

Hedda's reaction shocked even him. As soon as he lifted the hamsa up so that she could see it, she gave out an eerie, hollow howl, like wind blowing down a chimney. She staggered two or three steps backwards, and threw up both hands so that she flung the shovelful of charcoal briquettes straight into her own face, and scattered them all over her shawl and down the front of her coat. They were glowing only red now, rather than white, but they were still hot enough for her face to crackle and her shawl and her coat to catch fire.

She spun around and around, howling and blazing, still swinging the shovel so that it banged against the ovens. The squatters all around the table shrank away from her in horror, almost falling over themselves, none of them thinking to throw a coat over her to stifle the flames. Some of them stared wide-eyed at Jerry, and he could see that he had terrified them even more than Hedda.

'Hed-dah!' wailed John, but now Hedda had collapsed in front of the ovens, and was lying face down, her coat smouldering, her boots twitching as if she were having a nightmare about running.

'Right, let's get the hell out of here,' said Jerry. 'Linda! Don't just stand there! Let's go!'

Linda seemed to understand him now, because she went out through the kitchen door. John said, '*Muh-muh?*' and followed her without any further kicking or struggling. As he stepped out into the reception area, John saw Edward lying on the floor, naked, his eyes still closed, his hands and his elbows and knees marked with stigmata. He looked up at Jerry as if he recognised Edward for some reason, but couldn't think why.

They were crossing the reception area toward the door that led to the cellar when every candle in the kitchen was abruptly snuffed out, and even the faint light from the first-floor landing was swallowed up in darkness.

Now the only illumination in the reception area came from the kitchen door, where the ovens were still open. There was a brief flicker of flames from Hedda's coat, and then even that died out.

Jerry ushered Linda and John toward the cellar door, and bent down to pick up Edward. As he stood up, though, heaving Edward over his shoulder, the cellar door burst open with a splintering crash. It was ripped with a piercing squeal clear off its hinges and cartwheeled across to the other side of the reception area, where it clattered flat onto the floor.

Out of the door, barely visible in the gloom, Mody came shuffling out, with his bandage over his eyes. Two hands with clawlike fingernails were resting on his shoulders to guide him, and behind him, in the blackness of the cellar, two yellow eyes were shining, with the horizontal pupils of a goat.

34

'Hedda!' shouted Mody. 'Where are you, Hedda, you bitch? I've fetched someone to see you!'

He groped his way toward the middle of the reception area, steered by Balaa. Jerry pushed Linda and John flat against the wall and gently lowered Edward to lie down with his back against the skirting board.

Linda made a soft growling sound but Jerry pressed his hand over her mouth and whispered, '*Sshh!*' John sniffled but said nothing.

Jerry could make out nothing but Balaa's eyes and the curved gleam of his goat's horns and his hands on Mody's shoulders. His body was invisible, darker than the shadows from which Mody had summoned him. He could hear him breathing though – that steady, leathery rasping sound, punctuated with an occasional wet click as if he were licking his lips.

'Hedda!' Mody repeated. He was speaking in fluent English now, although his voice was very rough. 'Where are my people, Hedda? What have you done with my people? I've fetched the great one to see you! He's *angry*, Hedda! My people are *his* people, as well as mine! *He* decides what their fate is going to be, not you!'

Jerry heard soft, frantic growling coming from the kitchen, and Mody must have heard it too, because he started to make his way toward the kitchen door, with the tall dark shape of Balaa close behind him. When they entered the kitchen, Jerry heard desperate shouts from the men and screams from the women.

He thought of picking up Edward again and making a run for the cellar, but Balaa was standing in the kitchen doorway, and kept swivelling his goat's eyes around. He didn't know what Balaa would do if he caught sight of them, but he didn't want to find out. He had seen enough gruesome butchery for one day.

'Where are my people?' Mody demanded. 'Have you been eating my people? Where are they? Where's Hedda? *What?* What – she's *what?*'

There was a heavy thump, which sounded as if the table had been turned over, and more screams, but then abruptly the screams were silenced, and there was no sound out of the kitchen at all. After a minute or two, Mody reappeared in the kitchen door, with Balaa behind him. He made his way over to the staircase, but he had only mounted the first stair when he stopped. Balaa was sniffing like a bloodhound, and his eyes were flicking around the reception area as if he could sense that there was somebody hiding in the darkness.

Linda sucked in her breath and John let out a tiny squeak. Jerry said nothing, but he could see that Balaa was staring at them through the gloom. Mody had to wait where he was, with one foot on the stair, because Balaa was gripping his shoulders and holding him fast. Apart from that, he must have been able to sense that the demon's attention was fixed on somebody or something in the shadows.

'Who's there?' said Mody. 'Is there somebody there?'

Jerry didn't answer, but slowly lifted out his hamsa necklace again. He held it up high and angled it slightly toward the kitchen doorway so that Balaa would be able to see its silver fingers reflected in the darkness.

There was a long, aching silence. Balaa's yellow eyes didn't blink, although his horizontal pupils appeared to narrow until they were nothing more than black slits.

Jesus. It worked for Baggy Nell. Please let it work for you. I don't know what the hell you are but if you expect people to pull their eyes out when they let you down, and eat each other to show you how much they love you, then believe me I don't want to know.

Mody stepped down from the stair, and it must have been because Balaa was pulling him back. Oh God, he's coming over here, thought Jerry, and he started slowly to bend his knees so that he could pick up Edward and try to make a run through the cellar door. His knees, though, felt stiff and arthritic, and he couldn't manage more than a crouch. His elbows too felt as if they were locked, but he managed to keep the hamsa raised.

He tried to warn Linda and John to stay completely still and silent, but his lips were numb.

Balaa seemed to be wary, tilting his horns to one side and then the other, as if he couldn't make up his mind whether to come over and attack them or leave them alone. Maybe he could sense that Jerry wasn't one of his own worshippers, one of Hedda's or Mody's tribe, but then again maybe he couldn't.

'Who's there?' Mody repeated. 'Where are my people? What have you done with them?'

He took a step toward them, but then Jerry suddenly heard that groaning and wailing from upstairs. Balaa twisted around, and let out a deep grumbling sound, followed by a keenly whistling exhalation of breath. Mody started to scramble blindly up the staircase, on all fours, like an excited dog, with Balaa flowing up behind him, darker than the darkest shadow, so that when Mody reached the first-floor landing he was swallowed up into the blackness.

As Mody and Balaa rushed away along the upstairs corridor, Jerry felt a tingling sensation in his knees and his elbows, and that he could bend them again, and that his lips were no longer paralysed.

'Right – let's go!' he said, hoisting Edward up over his shoulder again.

He took a step toward the cellar doorway, but as he did so Linda snarled and pushed against him, and with Edward hanging over his shoulder he almost lost his balance and fell over. John barked at him too, and pulled at his trouser leg.

'What the *fuck* are you doing?' he yelled at them. 'We have to get out of here! Didn't you see that fucking great shadow? That's a demon, or a devil, or whatever you want to call it! It's Balaa, and he'll kill us if he catches us, and he'll probably fucking eat us too!'

Even in the gloom, Jerry could see both Linda and John clamping their hands over their ears. *Balaa!* He had spoken the name of the great one out loud, and that was blasphemy!

At that moment, he heard a shout that was louder than almost anything he had ever heard in his life, except for a sonic boom. He could guess what it was. Balaa had reached the end room, where his own image was painted on the wall, and he had discovered Mody's tribe nailed around the walls, and onto the floor. He heard Mody cry out too, but that was a cry of terrible grief, rather than cataclysmic fury.

He heard more shouts, and then doors slamming and feet running. The squatters in the Duchy's bedrooms must have woken up and were trying to escape. Before any of them could reach the staircase, though, the entire hotel was shaken by a devastating tremor, like an earthquake.

'Come on – we have to go!' shouted Jerry, grabbing Linda's arm with his free left hand and trying to push her toward the cellar doorway.

But then the hotel was shaken again, and this time it felt as if a high-explosive bomb had detonated on the upper floors, where Balaa was raging. The kitchen ceiling collapsed, and it must have crushed everybody in there, while a swarm of orange sparks flew up from the ovens. Next, the staircase dropped away from its moorings and crashed to the ground. There was a wrenching noise that resonated through Jerry's jaw like having his wisdom teeth pulled out, followed by a thunderous bellow as the entire first-floor landing tilted sideways and then came lurching down.

Balaa shouted again, ranting on and on, one sonic boom after another, and Jerry could almost understand what he was shouting. *This is my punishment! This is my revenge! I am the master of the shadows and nobody can use my authority to satisfy their own greed and their own lust for power! No man, no woman, no matter what century they come from!*

I brought you out of the shadows when you were born! I granted you light and life! Now I can send you all back to the shadows, where you belong! You are the shadow people!

There was an ominous splitting sound, and a wide crack snaked its way from one side of the ceiling above Jerry's head to the other. The chandelier dropped down onto the floor and smashed, and the glass glittered even in the darkness.

Linda was still standing in front of him with both hands raised as if she wanted to stay here and sacrifice her life. John seemed much less certain now, although he kept waving his right hand up and down and twiddling his fingers and letting out little yaps.

'What the hell are you doing? Let's *go!*'

John looked up at him and screamed, '*Sowber Sek! Sowber Sek!*'

There was another loud split, and a huge triangular lump of plaster fell from the ceiling onto the reception desk. It must have weighed a third of a ton.

Jerry tried to shoulder Linda toward the cellar doorway but she still resisted, staring at him as if she were mad.

'*Go!*' he shouted, almost hysterical. 'This isn't the Third Fucking Reich! We don't all have to die here along with the Führer!'

He heard the second and third floors collapsing, one on top of the other. It sounded like an avalanche. In a matter of minutes, the entire Duchy Hotel would be reduced to a demolition site of concrete, timber, bricks and dead bodies.

He lifted Edward as high as he could, ready to hurl him bodily into the cellar doorway. Then he could seize Linda and John and force them through the doorway too. Before he could throw him, though, bright flashlights appeared, criss-crossing up the cellar steps.

'Jerry! Jerry, is that you?'

Jamila came panting through the doorway, holding a torch. The leading armed officer was close behind her, followed by the rest of the armed unit.

'*Hey bhagwan!*' she said, as more of the ceiling came thundering down, and her torch lit up clouds of swirling plaster dust. 'What's happening?'

'We need to be somewhere else fast, that's all! Take Linda, will you? She's still a bit brainwashed so don't take any crap.

And – Col – look after this little lad, could you? He's gone a bit screwy too.'

Jamila took a firm hold on Linda's arm and said, 'Come along, sweetheart.'

Perhaps because Jamila was a woman, Linda nodded and followed her silently and obediently down the cellar steps. When John saw that 'Muh-muh' was going quietly, he allowed the leading armed officer to pick him up and carry him like a small child down to the cellars.

As he made his way down the steps with Edward slung over his shoulder, Jerry heard another stentorian shout from behind him. It sounded less like a shout of rage now than a roar of triumph.

Jamila turned around to look up at him. 'Was that him? The demon?'

'Don't worry, skip. I reckon this is the last we'll ever hear of him. With any luck, he'll go back to shadowland now, where he belongs.'

35

It was thundering on the morning they all met again, almost as loud as Balaa's angry shouts. They hurried out of the hospital car park in a heavy downpour, through the temporary plywood doors, and along to the conference room.

They had agreed to confer at St George's, so that they could bring police and forensics and doctors all together, and at the same time they could visit Edward to see how he was progressing.

'Well, ladies and gentlemen, we have a good idea now how this cult started,' said DCI Saunders, standing by the window and staring at his rain-bejewelled reflection. 'That bomb has been lying there ever since September the thirteenth 1943 and if that Baggy Nell woman hadn't gone nosing around in the cellars at the Duchy, it would still be there now and a considerable number of people would have gone uneaten.

'The bomb disposal squad told me that it's the largest size of bomb the Germans ever produced. It weighs two thousand five hundred kilos and they called it a Max. Even bigger than a Satan.'

Tosh said, 'We've now pretty much agreed on the opioid's formula. I've been in contact with the German forensics people in Wiesbaden – the Abteilung KT Kriminalistisches Institut, if I can say that without spitting all over you. They're trying to see if they can find any more records of the Nazi chemical warfare programme during the Second World War.

'Apparently this project was a brainwave of Goebbels himself and he called it the PG Programme – PG being short for *Primitiver Gehorsam*, which means Primitive Obedience. But the chemists who worked on it called it *kala jadu*, black magic, because it contained soma, the psychedelic drug used by the Urdu for conjuring up visions of gods and demons. Hence "calla dew".'

'But what we saw – the apparition with the yellow eyes like a goat – that was not a psychedelic vision,' said Jamila. 'And neither was the effect that it had on all of us. While it passed us by, it paralysed us. We could not move a muscle! We could not speak! And what was it that brought down the Duchy Hotel? A psychedelic vision could not have done that.'

'We're still working on that,' Tosh told her, glancing uneasily at DCI Saunders. 'You know yourself that the Stone Age culture in Germany originally came from India and the Middle East. The gods and demons that the cave dwellers worshipped in the Swabian Jura were pretty much the same as gods and demons that were worshipped in India, or Jambudvipa as they called it in those days. That Balaa painting – you can find almost identical figures in Neolithic caves in Germany.'

'This aspect of our investigation is remaining confidential for the moment, DS Patel,' said DCI Saunders. 'Until we know exactly what it was that we were up against, we're not releasing any media statements except to say that the Duchy Hotel was demolished without approval from Lambeth Council, and that we suspect there may be some casualties.'

'*What?* About fifty people were crushed to death in that building, by an angry demon!'

'Exactly,' said DCI Saunders. 'And you can imagine how that would look on the front page of the *Daily Telegraph*, can't you? After some of the investigations that you and DC Pardoe have been involved in together, I would have thought you had come to understand that we never release the details of anything that makes us look like raving lunatics.'

He paused, and waited for her response, but she shrugged and sat down. Without taking his eyes off her, he said, 'Go on, Dr Seshadri, if you would.'

Dr Seshadri stood up. 'Our laboratory here has also isolated the drug that affects the area of the brain controlling speech and language. But although this component mainly deconstructs speech to the level of a Stone Age vocabulary, which sounds very animal-like, it also allowed for the understanding of certain German words. We assume that this was intended to make it possible for Nazis to give instructions to British slaves once they had invaded Great Britain.'

'As we know now, they called the two Willow boys "Erst" and "Sek",' put in Professor Walmsley. 'John was able to tell me that he performed some simple magic tricks for them, which impressed them so much they treated him like a god, almost, and called him "Sowber Sek". The German word for magic being *Zauber*.

'I still have hours of Stone Age language to decipher,' she went on. 'And Detective Pardoe has told me there is so much of that calla dew still stored in that bomb that it might be possible to carry out some controlled experiments on volunteers.'

'We're testing it on hamsters to see if it's safe to try out on human subjects,' said Tosh. 'I mean, it's been down in that cellar since the Blitz, so it might be past its sell-by date.'

'You told me on the phone, Tosh, that you'd found out

more about this mourning thing,' said Jerry. 'Me and DS Patel began to get the idea quite early on that this cult was hunting for people who had recently been bereaved. Linda had only just lost her dad and it was like this geezer could smell it as she walked along the street. And all those Holocaust survivors, they were all grieving for that Russian bloke, even though it turned out that he didn't deserve it.'

'We have discussed this at some length together, Mr Brinkley and I,' said Dr Seshadri. 'It is a fact that when people are bereaved, it can have a dramatic psychological effect on them – depression and so forth – but it is less well known that it can also have strong physical consequences. The most pronounced of these is inflammation, to the point where some mourners have to take a gout medicine such as colchicine to calm it down.'

Tosh nodded. 'One of the results of this inflammation is, they taste much better. Sorry to put it so crudely, but it's true. Sad people are infinitely more delicious than happy people. That's why your cult went scouting around for mourners. I don't know if they had any idea that those Holocaust survivors had been used as guinea pigs during the war for this calla dew. It could have been nothing more than coincidence. My guess is that they were simply hanging around places where bereaved people got together, like churches and cemeteries, because they were looking for prime cuts of meat.'

'That is so sick,' said Jamila, and Professor Walmsley shook her head to show that she agreed.

'I'm sorry to say that life *is* sick,' said DCI Saunders. 'But that's why we're here, isn't it, to mop up the vomit. Sometimes it's better, though, if we don't let the general public know quite how sick life can be. We don't want them to get ideas, do we? Don't want another tribe of cannibals going around south

London, do we, looking for funeral guests to cook for their dinner?'

DS Bristow was there too, looking tired.

'We've checked most of the abandoned Tube tunnels now, guv, and we're blocking off as many as we can. There was access behind a row of garages right across the road there from Lambeth Cemetery. There was access round the back of St Anselm's Church in Stables Way. We haven't located them all yet, but we've got the old map now, so it shouldn't take us too much longer.'

After the meeting had concluded, Jerry and Jamila went to visit Edward. He was still very pale, and his hands were bandaged after surgery to repair his tendons, but he managed to give them a smile and a weak salute. His mother, Elizabeth, was there, and she smiled at them too. She had already thanked them for bringing both Edward and John out of the Duchy Hotel before it collapsed.

As they drove back to Tooting, with the windscreen wipers frantically flapping, Jamila said, 'How's Linda?'

'Gone to stay with her mum for a while. It really shook her, all this.'

There was a long silence between them. Then Jamila said, 'I'll be going back to Redbridge this afternoon. So I suppose this is goodbye. For a while, anyway.'

'Yes. I suppose it is. You know that they're selling off Tooting nick, don't you? So I don't know where I'm going to be stationed next. Wimbledon, maybe, or Walworth. Who knows?'

'With any luck, they won't need us again. Not as a team.'

'I wonder what happened to that Balaa. Did he just vanish, do you think? I hope he's not still squashed under all that rubble, like all of those squatters.'

'I doubt it, Jerry. That Moe Dee raised him out of the shadows. I expect he has gone back there, into the dark, where we all go one day.'

Jerry turned into the station car park and switched off the engine. The rain continued drumming on the roof.

He looked at Jamila and thought that he almost loved her. She reached out and lightly touched his shoulder as if she understood how he was feeling. But then he had Linda to take care of, and he couldn't be sure that she felt the same way about him.

'Why is life so bloody inexplicable?' he asked her.

'I do not know, Jerry,' said Jamila. 'There is no explanation.'

When he went upstairs to their office, he found Edge sitting behind his computer playing *Grand Theft Auto*.

'You're looking a bit serious, mate, if I might make so bold,' said Edge. 'Cheer up. There's a souvenir for you on your desk.'

Jerry hung up his jacket and then looked at his desk. Resting on top of his keyboard were two black wide-brimmed hats, one on top of the other, covered in fine grey dust.

Edward was well enough to return home three days later. On his first night, Elizabeth cooked him lasagne, which was his favourite, with chocolate ice cream for pudding. He was still a little subdued, and before he went up to bed he stood staring at the framed photograph of his father for almost five minutes. Elizabeth didn't disturb him, although John kept calling him from the bathroom to come up and brush his teeth.

When they were tucked up in bed, Elizabeth came to say goodnight to them and switch off their lights.

Edward lay in the darkness staring at the ceiling until John whispered, 'Are you asleep yet?'

'If I was, I couldn't tell you, could I?'

'I didn't know it was you, honestly, when I was Sek.'

'I know. I didn't know it was you either, when I was Erst.'

John sat up and said, 'I was Sowber Sek. That's what they called me.'

'Sowber Sek? What does that mean?'

'I did magic tricks for them, so they said I was magic.'

'You can only pretend to bend spoons and do that disappearing mug trick. That's not magic.'

'I can do magic now though.'

Edward turned over and punched his pillow to make himself comfortable. 'Go to sleep. You can't do magic.'

'I can. Mody taught me.'

'Oh, go to sleep.'

John started to clap his hands, very softly, and lean from side to side, so that his bedsprings creaked. He made a purring noise in the back of his throat, which gradually grew louder and louder.

'Shut up, John,' said Edward. 'I'm tired.'

'Look!' John insisted. 'You say I can't do magic! Look!'

He jumped down from his bed and went to the window, stumbling over the Lego scattered on the floor. He dragged back the flowery curtains and said, 'There! *Now* do you believe me?'

Outside, in the darkness, two yellow eyes were staring into their bedroom, two yellow eyes like a goat's.